*Dedicated to*

Ellen DeRiso
My Empress and my High Priestess.
How can the ocean thank the clouds for the
rain? Our adventure together continues and
my love for you only grows with it…
always, in all ways.

Books are nothing without readers.
Special thanks to the following for their
invaluable assistance:

Dan & Angelique Schmidt
Michael Waterman
Sean Haggans
Mom & Dad Waterman

Rob Condon
Joe Healy
Neil Trivedi
Marie Isenberg

# Ends of the Worlds

ISBN 978-0-9967962-1-7

Cover design by Matthew Waterman
Inset cover and image courtesy of Dan Schmidt


EOTW Publishing

www.MatthewWaterman.com

# by
# Matthew
# Waterman

# MATT

The next day Matt went back to work. Because, really, what else was there to do? It's not every day one is stalked and nearly killed by a knife-wielding lunatic. He'd returned to his apartment the previous night and been confronted by the abject normalcy of it—dirty dishes from that morning's breakfast still sat in the sink and his unmade bed was just as he left it. Such a harrowing encounter left him innervated and the impulse to take some sort of action screamed for his attention. Yet, at that moment, there was no course of action to pursue. Reporting the incident to the police wasn't an option after what he did at the library. And that assumed he had a description of the assailant in the first place. Instead, for the time being, he needed to act like nothing happened. As far as he was concerned, the world hadn't come to an end and he'd still be expected back in the office.

Reality returned in force the next morning, however. Upon his first step out of bed, he crumpled into a heap on the floor. His sprained ankle announced itself like a cymbal crash and, only half-awake, he remembered the injury too late. Adrenaline had masked the worst of the trauma but, after sleeping on it without medical attention, the merest touch of pressure jolted waves of agony up his calf. With a growl, he gathered himself up off the floor and began the battle with his pain-suffused morning. His shower required an extra ten minutes, the inefficiency of dressing on one leg added an extra five, and, collectively, such little difficulties meant he was already late for work before he reached the subway.

Matt was a writer and his current novel was titled, *Ends of the Worlds*. In a literal sense, the collection of stories, each sixteen pages long, featured an apocalyptic cataclysm experienced by multiple protagonists. The work's true theme, however, was an exploration of the ends of peoples' inner worlds—the loss of their previously held expectations or beliefs. Matt sensed a zeitgeist of disappointment growing across people and cultures: kids were graduating college with zero job prospects; technology was making entire employment sectors obsolete; social media was promulgating aspirations that continually slid out of reach. He didn't intend the novel to be a drab, depressing ode to unfulfilled dreams. Rather, he hoped to examine the watershed moments in peoples' worldviews. That college graduate might realize too late she pursued the wrong major; that newlywed might realize fatherhood isn't all it's cracked up to be. Such pivots might send characters down new paths in life yet, on the same token, this transformative growth couldn't always guarantee a happy, comfortable ending.

This morning, Matt's energies were focused on the tale he intended to tell his co-workers. He needed to concoct some sort of explanation for his limp and, by the time he reached his subway stop in Manhattan, the rudiments were complete. He exited and hobbled up the stone staircase into the grey of the morning—the Fall air was sharp, the sidewalk hard. Normally the concrete of the city held on to the summer's heat well into September and, sometimes, October. But a mild summer meant that battle had already been lost; winter was on its way.

The first person Matt encountered that morning was Conrad, his cubicle neighbor across the hall. Matt held his story on his hip like a six-shot, ready to un-holster it and fire at a moment's notice. He took his time limping to his cube in anticipation of such inquiry.

"Hey Conrad," said Matt. "Sorry I'm late."

Conrad didn't look away from his screen, though, and responded to Matt's initiation of conversation with a simple, "Hey Matt." Then, as an afterthought, he added, "I think Chicken Little was looking for you."

Conrad was referring to Abby, their high-strung co-worker who seemed permanently locked in disaster mode. In her world, the sky was perpetually falling. Hence, the nickname.

Matt dropped his bag in his cube, unsure if he felt disappointed or relieved he wasn't forced to explain his injury. "Did she say what she wanted?"

"Nah."

Matt frowned. So much for his grand preparations. He was about to sit when, over his cubicle wall, he picked out his boss marching his way. Louise didn't emerge from her office often but, when she did, she was on a mission. As misogynistic as the culture at many investment firms could be, she lived through the days when they were exponentially worse—her no-nonsense attitude had been forged the hard way.

"Matt. I thought you did a great job with the review last week." Matt began to offer polite thanks but didn't get the chance. "Listen. We've got a big project coming down the pike. I know you have a lot on your plate; I was originally going to give the assignment to Abby but she's all worked up over some issue with Datachariot. Therefore, I need you to spearhead it."

"Okay," said Matt. As if there was any choice.

"Great. It's called Project: Saturn. Tom Sussex will send you the details. Thanks."

And, just like that, Louise was gone.

Working in the back office of an investment firm was not the way Matt had envisioned spending his life. Crafting fiction was his true passion, his true focus. But he needed to pay the bills. His work at the firm stood in stark contrast to the nights spent writing and, he reasoned, it was a good division of labor. His workday role involved hard numbers and the mitigation of red tape. With his creative energies largely untaxed by such work, an inspiration reserve could be kept at the ready. The fact that he was often too exhausted to conjure any worthwhile writing after a stressful day was the logistical serpent he battled, the conflict rarely producing a decisive winner.

"Matt." The word was issued like a bullet. He'd logged on and begun responding to a few emails when, out of the blue, his name was fired at him. The source was Abby—she'd materialized out of nowhere at the entrance to his cubicle. "I heard you're going to be working on Project: Saturn."

"Um, yeah," said Matt, shaking off a cobweb or two.

"That. Is. Great," she replied, in her deliberate, overly-enunciated tone. It was obvious to Matt it wasn't great, however. She was speaking through gritted teeth and if her shoulder blades were any tighter they'd be touching her ears. For whatever reason, Abby must've been looking forward to the assignment and he'd unwittingly stepped on her toes. "Perhaps we could work together on it?"

No, no, no. Matt's demeanor betrayed no emotion but a rabble-rouser in his mind had already formed a picket line to protest the idea. He tolerated Abby. In truth, she was quite good at her job. Her working style, however, was the antithesis of his and she had a knack for transforming a molehill into Mount Everest wherever she went. He would gladly hand the assignment back to her—to complete alone—except Louise had specifically asked him to field it.

A second of awkwardness passed and, when Matt didn't respond, Abby added, "The project was supposed to be mine anyway, y'know. But I was on the phone with representatives from Datachariot. Absolutely annoying. Then you arrived late. So...."

She trailed off and Matt resisted the urge to comment on her passive-aggressiveness. "I think I can handle it."

Her smile dropped. Then, just as quickly, it rose anew. "Oh. Absolutely," she said. She lingered for a second longer, as if searching for the right words, and then shrugged mechanically. "Well, y'know. Just let me know if I can help."

It seemed as if she was about to depart when she cast a quizzical glance at Matt's outstretched leg. "Did something happen to your ankle?"

How could she have noticed that? He was sitting down! "Yeah," said Matt, caught off guard for the second time. Earlier, he could've deployed his tale in a moment's notice. Now he was drawing a blank. "I, uh, sprained it last night. How did you—how could you tell?"

"That's terrible!" she gushed, ignoring his question. "How did it happen?"

"Ah, it's a funny story, My friend and I were stargazing last night. Out in Long Island, to get away from all the light. My friend—he was about to fall in the water—so when I saw him lose his balance I jumped to help and landed on my ankle at an awkward angle."

He only barely kept from laughing at his gullible co-worker. Stargazing? Where did that come from? It certainly wasn't the story he prepared on his commute.

Then: "What constellations?" asked Abby. It wasn't a question Matt would've expected.

"Ah, I'm not really sure. My friend's the expert. I was just there to keep him company."

"I see," said Abby nodding. Her mannerisms were often grand, as if performing on stage, and Matt couldn't tell if her ponderous air was borne of skepticism or if she was just adding gravitas out of habit. "I minored in astronomy. I bet it was very hard to get a good view last night. All the clouds."

"That would explain why we had such trouble," declared Matt with a nervous giggle. He scolded himself for going off script—how was he to know she studied astronomy? Before Abby said another word, though, Matt motioned to his computer screen and added, "Now, if you don't mind."

"Absolutely!" said Abby, overly animated. If there was one ace up his sleeve Matt could always play, it was the need to get back to work. "You're busy. You have stuff to do." She vanished just as quickly as she appeared and Matt swiveled back to his computer. What an odd exchange to start the morning!

As transfer request specialists, it was their job to be a bulwark when machines failed. Most transactions requested by retail investors happened via straightforward computer-driven programs but, on occasion, quirks occurred outside the normal processes. Transfers might go to the wrong account; reallocations might not process before the close of business; that sort of thing. Matt's group was charged with navigating a labyrinth of accounting standards, technology interfaces, and SEC rules to ensure the dollars and cents of all transactions were fully reconciled. The investment gods located upstairs in the corporate offices of Fitzgerald Tower might be paid the big bucks to enact their investment schemes but somebody had to ensure the client's money actually moved to the right spot at the end of the day.

Matt ate his morning granola bar, organized some plans, and, once settled, took a look at the project Louise mentioned. The documents were so voluminous and the file sizes so large Sussex sent them in six separate emails—perhaps it wasn't too late to hand it over to Abby? In fact, after reviewing for over an hour, he was no closer to getting a handle on it. Apparently, the compliance team was implementing an updated data management system due to new fiduciary regulations yet the practices used for decades by the accounting team only barely aligned. The project was no single group's responsibility so, predictably, it'd been pushed off on the reconciliation group— if crap flowed downhill, Matt's group existed near the brown mouth of the river's estuary. He was vaguely proud Louise trusted him with such an assignment but it wasn't exactly the type of work that catapulted one to the corner office.

Initially, he assumed the project would be straightforward albeit mind-numbingly grueling. Multiple information systems utilizing entirely different jargon and code across hundreds of thousands of accounts needed to be synthesized over myriad fields. After opening the assortment of documents, however, Matt's sense of dread compounded. The material wasn't only misaligned, it was flawed in utterly unpredictable ways. Some of it was stored in outdated systems that forced Matt to locate and download antiquated applications to access it—but at least that data could be manipulated. More troublesome were files stored as screenshots or pictures, requiring manual re-creation. Even if he went through the arduous process of re-entering the material in workable formats, what was the veracity of a screenshot?

Simply appraising the deluge of information ate up half of his day. The other half disappeared into a void of failed reconciliation. Matt hoped to crunch some of the numbers at a very high level to ensure he was aiming for a correct, verifiable point. Yet even that eluded him. How could he square up the granular back-up equations when he couldn't formulate a simple definable goal? He understood why certain fields might differ when factoring for variables such as non-executed swaps or currency exchange difficulties. But dollar value totals at a specific point in time shouldn't diverge. And every time he thought he found the cause of the discrepancies, three more problems arose. By the time 6:00 rolled around, his short-term memory was shot and he wasn't positive he could form a coherent sentence. Worse, he'd made no headway on the ridiculous project. With grudging acceptance, he stood and prepared to leave for the day, hoping for better results on his novel that night. Then:

KRACKOOM!!!

Matt ducked on sheer instinct. Abby yelped. In the cubicle opposite him, a co-worker cursed. In the immediate aftermath, he took stock. It sounded like a bomb had exploded. Yet there was no devastation, no smoke or fire. The floor had shaken but no one cried as if injured. He stood up and found others popping their heads out of their cubicles in similar fashion, each wearing expressions of concern and confusion.

"Is everyone okay?" asked Abby to no one in particular.

A gradual murmur began to grow and, out of the buzz, Matt heard someone describe a bright flash. That's when he realized what it was: Lightning.

"I think it was lightning," said Matt.

Wait a minute, that doesn't make sense. He began to doubt himself. He'd experienced countless thunderstorms in his office building yet he'd never heard such a loud thunderclap. Normally the sound of thunder rolled down the Avenues, slow-moving and growling. It was never so acute. Also, skyscrapers were designed with lightning rods on top for safety, weren't they?

"You think so?" asked Abby, appearing outside his cube.

"I'm—I'm not sure," he said vacantly.

"It was a heck of a flash," said Conrad, approaching from the cubicle across the hall.

"You saw a flash?" asked Matt.

"Yeah. Definitely. I can still see the image when I close my eyes. It hit right outside the window there."

At that the trio turned their gazes to the location of the purported lightning strike. The floor-to-ceiling windows of the office reflected the artificial light inside, making it hard to see the world beyond initially. After staring for a moment, though, the three discerned the sheets of rain slapping the side of the tower. Like the starting gun of a race, the bolt had signaled a torrential downpour. At the same time, the commotion on the floor was only increasing. Matt glanced around, saw that certain co-workers were donning their fire warden vests, and he put two and two together—someone had made the decision to evacuate the floor.

"I thought towers were built with rods on top to absorb lightning strikes," said Matt, despite the growing din. It didn't make sense to him that lightning should strike the side of a building and his mind was unwilling to dismiss such an odd occurrence out of hand.

"I don't know, man. I saw it," said Conrad.

Just then, Bill Nevers, the officious twit in charge of omnibus transfers, appeared, wearing his cheap orange vest like he was a state trooper. "We have reason to believe the tower was struck by lightning. Security has asked everyone to move to the ground floor for their own safety," he declared robotically before moving on.

Matt rolled his eyes. Though his day had been wasted, getting work done on his novel would've salvaged something positive. Now, with the elevators taken out of service, the entire floor would be forced to descend the stairs. Making matters worse, many were gathering their coats and bags to leave for the night, further delaying the evacuation process. Contrary to expectations, getting thousands of people in twenty-nine floors of offices down to the ground level could actually be done in an orderly manner—it just took forever. With decorum at a maximum in such a situation, no one panicked or descended the stairs recklessly. Instead, it was a tiresome procession that moved one halting step at a time. Matt surveyed those around him grimly as he envisioned the evacuation taking well over an hour to complete.

By the time he reached the ground floor he was beside himself. His ankle felt like cracked ceramic suffering microscopic fissures that'd spider-webbed out with each pain-shocked step. The stairway's railing had helped him keep his balance multiple times as people brushed past. Once in the lobby, however, he found no similar respite. Worse, he was reminded that his journey was far from over, that he still needed to navigate the downpour. Wearing a furious grimace, he shoved open the door and charged outside. He limped down the sidewalk, fumbling with his umbrella and struggling to locate nearby objects for support. And, when he finally made it to the subway entrance, he was drenched anyway.

Thankfully, the worst of rush hour had passed and the arriving train was nearly empty. The previously-packed subway car full of rain-soaked passengers still carried a noxious, wet-dog odor. But Matt didn't care. He collapsed into the seat with a heavy sigh. His ankle throbbed angry and, due to his hobbled gait, a dull ache had taken up residence in his lower back. Yet he was consoled to be headed in the right direction, at least.

And at the opposite end of the train a dark figure remained unnoticed, cataloguing Matt's every move.

## MEDA

Two days down. Only two days down in this crappy week. While Matt trudged the streets of Manhattan on an injured ankle, his girlfriend, Meda, found herself sloshing through the frigid rainstorm to her apartment in Astoria, Queens. It was too early in the week to be this tired. Worse, she wasn't even halfway finished with the campaign and it was due to the client next Tuesday (a thought that produced a mental explosion of stress). She struggled into her apartment, dropped her bag at the door, and only partially succeeded at keeping the water from her coat and umbrella confined to the welcome mat.

It wasn't supposed to be like this. If anyone told her when she shipped off to college that she'd still be a Senior Associate in her early thirties, she would've picked a different major. The role at her firm wasn't awful; she enjoyed diving in and creating public relations campaigns, particularly for enthusiastic small business owners. The problem was her co-workers. For every project that went smoothly, five were nearly derailed by her misogynistic colleagues. The stars needed to align in serendipitous convergence for her to complete an undertaking without one of them taking credit for her work. Then, following all those battles, someone might advise her with doe-eyed solemnity that she should be thankful simply to have a job.

With a moment to compose herself, she slung her jacket onto the coat rack and retrieved her phone from the inside pocket. (Nine new work emails. Great!) Then, thinking better of checking her messages, she eyed up the pack of cigarettes at the kitchen window. Though she wasn't a smoker in the classic sense, she sometimes enjoyed one after yoga. She stepped into the kitchen and the Native American woman on the cover of the White Buffalo pack beckoned with her tranquil smile.

Then the phone rang. "Oh, come on," she moaned.

She picked it up and, to her relief, saw that it was Matt. Upon answering though, before either spoke a word, she discerned the copious amount of background noise. Matt's breath was ragged and a whistling sound was omnipresent, as if he'd called from some windswept landscape.

"Meda! Can't talk! I need to come over," said Matt, spitfire. In the background, she caught the sound of his loping footfalls and fabric susurrating in quick, repeating bursts.

"Of course, baby! Is everything okay?"

"Yes! It will be. Don't call back. I'll be there soon."

And, before she could utter another word, he hung up. Meda very nearly returned his call despite his exhortation to the contrary. The conversation (all three seconds of it) was so sudden, so abrupt and she yearned for more information. It was obvious something was wrong yet he'd provided no clue about the nature of the emergency. Should she call 911? Would she need bandages when he arrived? Or a weapon?

Matt showed up almost thirty minutes later. By then, Meda was fuming. Three times she'd picked up the phone only to resist calling. Her trust in Matt battled imagined worst-case scenarios. She paced, with nowhere to put her nervous energy. And, when she heard him downstairs at the door of her apartment building, she rushed to her second-floor landing. "Matt? Is that you?"

"Hey hon," he said nonchalantly.

"Are you okay?"

"Yeah. Why wouldn't I be?"

He took his time going from the front door to the stairs (any day now, Matt) and many seconds passed before he came into view. Meda, vexed, was at a loss for words. He arrived at the bottom stair, flashed a quick smile, and began a ponderous, unhurried climb up the stairs.

"Matt! What's going on? That phone call?"

"What about it?" said Matt guilelessly, leaning into the banister with each lumbering step.

"'What about it'?" she repeated. "You had me worried half to death, you idiot! You told me not to call back! Why were you running? I thought something terrible happened."

Matt reached the top of the landing and, exhibiting a breezy lack of urgency, said, "Running? I wasn't running."

He gave her a peck on the cheek but she wasn't interested. She stared him up and down. He wasn't huffing, he didn't appear sweaty. He ambled inside but Meda remained frozen, her fingers splayed in what-the-hell astonishment.

"Wait, wait, wait," she insisted, stalking him from behind. "What's going on here? Is this a joke? When you called me, I heard you. You were out of breath. I could tell you were running. Why would you lie about that?"

Matt plopped his bag on the couch and, wearily, said, "Hon, I don't know what you're talking about."

At that, Meda was forced to re-appraise him. She'd been so distressed that she hadn't taken stock of Matt's appearance. For the first time, she registered the bedraggled air about him and the unnatural stance. "Matt, are you limping?"

He acceded with a dour nod. "My ankle. That's why I stopped here tonight."

"Oh no! What happened?" Residual alarm from the call entangled with new worries inside Meda.

"I sprained it last night."

"Sprained it? That could be serious." Meda rushed to him and bent to get a closer look. He was leaning against the sofa with his weight shifted to the other leg, however, foiling her attempt at proper inspection.

"It'll be fine. It's just healing slower than I expected."

Meda stood up straight again and eyed his dress shirt and slacks. "You went to work today?"

Matt's gaze shot skyward, effectively admitting it was a dumb idea. "Yeah. Like I said, I thought it'd feel better. I figured if I just made it to the office it would take care of itself."

Meda frowned. Then, putting her hands on his shoulders, she took control of the situation and guided him to the couch. "Here, lie down." There was a pause in the conversation and, while rolling up his pant leg, she asked, "How did it happen?"

"I was at the library. Of all places. And it's weird, my memory is a little hazy. I lost track of time. You know how I get when I'm writing. And then there was this—"

"Matt!" cried Meda, cutting him off mid-sentence after rolling down his sock. His shin lacked its normal curvature; the bottom was swollen nearly as thick as his calf. And, due to this engorgement, his sock left imprints in the skin, bands of concentric circles notching choke points above his ankle. Along these purple subdermal lines, the blood had nestled in bleak ridges. Meda shot a wide-eyed glare up at Matt and then gave a final tug to pull off the sock completely. Matt winced. A miserable splash of black showed directly below his ankle—the blood displayed that unique hue of darkness only possible when viewed through the semi-transparent filter of flesh.

"I was afraid of that," said Matt with resigned apathy.

Meda shot him another glare, this one incredulous at his flippancy. "Matt. This is serious. You need to get this checked."

"It'll be fine. It just needs time to heal. The building was evacuated at work today and I had to walk down the stairs. Twenty-nine floors. That's probably making it look so much worse than it is."

"No. It's black. Your ankle is black." She said no more, preferring to let the silence build and weigh on him.

"Well then? What do you want me to do?" he asked, his blasé coolness beginning to wane.

"You need to see a doctor, you idiot!"

Matt scowled. She'd shouted at him as if he was a child yet he could recall at least three occasions when Meda refused medical help after he suggested it.

"Matt, I'm just trying to help you," she added, more tenderly this time. "Your ankle looks terrible. It might be infected. Sticking your head in the sand is not an option here."

Matt remained defiant, however. "I told you. It's fine. It'll heal. I'm not in denial, if that's what you're suggesting."

"And that's it? You're not going to do anything about it? You're just going to fiddle while Rome burns?"

Matt rolled his eyes like a politician addressing an issue deemed unworthy of his time. "You mean Nero? In reality, that story is impossible. Rome burned in 64 A.D. but the fiddle wasn't invented until the 10th century."

"That's not the point," groaned Meda at the semantic distraction. She knew her insistence was wearing him down, though. "How's this? My friend, Hadad, is a bone specialist. I can ask her to come over to take a look. How does that sound?"

It was a veiled threat. Matt hated Hadad and her droll, lecturing tone. While technically Meda was offering him a choice, this path was far more irksome and both of them knew it. "Fine!" he blurted, caving to the pressure. "I'll go see *my* doctor tomorrow morning. It'll make me late for work. And this huge project just hit."

Meda sent him a sour, consolation prize of a smile. "I don't understand why it was such an issue to begin with," she muttered. Then, standing, she announced, "Okay. Now get your ankle elevated. You need to get the blood out of there. I have a hot pack and a cold pack. You'll need to alternate them to reduce the swelling."

She hadn't finished speaking before she was in the bathroom digging under the sink for a hot pack. Matt was left on the couch and dutifully followed orders by putting his ankle up on the arm of the couch. Then Meda buzzed to the kitchen to retrieve a cold pack from the freezer as Matt clicked on the television. The microwave began humming and she returned with the cold pack to find Matt pointing at a news report on the television. "Hey look. We'll be able to see a comet in the night sky soon. Without using a telescope."

"That's great," said Meda, unimpressed. She handed him the cold pack wrapped in a towel and, moving on to a more pressing matter, she asked, "How exactly did you hurt it anyway? What could possibly be so dangerous at the library?"

Matt smiled and bowed his head, a look of embarrassment creeping in. "You're not going to believe me. It's really stupid."

"Why am I not surprised?" The mood in the room recovered a bit and she smirked for the first time.

"You know how I go to that library out past East Elmhurst? Because it's deserted?"

"Right."

"Well, Monday night it was perfect. Completely empty. And I went to my spot, this place near the old reference books nobody checks anymore. And I got really swept away in my writing. It happens sometimes."

"Oh, I know all about that. Especially when it delays my carefully constructed dinner plans," smiled Meda, the atmosphere relaxing further. Matt appeared as if he wanted to add something, his grin lingering then receding. His eyes dropped, then the moment stretched into an awkward pause. Eventually, Meda said, "And?"

"And," Matt continued, "I must've been distracted—I went to stand up and slipped on a book on the ground."

Meda's expression broke anew, a mélange of emotion that combined pity, frustration, and mirth. "Oh no. Only you, Matt. How could you break your ankle on a book?"

"It was open! With the pages facing down. It was really slippery!" His tone was jocular, a subtle acknowledgement of the implausibility of his tale. For her part, Meda covered her face with her palm, shaking her head and chuckling. "My foot slid. It was like ice. I landed on my other ankle at an awkward angle. It twisted. And that's how I sprained it."

Meda pursed her lips despite her grin, issuing a mildly disapproving glance. "We don't know it's a sprain yet."

"I know, I know," said Matt. An easy silence settled in, Meda still in disbelief at her clumsy boyfriend. Then, as if on cue, the microwave dinged to alert the hot pack was heated. Meda retrieved it and, later, Matt called to make the doctor's appointment as promised. And despite various chances throughout the night, Matt never elaborated on the shimmering black figure at the library that caused him to slip on the book.

# MAGEE

The plan had been for Magee to meet up with Matt for drinks that night. From what Magee understood, however, Matt really screwed up his ankle and needed to cancel. Magee was concerned for his friend...naturally. The pair had weathered many storms together, dating back to college and their threadbare existence after moving to New York City. And he was disappointed they wouldn't hang out. Yet the change in plans did serve to open up an unexpected blank spot in his Wednesday night.

Magee was an artist and, often, finding the time to disappear into his studio represented half the effort. He also worked as a bartender and looming before him were Thursday, Friday, and Saturday...the roughest nights of his week. So, whereas previously he'd grudgingly accepted no painting would occur until Sunday, the newfound bevy of time was an unexpected windfall.

Magee's converted-garage studio below his apartment was more akin to a shack...yet depressingly expensive in his Brooklyn neighborhood. He descended the stairs and was greeted by the distorted specular reflection of himself, his scraggy beard, and surplus army coat. The source of the image was an ancient mirror he salvaged from a gutted building. Its age showed unmistakable in its exquisite weathering. In many spots, the silvering was flaked off the back while, in others, the world reflected back in a gold- or green-tinged hue. Less a functional mirror to check one's appearance, it'd likely been used as a display piece in a foyer or office board room. Magee imagined it being installed about the time Dickens published *A Christmas Carol*...only through divine intervention had he fit it through the studio's doorway without breaking it.

The problem was that he'd come to a standstill on the project. His vision for the final piece was clear...the paint was simply not cooperating. The timeworn areas of the mirror created a magnificent impact wherein viewers witnessed portions of themselves fade away or truncate entirely as they changed viewpoints. Magee grasped the inimitable artistic value in that. Yet, when he attempted to lay down a layer of paint, hoping to create a binary depth of color to play off that background, the result wasn't coming together as a unified whole. This created hesitation in Magee, a fear of moving forward until he was positive he could achieve the desired look. Forcing work on a project and achieving mediocre results could be worse than no work at all...especially with such a never-to-be-replicated canvas Yet such perfectionism also presented a different hazard. It was too easy to give up and get distracted by something else. And that was exactly what he did the last time he encountered the same dilemma.

This time, he eyed up the mirror as if it was an opponent on the other side of a boxing ring. Walking away in frustration was no longer an option. If he wanted to create something special, he needed to take a risk. With stoic precision, he approached his work table and laid out his paint, brushes, and rags. He didn't know what the end result would be but he hoped momentum alone would be enough to send him down the right path. Then, with nothing left to prepare, he moved to apply the mixed paint to the very corner of the mirror.

Immediately upon applying it, disappointment hit. The paint lay there, lifeless and flat. It was the polar opposite of what he imagined. Magee pulled away, appraising the dot with a scowl. What to do? What to do? It was now abundantly clear the paint wouldn't give the appearance he desired...the same thing happened last time! Expecting a different result was the very definition of insanity. With no outlet for his pent-up energies, he began to pace. He couldn't keep doing this! Angrily, he swiped a paint tube up and glared at it, as if it might offer some sort of revelation. He probably needed to buy a better brand of paint...with money he didn't have. But what if that didn't work? What if the brand of paint wasn't the problem at all?

Then, by degrees, his complexion began to change. Magee squinted at the mirror anew, only half of his face reflected back this time. If the idea was to take advantage of the duality created by the optical illusion, it dawned on him that he needed to step away...separate himself from the art. The effect must occur on its own, unimpeded. This wasn't some bathymetric map cataloguing the underwater contours of a lake. The impression's source was organic and needed to stay that way. In trying to maintain too much control over his creation's trajectory he was impeding its inherent potential. Put another way, he needed a second pane of glass. Laid over the mirror with the paint atop that, the bifurcation would allow the paint to achieve the height and weight to carry the visual while also giving the aged mirror free reign to create its own magic beneath the current.

Without conscious thought, Magee took a half-step backward, appraising the mirror with new clarity. A hint of a grin appeared at the edge of his lips and he cocked his head ever so slightly. Then, with his point of view now turned 90 degrees, he caught sight of the pair of eyes peering in at him from the window above.

It happened swiftly albeit with neurotic uncertainty...as if catching an insect's movement out of the corner of his eye. In the space of a second, he spotted the voyeur's eyes, frowned in disbelief, then fixed his stare more fully. Then the person disappeared, shooting sideways into the darkness.

"Hey," said Magee, a beat late. "Hey!"

The window was a tight sideways rectangle near the top of the twelve-foot concrete wall. Whoever was spying on him needed to climb to obtain such a view...meaning it was no accident, it wasn't simply someone walking past. Magee hesitated for an instant, unsure about the proper response. It wasn't exactly a situation he'd prepared himself for. Then, foregoing the urge to call the cops, he rushed to the door and scanned the immediate area outside.

Dusk in October crept in early, the clouds darkening the world before the sun truly set. It also made the world quiet...no chirping insects or blaring music from open-windowed cars. And that allowed Magee to hear the patter of distant footfalls. He homed in on them, then stepped farther out on the sidewalk to locate the source. It was a little boy. As he scampered away, his back to Magee, it was hard to ascertain his exact age but Magee guessed he was roughly nine years old.

A part of Magee readied to give chase and find out what he was doing. After registering the boy's age, though, Magee relaxed. He was probably just some neighborhood kid, bored and curious when the light in the studio flicked on. Magee stood staring for a long moment before peering back at the side of the building where he spied the boy. Sure enough, there was a creaky gutter pipe running alongside the wall. He was amazed it could support the boy to begin with...surely the weight of any adult would rip the contraption down.

Magee smirked anew. For a moment there his imagination had flashed worst-case visions of intruders breaking in and stealing his artwork...of confronting some leather-clad Eurasian guy with a gun...of being trapped in the burning studio after a Molotov cocktail was hurled inside. Instead, it was only a curious little boy wondering what that painter was up to. Hell, if Magee hadn't been so startled he would've invited the kid in to chat.

His heart rate slowing and his mind relaxing, Magee meandered back inside. He reacquainted himself with his previous breakthrough. While revelatory, the directional shift resulted in an immediate work stoppage until he got his hands on that second pane of glass. He pondered this, his hand on his chin. Before he could settle on a plan of action, however, a new interruption occurred: Taylor was calling.

Taylor was half Magee's friend and half an industry associate. Each hustled for odd jobs and maintained industry connections that often proved vital to the other. It was an odd relationship, resulting from years spent mingling in the same circles until, eventually, they realized they'd become more than mere colleagues at some blurry point along the way. They'd enjoyed a few adventures together yet, invariably, they defaulted back to their static, business-style arrangement afterward. If Taylor was calling, it was equal odds it involved either an opportunity for Magee or a favor regarding one.

"Hey, the permit came through!" announced Taylor. "The owner said we have until mid-November to shoot."

"Woah! That's great news!" It took Magee a second to figure out what Taylor was referencing but, once he did, his eyes lit up. A director with real connections was keen on filming at an abandoned warehouse up in the Bronx and Taylor had shown this director some of Magee's work behind the camera. Impressed, the director had hired Magee on the spot...a gig that would be both creatively stimulating and generate a nice chunk of change. Then, as offers such as these were wont to do, the project ran aground and production got snarled in red tape for weeks as the director haggled with the owner to get permission to film. Magee had all but given up on the opportunity so the call represented the second pleasant surprise of his day.

"I knew you'd be excited. Dante's going to need you there tomorrow."

Magee paused. "What? Tomorrow? Is the cast ready?"

"No, no. Not to film. To sign the paperwork. Just a formality. The owner needs you to be covered under Dante's insurance. In case you break your ankle or something. We probably won't be ready to shoot until after the 22nd."

Magee grimaced, peering at the mirror. Taylor's timing couldn't have been worse. While, yep, it was a great gig, Magee had experienced his epiphany regarding the mirror mere moments earlier. Creative inspiration like that doesn't happen often...yet neither do paying gigs that aren't tortuously boring.

"What? What's the matter?" asked Taylor, responding to Magee's silence.

"It's just," began Magee, "the timing. It's really bad. I'm juggling a lot of projects now. And tomorrow is the start of my long shifts at the bar."

"Come on, man. You're a professional juggler. You never have less than three projects going."

"I know, I know. This one is important to me, though. Sometimes when I overextend, all the projects suffer. I don't want that to happen with this one."

For a moment neither spoke. Then Taylor said, "How's this then? I'll bring the paperwork to you. No need to mess up your perfect day. You can just sit on your lovely, artistic butt and I'll ferry these contracts all around the five boroughs."

"Taylor," groaned Magee.

"Chill out," said Taylor, less sarcastic. "I'll ask if he can wait a bit. We can't film for two and a half weeks anyway. I doubt it'll be a problem."

"I'd be so grateful. I've got this piece I'm working on. I've got high hopes for it. The timing of all this is fully crap."

"It's okay. I'll let you know. It's just another line item in the growing, 'you owe me' column."

Magee chuckled, hung up, and took a second to process the orthogonal swerves in his night. Then he considered lighting up a joint. After being startled like that, and then receiving such great news, he deserved a break. Also, technically speaking, he'd made some progress on the mirror piece, if only through the realization he needed more materials.

One problem quickly became apparent, however. He had no weed. Years ago, he'd re-appropriated an old library card cabinet to store his varied paints and brushes. Ever since, the drawer in the lower left corner served as a safe place for his stash. Upon opening it, however, only the hollow, emptiness of the drawer was found inside...which was weird because he could've sworn he had some weed left. Normally, when he smoked the last of it, he left the empty bag as a reminder to procure more. Yet even that was missing. Could he've rolled a second joint the last time and forgotten to leave the bag? Entirely possible. But it was rare for him to be so sloppy.

Gradually, the disappointment receded, aided by a dash of guilt at his thwarted dalliance. He didn't need to get high. In fact, he possessed an obvious goal. It was still early and stores hadn't yet closed. There was no reason to get lazy now when he could position himself to kick ass on Monday. He glanced around the studio one last time...still bemused by his intrepid onlooker and still processing Taylor's good news...and then he headed out to find a large, sturdy pane of glass.

## MATT

That night at the library? Here's what actually happened. Monday night Matt had set out to the library to work on his novel. This branch wasn't the closest to him, geographically— that one was bustling and far too hectic. He needed peace and quiet and, after many experiments at divergent locations, he'd discovered this location farther out in Queens. Specifically, he'd isolated a secluded area tucked away and nearly out of sight. The room was technically connected to the main building. But most people—if they thought to peek behind a certain nondescript, commercial wooden door—would find only a barren hallway walled by boring old cinder blocks. Whereupon, they'd likely assume it was a passage to the employee break room or a storage room. So, when Matt located the dusty reference section beyond, he knew he hit the jackpot. It was tailor-made for uninterrupted contemplation.

The reason Matt required such solitude was the nature of his work. His novel comprised eighteen short stories that occurred simultaneously at the end of the world. The protagonists in each would rub elbows with those in the other stories and create a sort of synergistic mesh. One protagonist's narration may paint him as a lady's man—until the reader got the other side of the story in a different tale. Another character might miss an important detail—one that proves to be a pivotal element in another's story. Through this interaction, readers could devise their own deeper reasons behind the character's motivations and dreams. The multitude of viewpoints—some outright contradictory, others more nuanced—would offer a subjective tapestry for unique interpretation. In Matt's vision, this collaboration, fueled by readers' unique perspectives, would lead to a more personal experience with the characters and their stories.

To imagine such a panorama, Matt needed to step away from traditional linear thinking and, instead, envision every individual story coming together as a field of possibilities. It was a state of purposeful narration-Dyslexia wherein words lost their traditional attachments and the story arcs and characters' actions all transpired concurrently. Of course, it'd be impossible to literally write all the stories at once. Therefore, Matt required a place that presented no distraction, no connection to the real world, to get lost on such a meditatively collinear route. An empty room cut off from time and space would've been ideal; this forgotten corner of the library was a close second.

Matt arrived at his familiar spot, his footsteps echoing to no one but himself. He pulled out a chair, the same one he'd sat in numerous times, and then reconsidered. Better to change it up, stimulate his mind in a new way. On those previous occasions he sat facing a collection of encyclopedias that chronicled ancient Babylonian histories, each five-pound monstrosity colored a shade of puke green that could've been fashionable only in the 1970s. This time, he swung his bag around to the other side of the table before he fell into the seat facing the wall. The paint slathered on the concrete blocks was an inoffensive mauve and the visual was even less engaging than the volumes behind him—exactly what he wanted.

To establish some semblance of order around the characters' stories, Matt had created an ad hoc matrix to record the important details about each. He unfurled it on the table before him, flipped open his notebook, and began soaking in the minutiae of the various tales. He recalled a story he'd been plotting about a high schooler whose passion was live action role-playing. Her story seemed to encapsulate the notions of self-creation Matt intended to explore. He also mused that, at some point, he needed to write the story describing the literal end of the world—a fairly important element given its impact on every other story. But those tales could wait. Presently, he needed to move away from structural specificity and, not unlike the Buddhist notion of Sunyata, swell to a more holistic view of the universe of narratives.

His breathing slowed and, in no time, he lost himself in his work. Immersion resulted. His mind drifted into the ether of his stories and a dislocation took place. Matt didn't register the transformation—he merely left his egoistic attachments behind. Neural scientists might explain the experience as a unique engagement of certain areas of the brain; psychologists might describe the sensation as a sort of dissociative fugue state. But it was neither. It was the creation of a new self through the loss of the old self, everything and nothing, both states of being existing simultaneously.

Then, with his mental being fully lost in the fabric of his tales, Matt reappeared. His body continued to work—he watched it from above as it jumped from the matrix to the notebook, scribbling notes in each. But he was now processing thoughts away from that body, about topics wholly unrelated to the stories. The duality was striking—it was a sensation he'd experienced many times previously yet one that seemed new every time.

A sense of contentment settled in. Time, itself, rounded like a mesh covering a sphere or an enormous amoeba. Now tangible and existent, it lost its previously immutable power. Matt's transitive self experienced a stupefying sensation of everything happening at once—all the world's history, every moment from the Big Bang to that very instant—all of it happening at the same time. All was one and nothing was all.

In fact, contented to remain adrift as a bifurcated self, he very nearly missed the impending danger. It was his body, his sense of smell, that caught the pungent odor and roused him.

Previously, the isolated room had offered a pleasantly musty scent similar to that of a comic book store. The new smell stood in direct opposition, a stale aroma that reeked of brackish saltwater and rotting oysters. It arose gradually, despite its putrescence. And, concomitant with Matt's delayed awakening, arrived the fear that the odor was likely present far earlier than his cognition of it.

With this blurry awareness came a vision from behind the stack of books. It showed as a flicker and stirred the problem-solving part of Matt's brain. No one had entered the room since he began. The hallway behind him was the only entrance. Had this person been there all along? Worse, his dissociated state prevented him from gleaning key details of this shadow person's appearance. It was as if Matt was viewing the being through a telescope—catching a shimmering detail here, magnified nothingness there. It showed like ghostly images of snow billowing off a speeding train, appearing and disappearing in black swooshes of movement. Rather than witnessing a corporeal presence, Matt was seeing a liquescent shadow that flowed across and around the books.

Yet, even as he perceived this shadow figure advancing, his body resisted interruption. Just one more sentence, just one more sentence—that was the message Matt's body conveyed as it continued to write. From above, it was a sight to behold. The dark menace undulating closer while, wholly unperturbed, Matt continued to scribble. In some astral plane, he knew he should barge in and take control. Yet his body disallowed re-entry. The specter loomed at the edge of the book stack with serpentine patience. But Matt did not release his grip on the pen.

Then came the knife. From nowhere, it sliced downward at Matt's hunched body, narrowly missing the crown of his head. His body jerked. His consciousness returned, unified.

And Matt only perceived the event in the past tense—the weapon now standing upright before him, plunged into a mountain of papers with the tip impaled in the table beneath. Matt's eyes went wide. This was his current reality. Someone had tried to stab him.

On instinct alone, he shot upright in his seat. The shadowy menace crested above him, threatening to wash over everything. And, as if to confirm the danger once more, he glanced at the erect knife again, its white bone handle wavering slightly. Then Matt's body went into action.

Propelled by a hard shove on the table, Matt first fell away from his chair before twirling to his feet. It was an ungainly movement and he attempted to right himself by leaning into the stack. The tomes began to tumble off the shelf but at least he'd put distance between himself and the entity. Then, realizing he should press his advantage, he twirled yet again, this time in the opposite direction.

The movement was as drastic as it was desperate. It plunged him deeper into the room, away from the exit. As an impetuous necessity, though, it allowed him the respite needed to devise a plan. First casting a quick eye back to where he imagined the presence to be, he then ducked around another shelf of dusty books. The act was further commitment, plummeting him still farther into the darkened room. But he had an idea.

Once behind the stack, Matt began shoving the volumes off the shelves with all his might. The weighty catalogues required more effort than initially anticipated but adrenaline wasn't in short supply. Book after book careened out the other side as he blindly drove them forward. In his ears, Matt's heartbeat throbbed in carwash-like whooshes, pulsating alongside the smack of weighty spines and rustling paper. Books continue to crash and settle and, through the cacophony, he tried to discern any sign of the dark being's approach. Then, deciding he'd created a suitable obstacle, he bolted back around the opposite end of the stack.

He didn't get far. Upon rounding the corner, his foot—the one he intended to plant on—landed on the spine of one of the colossal encyclopedias. The pages of the book were splayed face-down, creating a slippery, almost aqueous surface and Matt's foot shot sideways when the book squirmed out from beneath him. The full weight of his body continued on its intended path, however, landing on his twisted ankle. Matt crumpled immediately.

In split-second succession, he crashed down hard on his hip, realized what'd happened, and imagined what was to come. He rolled slightly to get a better view behind, half-expecting to see the ephemeral being blotting out the room to black. It wasn't and he scrambled to his feet. And then the pain truly showed itself. The merest touch of weight on his damaged ankle nearly sent him sprawling anew. Instead, he managed to fall sideways into one of the tables. It provided temporary support, even as he felt the nefarious presence closing in from behind. Forced to hop, he used the table and then the stacks of books for support. And, despite the pain, he managed to hobble to the entrance and fling the door open.

The tunnel entrance beyond was a boon. While leaning his weight into the wall, it offered him the chance to think rather than merely react. The entire attack occurred in fewer than twenty seconds and he'd been yanked out of an otherworldly meditative state at the outset. As he struggled down the hall, he returned to himself more completely as a unified being. And, once restored, questions began to alight his mind with the unpredictability of a firework display gone awry: What the hell was that? How did it get in? What about my writing notebook? What about the knife?

The last thought was the most critical. It rendered all other concerns null with the tangible threat to his mortality. He didn't need to explain the shadow creature; he needed get away from that knife and whoever had wielded it. The thought propelled Matt forward and he slammed into the opposite door, clutching and turning the doorknob in the same motion.

It didn't budge. Confusion turned to anger, he struggled with it more vigorously. Still nothing. It was locked. He shot a terrified glare back at the other door. There was no window in it, no portal to see the room beyond. But he imagined the dark presence flowing around the doorframe and into the hallway, mercury-smooth through the merest crevice with no chance to escape. Panicked, he tried the door knob yet again, yanking up and down on it as if that might miraculously disengage the lock. Nothing.

"Help!" he called out, before following up with a second, even louder cry. "Help!"

He waited and listened, mouth agape. But there wasn't even an echo, a sense of a call unanswered. There was only him and him alone. He hollered again, more desperately than ever, "Help! Is there anybody there? I'm locked in!"

Again: Nothing. He frowned, shifted his weight. Then he flung up his forearm to check his watch. It was almost 2:00 AM. His world spiraled. How was that possible? How had he lost so much time? His mouth went dry. And his next breath inflated his lungs with the aridity of an Arabian desert. The library was closed. He was locked inside. With that thing.

All was silent apart from Matt's hoarse breathing. Previously, the hallway had been inviting, offering him privacy and solitude. Now, it felt like a purgatorial netherworld. The cinder block walls were lacquered bone-white and institutional in their severity—he'd need a jackhammer to get through them. Meanwhile, the door was solid oak—he could

31

spend hours trying to break it down and a fractured shoulder would be the only result. The prison-like ruthlessness only served to highlight the severity of the situation. He possessed exactly two options. He could stay in the stark but secure hallway overnight, eagle-eying the opposite doorway throughout. Or he could summon his resolve, re-enter the room, and hope to break through the windows on the opposite side before that thing bore down on him. Two divergent paths, each carrying axiomatic risks.

Matt's sense of absolutism grew. He glared back at the door to the room with a sneer. It represented a Rubicon-like, zero-sum threshold. If he intended to cross it, he needed to do so now, immediately, before that shadow creature used the time to prepare. He took a gulp of air and lurched down the hallway, glowering at the door with determined resolve.

Before he could reconsider, he threw it open. His imagination conjured images of the shadow creature at the precipice, a wall of shimmering black awaiting him. Instead, there was nothing. Only the familiar room and the familiar scent. He shot his gaze about like a SWAT officer clearing a room. He examined the corners, the crevices, the fields of empty space above the books. And only after taking in the entire room did he appreciate the chaos he created. In addition to the books he intentionally shoved off the shelves, others had tumbled free when he fell into the stacks. A virtual river of displaced tomes pointed the way from the door to the table. His stare followed the trail and he shifted to get a better view. That's when the absence hit him. Something was missing. Amid the clutter, the knife was nowhere to be found— the table was bare apart from his coat and paperwork.

Matt careened into the room, bouncing from fixture to fixture for support. He moved closer to the table and glared at his stack of papers. Only a neat puncture wound remained to bear witness to the impaled knife. If not for that shred of evidence he might've worried he imagined it all. But, for better or worse, the hole resided right there at the center.

The corollary to this proof, however, carried a sinister implication. If the knife disappeared while he was outside, that meant the being responsible for taking it still lurked inside. And with that revelation, his urgency exploded.

Initially, he'd staggered in and come to a halt about five feet away from the table. He sized up the nearby windows, then glanced back at his personal effects. Logically, his personal safety came first. Instead, his sense of purpose compelled him to hop back to the table. That writing was his whole reason for being there in the first place—he'd be damned if he just forgot about it like a scared little boy.

Matt reached the table and swept everything into his bag with one giant wave of his arm. Next, in one ungainly movement, he slung his bag around his body, hoisted up a chair, and sent it crashing through the window. He may've heard an alarm sound; he never checked for security cameras. Those matters were secondary observations, distractions from the escape portal in front of him. He cleared out the remaining window glass with his sleeves pulled over his hands. Then he launched himself through it, gracelessly heaving his body onto the frost-covered grass outside.

He staggered to his feet and, not unlike Lot's wife fleeing the devastation of Sodom and Gomorrah, Matt glanced back for the briefest moment. He witnessed no dark figure. He smelt no seawater stench. And then, still struggling for balance, he limped to his car and raced away.

## MATT

Matt broke his promise. Though he called for an emergency doctor's appointment Tuesday night—quite demonstratively in Meda's presence—he left a voicemail to cancel Wednesday morning. His spat with Meda was settled quickly and the rest of the night proved restorative. But that colossal project at his office was a beast and he'd made zero progress on it. Wasting time at a doctor's office wasn't an option. In fact, he left her apartment two hours early with the express notion of getting a jump on the work.

The assignment had commandeered an ominous place in his mind overnight and Matt knew why: his days were about to be engulfed. The project promised to be lengthy and rife with aggravation—such an endeavor would curl anyone's lip. More personally threatening, however, was the mental space the assignment would occupy. If his mind was a storage unit, it was essential that a large portion of that space be devoted to writing. It was virtually impossible to sit down to write without an existent well of ideas. Even if he wasn't literally at his desk typing, he needed to be obsessed with the craft of storytelling.

As a little boy, he chose to become a writer. After devouring the works of Alan Moore, Stephen King, and so many others, the field drew him in. He grew. The universities got ahold of him. And though it all began as a childish vision, lacking perspective and ignorant of the real-life implications, he remained determined to stay the course. In turn, an act of self-creation occurred—the process of becoming a writer doubled as both the direction and the result. So, if the storage unit of his mind demanded space for that little boy's dream, this project had all the makings of a leaking pipe ready to burst and flood everything inside.

Matt arrived at his office that morning and, after he clicked on the motion detector lights, discrete sections lit alive as he limped across the floor. The atmosphere at such an early hour was alien. Even most haunted houses exhibit an air of humanness in their weathering—the worn floorboards at a room's entrance, the scraped wall where the rocking chair used to knock. Empty office floors possess none of those details. The expanses are clinical and dour, drained of all humanity. Rather than the threat of some howling apparition, there is only nothingness. Two hours later, the landscape would be familiar and buzzing with activity. At the moment, however, this sense of estranged absence caused his moves to be tentative, as if something might crack should the silence be disturbed.

Then the being popped out of Tom Sussex's office. Matt experienced it as a rush of movement. Then panic. And, for the briefest instant, his spirit shuddered out of his body.

"Oh! Hi Matt!"

It was Abby. Goddamn it. Only Abby. Why was *she* here?

"What? Jeez," Matt muttered. He couldn't hide his irritation. In fact, he wasn't sure he wanted to. "Abby. You scared the crap out of me."

Abby cackled. It was far too loud at such an hour. Matt suffered visions of eggs shells cracking, light bulbs popping. "Sorry about that! What are you doing here so early?"

He couldn't speak. He was flabbergasted. How dare she ask *him* why he was there early? He'd struggled in on an injured ankle, purposefully carved out time to make headway on that infernal project, and now—before he even reached his desk—she was distracting him from his intended work. She was the interloper! Not him!

"I," said Matt eventually, still slack-jawed, "would ask you the same thing."

Again, she cackled. Again, it was too loud.

"Oh, y'know. There's just so much going on. Absolutely crazy. And like they say, early bird gets the worm. Any luck with the telescope?"

Abby's words were too quick, it was too early for this crap, and Matt was still too pissed at her presence in the first place. Telescope? What telescope? Then he recalled the asinine stargazing story he'd told her. Inwardly, he groaned—how did she remember that stuff?

"Ah, no. Nope. Haven't been out since."

"Got it. Absolutely. I was just curious. The moon can be brutal if you're not careful."

What? The moon? What the hell was she talking about? He started to say something, pursed his lips, then moved on. Yet she trailed behind nonetheless, prattling on and stalking him the entire way to his desk.

He tried his best to pick up where he left off but Abby's interruption rattled him more than he would've expected. Apart from the initial surprise, her very existence continued to distract. On an office floor spanning roughly fifteen thousand square feet, Abaddon Gupta resided a scant four feet from Matt—stapling reams of documents with workout-like intensity, squealing at texts, and engaging in shrieking conversations with friends. The distractions laid waste to his concentration and, by the time other co-workers began to trickle in, he'd accomplished nothing.

It was in this state that Louise appeared at Matt's cubicle. "How's the project going? I heard Amy in PR wants to take a look. Can't imagine why. Everything okay on your end?"

"Um, it's going well," said Matt, lying through his teeth. It was a reflexive response—he couldn't tell his boss he'd made no progress whatsoever. As soon as the words were articulated, however, he regretted issuing them.

"Great. Let me know if I need to get involved." She was like a car at a deserted stop sign, barely coming to a rolling halt. Before Matt even considered responding, she was gone.

Louise's drive-by only served to increase Matt's stress. At a certain point, he might need to admit the project was simply too big, that he was in over his head. But the shame at such an admission would be compounded by the fact that he allowed so much time to lapse—it was like going to the police weeks after committing a crime. He'd be presumed guilty.

In terms of silver linings, at least, Matt gleaned one small positive. He now appreciated how much he didn't know. Unlike his previous attempt to wrangle everything at once, he now began focusing on singular fields. By spotting common errors within certain groupings, he hoped to make those discrepancies predictive.

As an unintended consequence of this new approach, one particular account caught his attention. The investor, named Double Eagle Fusion Co., was based in Iran. It wasn't uncommon for foreign entities to invest in Fitzgerald's funds— approximately 9% of the firm's total assets were from non-U.S. investors. The vast majority of these were public or corporate pension plans in Japan or developed nations in Europe, however. It was rare to encounter an investor from Iran. And how many independent nuclear fusion companies existed in the world, much less Iran? While plants utilizing fission as the source of energy were common, Matt thought fusion technologies were still in development and limited to European countries.

The peculiarity sparked Matt's imagination. He began to ponder the allegorical notion of fusion in relation to the story he was writing about Edie. Thematically, her story was critical. If his intention was to explore forgotten dreams or unanticipated changes in life trajectories, then marriage, divorce, and parenthood were prime opportunities for such right angle turns. These events often did *not* work out the way one expected. Some partners might not pull their weight; some babies might abjectly refuse to sleep at night. And in his musings about fusion, he couldn't help but see a parallel taking shape.

As the source of the sun's energy, fusion occurs when two atoms come together to make a new nucleus, releasing energy as a result. This process works well for nuclei with lower masses. However, a pivotal juncture is hit inside stars as more and more matter fuses together. Once the nuclei reach a mass heavier than iron, everything changes. Fusion no longer creates energy but, instead, requires it. Could this not be analogous to parenthood? Could parenthood be a bond holding some marriages together and also be a disruptive wedge driving others apart? This relationship was the catalyst Matt needed to propel Edie's tale in a new direction. Once the idea hit, he couldn't stop obsessing about it.

Matt had begun his morning intending to focus on Project: Saturn. This new epiphany obliterated that plan, however. He made a couple lame attempts to put a dent in the project but, in the waning hours of the day, his heart was no longer in it. Eventually—workplace duties be damned—he threw in the towel and decided to take some printouts home for review later that night. He left work early, arrived home, and strode directly to his office where his half-completed story about Edie awaited. And then, fueled by this newfound inspiration, Matt disappeared into his writing in no time at all.

## EDIE

*Really? Seriously? Ten hours at work, an atrocious drive home, the fortitude to slave over the stove for an hour, and all Nick could think to say was, "You used too much butter on the asparagus." It'd required all of Edie's reserve to keep from leaping over the table and clawing his eyes out. And, as if to pour salt in the wound, he'd ensconced at the computer already and left her staring at a table full of dirty dishes.*

*After many minutes she sighed and throttled back her chair on their tile floor loudly enough for him to hear. She remembered when it was different. She recalled a time, only two years ago, in fact, when Nick surprised her with an extravagant meal after a particularly onerous work day. He greeted her at the door with a cup of hot chocolate and had her favorite song playing. Then, to top it off, he sent flowers to her office the next morning.*

*Now? Only a year into their marriage, it was an upset to see him after work for more than fifteen minutes before he disappeared. Oh sure, he eventually emerged for dinner and they might watch some television together. But the vibe was all wrong, so far from when they were dating. Spending time with his wife shouldn't be a damn obligation.*

*"What do you want to watch tonight?" she hollered from the kitchen. It was an act of rebellion. She knew perfectly well what they were going to watch. It was Thursday, the entire line-up was set in stone. But if forced to handle dinner without so much as a, "thank you," she was going to yank some sort of contribution out of Nick.*

*"Uh," came the distracted voice from the back room. "You know. The normal stuff."*

*Fine. That was all she needed to hear. She steadied herself, picked up Nick's dirty dinner plate, and then let it drop to the floor.*

*The ceramic disc shattered. Leftover gravy sprayed the cabinets; silverware bounced with metallic clinks across the floor. And when the shards settled in a gloppy mess, the clean-up appeared downright intimidating. Nick appeared at the threshold of the kitchen and Edie, as earnestly as possible, said, "Oops." Nick glared at her, then at the ugly clutter, then back at her. His concern withered and, gradually, an expression of weary disappointment settled in.*

*"Come on," he said simply.*

*She hadn't fooled him. She wasn't even sure if she intended to. Inwardly, she wanted to cackle at the ridiculousness of it all. But then, with his shoulders slumped, Nick simply walked back the way he'd come.*

*Edie didn't know what drove her to do that. It was so impetuous, so reckless, she hadn't even considered intentions or expectations. But his abject indifference wasn't a result she envisioned. With him back at the computer again, Edie was left alone with the mess. And, this time, she had no one to blame but herself.*

ⵉ     ⵉ     ⵉ

*Edie and Nick met through a mutual acquaintance at a series of parties. Both graduated college a few years prior; neither were working in a field related to their major. It wasn't love at first sight. In fact, the pair had attended similar events at least three times and Edie couldn't recall his presence at any of them. What eventually drew her to Nick was the way he concentrated when he listened. It was only after a few conversations, after he peered into her eyes with that stone-faced expression of his, that she started to experience the flutters. His singular focus made her feel like she was the only person in the world and this attentiveness soon shifted from flattery to physical desire. Many of their friends were also pairing up so it was easy for their relationship to move quickly. Friday nights at the bar gave way to quiet nights home on the couch and it all seemed perfectly natural.*

*Now, at twenty-eight years old, everything felt stale. It wasn't something she could easily articulate. Nick was still the man of her dreams. She made sure to remind herself of that often. And her job was fine. It was secure and paid well enough. Yet she hadn't spoken to her best friend, Jenny, in weeks. And she couldn't remember the last time Nick took her out to dinner. She had no reason to complain, particularly when she compared her life to the messes others had made of theirs. Yet a creeping lack of newness seemed to insinuate itself more strongly with each passing day.*

*Thankfully, the weekend's lunch with Ruzanna offered a welcome break in routine. Jenny had introduced her exotic, high-octane friend many years earlier and, for a time, the three were inseparable. Once Jenny settled down, however, her appearances grew increasingly infrequent with each successive newborn. Edie and Ruzanna tried to stay in contact but, with Jenny's incessant cancellations, their time together suffered collaterally. When Edie heard Ruzanna would be passing through town on business, she'd insisted they make time for lunch, with or without Jenny.*

*"How did we get here?" squealed Ruzanna upon spotting Edie. She then raced across the restaurant's waiting area and nearly bowled over an elderly woman in the process.*

*"Ruzanna!" Edie hollered.*

"How did we get here?" Ruzanna asked again, even more loudly. "How did we get to the point where a full year passes without hanging out? What is going on?"

"I know, I know," said Edie. "C'mon, let's sit down."

"I mean, how did we let it get to this point?" she continued, following the hostess to their seats. "What happened to us?"

"I don't know." Edie was beginning to feel vaguely awkward and feared they might be making a scene. "The important thing is that we're here now."

"But a year? Come on, a year? And where is that bitch, Jenny? Why couldn't she make it?"

"Oh, I think one of her kids has a recital or something." Edie wanted to remind Ruzanna that it was her decision to move to San Francisco. And that it was Ruzanna who'd dropped out of Jenny's wedding at the last minute due to an, "amazing Costa Rican expedition," thereby defaulting the Maid of Honor role to Edie. But Edie held her tongue. She was happy to see her hysterical friend; no need to spoil it with unnecessary ugliness. Instead, in a clumsy attempt to restart the conversation, she asked, "How has work been?"

"Ugh. It's driving me nuts. My clients are amazing and I love the travel and all, but it gets so old living out of a suitcase, don't you agree?"

Edie laughed. "I wouldn't know. I'll have to take your word on it."

"And Ronald. He's being such a baby about the whole thing. As if he can't live without me for three days!"

"Wait. Who? What about...?"

"Lucas? Oh, he's long gone. Decided his dirt bikes were more important than me. So, see ya! Ronald is much more mature."

Edie laughed again, differently than the previous time. She was actually thinking of Dylan. But, apparently, he was even older news than this guy, Lucas. She felt like she needed a spreadsheet to keep up.

"What?" asked Ruzanna, sensing Edie's camaraderie wasn't exactly in line with hers.

"Nothing. It's just...your life it's something else."

"Oh, you could have it, too, dear," said Ruzanna, reaching to clutch her hand, yet blind to the frown that flashed across Edie's brow. "You don't have to stay in this town if you don't want to. There is so much to see out in this world."

"I know. It's just," demurred Edie, her statement unfinished.

"Stop making excuses," Ruzanna pressed, still gripping Edie's captured hand. "I've always said that the only person that can stop you is you."

"I'm okay. Really, I mean it."

"Your words say one thing. But I see how you truly feel."

"Ruzanna. Shut up," said Edie. She rolled her eyes as she spoke, attempting to add levity. But the way she yanked her hand back from Ruzanna's grip told a different story.

"I'm sorry," said Ruzanna in a sudden moment of self-awareness. "You know me so well. Sometimes I get going and I can't stop. I'm sorry, dear. You know I love this town so much. But it's just, you know, not for me."

"Oh, I know," said Edie, summoning a laugh that required far too much effort. Edie admired her friend. But Ruzanna was a cartoon who sped through life on an effortless ability to ensure others cleaned up her messes. Edie had recognized the trait a decade ago. And, in the face of this lunch date conversation so immediately off the rails, she reminded herself yet again that it was a feat Ruzanna could pull off but she couldn't.

*By the time Ruzanna rushed out, tossing two twenties and sending an air-smooch, Edie was feeling contented again. Sure, it might be fun to visit places like London or even Paris, but to have a life like Ruzanna's? No, thank you.*

*Edie returned home that afternoon and life rolled on with dogged ruthlessness. Monday passed. Edie made breakfast for Nick on Tuesday morning and they discussed the weather. Then, that afternoon, she went to lunch with her work colleague, Kate. When they returned, however, they sensed something was up. Four of the other women, almost half of their company's female employees, were huddled in the hallway, their attention downcast. The area was cramped and, initially, Edie couldn't discern the source of the interest. When Samantha Dering saw the pair, though, she tapped D'Eisha's arm and the group parted to reveal a giant cupcake on Kate's desk. Though homemade, it was quite ornate, with a giant reservoir of toffee gobbed in the middle.*

*With plump cheeks and a happy squint, Samantha announced, "Brian was here. He dropped that off for you." All of the women were smiling and, when Kate caught sight of the dessert, her eyelashes began to flutter. "I'm sorry you missed him," added Samantha. "Doesn't he work almost nine miles away?"*

*Kate affirmed it with a glance and gushed, "He must've made it this morning. We were watching a cooking show a few nights back. I said how much I'd love to make one of those but I'd never have the time. My Mom. She would've been fifty-two today." At that, she swatted with her hand as if to wave away tears. A sympathetic coo arose from the women and Tina Loprete placed her palm on Kate's shoulder. "I can't believe he remembered. I don't talk about it much. I never expected this."*

"That's so sweet," purred Elaine, with murmured agreement from all.

"Let me give him a call," said Kate, suddenly animated. She motioned to move behind her desk and the happy group dispersed to return to work.

Edie was happy for her. She really was. Kate was five years her junior and, when she was hired, Edie had taken her under her wing. The trend that gave Edie pause, however, was Kate's increasing propensity to take liberties. She'd only been there six months yet she was already approving payments without consulting Edie. That wasn't against company policy, technically, but some might consider it a slight breach of protocol. At the very least, such recklessness was asking for trouble. And Edie sure as hell wouldn't be held responsible when something, inevitably, went wrong.

Nonetheless, Brian's gesture was very sweet and it reminded Edie of the old days with Nick. She noted that Nick often hadn't required a specific event to show his affection but then scolded herself for splitting hairs. The point remained that Kate's boyfriend was thoughtful enough to make her day better and he'd gone to great lengths to do it.

The workday ended without incident, Edie picked up some groceries on the drive home, and she pulled into the empty driveway. She approached the front door, the bag in one hand while fishing for her keys with the other. And she never heard or noticed the tree limb dropping from above.

⋈　　　　⋈　　　　⋈

Edie came out of the fog in a new place. She was in her home. She was on her couch. Yet, similar to the initial dislocation experienced upon waking up in a hotel room, something was missing. How had she arrived there?

*She blinked and peered about. Nick was in the kitchen, doing something at the sink with his back to her. The lights were on. The sun was down. What time was it? She twisted to sit up and the pain struck, a lash across the back of her head. She must've grunted because, despite the noise of running water, Nick took notice. "Oh hey. Take it easy," he said, drying his hands as he rushed to her side.*

*"What happened?" she muttered, her words thunderous inside her head. It felt like an iceberg had formed a ridge at the base of her skull that stretched up and over her forehead.*

*"Relax, relax. Don't move," cautioned Nick. He knelt down and peered at her with instructional seriousness. "You got hit by a tree branch. I found you outside. I don't think you were there long because the car was still warm. I called 911 and they walked me through everything. They wanted me to stabilize you first, in case it's a concussion, then get you to the ER. Most importantly, you're going to be okay."*

*It was a lot to take in. Nick's words were coated in cobwebs initially, foreign to her senses and in need of translation. Gradually though, Edie caught up as her immediate surprise subsided. She touched the back of her head gingerly, her fingertips instantly registering the large bump and eliciting further pain. She winced and, with steadying concern, Nick said, "Easy, easy."*

*Before her eyes, Nick morphed into Florence Nightingale. Gone was the disinterested computer nerd who'd become more a roommate than a husband. Yet also disappeared was the mysterious stranger who captured her imagination years ago. He explained that, though an emergency room visit wasn't absolutely necessary, they should go to the doctor's office to be positive she didn't have a concussion. He ensured she was warm, remained patient as she came to grips with the assorted details, and even carried her to the car.*

*Throughout it all, Edie's internal attention grew increasingly focused on the accident. It'd occurred out of the blue, on an ordinary day. She'd done nothing wrong, taken no unnecessary risks. She was right in front of her house, walking from her car to the front door. Yet. She could've died. Who knows how long she would've lain there unconscious if Nick got caught late at work? Or what if the limb struck a quarter-inch to the left or right? It could've been so much worse. If she died tomorrow, would she be proud of the life she lived? She was only twenty-eight yet it might've ended then and there.*

*Nick drove her to the doctor and stayed with her every step of the way. The staff did the traditional tests and took samples of her blood. Her pupils looked fine, she experienced no memory loss. Yet, though she showed no lingering effects, Nick's concern wouldn't abate until the doctor confirmed she'd be okay. Ultimately, the doctor prescribed a simple painkiller for her headache before telling her to take it easy for a few days. And on the drive home that night, Edie made a vow to divorce Nick.*

ᐂ        ᐂ        ᐂ

*Edie's follow-up appointment with her doctor was scheduled for three days later, first thing that Friday morning. In the interim, she'd surreptitiously packed some bags and dropped them with her sister, researched legal considerations regarding divorce, and made copies of her important paperwork. In fact, she'd nearly forgotten the appointment amid such preparations. Only at the last moment did she decide not to cancel. Better to wrap up loose ends before the coming tumult.*

*The appointment also served as a convenient explanation to Nick why their routine was disrupted that morning. And when he left at 7:00, she leapt to finish packing her remaining belongings. She darted about, tossing items in boxes with squirrel-like feverishness. Until finally, just as suddenly as she started, she stopped to dab her forehead and take stock of the room. The one remaining obligation revealed itself then, a goblin that crawled out from behind the couch to remind her she wasn't done yet. She needed to write her goodbye letter to Nick.*

*Mentally, she thought she'd conceived a decent structure to the note. She knew she couldn't convey the level of her frustration in person; pen and paper were required to express herself fully and, she reasoned, it would be kinder to Nick. Actual construction of this explanation didn't go exactly as planned, however. Four times she began the letter, only to get frustrated and crumple up the paper. While packing her valuables was liberating, reminiscent of the last day of school, crafting the letter was the opposite. The act of leaving an institution was far different from the act of leaving another person. Her goal wasn't to hurt Nick. Yet the note's impact on him hit her harder than she initially anticipated. As much as she enjoyed the feeling of escape, the responsibility on her shoulders weighed like a bag of concrete.*

*She worked herself out of this malaise with a simple mantra, telling herself that she needed to do what was best for her. There could be no going back. She couldn't risk telling Nick in person lest she wither and decide to stay. Therefore, she had no choice but to make a clean cut and leave the letter.*

*Eventually, she finished it. She told Nick she needed her space and she didn't want to perpetuate a mistake any longer. She stressed it was neither his fault nor her fault.*

They were young and impulsive when they got married, and now she needed to move on. She wasn't proud of her decision. Yet the fact that she never shed a tear crafting it confirmed she'd made the right decision. She placed the letter on the banister and, after giving one final look around, she closed and locked the door.

There was still so much to do. Nick would doubtlessly be calling the moment he got home, meaning she only had about nine hours to get all her remaining affairs in order. Once again, she considered skipping her doctor's appointment; the office was in a sketchy part of town and parking was atrocious. However, with a change in her insurance providers likely imminent and her headache returning, cancelling was a terrible idea.

As anticipated, she couldn't find a place to park near the office and settled for a spot three blocks away. Her car was loaded with her most vital earthly possessions, however. Only after she stepped out of it did she appreciate how much she stood to lose.

She peered at it skeptically before scanning the immediate area. At night, she wouldn't be caught dead there. Now? She tried to convince herself that the place was different, safer in the daytime. The small patches of grass in front of the houses were weedy. No children played. It was hot for a late October morning and the sun made the area seem vast and open. If anyone tried to break into her car, the entire block would see. Fine, she frowned, locking the door. She'd probably be in and out in a jiffy anyway.

A block away from her car, she began to regret the decision. A derelict had shuffled onto the otherwise deserted sidewalk up ahead, directly in her path. The reassurance she'd formerly found in the landscape's openness now inverted in a sinister way, turning desolate and arid. She considered crossing the street before deciding that was silly. The guy hadn't even noticed her. And she'd need to cross back again to reach the doctor's office.

Edie and the man's trajectories remained locked and the predetermined path of the sidewalk underscored Edie's dearth of options. Either she stubbornly pushed forward into the man's path or she needed to take advantage of the upcoming corner's outlet and cross the street now. She didn't want to seem like one of those oversensitive ninnies that ran for cover at the first sign of trouble. And there was the principle playing into it, as well. Why should she be forced to cross the street? Why should she live in fear? She'd chosen her path and she shouldn't need to alter it because of some wino.

Their inexorable approach continued. Each entered the same block from opposite ends and Edie got a better view of the man. He looked terrible. Wholly wrapped up in his inner demons, the man was flushed with sweat and his pallor bordered on translucent grey. It wasn't merely a matter of being sick; the man looked fundamentally rotten.

A rusted chain-link fence boundaried Edie on one side and a tight row of parked cars formed a line on the other. The sidewalk's width allowed for two people to pass easily. Yet the man was careening down the very middle of it on stumbling, unsteady legs.

Claustrophobia and a dark sense of the inevitable overcame Edie. She'd made her choice. But now, societal judgment be damned, she wished she had crossed the street instead. The parked cars were bumper-to-bumper without a break in sight. The fence loomed with ferocious barbed wire atop. Edie felt like she'd entered a one-way exit ramp heading in the wrong direction. No way to turn around, certain doom bearing down.

Fewer than twenty feet separated the duo and the distance was rapidly disintegrating. Edie edged to one side. Then the other. But predicting where the man might stumble next proved impossible. She slowed a fraction, ready to pivot. Then, nine feet away, the man looked up. His eyes, jaundiced and haunted, went wide at the sight of Edie.

Five feet. Their momentum kept each hurtling forward. Her body stiffened in terror. He honed in on her. She readied to flee. He raised his hand, fingers twitching, towards her face. And on pure instinct Edie rotated to the opposite side.

"You're the woman," the man said.

The words, gravel-intoned and ominous in their simplicity, pushed Edie past her limit. She shuddered and, still twisted at the waist in avoidance, she nearly spun out of control.

Then she was past him. And, once steadied, she accelerated, racing away. Like the slow-motion terror of a near-fatal car crash, the encounter occurred in an instant and it was only afterward that she had the chance to appreciate what'd happened.

Her blood pounded in her ears, nearly cancelling out the spiking −click, clack− of her heels on the concrete. She exhaled through her nostrils and her cheeks brightened to red. A toxic rush of embarrassment that she'd overreacted crashed against feelings of fear, vindication, and basic self-preservation. She continued to march in tight, snapping movements. Then, finally deciding she was a safe distance away, she turned to glance back. The man wasn't following. He was stopped in the middle of the sidewalk and appeared to be contemplating something.

Edie hit the doctor's office in stride and barged through the front door into the waiting room. Once inside the safety of the practice, she took a moment to calm her breathing. Her palm went to her forehead and she found it sopping wet, blazingly hot. And only then did she register the alarmed expression worn by the receptionist. "Can I help you?"

"Hello. Yes," Edie said with an awkward giggle. "I'm sorry. I had a very weird encounter outside. I have an appointment with Dr. Han."

"Oh, Mrs. Dennis?" asked the receptionist, her demeanor doing a U-turn. A broad grin blossomed on her face, one that Edie found a little creepy. Then she intoned, "Come right this way."

Once in the examining room, Edie took the opportunity to mop the sweat off her brow. It wasn't the middle of July; she hadn't run a marathon. Yet the suddenness and the awfulness of the encounter left her flushed and wet all over.

Her doctor, Dr. Han, was an affable man who perpetually appeared both excited and surprised. When he entered the room with a sly smile, Edie thought nothing of it. "The good news," he announced, "is that your tests came back without any serious reasons for concern. Nothing." That was easy! Edie readied to hop off the table. Then Dr. Han added, "The even better news is that you're pregnant."

Her spine shuddered. It was involuntary. For a fleeting moment, she thought she misheard him. Immediately after that, she flashed mortified at how her reaction might be interpreted. Then all those concerns fell away, replaced by the undeniable, immutable reality of the doctor's announcement. She was pregnant. She was no longer herself. She was now living for two. And she doubted she could pull that off alone.

All her life she'd imagined hearing the glorious news. The expectation, the duty, the honor of becoming a new mother. Never, in her wildest imagination, had she envisioned receiving it like this. She'd just walked out on her husband!

*The revelation wasn't a miraculous, blessed event. It was an intruder, a stranger that barged in without invite or anticipation.*

*The silence stretched on. The room darkened. And Edie's eyes glazed over. Eventually, Dr. Han asked tepidly, "You seem surprised."*

*Edie shook awake, moving her head from side to side. "No. I'm sorry," she stammered. "Yes. I mean, yes, I am surprised. I didn't know I was."*

*"Well, it's very early in your term. You may not have noticed any changes in your rhythm."*

*His words offered no consolation. Edie didn't care about the timing. Two days pregnant? Two months pregnant? It didn't matter. The concrete reality of pregnancy was all that mattered. Full stop. Zero-sum. A one-way street.*

*Her thoughts shot to Nick. And their life together. Previously, she felt like she was spinning her wheels staying with him. As hard as she might floor the metaphorical accelerator on their relationship, the momentum nonetheless continued to wane.*

*This was worse. This was a brick wall. Sudden, jarring, and irrevocable. Smack into the windshield. She questioned how she arrived at this place, how she could make such a choice under such pressure. But then, she realized, it wasn't really a choice at all.*

*"I'm sorry," she muttered, as she sloughed off the examination table. The words, barely above a whisper, appeared but she didn't feel like they were hers. "I need time to think."*

*"Take your time, of course. We have services to help when you are ready. Many people need some time," said the doctor to the back of her head as she ambled past.*

*Edie emerged from the doctor's office into the harsh light of the morning. The sidewalk was desiccated and spotted with the briny outlines of evaporated puddles. The derelict she encountered earlier was long gone. It wasn't the same world she'd known.*

*No choice existed now. No alternate path. She knew she needed to go back. She needed to go back home, rip up that note, unpack all her things, and return them to their exact same spots.*

*How she wished she could go back even farther! Back, before she married Nick, before she ever met him. Before that, in fact. Before the expectations, and the fears, and the hesitation. Go back to that time when life was filled with opportunity and fun and hope.*

*She made her way home to begin the dreary task of replacing all the items she packed. Zombie-like, she marched to the car and back with her possessions, bereft of emotion. With desultory precision she placed her bathroom supplies in their former positions, her clothes in the proper drawers. Throughout, her eyelids hung nearly closed, focused only on the task at hand. And, without regard or notice by Edie, a light soon blazed up and over the horizon.*

## MEDA

Meda intuited something was wrong before she rounded the corner. Maybe it was the light reflected in that window, or perhaps the way that man stared down the street. On an otherwise uneventful commute home, she approached the edge of the stone building at the end of her block with an anxious apprehension. Her fears were confirmed when she made the turn and discovered a fire truck idling in the middle of the street. Worse, it sat in front of her apartment. Worse still, firemen were coming in and out of her building. This recognition unfolded in her mind both gradually yet with alarming celerity. Her conscious mind didn't want to believe it yet her instincts set her body in motion. Her pace cycled quickly from a beleaguered shuffle to a trot to a full-on sprint.

As she rushed to the scene she continued to soak in details, catching sight of her neighbor, Mrs. Javier, and the building superintendent, Mr. Goldt. Yet neither appeared particularly worried. Similarly, the firemen's movements were unhurried and lacked the urgency commonly associated with an emergency. She relaxed, but only slightly. Then, as she slowed her approach, a fireman at the perimeter intercepted her. "It's okay, it's okay," he said, his palms up towards her. "I take it you live here?"

"That's right."

"There's no fire. Everything is safe. The batteries in your neighbor's fire alarm were running low and he thought it was carbon monoxide. Everything is fine."

The fireman delivered the news with a practiced efficiency that suggested he might've recited a similar speech a hundred times. Fully disarmed, Meda uttered a simple, "Oh. Okay." The fireman flashed a brief grin and Meda asked, "Is it safe to go in now?"

"Give us a second. We'll be out of the way soon." Meda nodded and the fireman went back to work. Still invigorated by the surprise and without any obvious place to focus that energy, she pivoted on her heel, unsure what to do next.

Often, she felt like her entire life was spent marching back and forth between her apartment and her office. Today, however, both ends of her commute had become unexpected boondoggles. Apart from this scare, Matt had messed up her alarm clock and made her late for work. More aggravating, he still hadn't called to tell her about his trip to the doctor despite leaving yesterday morning. The pair had a standing 'Date Night' on Thursdays and she presumed she'd get the full report from him later. For now, though, she really could've done without this latest stress.

"You left the door open."

The gruff pronouncement hit Meda from behind. She turned to find Mr. Goldt, all 5-foot 3-inches of him, clad in the ever-present white undershirt. "Excuse me?" she asked.

"This morning," he said, as if the implication was self-evident. "You was running out and the door slammed. It didn't lock. Anybody coulda got in. You gotta be more careful."

"Oh. Yes. I'm sorry," apologized Meda, before slipping into an amused smirk. "Won't happen again."

Then: "*Actually*." The single word swooped down, like an avenging angel from heaven, and Meda could've sworn she saw Goldt wince. "I would say she did you a favor."

Mrs. Javier sidled up to Goldt, eying him as a nun might a naughty schoolchild. She exhibited a porcelain-like delicacy that often elicited offers of assistance from strangers. Yet her uncanny confidence and those eyes (those enormous, soul-piercing eyes) suggested she could handle herself just fine. "If that door hadn't been left open, the carbon monoxide might've built up quicker. She probably saved us."

Goldt glared and spit his way through a frothy diatribe. "Didn't you hear the fireman? There was no carbon monoxide. It was the batteries. The batteries! Mr. Webber didn't know no better so he called the firemen. There wasn't no carbon monoxide!"

Mrs. Javier wasn't buying it. Before he finished speaking she'd already started shaking her head in defiance. "You know full well how old that boiler is, Mr. Goldt. It was only a matter of time until something happened."

The pair continued to squabble and, effectively excluded from the conversation, Meda strolled away. Mrs. Javier (sweet enough to induce diabetes) was perpetually ready for conversation and always seemed to materialize on the heels of Meda's most frustrating days at the office. Meanwhile, Goldt was virtually invisible every day of the month apart from the first, when rent was due. To varying degrees, each was uniquely tiresome. So, while Meda appreciated Mrs. Javier's stout defense, she felt no inclination to get sucked into a battle between the two.

A few minutes passed and the remaining firemen began to pile into the truck. Meda had planned to go to yoga. She still had plenty of time to make the class, in fact. Yet the scare had put her on edge and worries about Matt's ankle continued to plague her (along with them, growing feelings of resentment at his lack of communication). How relaxing would yoga be with so many distractions cluttering her mind? She reached into her pocket to check her phone but, predictably, there were no new messages.

She recalled Matt mentioning something about a passing comet and, killing time, she craned her neck to peer up at the sky. It was futile. If the ambient glow of the city wasn't too much light pollution, the moon had been glowing brighter by the day. Unsure what Matt hoped to see up there exactly, she looked back to the street. Eventually, the fireman gave the 'all clear' sign and she readied to finally enter her apartment. Then her heart sank when she saw Mr. Goldt waddling back towards her.

"Another thing," he opened with. "What's the deal with that boyfriend of yours?"

"Matt?" she asked simply, put off by another brusque conversation starter.

"Bingo. Him. Why're people chasing after him?"

Meda frowned, then drew her jaw in to illustrate her puzzlement. "I don't know what you're talking about."

"Tuesday night. Didn't he come and visit you?"

"Yes."

Goldt registered her apprehension and, with a quick wave behind him, said, "I saw him on the security camera."

"Oh. Of course." Goldt envisioned the device as a foolproof deterrent to would-be burglars. Meda remained dubious. The field recorded by the camera didn't reach the end of the sidewalk and she was fairly certain it wasn't digital, implying Goldt recorded over the same tape every week.

"I saw him come running up to the building. He went through the door and this other guy comes right behind him. That guy slammed into it a second late. Like he was out to get your boyfriend. I don't want no trouble. Whatever your boyfriend's doing, I don't want it seeping into my building."

Goldt was trying to appear stern but Meda's reaction indicated only befuddlement. "What? That doesn't make any sense. Are you sure it was Matt?"

"Positive. I knew he was over Tuesday, didn't I?"

Meda scowled. Such knowledge offered a bit of credibility, she would admit, but it didn't conclusively prove anything. "Right. I'll ask him about it. I'm sure there's an explanation."

"Okay," said Goldt warily. "Okay." Then he plodded away.

Meda took a deep breath then scooted up the stairs to her apartment. While relieved the conversation was over, her disquiet lingered. Goldt's story didn't add up. How could Matt run on his injured ankle? And why would someone be chasing him? The superintendent tended to flourish his anecdotes with exaggerations. Yet such creative license usually involved casting former tenants in a bad light or forgiving his own supervisory shortcomings. (Mrs. Javier's theory about the door and the carbon monoxide was probably correct!) Bemoaning damage done by a previous renter wasn't the same type of embellishment as Goldt's bizarre tale about Matt. Together with Matt's frenetic phone call, it only further obfuscated the foggy narrative.

Absent-mindedly, she entered her apartment and dropped her bag at the door. She'd performed the same routine thousands of times, an act so automatic that no conscious thought occurred. The only thing to break her out of her trance was the old woman standing at the end of the hallway.

"Oh!" Meda leapt, her hand shooting to cover her heart. Then, almost imperceptibly following a taught second of caution, she relaxed. And a second after that, embarrassment gushed into her being. The "old woman" was Meda herself, reflected back via the full-length mirror at the end of the hall. Meda flashed the irritation of someone who'd had a fly buzz into their wine glass. The misperception was embarrassing on two levels, both the fact that she frightened herself so clumsily and that she considered the source of the fright, her own self, to be an old woman. She wondered how she'd avoided such a surprise until now and, as if to blame the mirror, decided to move it. It was an inauspicious start to her night and, as she took off her coat and shoes, her body language showed as a perpetual *harrumph*.

Along with the other surprises and frustrations that day, the scare convinced her to blow off yoga. Instead, she began preparing dinner while intending to hit Matt with those questions about Goldt's surveillance footage as soon as he arrived.

He never appeared, however. The minutes stretched into hours, over which a slow-moving, deflated acceptance occurred within Meda. And, left with only the leaky faucet (that she neglected to mention to Goldt) to keep her company, her various calls and texts to him went unanswered.

## MATT

"Where am I?"

**Nowhere.**

"Yeah. Okay. Where are you then?"

**A different nowhere.**

# MAGEE

It was fairly unprecedented to receive a call from Meda. Magee met her over a decade earlier...Matt's very first date with her, as a matter of fact. But apart from party planning or other oddball circumstances, communications from Meda usually filtered through Matt. There was no formal reason for this; it was a natural outgrowth of their maturation together. If Meda often acted as the wise, logical voice in Matt's ear then Magee represented the bellicose, rebellious holler in it. In fact, Magee might admit now with tepid embarrassment, that years ago the name, "Yoko," had come up on occasion. Most of this acrimony from their youth had faded over the years yet the communication structure between the trio nonetheless remained intact. Therefore, it was a bit of a surprise when Meda asked him to stop by Saturday afternoon.

He made the trek from the Astoria subway stop while listening to a voicemail from Taylor. Most of the time, Taylor used a speedy, fragmented speech pattern that cut to the chase. A dilemma with the film's paperwork, however, made this message anything but quick or tidy. Fall leaves blew past Magee's feet as he walked and, with Taylor in his ear, he spied a boy and his dog up ahead. The cherubic lad appeared lazily affable in a contended sort of way, a contrast to the excitability of the puppy. They were farther ahead on the sidewalk, frolicking beside two parked cars. Meda's apartment building stood at the end of the block so Magee would be passing the pair soon enough.

Taylor continued, "...you see how important this is? Dante's getting you added to his insurance. A week, likely. Then the property owner will need time, too. Meaning we'll need your signature on the day the paperwork is approved."

Magee's concentration waned as Taylor droned on and it found a new target in the boy...particularly when he placed the puppy atop a nearby ledge. The roughly two-foot-high barrier of fortified concrete and stone ran the length of the retaining wall behind them. This wall stood between them and a major expressway about twenty feet below them. The boy and his dog were safe up above but, if the puppy were to slip off the ledge, it'd plummet into the throttling traffic below.

Luckily, the puppy seemed to intuit the danger better than the boy and, after nervously nosing about for a moment, it hopped back to the sidewalk alongside the boy. With the crisis apparently averted, Magee shook his head at the boy's bizarre plan.

But then, to his horror, the boy proceeded to pick up the puppy and situate it on the stone perch again. Magee craned his neck and edged his steps sideways to get a better look. This time, the boy held the puppy in place for an extra second as the puppy's gaze shot to and fro. Concern welled up in Magee anew. What did the boy think he was doing?

Once again, the puppy hopped off and, based on the boy's disappointment, it was clear he intended to try yet again. Magee's pace quickened and Taylor's voicemail became a distraction rather than an actual focus. He didn't consciously decide to keep the phone to his ear...he simply never pulled it away as this slow-moving tragedy unfolded.

This time, the puppy grew more agitated as the grinning boy attempted to perch it on the top of the wall. It wriggled in the boy's clumsy fingers; its paws swiped at the air as if to avoid contact with the stone.

"Hey kid!" Magee shouted, sensing the inevitable.

Then the unwieldy canine squirmed free and the ham-fisted boy let go of it too soon. The puppy leapt. And, so high from the stone, its momentum propelled it too far.

The puppy tumbled over the top of the retaining wall and out of view. "No!" hollered Magee.

Still a half-block away, he galloped towards the boy, dropping the phone from his ear even as Taylor's message continued. Before Magee could reach him, however, the seemingly unconcerned boy moved beside the structure and peered over the edge. Magee readied to holler again, to tell him to wait. He didn't get a chance, however, when the situation swerved inexplicably worse. The boy, first throwing one leg over to straddle the barrier before then sending the other over, hopped off the ledge. It wasn't clumsy. He hadn't fallen. Rather, he just climbed up and over, casually and without hesitation. Magee couldn't believe his eyes. His logical mind resisted what his senses were conveying.

Magee sprinted now, yelling, "Hey! Hey!" By the time he arrived, though, both the boy and the puppy were nowhere to be found. Cars shot past, whooshes of movement across the motionless concrete landscape. Yet no evidence of the pair's existence remained.

"Hello? Little boy? Can you hear me?" He had no idea what to do. Should he call the cops? Should he continue to stand there bellowing at the highway? It was clear the boy climbed and leapt of his own volition. And no accident had occurred, no blaring horns or sounds of crunching metal. Perhaps, based on the boy's fearlessness, he knew of some secret passage Magee didn't see? The boy could be emerging from a storm pipe twenty feet away, puppy in hand and a pair of muddy knees as the only evidence of his journey. But Magee had no way of knowing.

Magee surveyed the area and started to question his recollection of the events. The boy had only commandeered his attention at the last moment. Could he trust his impressions in such a distressed state?

"Hello?" he called again, no longer expecting an answer.

Once more he soaked in his surroundings and listened. He heard no whimpering, no cries for help. Logically, that meant the boy and his pup were probably fine, didn't it? If the boy was scared or injured, he'd likely be screaming. In this instance, silence was a good thing, no? Magee wasn't sold on this conclusion. Yet he could craft no other satisfactory explanation. Gradually, the tension leaked from his body and, with an ornery grimace, he moved on to Meda's apartment.

"Hey Magee. Thank you so much for coming," said Meda, before recognizing his odd demeanor. "Everything okay?"

"Yep," said Magee. "I'm fine. Not sure I can say the same about that kid outside. It's going to sound crazy but this little boy...he jumped onto the Grand Central Parkway."

"Really? Was he okay?"

"I don't know! I couldn't find him afterward. He just vanished. Little butterball of a kid, he'd been forcing his dog to sit on the ledge above it. Then his puppy fell over and, well, the kid followed."

Meda frowned. "Carlos? From across the street? He wouldn't do something like that."

"I didn't get his name. I just...saw him jump." His comment was sarcastic, issued out of the side of his mouth. Then he added, "I'm sure he's safe. I listened for a while and didn't hear any screams. I'm guessing he knew of some place to avoid the cars. I considered calling 911 but...I don't know, it didn't feel like anything was wrong. Just weird is all."

Meda waited for him to add anything else. Then, given Magee's dismissive summation, she moved on. "Anyway, I wanted to thank you for coming over. Like I mentioned, I haven't heard from Matt in days and I'm getting worried."

"Yep. I don't blame you. He can be sorta hard-headed sometimes but it's not like him to just disappear. You mentioned he was injured or something?"

"His ankle. He insisted it was sprained. I wasn't so sure."

She stopped speaking, more abruptly than Magee would've expected. And when she added nothing else, he asked, "You think it might've gotten worse?"

"Well, no. Not exactly. There's more. For starters, he called me in a terrible panic. He sounded like he was running. I thought something awful had happened. Instead, he showed up cool as a cucumber. Not out of breath at all. That was weird but it wasn't the end of the world, right? Maybe I was mistaken. That can happen on a call when someone's walking. But then we took a look at his ankle. And Magee, when I say it was black, I mean it looked like a two-month old banana. Yet Matt didn't want to go to the doctor."

Magee smirked. "Actually, that doesn't surprise me."

"I know. His stubbornness knows no bounds," agreed Meda. "Tuesday night, he made an appointment with the doctor. Then he left early Wednesday morning. And that was the last time I saw him. I expected to get an update and, I'll admit, I was pretty pissed when I didn't hear from him. This is the guy who walked eight blocks to pass along someone's mis-delivered mail because he feared the pictures inside might get bent in a post office box. He's not normally this inconsiderate. But then he blew me off Thursday night, too."

"Your date night."

"Right. Now it's been over three days. I called hoping you'd heard from him. If only to know he's okay." Magee's solemn expression confirmed he hadn't and Meda took a deep breath. "Okay. Well, I've probably left him ten messages so far. I'm not sure adding another will accomplish anything." She hesitated, then asked, "Do you think we should call the police?"

It was a peculiar question inasmuch as Meda rarely asked Magee for advice, particularly on such serious matters. For an unsteady beat, Magee didn't know how to respond. Then, empathizing with the vulnerability inherent in her query, he said, "I don't know. It's not like he's a little boy. I wonder how authentically the police would take it. Maybe we could try some of his social media sites? See if he's checked in?"

Meda issued a mirthless chuckle. "If he posted a status update and didn't call me, he's going to wish he went missing."

Magee pursed his lips. There was no background noise, however, no traditional television chatter to fill the momentary, awkward silence.

Then Meda's phone rang. She snatched it off the table and peered at it. And once confirmed, she signaled to Magee with a bright-eyed glance, and answered. "Matt! Are you okay?"

He responded, "Meda, I think there are two of me."

## MATT

When Matt awoke he was surrounded by nothing. Gone was his desk. Gone was his computer. In fact, gone was the entire room. Normally, even during the darkest night, some infinitesimal quanta of light slipped in and outlined objects in the room. Matt detected nothing, however. Only darkness that may exist for five feet or may stretch to infinity.

Yet the awakening wasn't altogether jarring. Initially, at least. By degrees, he re-entered himself and foggy, disassociated memories returned. They were comforting in their amorphous haziness; mental images without context. He recalled writing Edie's story and dissolving into it—a mental state without a defined singularity.

As tangible thoughts formed, however, expectations and presuppositions arose with them. His sensate capacity grew, and as language returned, his mind exploded in a pandemonium of questions. Why was he on the floor? Why was it so dark? Was he hurt? A levy inside his mind burst and notions of past, present, and future overflowed his thought stream. How long had he been unconscious? Why was he out in the first place? He craned his neck to peer about. Still, he saw nothing. Then a chill ripped through him, a frigid and immediate gale. What if he'd lost his sight?

It was the first moment he felt properly frightened. Prior to that, the experience had possessed a certain naturalness— as if all would be explained in due time. The notion of blindness could be such an explanation. However, it was one that was terrible in its real-life tangibility. Frantically, Matt began to feel about. Could he truly be blind? He stretched in one direction, finding only a barren expanse of floor. Then, panicked, he hoisted himself on hands and knees and scrambled in the opposite direction.

"No. No."

He threw his hand up in front of his face. Still: Nothing.

"No, no, no," he whined, despair taking hold. He staggered to his feet and pain shot through his injured ankle.

It was both a terrible jolt and a measure of hope when he collided with the wall. There was something out there at least. Propped against it, he reached in one direction, then the other. His fingers collided violently with the bookcase and he finally gained some sense of direction. He steadied, recalibrated. If the shelf was there, that meant the door was over there. He skidded across the wall, unwilling to forgo its rigidity, and his fingers stabbed into the molding around the door. Matt traced it downward to the handle and he threw the door open.

Light burst forth. It washed over Matt, through him. He shouldn't have been surprised. Yet, he was. And despite the shock, it was one of the most refreshing blasts of illumination he ever experienced. He wasn't blind! He would be okay!

The reassurance caused a sea change in his outlook. For a moment he merely stood, leaning into the door frame as the immediacy of his quest faded. It was a startling position to find oneself. Then, with vestigial curiosity, he peered back at the room. Now fully illuminated, it looked as familiar as ever. His computer was in sleep mode, snuffing out its traditional glow. But the sun hadn't yet set—the halo around the blinds hinted that it was probably late afternoon, in fact. Why had it appeared so abyssally dark?

Matt continued to ponder and his relief transitioned to a peculiar nagging sensation. He felt embarrassed by his overreaction. But there was more to it than that. He was positive everything appeared pitch black. He'd held his hand inches in front of his face with no recognition whatsoever. And with each passing second, he grew more resolute. He wasn't mistaken. The darkness had been absolute. But how? Why?

Seeking an explanation, he hopped to the window and tugged the blinds sideways. Perhaps a cloud had passed overhead? No. The sky was blue. Matt grimaced, his theory disproven. And, while still troubled by the unexplainable darkness, he realized that myriad other questions remained unanswered. Most principally, how had he arrived there—wherever *there* was?

Retracing his steps, he'd come home from work with a healthy bit of inspiration. While he should've been exhausted after schlepping to the office so early, an idea had seized him and, once home, the writing poured out of him. The hours slipped away yet the creative juices continued flowing. He recalled being hit by a wave of transcendence, as if all was right with the world. And that's where his recollection got hazy. Words escaped him as he tried to summon a description of the retreating memories. In fact, he couldn't even remember if he finished writing the story.

Then, with that realization, a mundanely practical concern hit him. What time was it? If he was right about the afternoon sun, he was preposterously late for work. He hopped to the computer, jiggered the mouse, and waited with bated breath for it to spring to life. And, when it did, he was flabbergasted. Not only was it 3:19 PM. It was Saturday.

Initially, he didn't believe what he was seeing. The PC displayed it quite clearly. But there must be some other explanation. Perhaps a power surge? Or a computer virus? There was no way he slept for over two days.

Between his doubts about the luminosity of his room and this glitch in his computer, Matt grew agitated. Something was very, very wrong. He limped out to the living room and seized the remote control to the television. Then his vexation doubled at the confirmation that it was, indeed, Saturday afternoon.

How could he have lost so much time? The question, posed rhetorically in his mind, took on a second meaning when framed against the darkness he'd experienced. Physically, he came to a halt, lost in thought at this new consideration. What if he hadn't been in the room at all? While writing, he often experienced a sensation of dematerialization, as if the molecules of his body were drifting apart and his consciousness was disengaging from his corporeal form. He'd felt it Wednesday night, as intensely as the previous Monday at the library. What if he truly went someplace else?

Matt began to search for a rational, scientific way to explain this duality. He'd read an article detailing how the same photon could exist in two places at once, though the exact mechanics of this duality remained a mystery to him. He also recalled certain forms of meditation that allowed practitioners to remove their consciousness from their body for extended periods of time. What if he'd unintentionally married this theory of quantum entanglement with traditional spiritual projection?

Absent mindedly, Matt turned off the television. And for a long stretch he remained in this blank slate, weighing the possibility of such a wild theory. At face value, it was insane. Yet it explained so much! How could he sleep so long without waking up? How could he witness such a perfect void in his room? How could he go without eating or drinking for so long? These questions were all addressed by the notion that he simply wasn't there.

He bowed his head ever so slightly, as if giving himself some note of approval. Then he blinked, his features growing animated as he returned to himself. And, finally, he meandered to the phone to call Meda.

## MEDA

"What?"

The word was spit out. Venomous. Meda's eyes narrowed to slits as her concern for Matt sling-shot into vitriol at such an idiotic thing to say.

"I said I think I—"

"I heard you, I heard you," interrupted Meda. Gone for three days and that was all he had to say for himself? With her right hand white-knuckled on the phone, she steamed, "Matt, where have you been? You can't be serious. I've been worried sick about you!"

Across the room, Magee's expression morphed. Though relieved to learn Matt was calling, whatever he said had sent Meda on the warpath.

"I'm sorry. It's hard to describe," Matt responded. "I got lost in my writing. I'm not sure where the story began and I ended."

She barely registered his words. "This isn't right, Matt. You can't just disappear, blow me off, and expect some pseudo-science gibberish will placate me."

Magee took a step closer to her, palm raised as if to comfort her. Her glare stopped him in his tracks.

"I called Magee," she continued. The statement was targeted like a weapon, as if to depict the level to which she'd been forced to stoop. "He's here as we speak. We were just discussing whether we should call the police."

"Meda, today is the first time I woke up in three days!"

His desperate tone seized Meda. "What?"

Matt took the opportunity to lay everything out, rambling in his attempt to convey his side of the story. "I was writing Wednesday night. After work. Everything was going fine. Great, in fact. And then—it's hard to explain—I gradually lost consciousness. Not a blackout. More like skipping along the precipice of sleep. I still can't remember when I fully left. Then I woke up this morning on the floor. I was out the whole time."

As Matt spoke, Meda's body lost its affronted rigidity and an open-mouthed expression of concern took its place. Though Magee couldn't hear Matt's words, he registered the shift in her polarity.

"Oh Matt," she said, crestfallen.

"Let me finish. When I came back, I couldn't see anything. It was like I was in a black void. Absolute darkness. But this happened at mid-afternoon. Light should've been coming in from outside the blinds. And I realized, I wasn't waking up in the classic sense. Not like you do in the morning after sleeping all night. Instead, it was like I was coming back into being. My body was here all along. But the 'me' was somewhere else in the void. And that's why I saw such total darkness. There were two of me."

This time Meda didn't reply immediately. When she finally did, however, the words were deliberate and precise. "We need to get you to the hospital."

"What? No. I'm fine."

"Baby, you probably had a stroke. Or something else is wrong. I don't know. A person doesn't just pass out for three days if everything is fine."

Magee's attention spiked upon hearing this portion of the conversation. Why was Matt unconscious for three days?

"No really. I feel fine," Matt insisted. Then he corrected, adding, "Well, apart from the ankle, obviously."

"Your ankle! Of course! You've probably got an infection." Meda paused but, before Matt could interject, she continued, "That's it. We're coming over. Magee and I. We need to get you to the emergency room."

"What? No. C'mon."

"Matt, I'm serious. We're leaving."

Before Matt uttered another word, she clicked off the phone and looked up to Magee. "You heard?"

"Yep, most of it. Matt's been unconscious for three days?"

Meda shook her head, partly in disgust at Matt's cavalier attitude. "Yes. Since Wednesday night, apparently. And I'm willing to bet he didn't go to the doctor about his ankle. He's probably got an infection or a blockage. Who knows?"

"Okay, okay," said Magee, putting his hand on her shoulder, this time meeting no resistance. "Let's get over there and check the goofball's condition. If we gang up on him we might be able to convince him to get help."

Meda didn't need a white knight. But she was thankful for Magee's presence. They left and she attempted to summarize the nonsense Matt spewed, fearful she missed certain details. It didn't help matters that Magee appeared distracted, as if still looking for the little boy he encountered earlier.

When they arrived at Matt's apartment, Meda opened the door, quickly scanned the living room and kitchen, and issued a casual, "Matt?"

The expected reply never came, however, and the pair exchanged a quick glance. "Matt?" she asked again, more loudly.

Their concern grew. Meda separated to check his bedroom while Magee darted to inspect his office. The rooms were tiny, even by New York City standards; there weren't a million places for Matt to hide. The periphery around his bed offered scant room to maneuver and, in the office, the chair was so close to the wall it'd left countless scuff marks. Following their unsuccessful initial survey, Meda and Magee were at a loss.

"Unbelievable," said Meda in disgust.

"Yep," said Magee, agreeing with her sentiment. "He's not here."

They peered about again, as if to catch something they might've missed. Nothing seemed askance, however. His place wasn't a pigsty but it suffered from the traditional clutter of a single guy living alone: a small pile of magazines lay on the coffee table next to the couch, the kitchen table probably should've been wiped down five meals ago, and a dog-eared copy of a Plato's writings collected dust beside the television. But there were no signs of struggle, nothing in disarray to suggest he hurt himself or had an accident.

"His coat is still here," announced Meda. She found it in a heap next to a kitchen chair, as if it missed the mark when he tossed it. The immediate implication was that he hadn't gone anywhere. Upon further reflection, though, it only served to deepen their concern. Matt wasn't in the apartment. Yet, if he had wandered off into the cold, he'd done so wholly unprepared for the elements.

"Magee," started Meda, deliberately. "I'm worried."

"That goes for both of us."

# TINA

"It's common sense, y'know? Everybody's gotta take care of themselves first. Y'ever see those pictures at ball games, the moment the bat breaks and goes flying into the stands? Every single time, you can see it in the pictures, every time, almost everybody is jumping out of the way. Nobody's worried about protecting little Johnny over there or that baby up there. They see a bat coming at them, they've got a split second, they duck. It's instinctual. That's it."

"Except for that one fat-ass not paying attention. She's the one that gets clobbered."

"That's why I said, 'almost everyone.' Pay attention,'" corrected Roy, eliciting a Roman chorus of guffaws.

Tina sighed. She just wanted to eat her lunch in peace. In a breakroom the size of a glorified utility closet, however, it was impossible to avoid some of her more hooligan-esque colleagues. Complicating matters was the lack of an authentic reason to be angry; they weren't acting excessively obnoxious. In fact, they were only having some innocent fun. Yet she resented the arrangement: the four of them were over there, laughing it up after completing another survey, and she was over here, by herself, practically ignored in the corner. They hadn't even acknowledged her when they tromped in. To them, she might as well be another replaceable part on one of their rigs. Afloat in a virtual sea of single males, a 33-year-old divorcee like Tina should've been the envy of her single friends. But as the old poem lamented, "Water, water everywhere, nor any drop to drink."

Harlan Jakobs and Co. was a boutique engineering firm specializing in uniquely demanding projects. The company focused on speed and ingenuity, jobs that required specialized manpower to justify their higher fees. The head of

76

the firm had pioneered replacement technologies for unexpected or, sometimes, dangerous situations. Harlan Jakobs didn't design the replacement bridge; they designed the emergency repair to the failed pin and hanger before something catastrophic occurred. In Tina's hometown, steady jobs at such companies were rare and she recognized her good fortune. But she could do without the ruffian culture.

Tina dropped the soggy corner of her tuna sandwich into the tinfoil and crumpled it up. She tossed the wad in the garbage on the way out, avoided eye contact with the boys, and their conversation continued without missing a beat.

"Have a good lunch?" asked Phoebe. She was the other half of their human resources team. They shared an office and the sweetheart's bright-eyed vitality often provided a remedy to some of their more brutish co-workers.

"It was lunch," replied Tina with a smirk. What was she supposed to say?

"Um," began Phoebe, thereby calling attention to the awkwardness of her follow-up sentence. "Tim Park stopped by. He dropped this off."

"Oh," said Tina. She took the folder of papers, walked it over to her desk, then logged into her computer.

Of course, Phoebe knew about Tina's history with Tim. And of course, Tina knew that Phoebe knew. They'd never spoken about it in their two years working together. But it was simply impossible for Phoebe not to know.

It was all so exhausting. As if Tina didn't notice the wall of silence that dropped like a shutter when she entered a room, immediately followed by surprised greetings and awkward smiles. Tina preferred the tomfoolery of those boys in the breakroom to such false-pleasantries every time. The simple truth was Tina dated Tim for less than six months soon after she graduated college. That's it. But, since both still worked under the same roof at such a comparatively small company, the rumor mill's hunger remained insatiable. New hires might come and go, fresh faced graduates might morph into baggy-eyed parents, yet the rumors never aged. She made a dumb decision over a decade ago. How long would she need to be reminded of it?

Tina peeked at the paperwork in question and saw they were forms required to change beneficiaries. It was safe to assume Phoebe noticed likewise. This complicated matters. Because Tina would admit, yes, she did want to look them over immediately. Most employees filled out their beneficiary form at their date of hire and only changed it after two events: marriage and divorce. It was natural to be curious, no matter the employee. Yet, even though she trusted Phoebe, her younger colleague was prone to gossipy fits at the worst possible times. If Tina dug in too quickly, it might be mere minutes before the hyenas began circling. Instead, she bided her time in defiance of Phoebe's furtive yet clumsy glances.

The documents sat on her desk for much of the afternoon, practically glowing with radioactive allure. Phoebe steadfastly refused to leave her desk, however. Finally, mercifully, a light murmur began to grow outside their office. Tina and Phoebe exchanged a glance. Then, without saying a word, they stepped into the hall and found the receptionist, D'Eisha, with a young man they didn't recognize.

"Guys! Guys!" said D'Eisha, waving for them to come closer. "This is Kate's husband, Brian. He's here to surprise Kate with a goodie."

The guy's wide-eyed expression told a tale of sheepish awkwardness. He gripped the plate beneath the cupcake with both hands, as if holding on for dear life. That D'Eisha was corralling him like a circus animal didn't help matters.

"Hi, I'm Tina." She offered her hand to shake and the startled boy required a moment to reciprocate.

"Oh. Hi. I'm Brian. I'm Kate's husband."

"Yep, got it," smiled Tina. He was cute. The lug's intentions were noble but he clearly wasn't prepared for the rapidly flocking circle of hens. Their company's female-male ratio might be miniscule, but when a tedium-breaker like this occurred, all bets were off.

Samantha Dering, the busy-body, was relentless. She peppered Brian with questions about his relationship with Kate and her pregnancy, and the poor ingénue dutifully answered each without hesitation. How often had Samantha sprinted to the phone at the slightest whiff of a scandal to stir the pot with Tim's wife, Helen? Brian was getting eaten alive. And, on the verge of making a disparaging crack about Kate's preparedness to be a mother, Tina intervened.

"I think we should stop saying a woman is, 'having a baby.' 'Having a person,' is much more appropriate." Every lady froze, fully gobsmacked. Each appeared to be stymied by an inscrutable algebraic equation. If that wasn't the sound of crickets Tina heard, it was the echoing tick of affronted biological timeclocks.

Her gambit succeeded as planned, though. And, in the stuttering pause, Tina asked Brian, "Hey, how long does your boss give you for lunch break? Don't get in trouble."

A virtual light bulb lit above the boy's head. "Crap. Crap," he repeated. "I do have to go. I do."

Tina betrayed no sense of joy when she saw the precipitous drop in Samantha's mood; the hard blink, the suddenly pouting lower lip. Inwardly, however, it was as if the collected throng at a college football game had erupted in full cheer. And it was a rivalry game.

*Brian exited, the gathering broke up, and, predictably, it fell on Tina to clean up the small kitchen area when the day was done. Kate had taken her pastry earlier, of course. But the cardboard box, extra napkins, and a balloon were unceremoniously left behind. Tina tossed the box and the napkins in the garbage before rubbing some frosting off the edge of the sink. Then she located a plastic fork and prepared to stab the balloon. At the last moment, however, she wavered. The balloon wasn't intended for her. Her dream man hadn't stopped by to surprise her. And it would look downright weird if anyone saw her with it. Nonetheless, she walked it back to her office and let it hang over her desk. For now, she wasn't ready to pop it.*

⋈     ⋈     ⋈

*Tina dated a number of men before and after Tim, of course. She was married to Mike for over two years. Then again, that divorce only served to bump her out of the, "hasn't found the right man," category into the pathos-free, "she had her chance," club. No one knew about the infertility Mike hid prior to their wedding or the year Tina wasted unsuccessfully coming to terms with the pivotal omission. And surely no one knew she'd broken up with Mike and not the other way around. Yet Tina wasn't particularly keen to set any of those records straight. She wasn't sure such information would help or hurt her cause anyway.*

*The situation would be more tolerable if she could focus strictly on such external opinions. Those judgments were the easy part. Her internal strife was the true foe. It involved bedeviling double-thinks, rationalizations, and self-doubts that were infinitely more perilous. When battling the unfair perceptions of others, Tina could view those people as the* enemy. Applying the same approach to her self-confidence, however, resulted in logistical self-immolation. The best she could hope for was détente or, perhaps, distraction.

Did Tina want a child? Yes. Did she want to meet a handsome, loving man? Sure. Was she willing to settle to achieve either of those objectives? Ah, that's where things got tricky. Those two initial questions, cruising along on the highway without a care in the world, ran headlong into a twenty-car pile-up of societal expectations, rejection, definitions of femininity, and harsh self-appraisal. Tina might twist herself in knots obsessing on these questions, only to confront another well-meaning but ultimately boorish advice-giver. If one more old lady, her condescension dripping and her cloying perfume assaulting Tina's existential sense of self, advised her to stop being so picky, she feared she'd deck the unfortunate biddy.

She already lost one friend that way, in fact. "Tina, you're going to have to choose. Do you want a baby or do you want a husband?" The ultimatum had leapt out like a goblin in the middle of an otherwise humdrum lunch. Arlene, the source of such unsolicited wisdom, was over a decade older than Tina and, when she walked, she swung her arms as if to push the air out of the way. She regularly offered such advice that existed in that odd, nebulous region between helpful and pushy. At the time, Tina had sniggered nervously, unsure how to react. Then Arlene elucidated. "Because you can't have both. Back when you were twenty-five? Go ahead! Go get that husband first. You got your life in front of ya. Nowadays, darling? You don't got time to jump through all them hoops. Your priority should be a man who also wants a kid. That's it. You can always train him up later. Biology is your biggest enemy now."

It represented a watershed moment in the annals of unwanted, unneeded advice. 'Train the guy'? 'Bigger enemy'? It felt too conniving, too gross. No, she refused to reduce herself like that. Tina wasn't so naïve as to expect a fairy tale ending; she hadn't entertained such visions at twenty-three years old, much less at thirty-three. And she wasn't about to birth a child into some loveless relationship simply because she needed to create a new version of herself.

Tina and Arlene drifted thereafter and the responsibility for that landed squarely on Tina. Arlene would make overtures about lunch or drinks but, time after time, Tina always demurred. Finally, Arlene got the picture and stopped asking. It wasn't fair; Tina knew Arlene didn't deserve to be treated that way after one errant comment. Yet Tina also knew she'd be perpetually on-edge, in fear of what other helpful instruction her former friend might unleash.

Had Tina punished the messenger for what was merely a boorish opinion? Or had Arlene been insensitive and bull-headed in the face of Tina's very real turmoil? Tina had no answer. She'd tortured herself with these and similar quandaries. Yet her self-doubt remained the only clear winner from such ruminations.

Thus, with a certain salute to Arlene, a vocal fan of astrology and, "higher powers," as she liked to say, Tina decided to visit a psychic. That fateful lunch had occurred a year earlier and, logically, she knew such a trip wouldn't repair her broken relationship with Arlene. At best, it was a symbolic gesture of unsteady contrition. But with Tim's paperwork still on her desk, unread and unprocessed, she knew she needed to try something unorthodox. She parked her car and, smirking once again at Arlene's reductive manifesto, she made her way to the psychic's building before gingerly opening the front door.

*"Hello," came the soothing voice from the opposite side of the room. Though Tina entered with few expectations, those carried were immediately shattered. For starters, the elderly woman's clothes were quite understated and, some might say, dowdy. Tina hadn't expected a kerchief-wearing gypsy but she assumed some sort of flair would be evident. Instead, she got thrift store Jaclyn Smith from the 1990s. Beyond that, there were no displays, no countertops hawking cheesy merchandise and magic crystals. There was only the woman, a table, and a pair of extra chairs. The simple authenticity disarmed her on a certain level. Such brazen lack of showmanship signified supreme confidence in her abilities or else she'd be out of business soon.*

*"There is no need to be timid," said the woman, her words buttery and flowing. "Everyone who passes through those doors has their own story. That is why you are here."*

*Tina couldn't argue with that. Smiling, she said, "You're right. I thought I'd give this a try."*

*"Sit down," said the woman. Tina joined her at the table and, after some small talk, the psychic began laying out cards from the Tarot.*

*"You appear steady on the surface yet plagued at your core. This may be due to flawed communication between the external and the internal. It is likely still more complicated than that." The old woman's slow, vaguely European inflection enveloped the room as a mother's voice might a swaddled child. Tina melted in unison. "You need to identify the story you are telling your own self before you choose to believe it. Else, you may be listening to falsehoods or dangerous yarns without conclusion. In the case before us presently, the cards are the storyteller. And they can never be wrong. Because the act of communicating and the act of listening occur in unison."*

*As she spoke, the woman laid the cards in a formation similar to an addition sign but with an extra card across the middle. Then she placed four cards along the right side of the configuration. Tina didn't know each card's significance, of course, so she looked to the psychic's expression for insight. At one point, when a card showing the Devil emerged, Tina grew alarmed. The old woman's serene countenance assuaged her, however, and with a wave of her hand she finished placing the remaining cards.*

*The woman didn't speak initially. Rather, she gave Tina a moment to appraise the cards without intrusion. Tina recognized the Moon card and took a second glance at it. As if to read her mind, the woman said, "You are right to focus on the Moon. A powerful one, indeed. It is as if you don't need me here at all."*

*"Why? What does it mean?"*

*"Here," said the woman, motioning to the card, "it means you are likely only seeing half of the story. Your intellect is grappling with your dilemma. Your mind wants to wrestle it, beat an answer out of the problem with debate and rational thought. But there is a deeper portion of you that knows this approach will not work. Every time you get close enough to grasp this enemy, you realize it is not as near as you thought. It moves, slides through your fingers, and flows into the distance. It is only when you calm yourself that you will realize the proximity doesn't matter at all. The real key is the means with which you confront it."*

*Tina was rapt. Everything the psychic said was correct. She was exhausted from fighting the battle for so very, very long without any end in sight.*

*"This," said the woman more gravely, pointing to a card on the right side, adjacent to the Devil card. "This is the bigger concern. This is the warning regarding your*

approach. It is the Ace of Swords but it is upside down. Normally, this would be an exceptional card. It signifies breakthroughs and strength and purpose. Reversed? It represents confusion and missed opportunity."

Tina scowled. How long would she be dogged by life's missed opportunities?

"You see the single, uncluttered blade? How stark, how serene it appears? There is a reason it's double-edged. From the most perilous journeys come the most important revelations."

"Especially the journeys of the self," added Tina.

"That is correct," said the woman, smiling broadly at Tina's reciprocated attenuation. "There is a man in hell out there. He is coming for you. He is coming for everything. It may be too late to change your life now, my dear, but you can yet change your perspective. Before it's too late."

The woman hadn't concluded before Tina identified 'the man in hell.' The missteps in her life ticked off innumerable yet, if forced to isolate the single biggest regret, her misstep with one man cast a shadow larger than all others: Tim. Through all her anxiety-driven inaction and resultant self-loathing, all roads led back to Tim. If she ever hoped to come to terms with her life's trajectory, she needed to come to terms with her relationship with him. "Thank you. Thank you so much," Tina blustered, ripping two twenty dollar bills out of her wallet and slapping them down. And, though the old woman appeared as if she had something more to say, Tina was already out the door.

Tina didn't go home. Instead, she drove to the Harlan Jakobs office praying she'd finally have the privacy to read Tim's hitherto unaddressed request. The detour wasn't an option exactly; she knew she wouldn't sleep a wink until she investigated it properly. And, with the place as deserted as she hoped, Tina flicked on the lights and found the paper on her desk exactly where she left it.

She didn't know what she expected to find. When she opened the folder, however, the answer still managed to surprise her. Tim intended to change his beneficiary to his daughter, Dani Park. Why would he do that? It wasn't uncommon for people to change the beneficiaries for their 529 college saving plans, particularly if children changed schools or graduation dates. Life insurance was different, though. Life insurance companies don't pay the proceeds directly to minors. And Dani was currently only 15 years old. Also, if one hasn't made proper legal arrangements for someone to manage the money, the court appoints a guardian to handle the money until the child reaches at least 18 years old.

Initially, Tina felt relieved. All along, she feared Tim might be getting a divorce. Instead, it appeared he was merely changing his daughter's college savings deductions and he'd filled out the wrong form. Then she paused and re-considered. That couldn't be right. Tim was too smart. And the paperwork was too straightforward. If he intended to change the college savings account, he would've been alarmed by the comparative lack of detail requested on the life insurance form. He never would've confused the two.

Tina's conundrum mushroomed. The revelation received from the psychic provided the initial impulse to return to the office and she'd hoped reading the paperwork might quiet her demons. Instead, the opposite was occurring. She was no closer to mental clarity and now she had an ethical dilemma on her hands. She could do her job and process the request as instructed. But if Tim had, in fact, filled out the wrong paperwork, he and his family would confront a nasty surprise when his daughter left for college. She didn't hate the man; his presence at the company was a perpetual headache but she wished him no harm. In fact, if this occurred with any other employee she would've likely picked up the phone to confirm without hesitation. Yet such a perfunctory call to him held deeper implications, especially if his wife got wind of it.

She peered at the document, the office pin-drop silent. It was late. She was tired. And she couldn't process the request at that moment regardless. Anticipating Phoebe's prying eyes the next morning, she slipped the request into her drawer to give the impression she handled it. Then she left, fully expecting to conceive a plan of attack overnight.

That didn't happen. Fitful sleep resulted. As did a case of acid reflux. But a structured approach to the paperwork remained elusive. The request wasn't time-sensitive. Yet such a lack of urgency presented a double-edged sword, a chance for her to put it off, consequence-free, to another day. Hours ticked by and a dark resentment at her lack of decisiveness gnawed at her. For over a decade the albatross around Tina's neck was her indecision, her supposed inability to settle down with a man and have a baby. Now such accusations were coming full-circle. She was lobbing them at herself and adding weight to the already hefty anchor. She needed to do something. She needed to make a choice. And, after torturing herself through the night and into that Thursday morning, she decided she could take it no more.

"Hello Tim?" she squeaked, at the precipice of his office doorway. Of course, a handful of employees had seen her approach; those unaware of the significance would now know soon enough. But she didn't care. She needed to do the right thing. For Tim. And for herself.

Prior to her words, Tim appeared relaxed and distracted by some paperwork as if anticipating his visitor to be some junior colleague. Upon seeing it was her, his body stiffened rigid as a broom. "Oh. Hello Tina."

"I had a question about your form."

"Very well," he said, adding, "I dropped it off with Phoebe. I anticipated she would handle it."

Tina frowned, unsure how to take that. She summoned her courage a second time and, fully aware she might regret it, she shut the door behind her. "Tim, let's dispense with the formality. Is that alright?"

One of his arms shot up, his palm towards her. He appeared ready to leap across the desk. Then, open-mouthed, he hesitated and relented. "Yes. Okay."

"Thanks," said Tina, taking a seat across from him. The arrangement was still awkward: he residing behind his voluminous oak desk while she scrunched into the chair like an interview candidate. But at least prying ears were kept at bay. "I have no intention of starting a controversy. I'd have to be blind and deaf to be unaware of your wife's feelings towards me. That said, I have a professional duty. I need a confirmation about this request regarding the change to your life insurance."

"It's unique. I know," said Tim, his body language slightly more deferential.

His response and his tone caught Tina off-guard. She'd expected either a confirmation, firm and resolute regarding the request, or a confused realization he'd completed the wrong form. One or the other. She hadn't expected a weak-kneed shrug. "So, to be absolutely clear, you're aware this is a change to your life insurance beneficiary?"

"Why yes," he said, now appearing a tad puzzled. "I wanted to change it to Dani. From Helen."

"I see. Excellent," said Tina, agreeing quickly and preparing to stand. "That's all I need to know."

Then Tim probed. "Why? What did you think I intended?"

The question was a minefield, a Pandora's Box of potential wrong responses. She knew, upon entering his office, she risked undoing ten years of cold yet civil détente between them. Locating a proper response proved impossible and, in the face of her hesitation, Tim's air returned to authoritarian. "I would prefer," he said, "that you keep your nose out of my wife and I's business."

Her breath lodged a dry welt in her throat. It was clear he'd misinterpreted her concern. "Tim, I'm sorry. I wasn't sticking my nose into--"

"Please handle the request," he interrupted. "And there was no reason to close that door."

"I came here," began Tina, plaintive yet growing indignant, "to be positive the request wasn't regarding your 529 savings plan."

"What? No. It's not for that. Now please. Leave."

His hostility unnerved her. She felt the weight of expectation all around her. The weight placed by others. The weight she placed on herself. And she blurted, "I never meant to hurt you, Tim."

He froze, stunned. And something changed in his visage. The shift was minute, barely noticeable, yet the modulation from anger to sadness meant so much. "Your intention. Does not matter."

"We were kids!" cried Tina. She was sick of the weight, sick of the unalterable history. "How was I to know you'd get back together with Helen? Or that you'd become a partner here? Or that I'd still be here ten years later?"

Her raw emotion fractured Tim's stoicism. "You don't have to apologize for existing," he said, shifting in his seat.

"I'm sorry it came to this. I shouldn't have been so capricious. I thought...I don't know what I thought! But those

89

were my failings, my choices. I never once thought those choices would still be haunting both of us ten years later. It's all so stupid!"

Tim looked down, breaking eye contact, and stated, "Your decision is not haunting me."

Tina's lips pursed into an appreciative smile. "You're being kind. I know what your wife thinks of me and the trouble this has created."

"A moment ago, you spoke of choices," he said, his words slow and measured. "I have made mine, as well. That's why I was changing my beneficiary."

"But if anything were to happen to you, Dani wouldn't see the money until she's at least 18 years old."

Tim didn't blink. "All the more reason to respect the choice I'm making."

Tina's eyes went wide. She leaned back ever so slightly, as if no longer resisting a heaviness weighing upon her. She readied to say something, decided it was too clumsy, then reoriented. She concluded what he'd stated earlier remained correct. She should keep her nose out of Tim and his wife's business. "Okay. I'll ensure the request is processed."

"Thank you."

"And," she hesitated.

"Yes?"

"Hang in there, Tim."

Tina left and, as promised, she processed the paperwork. Phoebe could sense something different about her when she returned but, thankfully, she didn't pester her with questions. The irony was Tina could handle such inquiries now. Their formerly intrusive power had vanished.

Tina went home that night, made a few phone calls, and wrote a message to her boss warning she'd be late for work tomorrow. Artificial insemination was hardly a new idea.

*Yet, even in relatively straightforward cases like Gina and Tom's, it'd always been spoken of in careful whispers. Like conversations about gastric sleeves or addiction recovery, the discussion often concluded in awkward silence before a completely unrelated topic was introduced.*

*Now, however, the notion was different for Tina. No longer hovering at the edge of possibility, insemination felt more tangible. Tina didn't need to excuse herself anymore, didn't feel the need to change the subject in her own mind. Her path had been hers, and it still was, only now she intended to share it with a child. That's all there was to it. And, looking back, she wasn't even sure what she'd be excusing herself from.*

*The next morning, she glided to her doctor's office to begin the paperwork and the initial blood tests. Tim didn't factor into the decision. Neither did any of her other former significant others. It was entirely her decision. They were her past and she now existed in her present. And through the small vestibule window, as she sat pondering the long, fulfilling road in front of her, she witnessed a strange, brilliant light crest over and through the tree branches outside.*

## MEDA

Eventually Meda told Magee to leave (no need for both of them to waste their day waiting around for Matt). Hours had passed and Magee would be due for his shift at the bar soon. Initially he demurred but, when Meda insisted, he reluctantly agreed and promised to keep his phone handy.

It was far from the first time she was in Matt's apartment alone. Yet, given the circumstances, an air of foreignness made the situation unique. In virtually every other instance, she'd possessed an actual reason to be there without him; if she wasn't expecting him soon, she was picking up a forgotten item and leaving. Sitting around doing nothing was a new experience. (Had that yapping Chihuahua next door always been so infuriatingly persistent?) Her anxiety over Matt's status suffused the apartment yet there was nothing more she could do but wait. In turn, such a dearth of purpose offered too much time to obsess on life's pressures. She needed to finalize the Biendava account's focus group study on Monday if she expected to finish the project by Tuesday; she remained stumped on Janet's baby shower present; and, oh, she still had no idea what the future held for her relationship with Matt.

She loved Matt. Deep down, she knew that to be true. However, sometimes it felt as if she was a professional apologist for him and, to her great consternation, she didn't know if she'd taken on the role willingly or if it'd been thrust upon her. (How had it become her responsibility to explain why they weren't yet married or to divulge when they expected to have kids?) She told herself it didn't matter what people thought, it wasn't her job to do PR for their relationship. Yet the fact that it caused such insecurity remained a source of resentment. And when Matt pulled dumb stuff like this, her crown as Relationship Queen weighed all the heavier.

Listless, she drifted to the living room with no real destination in mind. She picked up the television remote control, slumped into the couch, and, in the same motion, spied a stack of papers on the coffee table. The logo in the corner informed her they were from Matt's job and, under normal circumstances, she wouldn't have given them a second thought. Something caught her eye, however, an item that made her glance again and then a third time. The paper on top displayed a series of data columns and Matt had scribbled notes alongside them to denote certain geographic locations. Virtually all of these were traditional, big-business centers such as New York, London, or Tokyo. Except for two: Exeter, New Hampshire and Araksavan, Armenia. (What activity could be occurring in those teeny cities that might be in league with the other multinational hubs?)

She clicked on the TV as an afterthought, yet her curiosity remained. And, after scanning a few channels and finding nothing, she leaned over to check out the paperwork once more. It felt foolish to get so invested in Matt's tedious office work. (How desperate was she for distraction?) Compared to the dullard news anchor rambling on the television screen, however, the oddity felt downright stimulating.

Meda picked up the report at the top of the stack this time. Quickly, she intuited Matt was attempting to reconcile the divergent figures into one master table. Based on the amount of scribbles (and, more tragically, the amount of crossed out scribbles), Matt probably wasted hours on the document. Yet those two towns were likely erroneous inclusions. He probably missed them in his attempts to make sense of the numbers.

She frowned. In the background, the news anchor droned on about the Burckle Crater and how a comet that struck the earth millennia ago may have been loosed by a binary star system light years away. But Meda's thoughts were even further out. She stood and, still staring at the paper, ambled slowly across the room. She intended to drop the report on the kitchen table as a reminder to show Matt the curious numbers (if she was still inclined to talk to him by the time he finally showed up). In the process, she passed the bathroom and caught a glimpse of herself in the mirror. Perhaps it was the late afternoon sun or the fact that she was distracted, but her reflection made her pause. She came to a halt, surprised at how good she looked.

This was not a common assessment on her part. More often, she only saw the flaws, the areas in need of improvement (more Hyaluronic Acid for her lower eyelids; more Vitamin K for her nose and cheeks). Despite her aggravation at Matt and her forced indolence, Meda found the serenity in her aura heartening. To be sure, this appreciation wasn't borne of vanity. Rather, after spending so many years at war with both the beauty industry and her own self-judgment, it was nice to see a version of herself that didn't make her wince.

She proceeded to the kitchen wearing the slightest grin of contentment. Then, after locating a Post-it note, she bent over to scribble her observation about the data. And, when she stood upright again, she found herself eye-to-eye with Matt as he emerged from his office.

## MAGEE

Magee left the bar that night exhausted; his clothes reeked of stale beer and the incessant twisting of liquor bottle tops had brutalized his hands. He reminded himself yet again that he needed to find a job at a different bar...some hole in the wall where his work was limited to tugging on a beer tap. Juggling the ten-ingredient cocktails, the neediness of the brats, and the loutishness of the drunks was too much to handle.

He stepped out into the night with the starlight as his only companion. At such an hour and such a dearth of activity, the streetlights timed off and the array of pinpricks emerged in the dark sky. He'd received Meda's texts during his shift and was relieved to learn Matt was okay. Yet, apart from her assurances about his physical safety...not much else about the story made sense. How could Matt simply appear in the apartment after they'd scoured the place so thoroughly? Magee yearned for answers. But it was almost 4:00 AM.

The subway platform was deserted when he arrived...a bad sign, indicating he probably missed the previous train by mere minutes. He found solace in the fact that another trio of Thursday-Friday-Saturday nights were complete, at least. He could finally get back to his studio. The previous Wednesday represented a frustrating tease. He'd isolated the problem with the mirror and purchased a pane of glass to correct it...yet he hadn't had time to start painting. As he stood, waiting for the literal light at the end of the tunnel, he was relieved to be at the metaphorical end of one, as well. Perhaps he could stop at his studio and begin prep for work tomorrow? Though his hands were too gnarled and jittery to attempt anything now, he could lay out his painting tools to save time in the morning.

Many minutes passed as Magee stood pondering this new plan. Then, very gradually, he started to hear something peculiar from the opposite end of the platform. It sounded like voices, echoes that were equal parts shouting and murmuring. The audio vibrations undulated, obscured by the cold stone acoustics of the station and he couldn't make out individual words or sentences. In fact, it was hard to discern if their tone was joyful or anguished to begin with. Magee listened, the ghostly murmurs waxing and waning in strength like a quick-moving, auditory tide. At times they would grow cacophonous, as if creeping closer. Then they'd lose vibrancy and sound like they were at the opposite end of the platform once again.

His senses newly attuned, Magee then caught a quick glimpse of movement between the station's pillars. By their nature, subway stations produced viewpoints obstructed by hulking metal columns and stolid concrete staircases. This meant Magee didn't see a specific person standing or pacing. Instead, he saw only a flash of motion, just enough to catch his attention. Complicating matters was the curve of the station...rather than a straight corridor, which might allow him to peer up and down the platform, the curvature forced Magee to crane his neck for a better view and lose his initial sightline. A transmogrified lensing occurred wherein his mind took snapshots of the station and then reconstructed the images afterward. He fixed his stare. His curiosity grew. Then, but just barely, he picked out a young boy as he dodged between the pillars. And immediately thereafter a different one appeared and disappeared on the opposite side of the platform. More and more boys darted to and fro and Magee's interest began to morph into something else. The boys' heads were down and covered by hoodies and he never saw the same kid twice. Quickly, he lost count of the total number in the pack. None appeared to be more than eleven years old and, bizarrely, they didn't seem to interact with each other as they ricocheted about. Coupled with the haunted reverberations echoing through the tunnel, Magee would admit he was getting severely weirded out.

He began to pace, restless for the train's arrival. On the one hand, he hoped to keep an eye on the mass of boys as they crept closer in fits and spurts. But on the other, he knew such attention was only contributing to his growing unease. What were those kids doing out so late? And how many of them were there? He scanned his surroundings anew, hoping someone else might've entered the station...if only to confirm the dark oddity of the experience. No one was there, however. It was only him, the boys, and that unearthly howling. This wasn't normal. Magee felt for his keys in his pocket, laced them between his fingers for self-defense, and prayed he wouldn't be forced to use them.

Finally, the rush of air came, heralding an incoming train. It didn't mean he was safe, necessarily, but at least he could vacate the station. Magee stopped pacing and took his position at the edge of the platform...as if entering the train quicker would make it leave quicker. Mercifully, it came to a halt and Magee leapt inside. He was pleasantly surprised to find a few haggard souls in the car. While they almost certainly couldn't be counted on for assistance in an emergency, their presence was preferable to an utterly vacant car.

Eventually Magee took a seat, still unnerved by the chilling encounter. What would've happened if the train hadn't come when it did? Were there truly as many little boys as he imagined? He felt relieved to be heading home but such questions persisted. Previously, he'd considered stopping at his studio first before proceeding upstairs...that notion was laughable now. He was too freaked out. Instead, he exited the train and went directly to his apartment. And with vestigial fight-or-flight energy in him, he nearly attacked the stranger in his kitchen before realizing it was Meda.

## MATT

When Matt emerged from his bedroom, Meda's outlook experienced a quantum reflection. Factually, she was positive Matt couldn't be there, standing before her. Yet he was.

"Matt? Wait. How?"

Matt, appearing befuddled in his own right, asked, "Meda? How did you get here so fast?"

The hesitant silence between the two ballooned with potential energy. What question to ask first?

"Wait. Hold on," started Meda, her palms up as if resisting the new data. "Were you in there the whole time? You couldn't have been. I checked. You weren't in there."

Matt scratched his head. "I was just writing."

He spoke in a near-mumble and Meda lost her patience. "Right. Okay. Let's start over. You look like you just woke up. Were you sleeping in there this whole time?"

Matt squinted at her, uncertain. "No. I mean—no, I wasn't sleeping. I was in there. But not sleeping. What time is it?"

Meda frowned. "6:33."

"Oh wow."

"Why? What did you expect it to be?"

Matt began to share Meda's disquietude more earnestly. "I don't know. Probably about 3:00? 4:00? I called you and you were really concerned about my ankle."

Meda rankled in silence. She was 'really concerned' because this idiot had fallen off the face of the planet for three days. She said nothing, though, allowing him to continue.

"You said you were coming over. I wasn't sure when you'd get here. So, I sat down to write. I had a new idea for a story and wanted to get started." Then, as if remembering something, he twisted and peered back into his office.

"What? What is it?"

"The story about Tina. That's the one I started." Matt stepped back into his office and Meda followed despite her ever-increasing annoyance.

Once inside, Matt nudged the mouse and the computer screen lit alive. A few clicks and he opened the document to reveal a complete, sixteen-page story. Neither Matt nor Meda uttered a word, stunned by what they saw. Matt scrolled down to the final page. Then, the anticipatory silence like a fuse with a millimeter left to burn, he clicked back to the folder. The document had been saved at 6:28. Mere minutes earlier.

The implications erupted like a starburst. How could Matt have written an entire story without even being there? Their eyes met, as if each hoped the other might offer some sort of explanation. However, their respective visages—speechless and mirrored back at the other—told each that no such revelation was forthcoming. Neither moved. Neither breathed. And when Meda eventually spoke, her words rippled the tension like a single droplet of water on a flat-as-glass lake. "Matt. How. On earth. Did that happen?"

Matt, as if enthralled by a specter, said, "It's like I was there. But I wasn't."

With that, Meda's attention snapped. She remembered something, a shooting star of an idea. "Wait. You said on the phone earlier that you awoke in darkness this morning. Did that happen just now? Did it feel the same?"

Matt frowned. "Yes. Well, no. Not exactly. The first time I came back I was startled. I feared I was blind. This time there was a calmness in the nothingness. I'm—I'm not sure I was there, technically. More like a notion *of me* was."

Meda collected his words with razor sharp attention. "So wait. Do you have a sense of time when this happens? You suggested earlier you don't."

"No, I don't. It's only after I put things together that I realize I've been out of action. It's like I'm just gone."

"What? What does that mean?" She was straddling the edge of cross-examination, her thirst for clarity unquenched.

"I can tell things happened. But I wasn't a part of them."

Meda paused, glanced at the computer again, and bit her lip. She was ready to believe anything. Yet Matt was giving her nothing to work with. "Right. So. Did you write that or not?"

"Yes. No." Then, after a pause, "I don't know."

"Matt."

"I know, I know!" said Matt, acknowledging her frustration and expressing his own. "Yes, that's my writing. But I wasn't here in this room when the story was written."

Meda glared at Matt. Previously, the factual part of her mind had surrendered, contradicted by the proof directly in front of her. Yet Matt was speaking in such vagaries. Despite her best efforts, she reverted to her familiar, stable state that required a tangible conclusion. "Is it possible you started writing that story previously? And you only saved it just now?"

"No, definitely not. On that point I'm certain," said Matt, his most confident statement since emerging. It was if he sensed Meda's return to logical process and reflected it back at her. "That story did not exist this morning."

The room suffused with silence again. Then, whereas Meda had dropped a single bead of water on the serene lake earlier, Matt now heaved in a boulder. "Pretty cool, huh?"

Meda first sneered, then dismissed his frivolity. "Matt, don't joke."

"What? I've got another story now. What could be better?"

Meda's countenance stuttered, a mix of irritation and disbelief. "Stop. C'mon."

"No really," Matt insisted. "I'm sorry I worried you but, physically, I'm fine. And hey, look—a brand new story!"

Meda registered his earnestness and recoiled in disbelief, outrage. "You. Can't. Be serious."

He was unprepared for this reaction. "It's," he began, "It's a good thing. To me it is. Why? What's the matter?"

Meda's lip curled. Moments earlier, she'd been prepared to accept whatever zany story he might concoct, even if it flew in the face of logic and physics itself. Such a concession required a conscious adaptation in her mind. She was ready to work with Matt! How could he be so cavalier?

"'What's the matter?'" she repeated. "Oh, maybe the fact that the man who supposedly loves me disappears for days at a time. And that he doesn't seem to care. And that, actually, he thinks, oh, it's kind of neat. You're right. I don't see how anything could be wrong with that!"

"Okay. I get it. Let me emphasize that everything is fine. I mentioned that sensation of contentment? It's like I'm assured nothing bad will happen because, if it did, I'd wake up. It's," Matt giggled, "logical in its own way."

Words, words, words. That was all Meda heard. How could she care so much about a man who couldn't muster the self-regard to care about himself? Or her?

She seethed and, too late, Matt realized he went too far. "Look, I'm sorry," he said, touching her arm as if to reassure her. She stared it down, glared back at him, and he continued. "I don't mean to be glib. It's just exhilarating to find this story completed. I struggle to find time to write these yet this one appeared out of the blue. For example, I started writing the first story the other night because I'd been inspired at work— this massive project got dropped on me and, in it, was a mention of a nuclear factory in Iran. That oddity started my mental juices flowing and, while writing that story, a theme to pair beside it also came to me. I started and, I guess, finished that story today. All due to that bit of information."

He'd lost Meda, however. Her exasperation had morphed as he spoke, gradating to a more concerned expression. "Wait. Hold on," she said, a lone finger in the air. "This project. Is it related to that report over there?"

Matt craned to identify the paperwork on the kitchen table. "Why is that on the—?"

"I moved it. I happened to glance at it when I was waiting for you to reappear," said Meda, visibly rankling at the last word. She didn't appreciate treating the still-unexplained event like it was an everyday occurrence. "I thought I'd found an error. My question: Is that report related to the project you mentioned? When did you receive it?"

"Yeah, it's a part of it. It hit my desk Tuesday. Why?"

"Because it's a connection. It's the only thing different," replied Meda, her knuckle moving to her lips. Matt said nothing but his skeptical smirk made Meda defensive. "Look, I know the difference between correlation and causation. I'm not suggesting this project at your office made you disappear. I'm just establishing a relationship. You were told to work on this project Tuesday and you disappeared Tuesday night. Then, Wednesday night you called me in panic, as if you were running from something." Matt began to protest but his words were snuffed out before they could appear. "I know what I heard, Matt! I haven't forgotten about your ankle. But I know what I heard. After that, my landlord saw some dark figure pursuing you on his security camera."

Matt's interest seemed to wane and Meda got the distinct impression he was appeasing her, rather than listening to her. Her fixation only grew. "My point is that nothing has been normal (in your life or mine) since you started work on that project. Let's rewind for a second. You mentioned a nuclear factory in Iran. Is that report your firm's client list? Something like that?"

"Yeah, that's exactly what it is. Fitzgerald is instituting a new data management and accounting system and it's up to me to reconcile the different platforms."

"Matt, Iran only recently restarted their nuclear program. World leaders were scared they may try to build nukes. It's very unlikely an Iranian company would have the funds lying around to invest so soon. Something doesn't add up."

"Okay, slow down," said Matt, his tone patronizing, as if speaking to a child. "I'm sorry. I think I misspoke. The only thing I know for certain is the client had 'Fusion' in its name. It could be an energy drink or hot dog factory for all I know."

"'A hot dog factory'?" she repeated. Frigid, shiv-like icicles hung from her words.

"I'm just saying we can't conclude anything from its name alone."

Meda said nothing.

Then, appearing weary of the discussion, Matt asked, "What's up? Why is this so important?"

"Because a lot of weird shit has been happening, Matt!" she cried, her frustration suddenly vulnerable, desperate. "I'm aware I'm probably grasping at straws. I'm not an idiot. But you've been disappearing. Your ankle is a mess. I'm getting creepy phone calls from you. My landlord's telling me someone's chasing you. And now this report surfaces! With weird cities and some place in Iran that might have nukes!"

"Honey, honey," said Matt, as soothingly as he could manage. "That report and the weird things you mentioned? They're not related at all. I totally understand you're feeling overwhelmed—I'm sorry for worrying you. But it's okay now. I know it."

Meda glared at him, resignation and disappointment rooted in her stare. "How can you be so sure? There are two of us in this relationship, Matt. It's not all about you."

"I know. I'm sorry. We'll both be fine," said Matt, effectively missing her point.

Meda shook her head. It'd been a long day and she could see she wasn't getting through to him. "Yes. Fine." She paused, then added, "I think I'm going to head out."

"Why? I only just got here," said Matt with a giggle. It pushed Meda entirely over the edge.

"Right," she said, taking a gulp of air and turning to go.

"Come on. I was just joking. I'm sorry." He cocked his head to the side, attempting to appear conciliatory. It was too late. She was already putting on her jacket.

"Got it. Great joke," she said, emotionless. "I'm tired, Matt. I'm glad you're safe. And I'm glad you wrote another story. But I'm worried and I need to be alone right now."

"Wait. Meda."

She took a step to the door before spying Matt's report on the table. "I'm going to take this, too," she added, almost as an afterthought, before shoving the paperwork in her bag.

"Meda, come on. You can't be serious."

"I *am* serious," she said, opening the door. "Let me know when you're ready to be."

## MEDA

Meda launched in before Magee got a chance to speak. "Magee, I know it's late. I'm sorry. But I think Matt's in trouble and he's not taking it seriously."

Though immediately relieved the person in his kitchen wasn't a burglar, Magee still appeared wide-eyed at the late hour intrusion. He'd only barely recovered from the surreal scene on the subway platform and that experience followed hard on the heels of an exhausting night spent bartending. His initial surprise receded but a sense of indignation began to take its place. "What? Meda? How did you get in here?"

Meda waved her hand, as if that was the least relevant question he could pose. "Matt and I snuck in years ago. I knew you kept a spare key underneath the drain pipe outside. I'm sorry, okay? I'm a Gemini; I'm resourceful."

Magee's pursed lips told the story of his chagrin. Meda and Magee's orbits had locked recently in their search for Matt. But she'd overstepped a boundary. This was an invasion of his privacy. Magee shot an embarrassed glance at his unkept bathroom and another at a pair of dirty underwear on his bedroom floor. It was clear he expected a damn good explanation for the intrusion.

Instead, Meda said, "Oh. Here." She produced a plastic baggie, tossed it to Magee, and smirked, "I found it outside. You should really be more careful."

Magee recognized the bag immediately as his missing stash of marijuana. His expression contorted, equal parts relief, disbelief, and annoyance. Then, with no time wasted, Meda picked up where she left off. "I sent you those texts. Matt re-appeared in his office. As if nothing had happened."

"Yep," said Magee, finally putting the baggie down.

"I couldn't summarize our conversation in a text. I wouldn't do it justice. Matt said he disappears off the face of the earth. And he senses that things continue to happen, whatever that means. And he finds it all completely normal."

"Wow." Magee remained out of sorts and seemed to lose more focus with every word Meda spoke.

Unnerved by his stoicism, Meda's tempo grew uncharacteristically spitfire. "And that's not even the weirdest thing. Apart from his disappearance and apart from his reemergence in a room we'd already searched, there's another really unexplainable part. Somehow, he wrote a sixteen-page story in the space of that hour."

She let that sink in and took a step towards him as if to impress the importance of what was to come. "Now we know something strange is occurring, right? Something without explanation. Well, I happened to spot an error in a report Matt brought home from his office. I figured I'd point it out to him."

Meda paused to confirm Magee was following, then continued, "During our conversation, Matt mentioned one of his firm's clients, a nuclear company that operates out of Iran. I thought it was odd given the tensions around Iran's nuclear program. And, then he mentioned a giant project he'd recently begun working on prior to his disappearances. Given the timing, I thought these things might be related. Matt had positively zero interest in discussing them, though. He was more concerned about his new story than his own well-being. It was infuriating. So, I left."

Magee shifted his feet and Meda registered his misapprehension. Then, holding up her hands as if clutching an invisible orb between them, she pressed, "Now that report? I mentioned how I found an error, the inclusion of those odd cities? Well one of the cities is in Armenia. It was a comparative blip on the report, the dollar amount dwarfed by others like New York or London. But I remembered Armenia shared a border with Iran and I went home to do some research. I'd known about Turkey's genocide of the Armenian people during World War I but I didn't realize the full extent of it. It was systematic, horrific. A million people were murdered. Some say a million and a half. Women, children. After reading that, I got worried. The timing of Matt's disappearances, the appearance of that report, and the geopolitical significance of Iran and Armenia scared the crap out of me. Each of those things seemed to originate at the same point but I couldn't imagine how any of them were related. I didn't know what else to do with myself. So I came over here."

Magee began to relax, finally taking his coat off and leaning against the wall as he settled on his words. "I see what you mean. That's a lot to take in. Now...assuming all of this is connected somehow, what do you want me to do?"

It was a stark question. The ruthless simplicity of it caught Meda off guard. "I don't know," she admitted, biting her lower lip. "I hoped you might know something I don't. Something weird Matt might've said or some different perspective."

Magee readied to say he'd experienced nothing out of the ordinary. Then he stopped, delaying for a beat.

Meda noticed. "What? What is it?"

"Well," Magee began, staring at the floor, "as I think of it, I've also run into some weirdness recently. Each event was bizarre but, unto themselves, each also had some sort of explanation. Put together in quick succession, though...."

He trailed off and Meda urged, "Go on."

He looked up, his eyes meeting hers. "I've found myself in some really surreal situations involving little boys."

It was hardly the bombshell Meda anticipated. Her chin dropped slightly. "Little boys?"

Magee scrunched his shoulders together, tortoise-like in his self-consciousness. "It started when I noticed this kid snooping on me in my studio. I thought nothing of it. Just a curious little boy with too much time on his hands. And then, this afternoon, it sincerely looked like that kid jumped onto the Grand Central Parkway."

"Carlos," Meda muttered.

"Yep, him. And then, on the way home tonight," Magee paused to frame his words. "It's hard to describe...there was this group of boys on the subway platform. They were hooting and hollering. At first, I thought it was just some rambunctious kids. There was something about them, though. The sound, the number of them. It really creeped me out."

Meda crossed her arms. "I don't know. I'm not sure those events have anything to do with Matt."

Her quick dismissal caused his enthusiasm to fade. "I know. I figured I'd mention them, at least. You asked about weird occurrences and I thought they might be related."

In the ensuing pause, Meda registered the air of exhaustion about Magee. It was late. The sag in his body was obvious. Sometimes Magee could pull a rabbit out of his hat at the most opportune times; other times he could only produce a raggedy stuffed animal. Meda knew it was unfair to expect some mystical elucidation from him but she'd hoped for something a little more tangible. "I'm sorry. I'll go. It seems like the only commonality of all these strange events is the timing of that damned project at Matt's office."

At that, Magee frowned ever so slightly. Lacking confidence, he began, "Well, that's not exactly true. There was something else that occurred before the report." Meda peered at him quizzically and he elaborated. "Matt's ankle. He injured it that night at the library."

Meda blinked. Then her visage went blank, lost in contemplation. Matt's injury was indeed the virtual starting gun to everything. "Right. Okay. You've got a point. But how could that be connected to all these other incidents?"

"I'm not suggesting his library visit is automatically related. I'm just saying, if you want to start at the beginning, that night is the correct point. It's not some report he happened to bring home from work."

Very suddenly, Meda's mood brightened. He was correct. Everything had begun earlier than she initially realized. (Matt's breathless phone call; Goldt's claim that someone had been chasing him.) If she could find out for herself what happened at the library, free of Matt's interpretations or hazy memories, she might discover the incipient source of the occurrences.

"The wheels are turning," said Magee with a wry smile, referring to Meda's silence and blank-stare expression.

"Yes," said Meda with a light snicker, suddenly self-aware. "You're right. I zoned out there."

"In a good way?"

"Yes," smiled Meda. "In a very good way."

## MATT

When Matt awoke Sunday morning it was an unexpectedly foreign experience. Under normal circumstances, waking in bed to start the day was as routine as it gets. Sleep created a natural beginning and ending to every day that was easy to take for granted. Matt hadn't experienced that sensation in days, however. Now something so mundane required an extra moment of recovery.

The previous night had ended badly with Meda. He hadn't intended to antagonize her. Yet, in his opinion, she was focusing on the wrong details. He'd leapt out of existence—the exact mechanics remained a mystery and, yeah, that was creepy. But what he couldn't articulate to her was his sense of contentment in the void. In fact, even that carried the wrong connotation. It implied he actively experienced such an emotion. Instead, he felt distant from all sensation, beyond physical boundaries and time itself. She was applying rational rules of physics and logic. Matt wasn't so sure they'd work.

In terms of real-life dilemmas, Meda was also forgetting a more practical concern. He'd missed three days of work. Matt had emergency days available, of course. But missing more than two days without contacting the office was grounds for termination. He'd need to concoct a whale of a story this time.

"Hi Louise," said Matt, his tone weak while interspersing practiced coughs throughout the voicemail. "I'm so sorry I haven't been in touch. I had an emergency when I was out of town. One of my childhood friends passed away. I was travelling to the funeral. I figured I'd call you once I got there. Well, my ankle flared up and I needed to pull over. It got really bad and this Good Samaritan found me, took me to the hospital. I was very lucky. Anyway, I wanted to let you know I'm okay and I'll be in the office tomorrow."

Matt hung up and took a breath. Was that too much? He'd planned the parts about the funeral and the ankle but the Good Samaritan tangent materialized out of thin air. That was the problem with his stories sometimes—while he was the one telling them, he often had no idea where they'd end up.

With that out of the way, he peered about his apartment. Outside, the church bells rang and the old ladies sloshed through the drizzle to get to Mass. Matt lacked such direction. Before he could settle on a path for the day, though, his phone rang. It was from a 917 area code—local but not programmed into his phone. "Hello?" he said, expecting a wrong number.

"Matt. It's Louise. I got your message." Matt snapped to attention. That was fast! She must've received a notification from the office's phone system and called from her cell. He needed think on his feet.

"Hey, Louise," he said, scolding himself for sounding so perky. He was supposed to be enfeebled, damn it.

"Sorry to hear about your loss. You'll have to tell Human Resources about it later. I'm calling about Project: Saturn."

Her words were locked in silos, fully cordoned off from interruption. She addressed three distinct topics in three sentences and, dumbstruck, Matt emitted a simple, "Okay."

"We should touch base on the project. Tomorrow, early. You had an emergency. I recognize this. Even so, I need an update. Corporate called Sussex, apparently. They're starting to get nervous. You know how it goes."

"Yeah. Okay," said Matt, nodding dumbly.

"Great. A lot of eyes on this one. See you first thing."

Then Louise hung up. Just like that, the chat over, completed at light speed. What had Matt agreed to? While he couldn't decline a meeting request from his boss, he might've been able to delay it. Now he was on the hook for a meeting with hardly anything to show for a week's worth of work.

111

Then it hit him: Meda took the report. He hadn't resisted at the time—he was more disappointed she was leaving in the first place and there was no reason to suspect such a crucial meeting would appear. Those notes were irreplaceable, however, and represented the scant work he accomplished.

Matt cursed, then glared out the window. It was such a stupid dilemma—what did Meda hope to find in the report anyway? She was likely still miffed and some time to simmer down would do wonders. Yet now he was forced to contact her the very next morning with his tail between his legs. He made coffee, collected himself, then bit the bullet.

"Hey hon, it's me. I'm sorry about last night. I was a jerk." Matt paused, recalling how he'd overdone it on the voicemail to Louise and decided against such flourish this time. "Anyway, can I stop by sometime today? I know you wanted to investigate that report but I need it for a meeting tomorrow morning. Give me a call when you get this. Thanks, hon."

He hung up and stared down at the phone briefly. Nothing left to do but wait, he supposed. He finished his coffee and, about a half-hour later his phone sprung to life. Presuming it was Meda returning his call, he answered without checking the caller. To his surprise, it was Magee.

"Buddy, you doing anything? I was hoping to hang out."

"Um, no, in fact. Come on over." And suddenly, Matt found his day travelling down a new, unexpected path.

Magee arrived carrying two six-packs of beer, one for their afternoon and one as a get-well gift. He made himself at home, tossed one to Matt on the couch, and mused, "I feel like I haven't seen you in weeks. How's the Apocalypse coming?"

Matt intuited the reference. *"Ends of the Worlds*? It's going well. Lately, I've been writing the stories in thematic pairs. Or, at least, that's how they've been coming to me. Some of the concepts are too nuanced for a single story. Putting them in opposition seems to create a better dialectic." Then Matt paused and eyed up Magee. It seemed obvious his friend hadn't made a special trip over simply to discuss the novel. "I take it you heard about my vanishing act?"

"Yep," Magee confessed. He grew somber and settled into a chair perpendicular to Matt, not unlike the classic image of a therapist treating a couch-reclined patient. "I have to ask, what's happening, buddy? Meda's really worried about you. She came by my place last night at four in the morning."

"She did?" Matt was taken aback. His gaze dropped.

"Yep. She's still grinding on that conspiracy of hers. So, I wanted to find out the real story. I figured...there must be something else going on. Something you can't tell her."

Matt looked up to his friend, doe-eyed. "No. I'm sorry. There's not."

Magee frowned, almost irritated. It was obvious he'd expected a better explanation. "You're honestly telling me you disappeared...off the face of the earth, no recollection whatsoever...twice now? And you're not at all weirded out?"

"Three times," Matt corrected.

"Three? You disappeared three times? Does Meda know?"

Matt thought back, his head tilting as if to inspect the ceiling. "Yeah. Kinda. Not really. It could've happened other times as well. I'm not really sure."

Magee peered at his friend in disbelief, bordering on disdain. He was appreciating Meda's frustration now. "How can you be unsure if you disappeared? And when did this third one occur? Only a day has passed since the last time."

"No, no," Matt said, realizing he'd given the wrong impression. "The first disappearance was last Monday. It was prior to the most recent two occurrences."

Magee put his beer down on the table. "Hold on. Are you positive that was the first one?"

"Yeah. Well, maybe." Magee's silence showed his contempt for such a timid response and Matt was forced to add more detail. "The first instance I can remember was Monday night. I was at the library, plotting the novel, writing."

Magee stared, still cautious.

"I didn't get a chance to tell Meda on Tuesday. She was so worried about my ankle. Little did I know I'd disappear again." Magee's scowl gave Matt only a crumb of the empathy he sought. "I was in the library and the best comparison is an out-of-body experience. I felt like I was falling asleep or boarding a plane. I knew I was leaving but it would be okay because I'd emerge somewhere else. I know that sounds strange."

"Yep. It does."

"I was in this state. Then something pulled me back. I saw a being behind the books—lacking a better description, a shadow man. It was semi-humanoid and it passed, like a wave, across the stack. I realized I wasn't the only living thing there."

Magee pinched the bridge of his nose, slowing the conversation to take stock. "Let me get this straight. You were zoned out writing. Then you saw a shadow man in the room?"

"Yeah. And, well, I panicked. I went to run but I stepped on a book. It slid out from under my foot and my ankle twisted. That shadow man? That's the part I didn't tell Meda. And that a knife impaled the table in front of me. She knows I slipped and twisted my ankle but she doesn't know why."

Magee's eyes bulged. "A knife? Why not say that earlier?"

"Because it didn't stay there."

"What?" cried Magee.

"The knife was there. I'm sure I saw it. I was jotting notes about Tina's story, her Tarot reading. And suddenly, I sensed the knife. I dodged it. But, when I looked back, it was gone."

Midway through Matt's words, Magee's body language changed. He'd been growing progressively incredulous at the tale but now something broke inside him. His shoulders lost their tension; his head tilted sideways. "Okay. Just to be clear, you're saying you had this out-of-body experience. Then this shadow man appeared. Then he attacked you with a knife. Except it disappeared seconds later. Is all that correct?"

Matt hesitated. Put in such blunt terms, it sounded like a silly story told by a little boy. He couldn't dispute the summary, however. "Well, when you put it like that."

It was a joke but it was also a deflection, a way to drain the seriousness from the conversation. And, despite his remaining misgivings, Magee smirked. Both remained silent until, feeling stonewalled, Magee assessed his friend anew. "You really are disappearing, huh?"

"As far as I know."

They broke eye contact, Magee grudgingly accepting no revelation was imminent. He also knew another explanation may yet be lying in wait, though. "Fine," he said, before taking a large gulp of beer. "But if I start disappearing, you better be more concerned about me than you are about yourself."

"How do you know you're not disappearing, too?"

A blast of laughter burst forth from Magee, guttural and jolly. "Because I'm not friggin' crazy. That's why."

"If I thought I was crazy, I'd at least have more fun."

Each chuckled and their attention moved to the television, hitherto ignored. Magee stayed until about 8:00 whereupon, Matt remembered the report Meda borrowed. He called her again, made dinner, and, feeling restless, called once more. He considered trudging over to her apartment unannounced. But that seemed like a bad idea. Instead he waited, perpetually expecting a call. And, by the time he went to bed, he resigned himself to an awkward meeting with Louise, made worse by Meda's silence. Apparently, it was now her turn to disappear.

## MEDA

Sunday morning arrived with a jolt. Meda snapped to attention, fearful she'd slept through her alarm and would be late for work a second time in the same week. Then, once she got her bearings, she remembered she went to bed only two hours earlier. And with a grunt she rolled over to sleep another hour. That hour turned into an additional hour. And another hour after that. And when she finally emerged, still sleepy-eyed and out of sorts, it was almost noon.

Over a cup of tea, she came to grips with the mechanics of her day. Following her late-night strategy session with Magee, she'd decided to investigate the library where Matt suffered his injury. Saying her enthusiasm was low, however, was an understatement; a root canal in a third-world country may've been preferable. The only reason for her quixotic investigation was because he couldn't summon the desire to care about his own well-being. Further, a cold drizzle had settled in and a trip to such an isolated library necessitated a cab ride (one she really couldn't afford). Yet the journey represented the only starting point available and she felt compelled to check it out.

While holding her umbrella aloft and dodging splashes from cars barreling through pothole puddles, Meda eventually lucked into an available cab. The driver, Rafiq al-Khwarizmi, looked to be of Middle-Eastern descent with a thoughtful yet affable air. Languorous in the driver's seat, he seemed to exist outside the rain and inhospitable driving conditions. Meda told him her destination and he replied, "Well, I fear this rain has turned the BQE into a parking lot. Traffic is very confounded. I saw the line of cars from the overpass and I must believe an accident occurred. I can deliver you to the library. But if you please, I might take a rather unconventional route. The service road might be our best option."

In the abstract, the city's large, six-lane highways always moved faster than the local roads running beside them. For cabbies who knew traffic patterns well, however, such shunpikes could be a godsend. Meda recalled Matt mentioning some secret shortcut to the library and, putting two and two together, she concluded this was probably the same route. With frigid sheets of rain still lashing her, she agreed and jumped inside.

In no time she found herself careening down the service road alongside Astoria Boulevard. Her mind began to wander and she recalled Magee's advice. While she had no idea what she expected to find at the library, she would admit Magee had a nose for these sorts of things. If he suggested she start from the beginning, the recommendation carried extra weight.

Roughly halfway there, the taxi stopped behind a row of cars at a red light. Meda was so lost in thought she almost didn't notice the image outside her window. She glanced up at it. Looked closer. Then stared wide-eyed as an expression of awe washed over her face. It was the Flower of Life. Spray-painted under an overpass. Right there in front of her.

The Flower of Life is a geometrical figure consisting of nineteen overlapping circles that, together, create a gorgeous symmetrical pattern. It appears in the records of disparate civilizations throughout history and instances of its use can be found in most of the world's major religions. Oftentimes used to symbolize creation itself, it also enjoys unique applications in creative activities such as music or architecture. Ordinarily, Meda encountered simple graffiti known as "tagging," the equivalent of painting one's initials. To see the storied, enigmatic symbol in such an unlikely location was baffling. Impulsively, she whipped out her phone and took a picture. She had no idea why (call it divine inspiration). She just decided the moment needed to be captured.

Eventually arriving at the library, she surveyed the modest one-story local branch, its architecture functional and spared of unnecessary flourish. The cab pulled up and, as she paid Rafiq, he said, "Ma'am, it is a treacherous day. Would you like to take my information? You may require a ride back later."

After years spent rejecting cards on countless street corners, Meda nearly declined. Then she stopped herself. He did have a point. Sure, she could just as easily summon another cab when she was ready, but what was the harm in taking his number? (And in this weather, avoiding surge pricing might save twenty dollars!) She agreed and, while engaging in chit-chat, entered Rafiq's number into her phone.

She exited the car, made a quick sprint to the front door, and, after ambling a few steps inside the library, she came to a halt. Though aware her plan was low on specifics, the act of entering the building highlighted her literal lack of direction. What now? She lazed over to the paperbacks, picked up one and then another, feeling no interest in either. She peered about, searching for anything out of the norm. Her field of vision allowed her to scan virtually the entire floor yet nothing stood out. After hovering almost ten minutes, she started to fear the journey was a dreadful mistake. Then a voice began to boom, growing in power as the source approached.

"I will categorically recommend we close that wing down. I don't care what Mr. Wells says." A tall woman with a hefty, box-like appearance emerged, the obvious source of the voice. An underling trailed behind her, peering up in apparent agreement. "We can't monitor it. Nothing worthwhile ever occurs there. This is the last straw."

Meda listened, staring blankly at the back cover of a random romance novel. Hadn't Matt mentioned a secluded room he preferred? Could that be the same place? The pair marched past and Meda traced their trajectory backward. If they were coming from the left, there were only two potential origins. One was a brightly colored room with children's bean bags spread about, the other a hefty wooden door that told nothing of its purpose. She opted to investigate the latter.

Meda crept to the door and pressed it open. The barren hallway beyond offered further proof she might be on the right track and, after a glance around, she scampered in. When she traversed the corridor and discovered a room full of stodgy tomes beyond, she was positive she located Matt's spot.

One surprise: a broken window hastily repaired with tape and plastic. Meda scowled. It was October. Matt must've been freezing. The librarian had sputtered about kids vandalizing the place. Maybe the damage occurred after Matt's accident?

Unless? Meda stopped that line of thinking in its tracks.

She meandered into the room and soaked it in. It was clean, insofar as everything was residing in its proper place. The lack of vitality, though, was unmistakable (it would be no surprise to learn it hadn't been dusted since last March). Unfortunately, this also meant nothing noteworthy stuck out. One table had an extra chair, another showed a deep divot at its center; hardly remarkable. Matt said he slipped on an open book yet there were no stacks on the floor. That suggested he'd put them there to begin with. (Leave it to Matt to slip on a stack of books he'd created.) No obvious clue presented itself, however, and, getting desperate, she peered into a garbage can to find a gum wrapper, nothing more.

Then the door beyond the hall outside opened. The librarian's unceasing rant heralded her approach and Meda had mere seconds to ready herself. "--not ha--time--esources to let these ruffians--" Upon crashing into the room, however, the librarian's surprise halted her mid-rant. "Gosh! Miss, I'm sorry, I didn't know you were in here. You'll have to pardon our appearance."

"Positively no worries. I was just looking around."

The librarian pivoted, fusing her sermon with an explanation. "It is truly a shame. These scoundrels nowadays. They think it's cute to trash an institution such as ours. Ungodly people." Throughout, her colleague peered up at her with silent unctuousness; Meda imagined him laughing at the woman's jokes but not necessarily the punchlines.

"Wow, what happened?" asked Meda.

"Some unruly kids broke in here after hours. Shattered the window. Knocked books all over the place. Luckily, the door to the main library was locked," she said, gesturing behind her. "Lord only knows what they would've gotten into out there."

To the naked eye, Meda's expression didn't change. Internally, however, she stiffened. At first sight of the room, she'd resisted the notion that Matt was the culprit. With this chronology of the events, though, circumstantial evidence mounted. What were the chances Matt slipped on a misplaced book and, afterward, these kids broke in the very same night?

"Rampaging. No respect for anything. Like they were out of their minds on drugs or something," the librarian continued to fume. The woman's words had largely faded into the background as Meda focused on Matt's culpability. After percolating in her mind for a moment, though, the woman's exact phrase seized Meda's attention. "On drugs."

Wait a minute. The lady might be onto something. From the outset there were parts of Matt's explanation Meda found suspicious. How could a slip on a book injure him so severely? Why hadn't he sought help while at the library? And why had he resisted medical attention so stubbornly? Something always seemed a little unfinished about his tale.

"Pardon me," began Meda. "Do you have pictures or videotape of these kids? Any proof?" She wanted to be sure, to cover all bases before going too far down this train of thought.

"No, unfortunately," said the woman with a deep sigh. "Our budget does not allow for that. I will tell you this, though. I'd give anything to find them. I'd press every charge in the book. In fact, I might well invent a couple."

Hearing this, Meda took a mental step back. She realized for the first time that Matt could be in serious legal trouble if he was, in fact, responsible. Her brief silence, however, elicited another shift in the librarian's demeanor and, now appearing suspicious, the woman squinted down at her. "Why do you ask, miss? Do you know more than you're letting on?"

Meda felt the room close in around her. The woman stood between her and the door. Her suddenly accusatory eyes shone as unrelenting as the sun on the Sahara. "No. Me? No," stammered Meda. "I was just commiserating. It's such a shame. This seems like such a nice little area to write."

A single eyebrow rose. "You're a writer, miss?"

Meda cursed her imprecise language. "No, not a writer, per se. I meant that this would be a good place to think, to get research accomplished." She paused, regained her footing. "I work in public relations and sometimes it's next to impossible to concentrate. There can be so many voices and opinions. A little nook like this is perfect for quiet introspection."

The librarian's body language gradually reversed course and, by the time Meda concluded, she appeared placated. "It sure is. It's just a damn shame some people needed to ruin it."

"Kids these days," agreed Meda, moving ever so slightly towards to the door and hoping the librarian got the hint. "Well, you guys have a good day."

"You too, miss," said the librarian, finally stepping aside. And throughout the exchange, Meda barely kept from bursting at the singular conclusion tying everything together: someone had drugged Matt.

## MAGEE

"Drugging him?" Magee was still out of sorts at the call, his second communication with Meda in as many days. At least she didn't break into his apartment this time.

"It's the only explanation. Remember we were discussing how disjointed all these weird events seemed? How none of it made sense? Well, we were relying on Matt's interpretation of these things. If he wasn't in the proper frame of mind, the inconsistencies become more understandable. And what would cause such a mindset but drugs?"

It was ten o'clock and Magee had begun to drift off. His late nights at the bar combined with the beers at Matt's place had left him mentally fuzzy yet Meda was moving at lightspeed as soon as he answered the phone. If she just gave him a moment to think he might appreciate her point better.

With only dead air, Meda tried a different tack. "Look, all of this comes back to Matt's night at the library. I went there this afternoon as you suggested. Apparently, someone trashed a room recently. I didn't want to believe Matt was responsible at first. If he did it, though, that might explain some things. It never made sense how he hurt his ankle, right? I mean, who sprains their ankle slipping on a book? I think something must've happened to him, to his decision-making."

Magee couldn't resist a joke. "Well, he wouldn't have twisted his ankle if he wasn't running from the shadow man."

A silence ensued, rife with potential energy. "What?"

"Sorry, I...I shouldn't have just thrown that out there like that," fumbled Magee. He forgot Matt hadn't told her about it. If only he had a chance to wake up! Cursing his loose lips, he tried to explain. "Matt told me about a shadow man this afternoon. He claims to have seen a figure at the library. He tried to run away and that's why he slipped on the book."

"Hold on. You saw Matt today?"

"Yep, I was over at his place. I wanted to check in on him. And you're right. We're not going to reach him. Some of the things he said? They were strange even by his standards."

"Why? A shadow man? What do you mean? What did he say?" If Meda's words were speedy before, they were downright kinetic now. It was as if she couldn't settle on the right question to ask quickly enough.

Her nervous energy entangled Magee and he began to pace about his apartment. "He gave me more details about that night at the library. He meant to do the same for you earlier but he disappeared again before he got the chance. Obviously, he didn't tell you about the shadow man. Did he mention the knife?"

"No. What knife?"

"I was afraid of that. He told me he became lost in his writing...in another world entirely."

"Yes. Right. He told me that, too."

"And he said something had drawn him out. He mentioned some sort of presence, like a shadow figure. It appeared behind the books. Then this figure tried to stab him."

"Stab him? Did I hear that right?"

"Matt moved, he dodged it. And that's why he slipped on the book. He was scrambling to escape." Meda remained silent, soaking it all in. Magee continued, "I'll admit, it sounded totally irrational to me. I figured he'd probably had a nightmare after drifting off to sleep and startled himself awake. Something like that. But you know Matt. Once he gets an idea in his head...."

"Yes. Indeed, I do."

Magee could sense Meda digesting this new information and he gave her a moment to organize her thoughts. In the interim, he peered across the room and spotted his bag of weed...he'd left it on the shelf last night after Meda found it. He still had so many questions about the recovered bag. How did it end up outside? And how had it survived the freezing rain on Thursday? After writing off Matt's story as a simple nightmare, the bag served to remind Magee that some explanations don't wrap up everything as neatly as one hoped.

"That seals it," said Meda, snapping Magee back to the conversation. "We need to do something. He obviously doesn't care about his own well-being. Who knows, this apathy could be a result of the drugs. But if he's unable or unwilling to help himself then we need to step in."

"Okay," said Magee, pondering. "What do we do, though? I don't think we'll be able to change his mind."

"Right. We need to find proof. We need hard evidence to convince him he's in danger. And I can't shake the feeling that the timing of that project at Fitzgerald and the timing of his drugging are somehow related," said Meda, invigorated by the prospect of putting a plan together. "I'll call him first thing in the morning. I have a hard copy of that paperwork but, from the sounds of it, there's a lot more involved. Who knows? Maybe that Iranian company with the connections in Armenia is drugging him to avoid discovery. I'll tell him to get us all of the material. In terms of tangible evidence, it's probably our best bet."

Magee gulped. He wanted to help Matt and he wanted to help Meda help Matt. But he doubted how much assistance he could offer with starchy corporate ledgers. "Yep. Sounds like a plan," he said, before adding, "I sincerely hope you're not correct on this, though. I hope everything's fine and we discover a better explanation. Because Matt's in denial. And he won't see the danger even if it's right there in front of him."

## MATT

**Technically, it's impossible to pull out someone's eye. The optic nerve is too strong. A person could wrench with all their might and, eventually, the eye would merely pop. Then there'd be nothing left to pull out.**

"You're threatening me now?"

**I am only telling you something you already know.**

*The darkness stretched on.*

## MATT

Matt awoke Monday with an emotional wreckage inside him. This dread had no point of origin, no clear source. And unlike an ordinary nightmare, the sense of foreboding didn't fade as the fog of sleep receded. It lingered. The image he recalled most vividly was of a fetid, brackish puddle. It appeared unremarkable to the naked eye, like a water-brimmed pothole in any street, in any town. Somehow Matt knew it was deep, however. So very, very deep. The sinister puddle plummeted to abyssal depths below while the black water disguised its true nature. And the memory of it haunted his morning.

Matt struggled on his ankle to the subway station—his first such trip since disappearing the previous Wednesday—and boarded the next train. Within moments he recognized a familiar character: The Foot Tapper. Matt often encountered such figures on his commute. There was the Foot Tapper, of course. And the Angry Consumer. And, perpetually lurking, the Stoic Man. He didn't know these people; he'd never spoken a word to any of them. Rather, they were distinctive entities who kicked his imagination into gear. They offered him the raw materials for his writing and he, in turn, pieced together their histories, their stories, and secret desires.

The Foot Tapper, for example, was some type of scientist, likely a chemist. While conducting trials day-in and day-out at some nameless corporation, however, his real passion resided in music. It was evident in the way his feet carried the beat—he tapped and padded continuously, without conscious effort. Distinct from the rhythmic thrashing of the train, the perfect meter of the man's tapping was a seraphic constant. Each footfall dropped on the train car's floor and then scraped back like a snare drum. The tapping existed in the ether, both diffused within and lost behind the everyday bustle.

The greatest irony about the Foot Tapper? Matt had no idea what he looked like. Actual sight of the man was perpetually obscured by other passengers. In fact, Matt only noticed him the first time due to the absence of his tapping—halfway up the stairs he realized the sound had disappeared. Since that moment, he became more attuned to it.

Tsimm-Tsuum. Tsimm-Tsuum. Tsimm-Tsuum.

Neither a complicated jazz beat nor an annoying, repetitious throb, its simple cadence was its most memorable quality. Once Matt heard it, he couldn't get it out of his head.

Tsimm-Tsuum. Tsimm-Tsuum. Tsimm-Tsuum.

On this particular morning, however, it irritated Matt. The meeting with Louise loomed and he remained unnerved by the visions haunting his sleep. He tried to reassure himself that the tapping meter was nothing—of course it was nothing. It would be gone soon.

Tsimm-Tsuum. Tsimm-Tsuum. Tsimm-Tsuum.

Yet it persisted. In fact, the pulsation seemed to encompass the whole of the train—as if somehow hovering in space around the vessel as it throttled through the tunnel. How could no one else hear it? Matt glanced at the other zombie commuters but they showed no reaction.

Tsimm-Tsuum. Tsimm-Tsuum. Tsimm-Tsuum.

The white shuffling insisted itself upon his mind. He contorted to discern the source, craning his neck and twisting side-to-side. But no candidate presented itself.

Tsimm-Tsuum. Tsimm-Tsuum. Tsimm-Tsuum.

The train began to slow and, outside, colors burst forth as it careened out of the dark into the station. So caught up in his quest, Matt found himself leaning into the person beside him. He disguised his ungainly stretch as an attempt to confirm the train stop but the ruse mattered little. The sound continued unabated with no incipient cause.

Tsimm-Tsuum. Tsimm-Tsuum. Tsimm-Tsuum.

The ping of the subway doors sounded and a wave of passengers crested toward him. Matt got caught in the groundswell and, frowning, he threw one last furtive glance backward. It was no use, though. The identity of the Foot Tapper would have to wait for another day.

Once at street level, walking proved difficult. The injured ankle remained as stubbornly painful as ever. He hobbled into his office, clammy from the exertion and still suffering the pernicious doom haunting his psyche. Louise was right there waiting. He'd intended to rehearse his story on the commute. Between his preoccupation with that all-consuming sound and the effort of his walk, however, Matt forgot. The moment they made eye contact, Matt felt a veritable shudder ripple across the office floor.

"Matt, can I see you?"

It wasn't a question. It was a command. And, after tearing off his coat, Matt proceeded directly to Louise's office.

"How was your weekend? I'm double-booked for another 8:30. We'll have to make this quick."

"Um, okay. It was good. Okay."

Matt took a seat, already flustered by the stilted exchange. There was the briefest pause, then Louise lost patience. "Well? Catch me up. How is everything going? You think you'll be set with Project: Saturn tomorrow? Maybe Wednesday?"

Matt only barely kept from blurting a startled, "What?" Instead, stammering, he said, "Um. No. Definitely not Wednesday. Probably not this week either."

"Oh? Why not?"

Matt could never fully gauge Louise's expectations in instances like these. He knew it was her negotiation tactic—set an unrealistic deadline of an hour and she'd receive the work in two hours—yet some of her timeframes were farcically tight.

"Well, this project is a beast," said Matt somberly. "The universe of data. It's just...."

He trailed off in an effort to illustrate the vastness of it all. Louise bristled. "Okay. Where do you stand on it currently? I notice you didn't bring any paperwork."

Matt's eyes dropped, a concession to her pointed observation. "I'm sorry. I should've prepared better. I'll come clean. I don't have as much to show as you likely expect. It took forever to organize the material. That may sound lame but I think my work will accelerate going forward."

Matt didn't expect to get a clean pass with his mea culpa but he thought it might buy him some time. Louise was too sharp to bullshit so he prayed unabashed honesty would be his best bet. Instead: "That is very disappointing."

The words emerged from the grave—emotionless, pitiless. Their frigidity startled Matt and the ensuing seconds seemed to lengthen to infinity. Eventually forced to speak, Matt fumbled, "I'm sorry, Louise. Please understand, I wanted to get more done last week. That emergency trip derailed me. I planned to use the overview I created as a framework for future progress. With last week lost, I didn't get the chance."

Louise leaned forward. The movement was virtually imperceivable yet the pressure on the atmosphere between them forced Matt back in his seat. "Matt, I need you to understand how deadly serious I am when I say this. There is no more important work now than Project: Saturn."

Panic set in. What to say? A simple response of, "Sure thing, boss," felt suicidally lame. Yet vague assurances seemed far worse. Clutching for any excuse he could muster, he blurted, "My girlfriend found something strange. I mentioned a client, uh, a fusion company in Iran. She, um, pointed out that it probably shouldn't exist. I was going to look into that. I thought maybe it was the source of the problems."

Louise might as well have been a statue. Impassive, unmoving. When she finally spoke, her lips barely separated. "You showed this to your girlfriend?"

"Well, my fiancé, really. I mean, I haven't proposed. But we've been together forever."

At that, Louise let loose, her words throttling the air, the walls, the floor. "How dare you? What kind of an imbecile are you? I gave you this project expecting you to step up. I thought you might show the big guys what you're made of. Did you know Sheffield Snow, the Head of Operations, is involved now, too? This endeavor is bigger than any of us. And, and, not only do you accomplish nothing, you make matters worse. You show the proprietary data to your girlfriend! You have literally done negative amounts of work. I am at a loss. I am stunned. I cannot believe this."

Matt daren't interrupt. The onslaught continued.

"What were you thinking? Were you thinking at all? Did you want your girlfriend to complete the work you couldn't? What kind of a man are you? I am flabbergasted. I simply do not know what to say."

Matt's emotions roiled. This was out of hand. But what could he do?

"Well, clearly I made a gross error in judgment. It's obvious you can't handle a project of this magnitude. Showing it to your girlfriend? Preposterous! You needn't worry about Project: Saturn any longer. I intend to shift this to Abby. Hopefully you'll have something of value to offer her after all this time wasted. Connect with her. I expect the transition to be seamless. I'll talk to her separately." She peered at Matt and, unclear if he should speak, he wavered. Then she snapped, "Well? Go!"

Matt hesitated, as if to apologize. Then he fled the office like a scolded puppy.

That was horrible. Louise would never be confused with a pushover but in all their years working together he'd never been the recipient of such a lashing. A voice in the back of his mind told him he should be happy to be rid of the project, no matter how the abdication occurred. The voice sounded shaky, however, and its silver lining had a very sharp edge.

Tsimm-Tsuum. Tsimm-Tsuum. Tsimm-Tsuum.

Though the Foot Tapper was nowhere to be seen, the familiar shuffle-tap returned to Matt. It seemed to emanate from a vein in his forehead—throbbing as if it'd resided there all along and he'd only noticed it now.

He returned to his cubicle, took a deep breath, and attempted to settle in. Still rattled by the encounter with Louise and with cheeks flushed to red, he noticed something odd on his phone, however. Meda had left two voicemails. She never returned his calls yesterday so Matt felt relieved to see the silent treatment had ended. Before he had a chance to listen to them, though, his phone lit up with her number.

"Matt! Did you get my messages?"

"I did but I didn't listen to them yet."

Meda sighed. "Right. Listen, I need you to get me a copy of everything related to that project of yours."

"What? Why?" In the wake of Louise's thrashing, the last thing he needed was to get caught making copies of sensitive information.

"Damn, I wish you listened to my messages." Meda paused and he felt her irritation in the silence. "I need to see those materials. I think you're being drugged. It's the only explanation for your blackouts. And, given the timing, I think they're related to information in that paperwork."

"Hold it. Slow down. Drugged? Nobody's drugging me. And they're not blackouts either. They're different."

Meda remained undaunted, however. "What if I could prove you were drugged? What if I could show you the connections?"

Matt felt overwhelmed. Still shot through with adrenaline and beleaguered by the incessant pounding in his skull, he said, "Hon, you have these theories and I played along with them because they were important to you. But, since you took my notes, I had nothing to show my boss this morning. Louise ripped me a new one. In fact, she kicked me off the project. So, you'll be pleased to hear, there's no need to worry about the project anymore anyway."

Matt assumed that would put the matter to rest—Project: Saturn was history, there was nothing left to discuss. Instead, Meda asked simply, "Just trust me, okay? Do it for me."

It tore through Matt's defenses. She was dug in. He could see that now. He could debate all the fallacies in her theory for the next two hours but, if she asked him to trust her, he had no choice but to do so. "Sure. If that puts an end to all this, I'll do it. I can drop off a flash drive tomorrow night."

"Tonight," Meda insisted.

"Okay. Fine. Whatever."

They hung up and Matt immediately regretted his lack of resolve. He remembered Fitzgerald's IT department had deactivated the USB ports on everyone's computers to keep disgruntled employees from stealing sensitive information. Luckily, Abby had protested and received an exception. Matt feared getting caught using her computer but, now that he made that promise to Meda, he saw no other option.

He peeked over the wall of his cube, confirmed Abby wasn't there, and lazed to her desk as if looking for something. Then, once sure he was in the clear, he went to work. Though reluctant to disrupt anything, slipping in the flash drive forced him to move her ridiculously oversized purse. While lifting the unwieldy bag, however, he uncovered a garish, remote-controlled car beneath. Why such a tiny, hummingbird of a woman required such a voluminous sack was anyone's guess—bringing a little boy's toy into the office was even more logic-defying. The holiday gift drive was still months away. But, Matt reconsidered, it wasn't entirely irrational to find Abby so overprepared. Regardless, he had no time to waste on such questions and he moved on quickly. The sheer size of the documents necessitated extra time to transfer but, thankfully, she remained out of sight. He copied the material, yanked the drive out of the computer, and put the bag back in some semblance of its original position.

He left that night without incident and stopped at Meda's apartment with a vague sense of mission-accomplished pride. She wasn't yet home, unfortunately, creating a strangely anti-climactic finish. He waited a moment, peered up and down the block, as if he might've forgotten something. And, with a shrug, he dropped the flash drive in her mailbox before calling to leave her a voicemail. Consoled that he'd lived up to his side of the bargain, at least, he strode away. And then, upon reaching the crossroads at the end of her block, he winked out of existence.

## 19 CORNET STREET

*Hope serves as the foundation of every house. While a concrete slab may be the literal base beneath a structure and the frame may bear the weight of the edifice, the longing for a better future metaphorically supports it all. No house was ever built with the intention it would go to seed. That boarded up flophouse with the crack addicts on the porch? It was someone's first apartment out of college. That dilapidated wreck in the middle of nowhere that's almost certainly haunted? It was raised by a village and sheltered four generations of farmers.*

*When Earl and Jeanine Dering began building their house at 19 Cornet Street, they only had enough money to pay for the foundation and the framing; everything else was up to them. Friends and family pitched in to do the plumbing, the insulation, the drywall, and the assorted detail work. Earl did the electrical wiring himself, of course. They'd been scrimping and saving while living in his parent's basement and the house was a true labor of love, made possible by literal blood and sweat.*

*It was 1963 and Earl and Jeanine married three years prior to construction. With increasing frequency, their friends joked how the United States could put a satellite in orbit but Earl couldn't escape his parent's house. The digs weren't mean-spirited but, as Jeanine's smile stiffened with each repeated barb, Earl bristled more and more. It was only when his father offered to loan him the final $2,000, a sort of umbilical cord that Earl both appreciated and resented, that they could finally begin work.*

*It would be generous to say construction moved in fits and spurts. More appropriately, it often entailed a week of harassment before a given friend finally showed up, followed* by a week or two of manic activity each night. The contractors fell out of contact for two weeks; Earl's friend Dizzy, who'd promised to do the plumbing, twice showed up so drunk that Jeanine told him to leave. With such meager proceeds and increasing time pressure to get the house built before winter, the uncertainty and the interruptions frayed the young couple's nerves. Ultimately, construction went so late they moved in without the living room painted, much less furnished.

It didn't matter. The fact that some drywall was visible did nothing to diminish the couple's joy. They had a house! The wallpaper, the paint, the trim could all wait; those were simply decorations. They finally had their own house!

At certain points in the gestation process the terminology had changed. Initially referred to as, "the site," when it was weedy land, it became, "the project," when the frame was erected. When Earl and Jeanine moved in, however, the shift was more dramatic. Rather than a mere semantic switch, the entire feel of the place changed. 19 Cornet Street stopped being a house and became a home.

From that point, 19 Cornet Street became a joyous figure. Though there were only two other houses on the block initially, that changed as other couples in similar situations moved in. Earl and Jeanine may've been one of the last in their circle to build a home but they made up for lost time by entertaining friends, old and new alike. Dick and Rosy were parents of twins and needed an outlet to blow off some steam; Sharon and Pete were splitting a duplex with their in-laws and needed an escape from her insufferable brother-in-law. Earl and Jeanine loved the activity. After relying on friends and family for so many years, they could finally offer a safe harbor to others.

"Say Earl," asked Pete one night over a game of gin rummy, "when're you going to move out to the country? I heard Stan's got a real doozy of a property out in Harlsburg he's looking at."

"What're you talking about? We only built this place a year ago," said Earl.

Everyone at the table looked at Pete like he was off his rocker for asking such a foolish question. Though all were imbibing, Pete's drinks seemed like they were going to his head.

"I'm just saying," responded Pete. "When you and Jeanine have kids. You're going to need a bigger place. And the west side...all those Polish moving in. Not good."

Earl scowled. He and Jeanine had disagreed about the size of their home from the start. She recognized, with only one extra bedroom upstairs, they'd either be limited in their number of children or they'd be forced to move to a bigger place eventually. Though never contentious, the topic remained a sore spot. At the end of the day, though, they simply didn't have the money to build a larger place.

"The Polish?" said Earl, laying his cards face down on the table. "You're telling me you're scared of them? What'd they ever do to you?"

"Hey, I mean the property value, you get me? This house you got is swell. I'm just saying, if those Poles keep coming...."

"I've met the Buczynskis and they seem very nice," inserted Sharon.

Pete flashed a quick harrumph at his wife's contradiction and, sensing those around the table turning on him, he stood up. "I'll tell you what. I'll call my buddy, Phil. He works in real estate. He was just telling me the other day how houses over on the west side are going downhill. Where's your phone?"

136

"Oh Pete, stop," said Sharon.

Earl, however, was smirking and emboldened by the table's shared reaction. He wasn't about to let his friend crap all over his new home. "My phone's right over there, smart aleck. Be sure to give Phil my regards."

"You'll see," said Pete, advancing towards it.

"Pete, stop being so stubborn and get back here," said Sharon, appearing embarrassed on his behalf.

Pete was already at the phone, however, picking the receiver off the cradle. He held it to his ear and readied to dial the numbers. He paused then, frowned, and tapped the hook mechanism a few times. In a different, less glib tone he said, "Hey Earl, you ain't got no dial tone."

"Oh shucks," said Earl, unconcerned. "Looks like we won't receive the expert instruction from Phil after all."

Everyone at the table laughed and, for a moment, Pete hesitated. He shot a final glare at the phone, as if it had purposefully skunked his plans, and waddled back to the table. The topic fell away and they resumed their game without incident. And, later that night after everyone left, Jeanine remembered to check the phone. Sure enough, she heard a dial tone immediately. She told Earl and they joked that Pete had probably faked the whole thing to avoid making the call. For a moment, Jeanine worried something might be wrong with their line but it was late and they still needed to wrap things up. 19 Cornet Street wasn't going to clean itself.

Samantha was born a little over a year later, a healthy baby girl who arrived with a full head of hair. 19 Cornet Street was overjoyed. As Jeanine's pregnancy had advanced and the pair began to entertain less and less, the guys playfully groused they'd need another place to hang out. In reality, of course, the loss of their weekly gathering spot didn't compare to the joy of a newborn and there was no shortage of attention for Sam amongst the family and friends. Afternoon play-dates soon replaced Friday night card games and, as even more new houses popped up, the block teemed with local playmates for Sam.

19 Cornet took a beating over the ensuing years. It never resented a moment of it. Where once Jeanine would've scrubbed mercilessly to ensure her new home remained in pristine shape, keeping up with Sam became the new priority. Crayon marks on the wall weren't unheard of. And who could forget the infamous turpentine spill that caused the edges of those kitchen tiles to curl? Throughout the first years of school, and the measles scare, and the loss of Earl's job before landing an even better one, 19 Cornet remained a happy home.

In 1977 Samantha left for college. "Promise you're going to move back when you graduate?" Jeanine asked from behind barely-welled tears. Earl sat in the driver's seat of the packed car, ready to drop off Sam at the state school two hours away. 19 Cornet had only existed without Sam for about two years; it was going to be a challenge for everyone to begin this new stage of life.

"Mom," Samantha moaned in response. She was barely holding back sobs of her own.

Both knew she had no intention of moving back. And that was okay. Someday Samantha would have her own home and her own family, but that did nothing to diminish her love for 19 Cornet.

Jeanine decided to stay home for both practical reasons— the back seat was fully loaded with Samantha's gear—and because she feared making a scene at her daughter's new school. Samantha and Earl pulled away and, after lingering in the driveway for a time, Jeanine meandered upstairs to her daughter's former bedroom. Most of Sam's clothes were gone yet high school awards sat untouched on the shelf. A poem she once adored was left crumpled in the garbage while a favorite teddy bear could be found artfully stashed in her closet. Her internal dissonance was obvious. It was as if she wanted to move on to her new life while nonetheless keeping the room as her own. Jeanine didn't mind. Apart from making the bed and emptying the trash, she left the room in the exact same state.

Everything changed when Earl finally retired. After decades of contorting in odd positions while running wire, his knees and lower back were shot. Over the years, the stairway to their bedroom had come to represent a dispiriting obstacle at the end of each day. And, once free from traditional morning wakeups, Earl began sleeping on the couch downstairs most nights. 19 Cornet felt terrible as Jeanine trudged up to bed alone, one ponderous step at a time. It wasn't 19 Cornet's fault. Yet its heart ached at the sight.

Eventually the pair decided to take the plunge and buy a condo in Florida. 19 Cornet had heard the whispers, of course. As their health deteriorated and as the neighborhood changed, it recognized the pair would move out sooner or later. That did nothing to assuage the hurt, however. Whenever Samantha and her then-husband visited, they pressed Earl and Jeanine about their plans for 19 Cornet. Each time the retired couple insisted they weren't ready to sell. Yet they stated it with ever-weakening resolve. The inevitability tugged at 19 Cornet's heartstrings and, on occasion, a very small pool of water would swell in the basement, unnoticed by anyone.

After some time, a compromise was reached. They decided to rent out 19 Cornet in case Earl and Jeanine changed their mind about Florida. Samantha's husband wasn't overjoyed with the arrangement but, anticipating the eventual sale of the house, Samantha convinced him to go along with the plan. And that was when 19 Cornet met Rick and Maria Gelt.

In many ways, Rick and Maria reminded 19 Cornet of Earl and Jeanine. They were also a young couple, married but not yet parents, and full of optimism. Rick appeared earnest, albeit a little rough around the edges, and he habitually failed to leave his work boots at the door. Maria was Latino, a fact Samantha and Jeanine hid from Earl until the last moment. And she worked at a tattoo shop. 19 Cornet tried to remain optimistic. Yet, when they moved in, they banged into the baseboards and scored deep cuts in the hardwood floors when dragging furniture across it. In that way they differed from Earl and Jeanine. While good people, Rick and Maria seemed to take certain things for granted, like a hungry person at a buffet lunch.

Around the same time, the neighborhood began to change. Through the 1970s and 1980s the city lost jobs in droves as manufacturing shifted overseas. By the mid-1990s, good employment could still be found but the downward pressure on wages was endemic. Many of the homes on the block reverted to mere houses; some were inherited by children while others were sold outright. The backyard of 25 Cornet became so overgrown with weeds they caught fire one day and the mangy dogs at 31 Cornet never stopped barking.

For the first few years at 19 Cornet, Maria and Rick did a decent job keeping the house together. Rick handled simple fix-its and Maria kept the place tidy, even as certain long-term problems went unaddressed. It was easier to shove a rock under a sagging porch plank than it was to call Samantha for repairs.

One night, after dancing around the topic like a fidgety child, Rick asked Maria, "Do you think it would be okay if my mother moved in?"

19 Cornet Street knew immediately it was a bad idea. The lights flickered. From the dusty attic came a jarring crack. Yet Rick barely registered any of it. "Her health isn't doing so good, actually. And I don't think she can be left alone. So, it's like, we'll probably be going up to her apartment almost every day anyway."

Maria remained unconvinced but it was a challenge to articulate her feelings. What Rick was proposing was noble; it was his mother, after all. And Maria was well aware of the woman's ever-increasing dependence on him. Yet she also knew certain financial incentives remained unspoken in his plea. "I worry," began Maria, while nervously tugging on her index finger, "it might hurt our relationship."

She stopped there, the implication evident. And Rick's reply sounded as rehearsed as the lines from a third-grade play. "No. Don't worry about that. I'll be around here even more. I won't need to spend so much time at her apartment. And, actually, if I'm not helping Mom with her rent anymore, that's more money for us."

19 Cornet shuddered. It'd suspected Rick's true motive but his spiel confirmed it. A moan emanated from the walls that no human ear could detect. Outside, a dog howled.

Maria reacted differently, though. She appreciated Rick's honesty. For once, he was taking initiative and thinking about their future together. She didn't like the idea of his mother moving in but she felt like she should give him credit for thinking things through. With extreme reticence she whispered, "okay," as if her low tone might somehow absolve the responsibility.

*Two weeks later, Rick's mother arrived. It was a disaster, of course.* What became apparent quickly, though only after her former apartment had been rented, was that Rick hadn't been altogether forthcoming. He'd given Maria the impression that his mother should live with them due to her ever-worsening dementia. Yet the only way he'd convinced his mother to move in was by telling her their marriage was in trouble because Maria needed help around the house. It didn't take long for this chicanery to come home to roost. Almost immediately, Rick's mother began offering unsolicited advice and taking over in the kitchen. Maria, unprepared, felt ambushed by the newfound intrusions. Making matters worse, Rick never fully copped to the deception after Maria put two and two together. Instead, he used vague allusions to his mother's mental state to sweep the topic away. A new, wholly unneeded jet ski appeared in the backyard one day and, in Rick's increasingly frequent absences, his mother and his wife were forced to sort out the new arrangement on their own.

A new, harsher ecosystem formed. Rick's mother stayed in the small den off the living room, creating a claustrophobic atmosphere which afforded neither her nor Maria privacy. Rick began spending more time at the bar after work and, with his mother's presence unavoidable in the living room, Maria retreated to their upstairs bedroom virtually every day. The elderly woman's mental state continued to decline and, with layers of resentment at their virtual imprisonment heaping ever-higher, Maria gradually stopped attending to her. Tissues full of excrement clogged one of the vents; an unaddressed leak rotted an entire corner of the room. And by the time Rick and Maria divorced in 2000, portions of 19 Cornet were reduced to filth.

*Samantha only barely kept Earl and Jeanine from inspecting. She suspected 19 Cornet might not be in the best shape when Rick and Maria moved out but nothing could've prepared her for such squalor. Her voice cracked on the phone and Earl intuited something was wrong with 19. Yet Samantha managed to convince him a flight from Florida was unnecessary.*

*Unfortunately, Samantha was also going through a divorce at the time. She didn't have the resources to hire professionals to fix 19's myriad ailments and, instead, relied on favors from friends. Some were professionals and their work was spot-on. In other instances, she needed to settle for the best available option. And she did most of the cleaning herself, in even the vilest, most disgusting corners of the house. Witnessing the indignity of her drudgery on its behalf made 19 Cornet despair.*

*How it missed Earl and Jeanine!*

*Samantha rented the house to a string of tenants yet, after that experience, she became noticeably less discerning. Whereas previously she would peer at her former home wistfully, with obvious reminiscence in her eyes, that sense of wonder diminished with each successive appearance. A pair of college students rented the house for a couple years; another couple lasted all of three months before breaking the lease and disappearing. Samantha might visit, wiggle the loose banister, and then move on with a sigh. Eventually, she ceased making any repairs unless absolutely necessary.*

*When Earl and Jeanine died, 19 Cornet found out three months after the fact. Samantha arrived to collect the mail after yet another pair of tenants moved out and 19 overheard her informing a neighbor. 19 was devastated. Of course, it understood that Earl and Jeanine couldn't live forever. Nonetheless, a part of the home fractured at the news. The late arrival of such a heart-breaking revelation only made it that much worse. Even if 19 Cornet hadn't seen Earl and Jeanine in decades, it always possessed the comforting knowledge that they were out there, somewhere. Now 19 was fully alone.*

*By the time Nick and Loreen moved in, 19 Cornet had just about given up hope. Geriatric, and with too many ailments to count, it was barely a house much less a home. Nick and Loren only made matters worse. They were different. While previous itinerants might've been decent people with lazy or careless tendencies, Nick and Loreen were the first people 19 truly loathed.*

*19 became a captive audience to Nick and Loreen's abuse. Like two drowning victims dragging each other down, they shared their misery freely, compounding it exponentially. With people like that, 19 possessed very little ability to influence. The house might stretch its joists until the beams emitted a nightmarish wail but Loreen would remain oblivious if careening into another tirade. It could turn off the refrigerator on Nick but, if he was opening his tenth beer of the night, he might not even register the can's warmth.*

*Worse, 19 Cornet could see the future. And it wasn't good. Shyla, eleven years old and born when Loreen was seventeen, was already a bully and a thief. 19 feared it might be too late for her already. Kaysie, though, was still young. Not quite a year old, she was Nick's biological daughter and his obvious preference for her guaranteed a wedge between the girls for the rest of their lives. 19 saw the sneers of resentment Shyla shot the infant and knew, if Loreen's rage or Nick's drunkenness didn't ruin her, then Kaysie's step-sister was waiting in the wings to finish the job.*

*"You hid them! I know you did! You're such an asshole!"* cried Loreen.

"I didn't," said Nick with a burp.

Nick slouched on the sofa in the living room, making no effort to move, as Loreen tore through the kitchen. She was threatening to leave them yet again but the rage-multiplying fact that she couldn't locate her keys was foiling her plan. To avoid the drama, Shyla had sequestered herself in the den formerly occupied by Maria's mother. And Kaysie lay unattended on her back in the middle of the hardwood living room floor.

"I swear! You have no idea what I do around here. You'll see!" Loreen picked up and slammed down any item within her reach. An empty fruit dish, a tin can filled with screws and bolts, and a stack of junk mail all fell victim. What started as a search for the missing keys quickly lost focus in the face of such fuming ire.

19 saw her fury spiraling ever-higher. While the house was as tired of her antics as Nick was, it wanted to beseech him to do something, to show some passing interest. Couldn't he see that his aggressive indifference only fanned the flames of her rage?

"You can't do this. You can't keep me here!" A cabinet door slammed shut. A dusty phone book flew across the kitchen countertop. "It's, it's illegal!" A chair fell sideways. "You can't...can't...." A kick to the side of the garbage can. "Are you even listening, you asshole?"

An abrupt, eerie silence replaced the commotion. Then broken by a guttural snarl, the slightest -whoosh- of air, and the shattering of a beer bottle on the living room floor.

Momentary shock dominated in its wake. Then Nick barked, "Did you throw that? Are you crazy?" Finally spurred to action, he charged into the kitchen.

"You're damn right I did! You deserve it. It's self-defense. You can't keep me here!"

*Though Nick didn't notice or didn't care, the bottle missed Kaysie by mere inches. The glass shards left a jagged trail across the floor and the glinting edge of the bottle's neck came to a rest directly beside the baby. Her eyes, wide and curious, fixed on the glistening curiosity. Then the infant attempted to reach for it, again and again. And against the backdrop of the escalating rancor in the kitchen, 19 Cornet decided something drastic needed to be done.*

M　　　　　M　　　　　M

*Causing the electrical wire to come loose would be easy. 19 Cornet had been holding it in place for years and no one would notice that a barely-used basement light was on the fritz. The real dilemma was the timing. Once 19 committed to an act as irrevocable as suicide, it needed to be positive the children weren't present at the time of the fire. Given such variables as the dryness of the wood, the speed of the fire's spread, and even the humidity on a given night, timing it correctly was like trying to hit a moving target while wearing a blindfold.*

*Thankfully, Loreen's sister would be visiting soon. She'd promised to take the kids off her hands for the day and even the normally sullen Shyla had lit up with excitement. Of course, Loreen was tickled pink to have a day free of the kids and likely wouldn't leave the house all day. Twenty years earlier 19 Cornet would've never considered suicide, much less murder-suicide. But every day it sat idly by doing nothing represented another day Kaysie's future grew darker. She didn't stand a chance on her current trajectory and this would be the one opportunity when Loreen would be home with the girls.*

*That Thursday night, the exposed wire touched the wooden beam. The contact was brief but enough to form an ember. 19 Cornet remained nervous, of course, fearful the flames would erupt in earnest either too early or too late. A twelve-hour cushion seemed best. But 19 couldn't be positive.*

*The next morning opened ominously, however. Loreen's sister was close to an hour late. Shyla took the delay in stride, texting with friends to pass the time while milling about. Loreen didn't handle the situation nearly as well. Following another fight with Nick that saw him storm off, her enthusiasm for her day took on an anxious quality. The uncertainty over her sister's arrival time gave her too much time to stew and, with gradually dawning horror, 19 sensed her demented indignation rising. She jumped to the paradoxical conclusion that Dina wasn't going to arrive at all, even as she continued to wait and seethe at her little sister's tardiness. And by the time Dina pulled into the driveway, Loreen was at full boil.*

*"Where the hell have you been? You said you'd be here two hours ago," cried Loreen, charging out onto the dirty porch in her socks.*

*Dina's car windows were still up and, hearing nothing, she emerged with a cheerful, "Hey sis." Then, registering Loreen's expression, she stiffened. "What's up?"*

*"That's all you can say for yourself? You're late!"*

*"What? I'm sorry. I didn't think it was a big deal," stammered Dina, unprepared for such hostility.*

*"You always do this! God, why do I trust you? I shouldn't be surprised any more."*

*At that, Dina sneered and drew her chin tight to her throat. No longer ambushed, she became defensive and agitated instead. "Hang on. Where is this coming from? I'm doing you a favor."*

"Oh, so I'm supposed to bow down and thank you? Is that it? All praise gorgeous Dina because she can spare five minutes for her sister?"

"Are you kidding? I don't know what's going on here or what you've been smoking but this is bullshit."

Behind them, at the window, Shyla stood frowning. Then, though neither took notice, she quietly slipped away through the back door to go to the playground down the block.

19 Cornet was aghast. It wasn't supposed to happen like this! It could already feel the ember of heat growing in its belly, too late to extinguish. Once the ash landed on the beam below it, the resulting flame would start to lick the underside of the floorboards.

"No, it's bullshit that you show up two hours late! You never could handle responsibility."

"It's not two hours, you liar. It's barely an hour."

"Whatever. You're still late. It's always the same with you. You're always going to be a goddamn loser."

No. No! 19 Cornet howled from the attic, growled guttural from the basement.

"That's it. I'm leaving. This is nuts."

Loreen's rage nearly erupted her eyes from her skull. "You're leaving? You're actually leaving?"

Dina didn't reply. She simply fell into the driver's seat, dropped the car into reverse, and screeched out of the driveway. Loreen trembled, incensed at her bitch sister's audacity. For a fraught moment, she stood motionless, her glare afire as it followed the car roar out of view. 19 Cornet watched, waited. Then she barged into the kitchen. Her veins throbbed, pounding with fire and wrath. She yanked on a pair of shoes and, before 19 could attempt to stop her, she snatched her car keys off the table.

19 bellowed in horror. Everything was wrong! What about Kaysie? The house twisted and contorted. Planks ripped free of their studs and baseboards grinded against the floor beneath. Yet Loreen's red vision registered none of the chaos. She flung open the front door and, exactly like her sister, she tore off in her car.

Time halted for 19 Cornet. The immutable reality of the situation hardened to concrete and its sense of alarm, once a string of exclamation marks, went silent. There was nothing left to do now, no urgency in the face of the inevitable. Tortured anguish seeped through the house. Down the wall where Earl once kissed Jeanine so tenderly, through the floor where teenage Samantha fell in a heap sobbing after a boy's callous rejection, across the ceiling that Rick's mother stared at for years on end. 19 was helpless to stop the murderous fire it started. And it realized there were no heroes here. Only villains.

It was too late. It was all too late. And, though the world would end in two hours, Kaysie slept upstairs, blithefully oblivious to the dual conflagrations coming to engulf her.

## MEDA

Seven days. Matt had been gone seven *goddamn* days. In fact, Meda's last interaction with him hadn't even occurred in person; it was when she found the flash drive he dropped off in her mailbox. That night, she proceeded inside and listened to his voicemail (that inscrutable, terrifyingly bizarre voicemail) with no reason to suspect it'd be the last time she heard from him. The first time she heard it, she hadn't listened to the end, in fact. She'd begun sorting the mail and, distracted, she'd simply hung up when Matt went silent. (You remembered the flash drive, Matt. Got it. Great. You want an award?) It wasn't until Tuesday night, following a miserable, rain-sodden trek home, that she looked again and realized the voicemail was over nine minutes long. Still not alarmed exactly, she went back to the message and listened again.

"Hey hon. It's me. I just wanted to let you know I dropped off the flash drive of those reports from Fitzgerald. It's a lot of material, to be honest. I have no idea what you plan to find. But hey—you asked for it. Anyway, you weren't home so I dropped it in your mailbox."

What followed was almost eight and a half minutes of silence. Complete, unadulterated silence.

Then: "I hope your day went okay, at least. I'll talk to you soon. Love you."

Meda nearly dropped the phone. Several times during those five hundred seconds she considered hanging up. Yet, when his words finally came, chipper as ever and oblivious to the lost time, they made the absence all the more terrifying.

Wednesday night she called Magee. 48 hours had passed since Matt's voicemail and, together, the pair investigated Matt's apartment yet again. This time, Meda was ruthless. She scoured the rooms, stood his mattress on end, ripped drawers out of his dresser and tossed the contents on the ground. Yet they discovered no new clues to his whereabouts.

On Thursday, she called the police. She'd been avoiding it for a couple reasons. Firstly, Matt's wallet, phone, and every other significant personal effect remained in his apartment. If he'd run off, he wouldn't have gotten far. Secondly, there was no foul play apparent. He was a grown man with no unsavory dealings and no history of mental illness. Meda described how he'd been acting strangely and, when the police officer remained unmoved, she blurted her theory about nefarious entities at Matt's office. That brought the conversation to a quick end and Meda was back to square one.

By Saturday, she'd re-visited Matt's apartment two more times and, on Sunday, she resorted to calling his parents. It was a delicate edge to ride. She didn't want to scare the elderly couple but she felt a responsibility to inform them. Further, if they'd communicated with Matt, she needed to know. They had no clue anything was amiss, however, and she spent the rest of the call reassuring them he was probably okay. It tore Meda in two. They had every right to be concerned but, given the myriad uncertainties, she didn't have much in the way of answers (which was the exact reason it'd taken her so long to call them). It was a terrible position to be put in and, compounding her anxiety, the rare chance to leave work early that Monday afternoon only gave her more time to obsess.

In the past week, she'd pored over the Fitzgerald data numerous times. Meda would admit she didn't understand all the talmudic jargon and it wasn't realistic to think she'd locate an obvious smoking gun in such a deluge of information. Yet, even to her inexperienced eyes, it was obvious Matt was correct on one count. For such a vaunted financial leader, the firm's accounting practices were a mess. The filing styles were haphazard and non-uniform. And the actual data contained within those divergent styles was often worse. Short positions appeared and disappeared with no apparent cover, the EBITDA here wouldn't match the corresponding earnings there, and losses were swept into one omnibus vehicle with no matching notation. Keeping track of it was like trying to predict the oceanic movements of a shoal by focusing on individual fish. The mind couldn't fathom it all at once.

Despite all this, she decided to take one last crack at it. With this newfound bevy of time she needed something to occupy herself and some constructive activity was better than nothing. She opened a pair of spreadsheets and, as she anticipated, the data across each didn't correspond in the least. Then she opened a third to reveal an entirely different set of numbers. For over an hour she continued scanning the data, still unsure what she was even seeking. The lack of cohesion made her doubt herself, and, at a loss, she returned to the paperwork that'd piqued her initial curiosity at Matt's apartment. She picked up the hard copy report and stared. There sat Double Eagle Fusion Co. in Iran. And there sat ENKI, operating out of Armenia. And, as usual, their numbers were the tidiest of the bunch.

Meda continued to clutch the report. Yet, following that pithy observation, her thoughts shot a million miles away. She froze, blinked once, and leaned back into her chair. Then, in a flash of movement, she pushed herself bolt upright and began hammering on the keyboard. She searched the various reports for Double Eagle Fusion and ENKI. One result appeared, then another, and another. And, as she suspected, a peculiar trend began to take shape. Even as she saw her theory play out, she doubted how long the pattern would hold. Yet it never wavered. There were no inconsistencies in the data tied to Double Eagle or ENKI. Whereas every other entity had some metric that diverged, their numbers remained spot on.

Meda pursed her lips. She focused laser-like on the data, the values mirrored across each and every document. If she was looking for a discrepancy from the norm, this was it. She realized, however, it was also proof by a negative. The fact that Double Eagle and ENKI were the only ones with their accounting houses in order didn't vilify them automatically. It merely made the companies stick out (or, as the saying goes, "absence of evidence is not evidence of absence"). Yet, why would they be the only outliers?

She remained stumped, her thumb at her lips as she pondered. Then the answer hit Meda, like a black swell of saltwater that drowned her investigative gusto. The data had been altered. What were the chances that she and Matt would discuss those exact items and, presto, they were suddenly the only two companies in sync across the document? More likely, Matt had likely overwritten the correct values accidentally while wrangling the metrics. He was the only one with access to the material. And he complained from the outset about his frustrations organizing it. He'd probably made matters harder on himself by unwittingly modifying it.

Meda slumped back once again. It'd all been a wild goose chase. Not because the data was wrong, but because Matt had tainted the files. She remained locked in her seat for a long time, morose and staring at the screen. Better to have no inspiration than to receive it and see it washed away. Eventually, she shuffled to bed, telling herself to be contented at her minor discovery. Yet, even as she drifted off to sleep, a nagging voice inside warned that she hadn't yet seen the entire picture.

## MATT

"Where am I?"

**Nowhere.**

"Yeah. Okay. Where are you then?"

**A different nowhere.**

"That explains nothing. We seem to be going in circles here."

**You are much more correct than you realize.**

"I have to admit, I was hoping for a better explanation. Because—if I'm not mistaken—the last time we had one of these little discussions, you threatened to pull my eye out of its socket."

**That was merely to get your attention. You are more focused now.**

"If you say so. It's like you can't answer a basic question without either sidestepping the topic or threatening me. I'm talking to a disembodied voice and I can't see or feel anything. Please pardon me if I'm grasping for some clarity about my corporeal existence here."

**We're all made of something. Houses are constructed out of wood and plastic; homes are created out of those same items—and something more. The building blocks of every human, every mountain, every breeze are substances birthed in stars eons ago. The oxygen molecule carried by the hemoglobin in someone's blood may be same oxygen created by the tree that later became George Washington's favorite childhood book. Atoms, ideas, molecules, dreams: these are what create us.**

## MAGEE

With each passing day, the situation grew more dire. No one had heard from Matt in a week. Meda appeared to be on the verge of a nervous breakdown. And, among such life-and-death concerns, Magee's mama wouldn't stop hounding him about some woman in Rhode Island. The only thing that wasn't a total disaster was his painting...the use of a second pane of glass proved to be the perfect solution to his dilemma. He painted on the pane as it lay horizontally, which kept the larger droplets from running. Then, to view the results under the proper light, he aligned the piece upright against the mirror. Though painstaking and replete with inefficiencies, this two-layered style finally achieved the effect he envisioned.

Creatively, he was on a roll and Tuesday afternoon passed in a veritable blur. There was something in the air...either the precise humidity, the low temperature, or something else entirely...that made the paint set exactly as he hoped. No smudging, no watery rivulets that took the paint on a surprising, unintended path. Opportunities like these were rare and Magee knew to take advantage.

He finished wiping down some brushes and, after allowing some of his recent work to rest, he felt ready for another comparison. Tenderly, he picked up the pane and carried it over to the ancient mirror. His vision required anachronistic color variations to play off the timeworn splashes of gold and green on the mirror below. If all went as planned, the latent, nearly imperceivable shadows created by the paint would guide the eye of the viewer in a full circle. He held the pane up, pressed it ever-so delicately against the mirror, and held both aloft. Then, in the reflected image, he saw the little boy standing behind him. And he almost dropped the twin panes of glass.

155

"Holy!" His body jumped at the sight before he returned to himself...the immediate priority was the protection of his work. Though startled, he turned and placed the mirror and the glass on his worktable with hurried care. Then, with them secure, he snarled, "You little shit! What're you doing in here? I'm calling the cops."

He was thinking aloud, expressing his shock and issuing dictums at the same moment. The boy, however, remained unmoved. Clad in raggedy clothes two sizes too large and cloaked in a wan complexion, the boy conveyed a morose, subliminal air of threat. He eyed up Magee with sunken eyes and his body language betrayed none of the hesitation most children displayed when confronted by an adult.

"Well? What are you waiting for? Beat it!"

The boy remained anchored in place and, unnerved by the boy's utter impassivity, Magee moved to locate the closest thing resembling a weapon. Then the boy spoke. "I'm glad you got your weed back."

It stopped Magee in his tracks. He stuttered, unable to form the right words in the proper order. In rapid succession, his mind cycled from surprise to affronted hostility as he connected the dots. Those kids had stolen his weed! One had distracted him by appearing at the window. Then, when he went to investigate, another ducked in and grabbed it. In retrospect, it made perfect sense.

"You? That was you? You stole my weed?"

"I wouldn't say we stole it," said the boy, losing a touch of his laconic demeanor. "We borrowed it. Worst case, we hid it. Y'see? You got it back."

"That's not the point, kid. You broke into my studio. I could call the cops on you."

"And what? Press charges on a minor for stealing your dope? Y'see, last I checked it was still illegal."

Magee frowned, silent for a beat. "What do you want then? Why are you here?"

The boy widened his stance and, though his words were banal, they were issued with brazen confidence. "I'm here because someone sent me."

"Who? Who sent you?"

"Someone who wants to keep you on track."

Magee's eyes narrowed to slits. The use of the word, 'track,' conjured memories of that gang of hoodlums on the subway platform. "What's that supposed to mean? Keep me on track for what?"

"Last Wednesday, you were gearing to get stoned rather than paint. Instead, y'see, one of my friends grabbed your dope before you went down that road." The boy paused and gestured to the mirror beside Magee. "You're welcome."

Magee recoiled. From the start of the encounter he'd been on unsteady footing, surprised and perpetually lagging behind. This boy...this creepy, sinister little boy...knew so much. Too much. It was obvious he and his friends were spying on him and Magee's knee-jerk reaction to such surveillance was resentment. Yet the boy's words, so cocksure and irrefutable, gave Magee pause. "Yep. Fair enough. You got me on that one," said Magee, beginning to pace. "Except...you still haven't answered my question. You said someone sent you to keep me on track. Who is it? And why?"

The boy sighed. "You know and I know. Matt is in trouble. It's well worse than you think. We have to be sure you're ready to appear when the time is right."

The explanation punctured Magee...a twelve-inch bowie knife to the side of a car tire. He'd told Meda about his odd encounters with little boys and she doubted their relationship to Matt's disappearances. Yet now this strange boy was referencing Matt directly. Initially, Magee felt his suspicions validated. However, a stubborn, wary part of him resisted. Wasn't this how psychics lured in clients? By offering some vague prediction before allowing people to fill in the rest of the details on their own? He decided to test the punk's meddle. "So that night on the subway tracks...that was you, too?"

"Not me exactly," said the boy without hesitation. "It was a bunch of my friends. Y'see, it was too late for me. Couldn't get all the way down to the Prospect stop. Heard they caused quite a racket?"

It wasn't the response Magee wanted. He'd hoped the boy would be confused or give a conflicting detail, thereby blowing his story. Instead, he didn't bat an eyelash at the accusation and went so far as to corroborate specific details. "Yep, fair enough," said Magee, his pacing quickening. "So why didn't they attack me? Did the train come too soon?"

"Attack you?" the boy snorted. "Who said we wanted to attack you? Are you even listening? I just proved how we kept you focused on your painting rather than lighting up. Still don't believe I got a 'thank you' for that, by the way."

Magee's hands shot to his hips. "So, what then? Why scare me like that? What purpose could that possibly serve?"

The boy's lips pursed, as if irritated at the need to address such details. "You intended to come here to the studio? That Saturday night. Didn't you? Y'see, if you had, you would've missed Meda upstairs in your apartment. And that would've been bad. You two needed to talk."

Magee all but threw his hands in the air...was there anything this kid didn't know? "Well, mission accomplished. You guys funneled me upstairs instead. Meda and I talked. Great. Why was that so important? Why do you or...whoever it is that sent you...care?"

"Because you needed to hear Meda's theory about the threat at Fitzgerald."

"What? Matt's office? What does that have to do with this?"

"There is a woman there. She will destroy *everything*."

Previous to that pronouncement, the boy had been cool, practically disinterested. The gravity with which he uttered those words, however, sent a shiver through Magee. It cleaved the conversation in half...having proven his veracity, the boy now vanquished any pretense. Magee's eyebrows raised at the abrupt tonal shift. The boy added nothing more, however, and let his words hang in the air undisturbed. Magee started to pace anew, frowning and burdened. Yet still the boy didn't budge. He pivoted on his heel, then raked his fingers through his hair. And, when he finally came to a halt, he asked, "So...what am I supposed to do?"

The boy smirked. "You're supposed to stop her, y'see?"

## MEDA

A sense of incompleteness shaded everything in Meda's world. Every effort remained half-finished; every puzzle lacked a final piece. She'd located that spooky symmetry between the two companies in Matt's reports the previous night and printed up hard copies of the paperwork that morning. But, while it seemed obvious he'd mistakenly altered the data, a part of her couldn't escape the suspicion she'd overlooked something obvious. Similar to the preying worry when one accidentally leaves the house unlocked, her obsession had a focus but no means to act upon it.

Her work duties that Tuesday provided a temporary distraction, thankfully. Every so often she'd peer at the stack of reports with a glum air of helplessness. Yet, inevitably, a new office crisis arose to take her mind off them. Towards the end of her workday, fried and preparing to leave, she saw her phone light up. The call was from outside the office and, thinking it might be a client, she cleared her throat to answer.

"Hello. Is this Meda?"

"It is."

"This is Louise Napier. You were listed as the emergency contact on Matt's employment papers. I'm his direct supervisor at Fitzgerald Associates and he's neither reported to work in a week nor has he returned any of our calls."

The woman was all business. Matt had relayed anecdotes about Louise but Meda had never spoken with her directly. Over the time he'd been gone, Meda considered calling his office many times. But she'd always come to the conclusion that he definitely wasn't there (he wasn't sleeping in his cubicle) and such a call would likely do more harm than good. Based on the speed and the perfunctory nature of Louise's words, Meda quickly concluded her suspicion was correct.

This conversation wasn't going to be pleasant. "Yes, he's been going through a hard time lately," said Meda, attempting to rally some sort of defense.

"Quite," Louise sniffed. "This is the second occurrence in a two-week period. At the first instance, I gave him the benefit of the doubt despite his preposterous excuses. However, our policy is that any absence greater than two days requires a doctor's note. Lacking such a note is grounds for dismissal."

Meda took a breath, now positive where this conversation was headed. She surmised she probably couldn't save Matt's job. And like everything in her life recently, it created a split within her. On the one hand, she'd been suspicious of that Project: Saturn from the beginning and this latest, lengthier disappearance came on the heels of her insistence he copy those files. On the other hand, if the two were truly related, his continued employment was the only way to ascertain the cause. Buying time, she asked, "What are you saying?"

"I'm saying Matt's services will no longer be needed. Our Human Resources department will be sending his exit paperwork. Given his utter lack of communication, we are left with no other option. While I would've preferred to tell him in person, I requested your contact information to alert you. It's not customary but I thought it was the least I could do."

Meda roiled. She felt stymied by the concrete certainty of the situation (what could she possibly say to win Matt's job back?), by her comparative uncertainty (was he better off without the job anyway?), and by her resentment at the morsel of sincerity in Louise's tone (did she honestly expect appreciation for such a call?) "When," Meda began haltingly, "Matt gets through this, can he come back? Is there a way he could be put on a furlough? Perhaps a medical reprieve?"

"I'm afraid not. He needed to tell us prior to this absenteeism. That is also Fitzgerald's policy."

Meda shook her head. Enough with the firm policies, lady! "I'm sorry to hear that," was all she could manage.

"I'm sorry as well. Please give him my best. Also, please let him know, if he needs a reference, I'd be happy to deliver a personal one."

"I will," said Meda through gritted teeth.

They hung up and Meda felt more conflicted than ever. If Matt needed to quit his job, if only to get away from that project, she would've preferred he leave of his own accord. The worst of all worlds was termination with cause. Sure, Louise offered to provide a personal reference, but that was a far cry from a professional one. In fact, if she hadn't assigned him to that project to begin with, she wouldn't need to concern herself with such a reference!

Meda froze at that thought. Bodily, not an atom budged. Mentally, however, an explosion occurred. Her hands clutched the edge of her desk. The knuckles turned white. She sucked in a full breath, deep and necessary, then exhaled it through flared nostrils. Quaking, feeling ambushed, she began to piece everything together.

Louise's call had come out of nowhere, lasted twenty seconds, and concluded in an instant. So unprepared, she'd been most concerned about Matt's job. Only now did she realize the depths of the call's menace. It was the epiphany experienced when the unthinkable becomes real, when the stranger in the parking lot pulls out the knife. All logistical implications led back to a singular stark conclusion: Louise was responsible for everything. It was all her doing. She'd been the one to assign Matt the project. She'd been the one to drug him, to make him disappear. And now she'd used his absence as an excuse to fire him. It was the perfect set-up.

Her grip on her desk still ironclad, Meda's mouth went dry at the enormity of the conspiracy. If Napier was engaging in a scheme involving potentially hostile overseas entities, she would recognize the danger inherent in this new firmwide data overhaul. Such an audit could easily expose irregularities in Iran, Armenia, or both. Yet, if she hoped to keep her dealings under wraps, she needed to remain at arm's length while the reorganization took place. Or, at least, she needed it to appear that way. By enlisting Matt and subsequently discrediting him, she could take over the project later and blame him for any errors. She'd have free reign to not only cover her tracks, but eradicate those tracks entirely. And, Meda realized, this also explained why she lit into Matt so grievously at their meeting. She probably hoped he'd storm out or provoke some disciplinary action that would get him fired. Instead, when he took it in stride, she resorted to a larger dose of the drug she'd been using to make him disappear. Which also explained why he was gone so long this time.

Meda reeled. The plan was so obvious in retrospect. But now it was too late to do anything about it. Louise had succeeded. Matt was out of the firm and she'd be free to sweep her nefarious transactions under the rug. Except: The flash drive. Like its namesake, its existence burst forth to Meda like a starburst. Very suddenly, the power of it was manifest. Not only did she possess the largely unaltered data but, more importantly, Louise didn't know she possessed it.

By degrees, Meda released her hold on the desk. The stark rigidity in her body eased, gradually replaced by a new nervous energy. Her knee began to bounce (when did her knee ever bounce?), as if she was about to give an important speech. And, energized by this new impulse, she muttered to her co-worker, "Ann, I've got an emergency. I need to go. Can you give my apologies to Dayle?" And before Ann finished offering her generic sympathies, Meda was shooting toward the door.

## MATT

**I think the question to ask yourself is this: Where am I when I'm not here?**

"Easy for you to say. I don't know where 'here' is."

**In the end, it's all the same place.**

"That explains nothing."

**Was it not Shakespeare who wrote, "Nothing will come of nothing"? Ponder it. Where are you when you're not here? Where were you before you were here?**

"Before I was here, I think I was writing. That seems to be the common theme. After I'm here, though? Nobody knows."

**Exactly.**

## MAGEE

Magee's timing wasn't altogether terrible. While 7:00 was still technically rush hour, he was going against the commuters, toward Manhattan rather than away from it. Earlier, a stray glance at his bag of weed reminded Magee of his conversation with Meda. He'd suggested she start at the beginning by simply going to the library. What if he took his own advice? If he intended to locate the woman who would, "destroy everything," the logical place to start was Matt's office.

Magee spotted the gigantic address numbers illuminated in the ground floor windows of Fitzgerald Tower from halfway down the block. Midtown Manhattan was lined with corporate offices that presented comparable architectural features: booming marble atriums, frenetic people in suits charging across them, and, of course, the customary security desk at the rear. Magee's pace slowed upon his approach...he realized he hadn't fully considered the security issue. Obviously, he didn't expect to simply saunter up to Matt's floor and start poking around. But the security personnel he encountered most often consisted of a lone elderly gentleman manning the desk at a boutique art-house. These corporate gatekeepers were a different species. They weren't warriors trained in a litany of fighting styles, they were worse...automatons laser-focused on "procedure" who would not, could not, deviate from script. Magee ascended the concrete steps outside the tower with growing trepidation and, once inside the glimmering hall, he came face-to-face with his glaring lack of direction.

For a moment he stood, locked in stasis and uniquely out of place in his green army coat and scruffy beard. Then, when three ruthlessly groomed businessmen passed and eyed him up as they might a wet possum, he knew he needed to do something. He couldn't just stand around and hope for inspiration. With a gulp, he puffed out his chest and approached the security desk.

"Hello, I'm here to see Matt at Fitzgerald. I believe he's on the twenty-ninth floor."

"ID?" The woman's jacket was starched as rigid as her demeanor.

Magee pulled out his wallet and, in a fortuitous surprise, he discovered a ragged copy of Matt's business card. "Here you go," he said with a smile, handing over the card and his driver's license.

She remained unimpressed. "Do you have an appointment?"

"Ah...no. He and I met for lunch and I think he accidently took my bag. I hoped to run up and grab it." The story appeared to Magee out of thin air...Matt would've been proud.

"I'll need to call reception. She's probably gone," said the security guard. She picked up a phone and began dialing as Magee's discomfiture swelled. With the discovery of Matt's card, he presumed he was home-free. This call, however, might not only reveal that Magee's appointment was nonexistent but also highlight Matt's absence. A second passed as Magee struggled for the right words. "I mean...it'll only take a second. Matt doesn't need to be at his desk. He works in the transfer department. I know where it is."

Then, out of nowhere, a new voice was heard. "Excuse me. You're looking for Matt? At Fitzgerald Associates?"

Magee turned to find a curious young woman of perhaps Indian or Middle Eastern descent. While tiny in stature, a certain manic energy radiated off her. "Yep," he said, attempting to quell his nervousness in the face of the sudden swerve in the situation. "He's the one. Do you work with him?"

"I do. I sit right beside him. Can I help you with something?"

"Ah...yes, in fact. I'm a buddy of his. My name's Magee," he said, offering his hand to shake. With the security guard looking on, he continued, nearly rambling. "We go way back. He might've mentioned me. Not sure how tight you two are. I think my bag is in his cubicle. I hoped to pick it up."

"I'm Abby. Nice to meet you," she said, shaking his hand. Then she frowned briefly and Magee, teetering in the conversation, feared she would mention Matt's absence from the office. Instead, she said, "No, he hadn't mentioned you. But, y'know, that's just Matt. I could absolutely take you up to his desk if you want."

Magee agreed eagerly and Abby, addressing the security guard, asked, "He doesn't need an appointment if I accompany him upstairs, correct?"

"Affirmative. But he'll still need his picture taken for the temporary badge."

Magee commenced the formality while Abby waited. He was grateful for her appearance yet also fearful of too much small talk lest she blow his cover. "You've known Matt a long time?" she asked eventually, the conversational emptiness apparently too much for her to bear.

"Yep. Since college. We moved to the city together."

"Oh wow," she said, newly animated. "I don't think I've known anybody that long. You guys must be really good friends. He must tell you everything."

She burst into a too-vigorous laugh...Magee wished the guard would hurry up with the dang picture. "I'm not sure Matt tells anybody everything. But yep, we've been friends for a long time."

"Our department would be nothing without him, y'know? Well, not exactly. I try to stay busy, too. But Matt was hired first. He's got seniority. It's absolutely a great place to work. I'm sure he mentioned."

Her words were borderline gibberish...Magee didn't even know how to react. What's the proper response to so many sentences with no cohesive message uniting them?

"Here's your badge," announced the officer to Magee's eternal relief. "Don't forget to turn it in when you leave."

"Of course," he said, preparing to go.

"He's a really good guy," continued Abby, oblivious to the exchange. "And he's so funny. Always making jokes, y'know? So funny."

Magee winced when it became clear she intended to tag along. While the access she provided was fortuitous, this distraction threatened his entire reason for being there. Each scanned their way through the turnstiles as she continued to prattle...he wasn't sure how long he could handle this. Then, perhaps ten steps from the elevator bank, Abby announced, "Okey-doke. I'm sure you can take it from here. I was leaving for the day anyway."

For the second time in two minutes a rush of relief washed over him. How many gift horses could appear in one day? "You're not coming up?"

"Nah," she said, with a wave. "I only came this far because security requires visitors to be escorted. Our office is on the twenty-ninth floor. The receptionist is gone but you might be able to find somebody to point you to Matt's desk. Worst case, start in the center and work your way out."

Magee tried to rein in visible signs of his relief. He was skeptical about his success. "Wow. Great! Thanks then!"

"No problem. Have an absolutely amazing weekend."

And with that, Magee was on his own. Gloriously so. Briefly, he felt a pang of guilt about his attitude towards Abby. She'd gone out of her way to help him yet he couldn't be rid of her fast enough. Then he reminded himself of his goal, hopped in an elevator, and was on his way up.

Abby was correct...the reception desk sat empty. In fact, upon a cursory view of the floor, everyone was gone. Magee moved cautiously at first, creeping out of the elevator and past the desk. The fluorescent light of the lobby truncated at the edge of the large hallway beyond and, when his movements failed to trigger any additional lights, he concluded the motion detectors were off. Once outside that main reception area, this meant the darkness was vast, broken only by the occasional glow of an EXIT sign, and the expanse ended at the unearthly full-length windows beyond. Magee peered out the faraway portals and mused that, with barely a meager glow of the city seeping in, it was probably one of the best spots in Manhattan to view the passing comet outside. Then he re-focused once more and got to work.

As he slithered down one of the floor's main arteries, he came to the first row of cubicles serving to partition the floor. He was attuned to his surroundings, proceeding stealthily and ready to detect any sound or movement. But there was none. In the abstract, this was the perfect environment to snoop without fear of arousing suspicion. With no one around he could take all the time he wanted. The catch? Locating Matt's cubicle would be no easy chore. It was too dark to read the name plates without putting his nose right up to each.

Magee continued to explore and his movements grew quicker, bolder. The cubicles stacked on, one after the other, each only marginally different than the last. Before long he grew disorientated and realized he needed a better approach. He could wander for hours and, if Matt's cube resided in a hidden alcove or isolated room, he might never find it. He stopped to take stock. A main hallway bisected the lobby and formed a 't' with another hallway that ran perpendicular. The result was four cohorts surrounding the reception hub. Offices lined the walls of the interior while those floor-to-ceiling windows wrapped the outside, punctuated only by select C-level offices at the corners. Magee re-appraised his mental map, finished exploring the remaining portion of the cohort he'd already started, then moved on to the next.

He crossed the main hallway; copiers and office supply depots lined it like stalwart guardsmen. During office hours, they were likely sources of buzz and activity. Now they were silent. For efficiency's sake, he headed to the innermost wall of offices to start his search anew. While still quite hard to read the name tags on the cubes, he was growing more comfortable with his mission.

It was only when he got within a few cubicles of the center offices that he registered the other person's presence. He'd caught it out of the corner his eye and his mind needed extra seconds to process it. Once he peered more intently and concluded he wasn't mistaken, however, his hairs stood on end. The mere sight of another human caused him to stutter-step then come to a halt. Initially, he remained frozen, unmoving. Then, after a moment in wait and confident he wasn't detected, he resumed his approach. With each timorous step, he grew more unnerved by the person's unnatural positioning. Something didn't look right.

After creeping closer, he identified what set his nerves on edge. The person was merely standing there, stock still, with his or her back to Magee. It wasn't the look of some poor office worker toiling away on a project after hours. This person was a statue. More eerie: the glow of the computer monitor back-lit the person in an ethereal emerald hue. The office was the second along the wall and, throughout his approach, a proper view of the inside was impossible. He didn't want to startle the person but the peculiarity of the situation compelled him to investigate. He slinked closer. The silhouetted being did not budge.

When he arrived at the office's doorway the grotesque enormity of the scene revealed itself. He'd been tip-toeing, ready to dive for cover should the person move. Then he saw the blood. The liquid, appearing black in the dimly lit office, was everywhere. On the carpet, on the desk, on the scattered papers...even on the walls. The smell of iron was unmistakable and overpowered the sterile scents of paper and toner ink. At points the blood lay in tidy pools, perfectly reflecting the ionic light of the computer monitor like tiny mirrors. In other areas, the gore was brutal and smeared across the wall in clawing hand prints.

The details assaulted Magee's senses. The elderly woman's body lay sprawled across the desk, contorted awkwardly, inhumanly. Her blouse was drenched in blood, not a stitch dry. And, ghastly in number, scores of stab wounds punctured her clothes in discrete, gruesome holes. Magee's gaze flitted in quick succession: first to the carnage, then to the woman on the desk, then back to the person standing beside it all. And, despite the horror before him, Magee was most shocked to see Meda.

## MEDA

Magee would later concede his first instinct had been to tackle Meda. It was an immediate fight-or-flight response and he was embarrassed to admit it. Meda understood, however, because she'd shared a similar reaction. When Magee stepped into the office, she'd jumped to the conclusion he was the murderer. Each experienced panic, their heart rates shot to adrenalized heights, and the situation could've easily spiraled out of control. The soundless, instant-to-impact singularity felt like an eternity. But it was only in that taught silence (nothing spoken, no movements made) that they created a modicum of trust in each other.

"We need to call 911," said Meda, each still locked in position.

Magee remained stiff for an extended second then, finally, relaxed. He reached into his pocket for his phone yet appeared conflicted. "What happened?" he asked, his voice quivering.

It was less a request for explanation and more an acknowledgement of the abject horror in front of them. "I have no idea. I just arrived myself," said Meda. "The only thing I know is this woman was murdered. Which means, if we don't call the cops, we might be considered accessories." It was enough to move Magee to action and he made the call.

The police arrived at Fitzgerald Tower in minutes. It wasn't enough time for Magee and Meda to sort themselves out and they struggled to find an explanation for their presence on the floor. Both had snuck in illegally, neither were employees of the firm, and neither could offer a substantive reason for their presence. Worst of all, Matt was nowhere to be found. With no one to vouch for them, one officer seemed ready to cuff them and ship them to the precinct as suspects.

"Look, at a minimum you're trespassing, right?" said the officer. He wasn't the first to arrive but, based on the eggshell-walking trepidation displayed by his fellow officers, he was clearly in charge. "You're going to have to give me something to work with. I'm losing my patience here."

In an attempt at full disclosure, both Meda and Magee had blurted out details about Matt's disappearances and their unfinished conspiracy theory about Fitzgerald. Magee was quickly realizing such honesty might not be the best policy, however. Whereas Meda had knocked him out of his stupor earlier, he could see he needed to bail them out now. He just prayed Meda would follow his lead.

"Officer, I know. This all sounds crazy," began Magee. "I can't believe this happened to us. We told you how Matt...my friend, her boyfriend...has been missing? Well, those two have tickets to the opera and Matt left them here at the office. Matt? He can be a little irresponsible sometimes. And we didn't want the tickets to go to waste while he was gone. I was trying to get my friend out of trouble. I had no clue Meda would come looking for the tickets at the same time. This has nothing to do with the woman who died. It's just atrocious timing."

Meda's gaze snapped to him, wide-eyed, and for a trembling second Magee feared she would contradict him.

"The opera?" said the officer, appearing skeptical yet also unprepared for such an unusual excuse. "What showing?"

"*Götterdämmerung*," said Meda without hesitation, much to Magee's relief. "By Wagner."

The officer jotted down something in his notebook then peered over it at Meda. "And when is the performance?"

Meda didn't falter. "Saturday. At Lincoln Center."

"Got it. Sure. Makes me wonder though, since today's only Wednesday, why the rush to pick them up?"

Meda double-clutched, her response stuck in her throat. Her mouth appeared to form a word but no sound came forth. Thankfully, Magee stepped up, exhibiting an air of embarrassment. "I know. It's a few days away. I thought, in case Matt didn't return, this would be my best chance to pick them up. The rest of the week is going to be very busy."

"Why not Saturday afternoon?"

"I've got a baby shower Saturday afternoon," snapped Meda before Magee could respond. As an explanation, it was technically correct. A friend's shower was indeed planned for that time. Yet it possessed a certain non-sequitur quality. If she was out anyway, wouldn't it be easier to pick up the tickets on the way to the opera? A shade of disappointment colored Magee's reaction and Meda scrambled to add, "The shower is ending late and I didn't want any complications. If Matt doesn't return soon, I wanted the tickets in hand ready to sell."

The officer stared at Meda. Then at Magee. The tick of the clock was his ally in such a tense moment. It was obvious his street-wise intuition was flaring at the sketchier details in their story. What wasn't clear, however, was whether those same instincts might lead him to conclude they killed Louise.

"Here's the thing: I gave you guys the benefit of the doubt and decided to interview you together, seeing as how you're not covered in blood and all. Thought I'd keep it informal, right? I have to admit, though, I'm sensing something is just a little off here. And, you know, this is a murder scene. I have to make sure I'm not letting a potential murderer walk unless I'm positive, *positive*, neither of you is a suspect. Now, if you'd prefer your preliminary statements turn into formal statements at the station, I can arrange that very easily. I can't help but wonder, though. If you two were in separate rooms, how many of your details would still corroborate? Like I say, this is murder we're talking about here."

The thinly-veiled threat wilted Meda and Magee's resolve. Yet they had no idea what details to provide to satisfy the officer. The whole situation was too crazy.

"Well?" said the officer. "Last chance."

Just then, another officer approached from farther down the hall, making a slashing motion at his neck as if to say, "stop." The officer who'd been interviewing Meda and Magee appeared surprised, almost disappointed. He shot his hands out to his sides and the officers began engaging in a sort of communication by expression, leaving Meda and Magee in the dark. Finally, the approaching officer moved within earshot and said, "Jim, we Luminol-ed the office. Not a trace. No clean-up. Only the footprints from these two. With that much blood, they would've had to strip naked to leave so cleanly."

The first officer wiped his hand across his brow, from temple to temple. "Did Zukher look at the wounds?"

"Uh-huh. And he agrees."

The officer pondered momentarily and Meda and Magee exchanged a glance, furtive and hesitant. "What...does that mean?" asked Magee.

"It means," said the officer, pausing for a deep sigh, "that you two are free to go. The wounds were self-inflicted."

## MAGEE

Magee wanted to kill that little boy. He wanted to take him, throttle him, and demand to know why he sent him on such a damnable journey. A woman died...brutally, gruesomely...and he'd arrived at the precise point it was too late to save her. What kind of sick cruelty was that? Why send him there knowing he'd be helpless to avert the tragedy?

It was late. By the time the police concluded Magee and Meda weren't suspects and they finished exchanging contact information, the time was approaching ten o'clock. The experience represented the longest Magee had been cooped up in a corporate setting in years...he never understood how Matt's creative fires weren't dampened by such an empty, spirit-draining place. Once finally free, he stomped across the asphalt, crossed the street against a red light, and narrowly avoided a cab barreling down on him. Then, when he descended the subway station stairs to find the train's doors closing, his already dour mood darkened further and he flung his half-empty bottle of water at the departing silver blur.

The rumble of the train receded into the darkness of the tunnel and Magee was left with too much time to think. Previously, he'd been concerned about Matt but in a vague, "Matt-will-be-Matt," way. The pair had survived many tough stretches and this seemed like another dilemma that would solve itself. Now someone was dead. Permanently gone, leaving friends and loved ones behind. He felt like he'd passed into some new reality where everything was more starkly concrete. All because that kid sent him on a wild goose chase.

Once again, he found himself as the only figure on a desolate platform. Agitated, he began pacing. The iron-sodden odor of blood remained embedded in his nostrils...the sight of the gore still flashed in his vision every time he blinked. He needed to get home, take a shower, and rinse it all away. Briefly, he considered going back upstairs to hail a taxi. If he encountered an especially talkative driver in his current state, however, he feared a confrontation. Better to take the journey free from conversation, even if it meant more time alone with his tortured thoughts.

He had never beheld a body so soon after a person's death. Sure, he'd attended funerals. And he saw his elderly uncle pass away in the hospital...but that was different. This woman had stabbed herself repeatedly, in the gut, in the lungs, in her arms and legs. What would make someone do that? Suicide was bad enough...why do it so viciously? While speaking with the officer, he'd been so intent on keeping his composure that he didn't have time to process what he witnessed. It was only as the night wore on, as his mind caught up to the trauma that Magee began to grasp the horrific implications.

What haunted him most was the timing. At one point, he overheard an officer say Louise hadn't been dead long; no more than ten minutes given the state of her pallor mortis, even accounting for the amount of blood lost. He wished he hadn't heard that. Working backward, from the moment Meda discovered the body to the point he dialed 911, roughly a minute and a half had lapsed...ninety seconds. Previous to that, he'd been exploring the office for about four minutes. And, before that, he spent probably three minutes at the front desk with Matt's co-worker. A grand total of about eight and a half minutes. Put another way, Louise's final plunge of the knife likely occurred as he entered the lobby. He was in the building! He could've stopped her! Yet, for whatever reason, the little boy chose late afternoon to confer his arcane prophecy. He could've shown up any time that morning...hell, any day preceding. Instead, sadistically, he chose the precise time at which Magee would be too late to intervene.

The train deposited him in his neighborhood and Magee, hunched forward with his hands buried in his coat pockets, tramped home through the brisk night air. He flung open the door to his studio, half-hoping and half-fearing the boy might be inside. He envisioned closing his hands on the boy's throat, his grip clamping tighter and tighter. He wouldn't give the boy the chance at an explanation...he didn't deserve one. The boy was nowhere to be found, however, and a certain back corner of his mind gave a sigh of relief.

He skulked about for a moment and was reminded of his halcyonic state earlier in the day. The mirror and the pane of glass still lay on the table, paint tubes were scattered about. He'd left in a rush following the conversation with the boy and Magee couldn't help but recognize the bitter irony...why such speed when the boy could've appeared sooner? He sneered at the thought. Then, as his gaze zeroed in on his work area, he stalked over to his brushes. In his haste, he hadn't cleaned them and he processed the implications with increasing ire. The paint had hardened solid in the bristles. He could clean them, of course. But their bend recovery would be impacted, a dicey proposition in the middle of such an important piece. Deliberately, he picked up one, then another. His body locked in place, trembling...a tension cable of rigidity.

Then he exploded. He flung the first at the wall. Then the second. They bounced off with mocking quietude, registering only a twinkling of sound. The futility magnified his rage, driving it ever-higher. He seized a paint tube and launched it at the wall. Its heft made it burst in a satisfying splat and he followed with another and another. The release was sudden and downright feral in its brutality. His lips peeled back into a snarl; his brow pressed his eyes into slits of rage. And when an easel leaning against the wall became loosed by the vibrations, he could only look on in horror.

The wooden device fell noiselessly in dream-like slow motion. Directly in its path...the priceless mirror. Yet, between Magee and it...his hardwood work table. His mind registered the imminent disaster. His arms shot up. He leapt across table. But he was too far away.

The easel clipped the edge of the mirror. The glass didn't break. But the heavy easel pressed on an overhanging lip, upending the precious relic. If the previous moment had been slow motion, this became an eternity. Gravity took hold as the smooth backside of the glass lost purchase on the precipice of the table beneath. Magee leapt in vain again...just in time to witness it career off the table and burst on the floor below.

"No!" Magee screamed, anguished, disconsolate. He knew he was too late to prevent the disaster. And by the time he sidestepped the table to reach the remains, it was already over.

The room re-inflated with fulsome, tombstone silence. Such a loud crash...such a wicked rain of glass shards splintering in unison on the concrete...all over in an instant. 500 seconds had meant the difference earlier; this tragedy was concluded in less than two. And now, staring down in disbelief at the shattered relic with electrified nerves ready to fire...Magee merely sighed. It was too late. It was just too late. His shoulders, formerly drawn as tight as a noose, plunged. Despondency filled him, swelling up and over his head. He needed to do something. Yet there was nothing to do.

For an unknowable amount of time he merely stood, his spirit in ruins. Then, by infinitesimal degrees, his vision began to liven. His gaze flitted to his work table. Then to the paint slowly oozing down the wall. Then to the exact-o knife laying on the table. And he picked it up. How easy it would be to end it all now. That mirror had been a godsend...he would never find another like it. If he was ever going to find any real success as an artist, it would've been through that mirror.

He held the blade up to the light. The razor's edge enticed him, so clean and so precise. There were no questions about symbolic intent or artistic integrity...there was only the blade. His eyes left it, moving to his wrist, to his forearm extended as if to donate blood. All was silent. All was still. Utter perfection. The mirror was gone...he could be gone just as easily.

Then he caught a glance of something. Behind his arm, insisting itself into his vision, was that bag of weed. If his mind's eye had been barreling down a linear, all-enveloping tunnel, the sight of the bag ripped the roof off that passageway. There were other possibilities. It wasn't so clean as he thought. The weed reminded him of the boy earlier and the way he felt when Meda tossed the bag to him in his apartment. Suddenly it wasn't only about the mirror and his artistic career...there were other parts of his life, other forces at work.

A vague resentment established a beachhead within him. It stood in contrast to the abject rage he experienced earlier. And he was overcome by the despicable sensation of being used...by the boy and his dementedly-timed warning; by the tumultuous emotions churning in his body; by memories that made him feel like a different person from one moment to the next. Moments ago, his fury had brought ruin to the most important piece of art he ever attempted. Immediately after that, he stood ready to take his own life. Magee felt like he didn't even know who he *was* anymore.

He put the knife down. The movement was calm, methodical. Then, exhausted from the roil of emotions, his eyes produced two salty tears. Dreary seconds passed. He no longer wanted to end himself. But that didn't save him from his current reality. Eventually, with leaden feet, he turned to make the bleak climb upstairs. And, never turning back to look at the destruction behind him, he failed to see the image of the little boy reflected back in the broken shard of the mirror.

## MEDA

Meda lingered almost nine minutes after Magee left. Whereas he'd turned inexplicably restless, Meda grew contemplative once everything settled down. In quick succession he'd called the cops, ushered her out of the blood-splattered office, and gone back inside to see if there was any hope of saving Louise. The cops arrived soon afterward, the police officer interviewed them, and Magee stomped off almost immediately afterward. Only then, in that sudden dearth of activity, did Meda get a proper chance to ruminate.

She'd been the first to stumble on the scene and she remained shaken. Mere hours earlier, she'd hated that woman. She and Louise had never met in person and that call was the first time they'd ever spoken. Yet, in the interim, Meda had become convinced she was the mastermind of some villainous plot involving foreign countries and Matt's blackouts. Meda had grown positive Napier set up Matt as the fall guy, fired him to cover her tracks, and was ready to enact her dastardly plan. It all added up. The whole reason for Meda's presence in the office was because she intended to confront the woman. Now, however, that storyline was utterly shattered and replaced by a sense of shame at her rush to judgment.

Complicating her tumult was the suspicion that Louise's suicide nonetheless confirmed her overarching theory. Something insidious was occurring at Fitzgerald. Meda had merely come to an incorrect conclusion. Her unique access to the office floor, put side-by-side with the dissolution of her theory, made her feel like she was caught between two warring impulses. She'd been offered this unique access to the office yet she still had no direction. Even momentarily disregarding her concern for Matt, she still carried the moral responsibility to do something with the unique knowledge gleaned from those reports. In a worst-case scenario, she was looking at the manufacture of nuclear or radiological weapons; she couldn't simply dismiss such information. Virtually alone and rudderless in the sea of cubicles, however, she couldn't decide what to do next.

In the process of saying goodbye to Magee, Meda had wandered with him for a stretch. As a result, the police on the scene seemed to half-forget her presence, so long as she remained clear of their activities. She shouldn't have been able to access the floor to begin with, of course. The spare badge was only available because Matt lost his ID once, received a replacement, and then found the original. When she first arrived, she'd worried a security officer at the front desk might be watching a monitor and notice she wasn't the person named on the card. But, with the lone clerk occupied by a young woman asking a barrage of questions, Meda had seized the opportunity and breezed through the turnstile.

It was only when a new cast of characters arrived on the floor that she snapped out of her languor. Three people approached the baby-faced policeman at the entrance of the main hallway. One crotchety man, his pocket adorned with aviator glasses despite the late hour, was trailed by a rounder man who was evidently his second in command. And a well-dressed woman with impeccable posture strode in beside the first man, her heels announcing the presence of the trio before they appeared. They introduced themselves, respectively, as the leaders of the firm's Operations department and the Head of the Public Relations department. Then they peppered the cop with eight question-demands in a commensurate number of seconds before he waved over another officer.

Meda accepted it was time to go now; she'd lost her opportunity. If the twitchy PR woman didn't spot her and demand she sign a Non-Disclosure Agreement, the Operations guys might demand she be arrested for trespassing. Any plan she intended to pursue was now a lost cause.

Meda crept back to the opposite hallway that bisected the first in an effort to outflank the Fitzgerald employees. Apart from the police activities, stillness pervaded the office and she didn't want to get caught on the way out. As she entered the elevator lobby, however, she caught a snippet of their conversation. She listened, then halted, her attention ensnared.

A woman's voice asked, "And there were no witnesses, correct?"

"No, there were two. A male and a female." Meda recognized the voice of the officer who'd interviewed her and Magee earlier. "Neither were employees. They apparently snuck in to pick up something off the desk of one of your employees."

"That's not correct," said a different male voice, though just as authoritative. "According the records from security, an employee had swiped his badge at the front turnstiles. His name was Matt."

# 8 ⅓ MINUTES

*As a firmly defined unit of measurement, an initial second is required to exist. Granted, this second would've passed long before any human, animal, or otherwise was around to record it. But that first second is necessitated before the second, third, and every second thereafter. Likely birthed in the immediate aftermath of the Big Bang, a strong case could be made that it was the most important second in the history of the universe. Thousands of years would pass before light, much less sound, came into existence; the churn of the immense forces may've even caused that initial second to pass differently than human's current conception of it. Yet, amid the indescribable chaos of that exploding plasma, that first second passed and all the ensuing seconds continued to march right along behind it.*

*And march along they did! In so doing, each second that passed also created a new set of seconds. There was the first second. Then the first and second ones. Then the first, second, and third seconds. These could be grouped into the omnibus set of all seconds passed, equaling the age of the universe. They could also be divided into dichotomous even- and odd-numbered seconds, each equivalent to half the universe's age. Or they could be put into a group of 60, otherwise known as a minute. And then those could be put into another group of 60 to create an hour. And so on and so forth.*

*Taking this one step further, a set could be established based on any requirement one pleases, be it ten seconds or ten millennia. And this continuum could begin at any point. One can imagine this set moving with each passing second, as if sliding along the timestream like a train on a track. While the respective set's length would be immutable, it could still exist at any point in the universe's history.*

*Today, we are concerned with the set of 500 seconds, or 8 ⅓ minutes. Obviously, the set of 8 ⅓ minutes (hereby known as "8 ⅓") is well aware of the myriad important events that occurred within its boundaries: Washington's cold contemplation after his near-disastrous Delaware river crossing; Caesar's horrific bleed out from 23 stab wounds; and, of course, who could forget Hammurabi's moment of divine inspiration in the moonlight. And such events don't even account for the whole host of world-changing zeitgeists set in motion, directly or indirectly, within its boundary.*

*To be sure, 8 ⅓ carried no reservations about its importance. While it couldn't compete with the clean precision of the single second or the sheer commonality of 60 seconds, it was humbly content to have such events transpire within its boundaries. Such recognition was the easy part. It longed for a vision of its appearance from the outside. 8 ⅓ often marveled at a human's compulsion to create an identity that blended self-assessment with inputs from the external world. In fact, many humans defined themselves more by others' opinions than by their opinions of themselves. 8 ⅓ had no conception of such a feeling or outlook. Therefore, it decided to set out into the world of experience. The path might prove perilous and, once embarking on it, 8 ⅓ might learn some transfinite truth it would rather not know. Yet it was a journey 8 ⅓ needed to take.*

*To enact such a plan, 8 ⅓ first needed a four-dimensional place to begin. The geographic location informed the decision but so did the timeframe. If 8 ⅓ wished, it could interview Grover Cleveland as easily as an ancient Mesopotamian. It wasn't limited in that manner. Ultimately, it decided the present day would be the best to start. And, once that was settled, 8 ⅓ decided to meet with a scientist, someone who might have the best grasp of its transitive existence.*

*8 ⅓ introduced itself to Talbot, an affable chum working at the particle supercollider at CERN. While technically a genius, he didn't always employ such mental horsepower in the most effective manner. 8 ⅓ thought it might glean a unique insight from the brainy, yet awkward fellow.*

*When 8 ⅓ appeared, however, Talbot wasn't prepared for such an interruption. Indeed, who would be? He was in the midst of analyzing some Tier 2 data from The Grid when 8 ⅓ materialized. "Hello! I'm 8 ⅓ minutes given physical form. How are you today?"*

*"Wuh? Huh? Oh no! Why is this happening?" Talbot's limbs shot outward; his thick forearm sent his coffee spraying across his desk. Luckily for 8 ⅓, no one else was present in the lab to witness the scene. It hadn't expected Talbot to lose his marbles so completely.*

*"Please. Calm yourself. I mean you no harm. I'm merely a defined set of seconds. 500 seconds, to be precise. There's also a set of 500 and 501, for example. In fact, there are lots of us sets; practically an infinite number. I come in peace."*

*"Um, okay," said Talbot. With only a portion of the coffee sopped up, he was doing an atrocious job righting himself.*

*Already, 8 ⅓ could see its path to awareness wasn't going to be as linear as initially hoped. It mused that it should've started with Talbot's maniacal colleague, Benedict, instead. Alas, that was water under the bridge. Best to settle the man further before making an attempt at any elucidation he might provide. "Talbot, have you ever seen an hourglass in action? Seen its sand drop with each passing second?"*

*"Yes. Of course."*

*"Great. Well think of me as one of those contraptions. Inside me are all those seconds. You can start me at any moment and I would represent the next 500 seconds. Does that make sense?"*

"Yes. Of course."

"Splendid. Well, the reason I'm visiting you today is because I hoped to get your thoughts on a few matters. Do you have a moment?"

"Yes. Of course."

8 ⅓ barely kept from chuckling at the man's repetitive, blank-eyed affirmations. It was as if the man was stuck on Repeat. "My main query concerns perception. You seem like an intelligent man with a good grasp of complex concepts. At the risk of putting words in your mouth, I'd hazard a guess that this is how you see yourself. Is that fair to say?"

This question elicited a more nuanced reaction from Talbot. Rather than the far-off veneer shown previously, a frown signaled deeper contemplation this time. "Yes. I suppose that's about right."

"Brilliant. My question to you, then, is twofold. How do you see me? And, just importantly, how do you think others see me?"

At that, the man became fully invested. He pondered and, after a second, his hand went to his chin. 8 ⅓ waited. And as Talbot's lumpy finger tapped away, 8 ⅓'s anticipation grew.

"Well, technically, you don't exist," began Talbot, torpedoing its self-esteem. "Time is simply a construct of speed and distance. It's all a matter of relative velocity. It doesn't matter if you're talking about 500 seconds or 500 minutes. These units of measurement, here on earth, are mutually agreed upon because everybody's moving at the same general speed. 500 seconds in Geneva will be 500 seconds in Hong Kong."

Now 8 ⅓ grimaced. It knew all this, of course. Talbot continued, "Time, as a universal concept, is far from agreed upon, however. It all comes back to the theory of relativity. From the perception of a massless particle travelling at the speed of light, a measure of time such as yourself would never even be seen. The closer one travels to the speed of light, the slower time will move. Theoretically, a traveler moving faster and faster would eventually hit a point where time stands still. Granted, this traveler would also become heavier and heavier at the same time, making such speed impossible. A proper view of you is nonetheless conditionally reliant upon the viewer's perspective."

8 ⅓ pondered this a moment. "Are you suggesting I wouldn't exist without other people to observe me?"

"Well, not exactly. You might still exist in your own way. But if there was no one there to record your passing, it wouldn't be defined. It's like that old paradoxical riddle about the tree falling in the woods. If there's no one present to hear it, does it still make a noise?" Talbot grinned, as if readying to say something funny. "When you think of it that way, your existence is almost fully defined by the person observing you."

8 ⅓ glanced at the floor ruefully. This was quite a literal interpretation of his question! When 8 ⅓ asked how it was seen, it meant to imply the abstract notion of summary observance. A person could be described as funny, or lazy, or kind-hearted; all static states of qualitative appraisal. In this conversation with Talbot, however, the semantic tail seemed to be wagging the dog. 8 ⅓ possessed a decent grasp of the workings of the time-space continuum. What it sought was something less textbook-y.

"I greatly appreciate your time," said the abstract set of 8 ⅓ minutes. "This has been educational but, alas, I'm not positive it's what I'm seeking."

"Oh, I see."

Talbot went back to his work and, with only days left before the end of the world, 8 ⅓ moved on with haste. The *conversation was informative but 8 ⅓ needed input from someone whose mind operated more dramatically outside the box. Rather than taking a bottom-up approach, 8 ⅓ decided to take a top-down approach and interview someone who specialized in high-level, macro data.*

*Billy was such a person. As an Opinion Optimization Architect at Helios Data, he was charged with taking untold quantities of information and transforming it into verifiable trends and actionable plans. As one would expect, he welcomed 8 ⅓ with open arms. "My word, what a unique opportunity!"*

*"I'm thankful your schedule was open," demurred 8 ⅓.*

*"Of course! Of course! I can make time for an entity such as yourself!"*

*Billy sniggered and, catching his time-centric joke a moment late, 8 ⅓ grinned in return. "Ah. Nice. Good one."*

*Soon Billy grew less jovial and, crossing his leg while perched atop his work stool, he asked, "Now I understand you're having an identity issue?"*

*"That's one way to put it," began 8 ⅓, growing more comfortable with Billy's enthusiastic response. The man's office was strewn with seemingly random objects. On his desk lay outdated electronic devices, an octopus-like action figure, and a musical instrument 8 ⅓ didn't recognize. And his hair stuck out in odd places, no doubt the result of wild rakes with his fingers and no mirror to consult. While unpolished, however, the Opinion Optimization Architect didn't lack for confidence. When he spoke, his maw often hung slack between sentences, making him appear equal parts a mad scientist and a chess master thinking eight moves ahead. 8 ⅓ continued, "As mentioned, the best way to think of me is like an hourglass. I'm a set period of time that can start ticking away at any moment."*

"Yes. Yes. I appreciate that," said Billy, blinking as if on Fast Forward. "I must admit, I'm quite intrigued. I have so many questions."

"Grand! I do believe discourse to be so much more efficient than simple questions and answers."

"Yes! Efficiency!" shouted Billy.

8 ⅓ leaned backward, wide-eyed at the man's stentorian pronouncement. "Yes. Well. Frittering away not a moment, my friend, let me pose my primary question. How do you see me?"

If earlier Billy moved on Fast Forward, now someone had hit the Pause button. 8 ⅓ recognized he was thinking; the mental gears were indubitably in motion. But the man didn't move, didn't blink. Until, just as abruptly, he sprung back to life. "Well! I think seeing you is less important than perceiving you."

8 ⅓ contemplated this assessment but said nothing.

"It's a key distinction. Forget, even, the particulars involving eyesight, retinas, and such. Instead, focus on the act of envisioning something, the act of imagining an event in the mind's eye. Ancient cavemen didn't create language by staring at a sabretooth tiger and assigning a label. They imagined the sabretooth out there, stalking them. And they needed a means to convey the threat to their hunting mates."

"So, you're suggesting people perceive me on a less conscious level. More in their mind's eye?"

"Well, yes and no. Let's not get ahead of ourselves," cautioned the man who ran mental sprints from the moment he awoke. "We can't automatically assume people are taking notice of you independent of your movements. For example, in my line of work, I need to disentangle consumers' actions from their lifestyles. I need to know why a person bought a specific item, at a specific store, at a specific time, in a specific *way. Call it 4-D consumerism, if you will. You see, on a granular level, a person creates a sort of vibrating string in their daily movements. Imagine a person's neighborhood from the sky, as a map. And imagine the movements of a person, day after day. Usually, most people go from their home to their workplace with reliable predictability. They may stop for various types of errands and, thereby, elongate the loop. Over time, however, particularly when their movements are sped up, the pattern becomes unmistakable. Certain people, such as those caring for an elderly relative or visiting a significant other, might create a more triangular route. Yet the pattern remains. You get the picture."*

*8 ⅓ gave confirmation.*

*"In your case, however, all that goes out the window. You have no starting point; only an end point. Imagine then, a person who can begin anywhere on this field. Like a firework, they appear from nothing and shoot across the map, only to disappear again. That's something most humans wouldn't consider in the course of their average activity. Their minds aren't conditioned to reflect on such a principle. You could force the concept upon them by, for example, discussing a drive to the store that should take 8 ⅓ minutes. But that's situation-dependent. Not entity-dependent. I hate to disappoint you but I fear most wouldn't stop to consider you as an autonomous entity."*

*8 ⅓'s spirits flagged a second time. Talbot concluded its existence was wholly dependent on the observer's position. Yet Billy concluded 8 ⅓ was unlikely to be observed at all due to human's preconceptions. How badly 8 ⅓ wanted to be free of such reliance on observation!*

*8 ⅓ thanked Billy and shuffled off alone. The rain outside made for a raw, glum afternoon and the few people who passed 8 ⅓ avoided eye contact. It couldn't help but wonder if this quest had done more harm than good. Previously, out there in the infinity of abstract concepts, 8 ⅓ felt no need to define itself. Every passing second signaled a new beginning. 8 ⅓ had been content to coast along like a car on the road of time. Does a vehicle need to know what the air outside thinks of it? No. It simply passes through on its journey, as independent from those molecules as the road itself. Why this sudden need for clarity?*

*It found a bench beneath a tree and tried to wipe away the beads of water on the seat. Only partially successful in its drying attempts, 8 ⅓ slumped down on it anyway. The journey to physical form required a leap of faith and, after two interviews, 8 ⅓ wasn't ready to give up quite yet. The problem was direction. It'd received macro and micro perspectives, views that didn't automatically contradict. Where to go after that? Did a transfinite path exist to reconcile the two?*

*8 ⅓ looked up. Through the fractal-like design of the leafless tree branches above, it stared skyward and registered the suffocating heft of the clouds. The dense nimbostratus blanket stretched from horizon to horizon and cloaked the landscape in drudging greyness. The opposite side of the cloud cover, if perhaps pierced by a jet plan, might be awash in sunlight and look downright heavenly. But, down here, the afternoon was dark as dusk.*

*8 ⅓ considered those rays, the incredible trip those photons had taken. It can require 20,000 years for the light at the sun's core to reach its surface. It's a complex, probability-dependent voyage and, technically speaking, it's not even the same individual material after such a violent journey. But for brevity's sake, the entire process averages about 20,000 years.*

*Following all that turbulence and that incredible passage of time comes the most important 8 ⅓ minutes of all: the time it takes for that light to reach the earth. Finally released from the bounds of the sun, that light, and all the life-giving properties it brings, requires roughly 8 ⅓ minutes to travel the incredible distance to the earth. 8 ⅓ was aware of the significance, of course. How could it not be? That evergreen 8 ⅓ minutes is the most important 8 ⅓ minutes in the history of humanity. Strictly speaking, the earth was 8 ⅓ minutes away from death at any moment. The likely end of the world would take far longer and happen millions of years in the future after the sun grew in size and swallowed Mercury and Venus. If something unexpected occurred, however, something cataclysmic that snuffed out the sun in an instant, the earth wouldn't even know until 8 ⅓ minutes later.*

*Few humans considered this. Through all of their plans, all their loves and losses, their vengeful machinations and their childish indulgences, they almost never acknowledged that everything could end in fewer than 9 minutes. Dependent upon how the sun was snuffed out, precisely, the earth would either freeze over or be thrown out of orbit in a maelstrom of environmental upheaval. Yet humans wouldn't know anything was amiss until 8 ⅓ minutes after the actual event, after it was too late.*

*8 ⅓ recognized the precariousness of the situation and lamented the journey of those individual photons. Following that perilous 20,000-year trek from the interior of the sun, the plucky photon shot out and completed the journey to earth in the comparative blink of an eye. Yet, on days like this, with the landscape swathed in cloud cover, that photon never reached its final destination. It played out like a Greek tragedy.*

*Yet. 8 ⅓ stopped. Then re-considered. With sudden self-awareness, 8 ⅓ realized it was viewing the plight of the photon through a distinctly human lens. Who ever said the photon actually wanted to reach the earth? Even assuming it was sentient and could feel an emotion like desire, it was a bold presumption to assume the earth would be its goal. In point of fact, it technically would've achieved this objective regardless. It arrived on the earth. It was only humans on the ground, beneath the cloud cover, who didn't see it. Further, it was only certain humans in isolated locations across the globe; 100% of the earth's surface wasn't ever covered by clouds. 8 ⅓ realized it'd over-subscribed to this self-created narrative and it was making human-like assumptions from an observationally-dependent perspective. Just as Talbot and Billy had done.*

*This shook 8 ⅓. Suddenly, an utterly new viewpoint of the situation shone forth. Perhaps the search itself was fundamentally naïve? 8 ⅓'s initial goal was a view from the outside to better understand its internal being. This not only assumed 8 ⅓ could impartially assimilate the judgments of others into the appraisal but that, within this quest, 8 ⅓ would know how and when it should accept those appraisals. Through different logistical means Talbot and Billy had surmised that the observer was the sole barometer of 8 ⅓. But what if 8 ⅓ concluded the observer's awareness was undefined? Or, more importantly, that outside appraisal incorporated through prejudiced internal criteria became an immediate logistical contradiction?*

*8 ⅓ set out again. The day might be bleak but that didn't mean it was bleak everywhere. For a being that could appear whenever and wherever it wanted, it was time to think outside the box.*

*Switching locations, 8 ⅓ appeared on a street corner far away. Here, the environs were scorched by the sun yet the dilapidated infrastructure still managed to appear more dispiriting than the previous rain-soaked area. Like so many Rust Belt towns in the America, the scenery brought to mind images of former boxers and washed-up hookers. The concrete may've looked terrific when first poured but, after years of use and un-corrected weathering, the crumbling edges now receded into the earth below.*

*8 ⅓'s destination was an old woman who possessed the ability to see through time itself. At least, that's what she told her clients. The decrepit location for her business could be seen as both debunking and confirming such a claim, depending on the person casting the judgment. In that sense, 8 ⅓ felt a certain kinship with her. While no one questioned her existence, her essence depended upon the view from the outside.*

*When 8 ⅓ entered her business, her disinterest in such opinions evidenced itself. "A specter, come to visit me." Her wry smile conveyed no fear, incongruous beside the literal words she spoke.*

*"Well," 8 ⅓ grinned, "that is a reception I've never received in the past."*

*"I am merely stating what I see. As in, 'specter', a terrifying ghost or apparition. Originating from the Latin, 'spectrum,' because light passing through a prism results in an array of differentiated colors."*

*"Ah. Of course," said 8 ⅓ with newfound apperception.*

*The woman's élan suffused the room with sage-like warmth despite her 1990s-era attire that made her appear more like a cosmetics saleswoman. "Come, come," she said, summoning 8 ⅓ to her table with a wave. "You've obviously arrived here for a reason."*

*8 ⅓ obliged and, with a mischievous grin of its own, asked, "How many people ask you to tell them the reason for their visit? Since you're the psychic and all."*

*"Far too many for my taste. If they harbor such antagonism to listening, how can they hope to understand the message? Better to stay home, I say."*

*"I agree. And yes, obviously, I've come for a reason. I'm in search of an identity."*

*The psychic winked, then casually eased the Tarot deck to the side of the table. "I don't think we'll be needing these."*

*On a certain level, 8 ⅓ was disappointed. The psychic noticed and reassured, "Do not dismay because the cards do not apply to you. The card's role is to tell a story. And that is exactly what most of my clients require. You, however, have the ability to be a part of any story, at any time."*

*8 ⅓ relaxed a smidge yet remained guarded. It felt like a child segregated from classmates, ostracized for being different. The child may learn the distinction was for an ostensibly good reason, such as IQ or reading ability. Yet the inherent question always lingered. Why must I be separated from the rest?*

*"Allow me put this conundrum another way. The identity you seek demands cohesion. You feel like a cipher, like you possess no individuality distinct from the moments that pass through you. Is that safe to say?"*

*8 ⅓ agreed.*

*"It's natural. Everyone feels that way at some point, as if one is merely sleep-walking through life, one day indistinguishable from the next. Yet you differ in one key aspect. You possess the ability to become any moment you want. You can start over as a clean slate, whenever, wherever. Do you know how many people would kill for a single chance to do that? I imagine a vast majority of people*

on this planet believe they could do a better job the next time if they could only start over again. It's natural. It's the double-edged sword of hope."

8 ⅓ acceded again, beginning to anticipate the woman's direction. She continued, "To apply the Tarot to a being like you would be akin to raising zero to the power of zero. Your indeterminate nature would give the cards fits. No, we don't require their wisdom at this juncture. What we need, dear specter, is illumination."

8 ⅓ recognized a slippery inference in her words but feared it didn't appreciate the full weight of them. For a long moment, it stared at the woman and her beguiling, Mona Lisa smirk. Then she continued again, "Hope is what keeps people going. It's why they come to see me; it's why they get out of bed in the morning; it's why a man risks his life charging into a burning home to save a baby. Empires rise and fall, the literal landscape of the earth is reshaped, all on the promise of hope. And what is most associated with hope?"

Again 8 ⅓ was stumped. But when the woman peered upward, at the lone hanging bulb above them, its eyes went wide. "Light."

"That's right. Of course, you know that. Which brings me to the truth that is directly in front of you, yet remains unseen."

8 ⅓ took a deep breath and pulled back. It had decoded the psychic's wordplay concerning light yet the allegedly obvious truth remained elusive.

The woman discerned his incomprehension and guided him once more. "Ask yourself, why did you, and you alone, come here for understanding? Why not the embodiment of, say, 400 seconds? Or 600 seconds? What makes you, 500 seconds, so special?"

8 ⅓ smirked self-consciously. "The sun's rays."

"That's right. You are well aware of the time it takes those rays to reach the earth. I'm guessing you've been thinking about it for quite some time. Yet, something was lacking. You possessed self-recognition while suffering from incomplete self-awareness."

"Yes. Yes. Yes," enthused 8 ⅓ as she spoke. It was as if she was reading its mind.

"You are well-acquainted with the notion of hope. The inconceivable number of photons that travelled in your 8 ⅓ minute time-set since the moment the sun first ignited can attest to that. Each journey built upon those preceding it, nurturing life in all its forms, millennia after millennia. Yet the humans you spoke with prior to this visit could only provide you with information about the physical world, notions of verifiable existence. As if such a concept could be so narrowly defined."

8 ⅓ remained rapt, trusting her guidance.

"I mentioned the elementary truth directly before you. Is there not another symbol of hope? The purification a dark cloud provides before the spectral light of the rainbow?"

8 ⅓ sat in stunned silence for a halted second. The psychic remained silent. Then, finally, 8 ⅓ uttered the word. "Water."

"Yes."

The wave of implications washed over 8 ⅓, filling its existence with the critical recognition it was lacking. Water, the giver of life, was the partner in crime to light's lifegiving hope. Whereas light is the particle that acts like a wave, water is the literal wave. It washes, cleanses, and streams through every epoch of human history. Metaphorically-speaking, if light provided illumination, water provided rebirth. And, like the petrichor tranquility that followed a storm, the psychic's parable became clear. Identity isn't set in stone. It originates from neither the inside nor the outside *but, instead, recreates itself constantly, moment after moment, through every regret, every victory, every choice.*

*8 ⅓ didn't require validation from the outside to construct its identity. It could invent its own identity over and over again. Much like a human's, its existence wasn't a steady-state; it was a journey, a constant recalibration of self-awareness while travelling on one's path.*

*"'When I am silent, I have thunder hidden inside,'" quoted the psychic with a smile.*

*8 ⅓ flashed a quick, embarrassed grin at its prolonged contemplation. "Yes. Sorry. I understand now. Thank you."*

*"Of course, my dear. The honor is all mine."*

*8 ⅓ thanked her again, departed, and re-appeared above the middle of the ocean three days in the future. It didn't notice the time shift; its mind was still fully enthralled by the transcendental revelation. The set of time given physical form stood on the quietly lapping waters under a cloudless blue sky. The sun's rays continued to bath the earth; 8 ⅓ appreciated every moment. And it watched as the second sun arose on the opposite horizon, signaling the end of the world.*

## MATT

"I feel strange. Like I'm in two places at once."

**Is that how you feel when you write?**

"Not exactly. This is different. When I write, it's closer to dispersion—I get so immersed in the stories that I'm no longer myself. This is almost an inversion of that. It's as if I should be somewhere else, away from this void and actually doing something."

**More writing, perhaps?**

"No. I don't think that would help matters. That's an activity, sure. But it's not the type of action I mean. This is going to sound strange but I fear something terrible has happened to Meda or Magee. I don't know where that knowledge came from, though."

**You feel like you should be there with them?**

"Yeah. It's like I'm feeling guilty for something I didn't do. Do you ever feel that way?"

**Often. I feel that way currently.**

*In the darkness, Matt paused.*

"Are you God?"

**No. I, alone, am not the God. Far from it. All of us are required for the God.**

## MATT

Matt returned Wednesday morning. Relative to his last emergence from the abyss, this return was more tranquil. He no longer felt so alone, so adrift. A lone beam of sunlight shone through the gap in the blinds above his head and specks of dust played in it like stars in the sky. He found himself focusing on them as he emerged and the darkness of the void receded.

It was when he consulted his phone that the anxieties of daily life came roaring back. Not only had he been non-existent for eight and half days, it was also nine o'clock in the morning. Startled, he shot up in bed, awash in the implications. Six days of work missed, already late for another. The last thing he remembered was walking away from Meda's apartment—how did he get back to his apartment in the first place? Adding to his vexation, he saw 19 messages in wait on his phone. Meda was going to kill him. He didn't have time to return her calls, though—if they hadn't spoken in almost nine days, what was an extra hour now? He rushed through a shower on his injured ankle, threw on some clothes, and scooted to Fitzgerald.

He arrived at 9:45, breathless and with damp hair still smelling of shampoo. He kept his head down as he moved to his cubicle, dodging eye contact with co-workers who appeared eager for chit-chat. He needed to get settled as quickly as possible—if Louise was angry at him previously, she was likely furious now. Sure, the project had shifted to Abby, but it was safe to assume Louise had expected him to facilitate the transition. Instead, he'd flat out disappeared for the second time in a two-week span. It would be a minor miracle if he could avoid getting fired.

One item buoyed his spirits. Out of the corner of his eye he spied some work being done in Louise's office. Her desk was missing and it appeared as if cleaners were scouring the rugs. In fact, the area surrounding her office appeared to be cordoned off, as well. Perhaps she was working out of a temporary office somewhere else on the floor? Or, even better, working from home? If she hadn't been around to spot his empty cubicle day after day, he might have a fighting chance.

Matt logged into his computer and, as expected, a bevy of unanswered emails awaited. To his great relief, however, he saw none from Louise. It was almost too good to be true.

Then: "Matt!" Abby squealed. "You're back!"

After the initial jolt, Matt smirked and turned to face her. Many such explanatory conversations awaited and he should've known the first would be with his hyperactive cube-neighbor. "Hi Abby. Yeah, I'm back. Sorry for such short notice. I'm sure people were looking for me."

Abby's eyes went wide. "They were. Absolutely. Oh. Wow."

"Yeah, life was just crazy." He'd concocted a story to explain his absence but, on pure devilish delight, he couldn't resist adding extra flourishes. "After the funeral and my ankle issue, I totally zoned it. I forgot about a trip Meda and I planned. I figured I could call Louise once we arrived. I intended to work remotely. But then the place's Wi-Fi was down. No cell service either. Each day they kept saying it'd be fixed but they never got it working. I had no way to contact anyone. In fact, have you seen Louise? It looks like her office is being renovated. I want to explain the whole mess to her."

Over the course of Matt's tale, Abby's demeanor morphed. Her attention focused and her brow furrowed, as if something didn't add up. It was an expression he rarely saw in Abby and, by the time he finished—his words slowing and losing confidence—his sense of foreboding had spiked.

"Matt," began Abby, her words enunciated with spelling bee precision, "Louise is dead."

Matt's breath lodged in his throat, stuck and unwilling to move. There were too many implications to process, too many ways to react. Before he could attempt a response, however, Abby added, "But...you already know that, I'm sure. You were here last night. When...she killed herself."

Now Matt's vision swirled. The entire office receded. He was still a part of this world; still seated in his chair, at his desk. Yet he felt nine feet away from it all. It was all too much to process at once and the best he could manage was a weak mumble. "What? I'm sorry. What?"

Abby's expression ticked, one eye squinting more than the other as she shifted from confusion to incredulity. "That's why everyone was looking for you. They're curious, y'know? Heck, I am too. The security guard leaked that you were here when it happened. What did it look like? Did you try to stop her?"

For an interminable second, Matt peered at her blankly. The story he'd fashioned disappeared in the zephyr. There were too many loose ends, too many ways to incriminate himself. "I'm—I'm sorry. I'm going to need a moment. It's all so overpowering." It was the best he could come up with.

And it worked. Suddenly self-conscious, Abby waved her hands in frenetic apology as she fluttered back to her desk. "Absolutely! Take your time. I'm sure it was terrible. I'll leave you alone. Just let me know if, y'know, you want to discuss."

She disappeared and Matt took stock. Louise was dead. Apparently, he was there when it happened. Yet he had no recollection of it whatsoever. The enormity of the revelations crashed around him, their heft quaking the ground. Contrary to everything he thought, he wasn't simply gone, away from existence during those disappearances—he was alive, functioning and mobile. And he'd witnessed Louise's death.

Then it hit him: Meda was right. All along she'd been trying to warn him about his disappearances, about someone drugging him. But he wouldn't listen. His eyes glazed as he peered out at nothing. What had he been doing during those black outs? What terrible actions might he have taken when not in command of his faculties?

Matt careened farther down in his tunnel vision. Abby stated that Louise killed herself. But what if she hadn't? What if it wasn't suicide? If he was present at the time, wouldn't he have stopped her? The binary conclusion was evident. Either he stood by and allowed her to kill herself. Or he murdered her himself.

Matt stood up and, without a word uttered, he walked out. On one level, he was aware how strange he appeared, brusquely plodding past colleagues as they offered innocent pleasantries. But on another level, he needed to extricate himself—if only to get time to think—before anything else happened.

He strode across the building's lobby, emerged onto the sidewalk, and immediately dialed Meda. "Meda, it's me. I'm back. And I want you to know that you were right. You were right all along."

"Matt! It's you!" she shouted, joyous before becoming concerned. "Are you okay? Where are you?"

"I'm outside my office. And—I don't know how to say it—but I think I may've killed Louise."

There was a long pause from Meda's end and Matt experienced visions of a computer crunching vast sums of data. Then, with an effortlessness he found unsettling, she replied, "You didn't kill anyone, you idiot. But you need to meet me at the police station. Now."

## MEDA

She didn't know whether to hug him or beat the living crap out of him. On a conscious level Meda recognized Matt's disappearances weren't his fault; he couldn't control when they occurred. Yet, for how badly her world had been upended, she felt like a couple roundhouses weren't uncalled for.

"Meda, I'm so sorry," he said, limping toward her on the busy sidewalk before hugging her.

Despite her reservations, she hugged him back. Then, almost immediately, she pulled away to re-appraise him. Apart from his ankle, he seemed no worse for the wear. "You look the same," she said, in disbelief. "How are you even alive? Did you eat anything? Drink anything?"

Matt shrugged. "I feel fine. Didn't eat or drink. I just wasn't there. That's what happens when I disappear."

Follow-up questions, too many to count, burst forth in her mind (Where did he go? What was he doing there? What about the missing minutes in that voicemail or the pursuer Goldt spotted with his security camera?) But there was too little time to pose them all. She closed her eyes and held them shut for a long second. Then she waved her hands at him, as if to dispel all the conversational clutter.

Before she spoke, however, Matt continued, "Now, can you please explain? How are you certain I didn't kill Louise?"

Meda huffed. She'd been deliberately vague on the phone and only convinced him to meet her outside the precinct with the promise of an explanation of Louise's death. Magee was supposed to go with her but, when she couldn't break him out of his suddenly crippling funk, she decided to go alone. With Matt now in his stead, though, she needed to keep her word.

"I'm positive it wasn't you because Magee and I were the ones who found her body."

"What? Why were you two at my office?"

"We went separately. I suspected Louise was responsible for your disappearances, that she was doing something illegal and she assigned you that project to cover her tracks. I jumped to that conclusion when she called to tell me you were fired."

Matt boggled at the number of events that he'd missed while he was gone. "Slow down. I was fired?" It was all too farcical and he almost giggled when he added, "And why did Louise call you?"

"Because you were nowhere to be found, you idiot," Meda snapped. "I was listed as your emergency contact."

"But then," began Matt, his cadence slowing ponderously, "that means I was in the office this morning even though I was fired. My access should've been cancelled."

Meda pursed her lips and nodded, signaling both that she recognized the discrepancy and that she was stumped as well. "The only explanation I can think is Louise never filed the paperwork. Our call was late in the day. So maybe she didn't get to it."

Matt contemplated the thought, peering at her askance. "And then she committed suicide?"

Meda caught his implication. Louise's actions, entangled by contradictory timing expectations, were at the very least suspicious if not outright spooky. Why bother firing Matt if she intended to commit suicide that night? Yet that was the exact reason Meda wanted to ensure the police knew Matt wasn't present, no matter what the ID-scanner recorded. If the police combined the scan of Matt's card with her and Magee's stories they might conclude there were three people on the floor (positioning Matt as the number one suspect for murder). She needed to halt that line of thought before it got started.

Meda could see Matt was still swimming in the details and, in a perfect world, she would've preferred to address all his concerns. But they were almost nine minutes late for their meeting and Meda feared irritating the police officer before opening such important dialogue. She motioned to the door, Matt assented, and they entered.

Inside, the waiting room was utilitarian, weathered but not unclean, and hallway-like in the way it funneled people to the back. A mustached officer sat behind Plexiglas and appeared to be scribbling in a large ledger. Though he gave no indication he saw them, Meda approached. "Excuse me. I gave a statement to an officer last night and I'd like to correct it."

The officer's gaze popped up and flitted between the two. "You're not here about the missing little boy, are you?"

Meda frowned. "Oh, no. This is concerning the suicide at Fitzgerald Tower. I spoke with Officer Ussher."

The officer relaxed then picked up a nearby phone. "Jim. You've got visitors."

Ussher emerged in short order, appearing a tad less wooden. "We meet again."

"We do," responded Meda, unsure how to react.

"C'mon," said the officer, before leading them to a back room and taking a seat. "It's not often I get follow-up visits."

"Right. We wanted to clear up a potentially bad misunderstanding. This is Matt."

"You're the one with the opera tickets."

Matt flashed a quizzical smile at Meda but she chose to forgo explanation. "That's right. That's why we were at his office to retrieve those tickets."

"Uh-huh," said Ussher, adding nothing more. It was clear he still held some reservations about her tale.

"Anyway, we wanted you to be aware the people you spoke to were me, obviously, and our friend Magee."

"I already knew that."

"Correct. But if you were to communicate with representatives at Fitzgerald, they'll say it was Matt and another woman. I heard them discussing this as I left. They think Matt was present because I used one of his spare ID badges. Therefore, I feared you guys might compare notes and conclude Magee and I were lying."

Ussher listened with a tinge of impatience, tapping his pen with his finger. "You don't need to worry about me talking to Fitzgerald." It was a blunt statement, begging for elucidation and he continued, "They stonewalled me every chance they got. Was stupid. No reason for it. Part of me wanted to re-open the investigation just to bust their chops."

Meda appeared perplexed, Matt more so. She asked, "Who isn't cooperating?"

"None of them. Initially, we spoke to representatives in their Public Relations department. Then Operations. Both pieces of work, let me tell you. I'm guessing the legal department grabbed them because now they clammed up. Technically, they don't have to cooperate, right? But if there's nothing to hide why keep us from investigating once more?"

Meda pressed. "Why? Did you see something suspicious?"

In a blink, the officer's body language changed, stiffening. It was as if Ussher caught himself and realized he'd revealed too much. "Don't worry about it. Our forensics had a few questions. If this is all you needed to tell me, that Matt wasn't at the scene, then we're all set here. Thanks for coming by. Appreciate the concern."

Ussher placed his palms on the table, readying to stand and leave. Meda resisted, however. "Officer, how many suicides have you seen where the victim stabs themselves repeatedly across their body?"

It stopped Ussher in his tracks. "None." he admitted. "But if you're thinking this was murder, you're wrong. The angles of the wounds were all consistent with self-infliction."

Meda shook her head. "I'm not suggesting it was murder. I'm just pointing out this isn't exactly a normal case. Can we agree on that?"

Matt peered over at her. It was hard to discern her endgame. Ussher cocked his head to the side and, eventually, admitted, "Okay. Fine. It's not something we see every day."

With the confirmation achieved, she swallowed and summoned her courage. "Officer, you're going to think I'm crazy but I think something really bad is happening at Fitzgerald. In a report from Matt's office, I saw a fusion nuclear factory in Iran. That shouldn't be happening. There are many reasons why it shouldn't. I think there's some sort of cover-up. Beyond that, there was no reason for Louise to kill herself, especially in such a horrible way. I think the events are related."

Throughout her monologue Officer Ussher's expression remained unchanged, skeptical and reserved. When Meda concluded, having rushed through her story, the sudden conversational void expanded inexorably. It was as if each was waiting for the other to make the first move.

"Miss, does the name Stuxnet mean anything to you?"

Meda's expression confirmed both her surprise at such a question and the fact that she didn't recognize the term.

"It was a computer virus allegedly, and I stress 'allegedly,' released by the American and Israeli governments to specifically target Iranian reactors. One of the first weaponized computer programs in history that could cause bodily harm. The virus made their centrifuges shred up like cheese when they tried to enrich uranium. It was discovered in the wild, infecting other systems a decade ago and, by that point, it'd spread to dozens of countries." Meda listened and, following a pause, Ussher summarized, "All of which is to say, countermeasures regarding Iran's nuclear capability have been in place for a long, long time. I appreciate your concern. But there's no way such an obvious Iranian connection at this firm would've been missed by federal agencies."

Meda's spirit fell. On a conscious level, she knew she should be relieved. The threat of nuclear disaster was gone. Yet, the closure for which she strived still hovered just out of reach. Matt's disappearances were still unaddressed; Louise's suicide remained unexplained.

Ussher provided Meda with an extra moment to gather her thoughts but, after a few seconds with no response, he asked, "Is that everything?"

Meda looked up at him. She felt Matt's anticipatory gaze. Each passing second pressed down on her further. Finally, her gaze vacant, she said, "One thing."

"Yes?"

"What did your forensics team want to check? You said Fitzgerald employees denied your request to return to the office. What did the team hope to find?"

Ussher leaned back and threw his arm out to cover the back of the chair beside him. Earlier, he'd evaded a different version of the same question. This time, weary and concluding Meda wouldn't leave until she got her answer, he replied, "Our guys use this stuff, Luminol, to find traces of blood, right? Spray it around the crime scene, it reacts with blood, and, *wa-la*, you get this blue glow. Well, Tuesday night, the guys sprayed some outside Ms. Napier's office as part of regular procedure. Didn't expect much. Just checking for foul play, making sure there weren't any tracks leading anywhere before we confirmed it as a suicide. The only ones they found were the plainly visible ones created by you and your friend."

At that, Ussher paused, seemingly at battle with himself. "Now, I have to stress, what I'm about to say is no reason to go re-open the case, especially one so tragic. This information doesn't exist, right?" Meda gave a nod and he continued. "The reason the guys wanted to go back was because they'd gotten an unusual result from the Luminol. It reacted with a different hue, apparently. They said it was strongest in the office and petered out in the hall outside. And the zinger? The residue grew in intensity as it went up wall. Again, this was out of the ordinary but nothing close to suspicious. They stopped spraying. There was more pressing work than a simple curiosity, right? I know their lead guy, Zukher, and he doesn't miss anything. He muttered something about buckyballs that are lighter than air. I don't know. When all was said and done, he couldn't explain the result either."

Meda and Matt remained captivated. Though attempting to downplay the peculiarity of the result, Ussher's efforts were falling flat. As if to get in front of their impending questions, he continued, "Look, this is no reason to go re-open a case like this. There are legal issues, ethical issues. You name it. Zukher admitted a million different things could cause the color shift, something as innocent as a cleaning agent with a weird amino acid profile. It was aggravating that we couldn't test it again. That's it. By now, the rug's been ripped up and the office's been scrubbed within an inch of its life. Even if we forced our way in, there's probably nothing left to check anyway." Ussher concluded, done with the conversation. He'd satisfied their curiosity. Now would they please leave?

Instead, laconic and measured, Meda asked, "What if I could get you an unsoiled sample from the office that night?"

Ussher said nothing but raised an eyebrow.

Then Meda pushed her purse across the table toward him.

211

## MAGEE

Wednesday was bleak. For the briefest moment upon awakening, Magee thought it was all a dream. No grisly death, no artwork destroyed, no contemplation of suicide...it was all too gruesome. Then everything came crashing down, stark and irrefutable. It'd definitely happened. All of it. He spent most of the morning moping about his apartment until, finally, he made the desultory walk downstairs to his studio. At some point the shattered remains of the mirror needed to be cleaned up.

He began by gathering the largest shards of glass first before attempting to sweep. A beautiful green-gold splinter lay atop a larger pane and, upon picking up the smaller piece, his own wicked visage confronted him in the second one. It was all so dispiriting. The mirror had been a gorgeous artifact to behold...literally one-of-a-kind. Once shattered, though, no hope of repair existed; the pieces could never remake the whole. The finality created a jarring end to possibility. How Magee wanted to go back in time! Go back and ensure the mirror wasn't situated so precariously! But that was impossible.

Not quite twenty minutes into the effort, however, his phone began to ring. Though he received a few calls from Meda and Taylor that afternoon, he hadn't summoned the willpower to call either back. This time, his mama was calling. He'd been ducking her calls for a week and, upon seeing it was her, his despairing state experienced a tidal shift. Already miserable and with all the time in the world to talk this time, the distraction represented a welcome break from his work.

"Hi Mama."

"I haven't heard from you in the longest time, dear." Her Greek accent was thick, despite living in the states for almost forty of her sixty-six years, and every word carried an extra ounce of flourish. "You should call more often."

"I know, I know. I'm sorry." Magee's mother applied the passive-aggressive arts with deadly precision...he fully expected the conversation to begin with such an entreaty. "I meant to call back. I just got busy."

"Well, I'm afraid you blew your chance again."

On the other end of the line, Magee recoiled at the gravity of her words. Perhaps he made a mistake answering. "Why do you say that, Mama? What happened?"

"I met the nicest young woman. You would've loved her. She was at liturgy this past weekend and—"

"Mama. Mama," interrupted Magee, his tone weary. "Please. I've told you a million times. I'm perfectly happy." This was a dance they'd repeated often, never with a different result. Despite living three hours away, Magee's mother would plead for him to go to liturgy with her in a transparent attempt to hitch him up with a woman of her choosing...as if he needed his mama's help finding a girlfriend. The most frustrating part of these entreaties was how they ignored all those made previously...as if she was going out on a limb, pleading for him to join her *just this once*.

"You didn't let me finish. She works at the museum at The Rhode Island School of Design. Since you wouldn't return my calls, I was forced to introduce myself."

Magee rolled his eyes.

"And you will never believe what she said."

The silence took up residence for a moment and the veins in Magee's neck below his beard protruded as he stared skyward. When he eventually accepted she wouldn't continue otherwise, he asked, "What did she say?"

"She said she knew your friend."

That was unexpected. "Really? She knows Matt?"

"No. Taylor." That was also unexpected. "The one who came with you that time you visited so many years ago."

Magee wanted to correct her...the trip she referenced occurred less than two years previous. Instead, with a smirk, he said, "Yep, that was Taylor. How do you even remember that, Mama? We were only at your house for a few hours."

"Oh, you two are in a picture in the living room on the mantel. That's how Ashley, the young lady from the museum, saw it. She helped me carry the groceries up the stairs. Very small world, no?"

Magee blinked hard. Then, frowning, he attempted to rewind the conversation. "Hold on, hold on. Mama...why is Taylor in a picture on your mantel? You met, like, once." Magee was ready to burst out laughing at the absurdity of it all.

"Oh, you looked so happy that night, Magee. Your smile, just like when you were a little boy. I adore that picture of you."

A shudder ran through Magee. In quick succession, he'd transitioned from utter depression to mild bemusement. Now, however, a blade of guilt cleaved those emotions in two. As best as he could remember, he and Taylor smoked a joint on the drive...they only stopped at his mama's house because they were passing through. Yet all this time she'd been clinging to a picture of him from that night, one he barely remembered. He felt like he'd betrayed her somehow, like he hadn't appreciated her love. The shame then multiplied at his lackadaisical phone habits. In her eyes, he would always be the little boy out there playing in the street with his big, dumb smile. Yet he barely made time for a phone call.

"I love you, Mama," he blurted.

"What? Well, I love you, too," she replied, clearly caught by surprise. "What brought that on?"

Magee went to say something, caught himself, then restarted. He wasn't prepared for the moment even though he instigated it. His cheeks tingled red, his eyelids slowly closed, and he stammered, "I.... I don't know. I suppose...I suppose I don't tell you enough. I feel sorta funny about the picture...I barely remember you taking one that night."

"Well, that's because you and your friend were a mess on drugs!"

Magee burst out laughing. It was all he could do. He may've even snorted. "Mama! Why didn't you say something then? Why take a picture of me like that?"

There was a pause over the phone line. Magee could imagine her shrugging. "I said earlier, you looked so happy. It was a nice picture. That's all. I didn't care what you two were up to."

Magee, still grinning, peered down at the remaining mass of shards on the ground. And, very suddenly, they didn't possess quite the spirit-draining power they held earlier. "Mama, I'm really glad you called."

## MATT

Matt went into work Thursday morning with a storm cloud overhead. The fulsome behemoth, colored a deep charcoal grey, threatened to drop its torrent at any moment. He was counting on no one knowing about Louise's intention to fire him but, if it turned out she had filed the paperwork, the situation could swerve from awkward to illegal in a heartbeat. The predicament could be almost humorous—pretending to work at a job he no longer possessed—if it wasn't all so lethal.

The night before, the police had accepted Meda's offer to Luminol her purse. Despite Ussher's repeated warnings to keep their expectations in check, his fellow officer's abject lack of a poker face undermined his efforts. To their surprise, however, Ussher recommended Matt continue to report to Fitzgerald. He said that the tests might turn up nothing and, if Matt hadn't officially been fired, he was better off keeping his job. Meda wasn't so keen. Her intuitive alarm continued to blare loud and red. But after being wrong about both the Iranian connection and Louise's nefarious plot, she backed down. She and Matt trekked home together but her misgivings remained in tow like a third, uninvited travelling companion.

Matt exited the elevator, reminding himself again to keep his head down and avoid unnecessary conversation. A unique balancing act awaited. On a normal day, there was enough work to keep him humming. Now he needed to handle that workload and a two-week backlog, all the while keeping his wits about him in the face of his nebulous employment threat.

"Where have you been?" Those were the first words spoken to Matt, issued by Conrad from his cube across the hall. Conrad was a schlub—the fact that he noticed Matt had returned today and not yesterday stood as testament. Yet this was the exact type of chit-chat Matt hoped to avoid.

"Yeah, it's been an incredible stretch of bad luck." Matt had rehearsed his story on his commute, of course. He knew its most important quality wasn't full disclosure but, more critically, concise believability. "First the car. Then the internet connection. It's been one thing after another. I can only imagine the stack of work I've got waiting."

Conrad bobbed his head slowly as if to appear lost in contemplation. "Well, I hope you feel better."

Matt almost burst out laughing. He readied to correct Conrad's flawed listening comprehension, then decided against the superfluous dialogue. Perhaps this whole charade would be easier than he imagined?

He reacquainted himself with his work and responded to the more urgent messages. And eventually, with such immediate concerns addressed, his thoughts returned to Project: Saturn. Though he no longer held any stake in it, he couldn't resist peeking in the folder. Large portions were saved late the previous night, meaning Abby was still hard at work on them. Good. Of anyone in the office, she was most likely to blow his cover with her incessant prattling. If she was still lost in that abyss, she might stay out of Matt's hair.

Though he feared rousing suspicions by inadvertently changing any of the files, he couldn't resist investigating the state of the project further. With a few clicks he checked some of the more confounding documents, snooping here and there to view her findings. In the process, the various files displayed the author responsible for the changes and, predictably, most revealed Abby. That is, until a new name popped up: ssnow. It took Matt a moment to piece the first initial and last name together. Then it hit him. Sheff Snow? The Head of Operations? The guy who wore aviator sunglasses indoors and spoke with in an inconsistent, exaggerated baritone? Why would he be editing the files? Matt seemed to recall Louise mentioning something about his involvement and, even back then, it hadn't made sense. The Operations Department was dedicated to the blue-collar, functional aspects of the firm: overseeing contractors, enacting disaster contingency protocols, ensuring carpets were cleaned and broken lights were replaced. That sort of thing. Their field of work was a vital component of an efficient office but there was no reason for him to be involved in a reconciliation project like Saturn. They were fix-it guys—not number nerds.

Matt grew intrigued and continued nosing around the various folders. If pressed, he'd admit Abby had enacted a pretty ingenious organizational system for the data. And, in total, he found only three documents indicating Sheff was the last person to make alterations. It wasn't preposterous to think he might've offered some edits on specific documents involving material storage, for example, or back-up systems. Yet it remained unusual.

Before he could investigate any further, however, the air was lanced through its core by the shrill approach of Abby's voice. Matt counted at least three, 'y'knows', in the space of four seconds. Yet one reason for hope existed. She was already embroiled in conversation. Perhaps she wouldn't notice Matt's existence? The pair approached, stopped at Abby's cubicle, and then her companion moved on. Matt cringed. A second passed. Then another. He remained still, reminiscent of a cautious bunny in an open field. And, when it seemed clear she'd returned to her work, he breathed a sigh of relief. No squeals of recognition; no interrogation about his absence. In quick order, he closed the files related to Project: Saturn and opened a couple unrelated ones. Then, the threat safely at bay, he began the anti-climactic task of sorting through all the work that'd piled up in his absence.

The afternoon passed with little fanfare and the quietude allowed him to ponder the confluence of odd events in his life more fully. He'd returned from the void the previous morning and raced to work, only to dart to the police station immediately afterward, and then commute home with Meda at night. He'd never, for example, had the chance to deconstruct the oddity involving the Tsimm-Tsuum rhythm of the Foot Tapper. And he'd never gotten to the bottom of the figure on the videotape Meda claimed was stalking him. Most importantly, he hadn't contemplated the changing nature of his disappearances. Whereas previously he'd experienced a total and complete loss of time, he was now carrying vestigial recollections from the other side—wherever that side might be. He'd begun to communicate with this omniscient, fluidic presence in banter that felt increasingly calming and instructive. At one point, Matt thought there might be two of himself; he said as much to Meda. Following his experience at the library, a sense of duality had filled him and he'd jumped to that conclusion. Now, as spooky as that concept might be, he wasn't sure it was even that simple. Ironically, it was only due to this vacuum of mental activity—the banal paper-pushing at his office—that his mind could wander and revisit the assorted loose ends.

The opportunity to return to himself was fortuitous and needed, especially once he received Meda's urgent call at the end of his day.

"Matt, I received word from the police. They want us to go to the precinct again, along with Magee this time."

"Okay, sure. Could you reach him?"

"Yes. There's a problem, though."

## MAGEE

"Did you know my mama has a picture of us on her mantel?"

"What? No. Why?" asked Taylor.

"It's from the night we went to see the Nine Inch concert up in Boston. Remember we stopped at her place on the way?"

"Uh-huh. I remember. You made us late because you didn't want to leave."

Both laughed but Magee's smile lingered, whimsical and reminiscent. The call from his mama had shattered his misery and that was crucial. He'd been ignoring calls from Meda and Taylor and, until their chat, he'd harbored no inclination to return their messages anytime soon. Only now did he feel like he was coming up for air out of the muck.

The eight voicemails revealed a nettlesome juggling of priorities. In his dour state, he entirely forgot about the movie at the warehouse...and Taylor needed his signature today. If the director didn't get it, he was prepared to move on. So, despite Meda's consternation, he'd agreed to meet Taylor quickly before rendezvousing with her at the police station.

"So how is Matt anyway?" asked Taylor. For efficiency's sake, they'd decided to meet on a street corner equidistant from each. The result was a choppy conversation spent dodging pedestrians. "I haven't seen him in forever. Is he still with that girl who always walked with her arms crossed?"

Magee snorted. "Matt's still crazy. And yep, he's still with Meda. As a matter of fact, I'm headed to see them after this." Matt and Taylor had met on a few occasions and Magee prepared to elaborate on Matt's disappearances and the recent bizarre events. Then he stopped. The image of Louise's corpse still lingered in his mind's eye. It was too fresh, too real.

"We should get together. You, me, him," said Taylor, inspired. "I'm free Saturday. You think he'd be up for it?"

Magee glanced down at the concrete, ready to enumerate the many reasons Matt couldn't be counted on for anything these days. Then he caught himself. "I don't think so. They're going to the opera Saturday night, the Wagner one up at the Metropolitan Opera. Meda's really looking forward to it."

"*Götterdämmerung*? They got tickets? How'd they manage that? Even I can't get my hands on those. I had to offload those requests to one of my buddies."

"Really? I didn't know it was so popular."

"Uh-huh. Apparently, some foreign royal families are visiting and bought up all the tickets they could find. Turkish and Saudi. They ripped the market, shelling out whatever it took. Most of the traditional internet sites needed to halt sales. The skyrocketing prices set off alerts."

"I'm surprised. It's not exactly a Springsteen concert."

Just then, a horde of pedestrians was unleashed from the opposite corner by a traffic light. The interruption forced them to take a step apart and briefly hold their tongues while the crowd passed.

"Anyway, here you go," said Taylor following the break. He handed Magee the paperwork before adding, "And hey, tell Matt, 'hello,' from The Dirty Lord."

It was a throwaway line, one that made Magee chuckle, even as it took him a transitive second to recall the reference. The Dirty Lord! Of course! The Dirty Lord was a deity he and Matt invented roughly a decade earlier. In the course of some drunken wandering, they'd happened upon this very peculiar graffiti underneath an overpass. Any other time they might've made a sarcastic remark and moved on, the image forgotten. Instead, they took a moment to appraise it. Then, lingering longer, they decomposed the nebulous symbol one letter at a time. And they arrived at...Dirty Lord.

It was an organic moment, as whimsical as it was unanticipated, and the term took on a life of its own. The pair concocted an origin story and an entire mythology around this fabricated demi-god and began inserting references about it into their daily lexicon. For a shining moment, the pair and many of their friends used the phrasings incessantly. But, as with any neologism, the novelty eventually wore off and mentions of the Dirty Lord faded away.

"Wow, the Dirty Lord," said Magee in a far-away whisper as if stoned. "I haven't heard that name in years."

"The Dirty Lord. How could I forget?"

"How could I?" emphasized Magee. He shook his head at the fond memory as he signed the papers. Then, telling each other they'd get together soon, he and Taylor went their separate ways.

It took Magee about twenty minutes to reach the precinct and, when he hit the lobby, he seized Matt in a giant bear hug. "Buddy! I'm so glad you're okay! You had us worried."

Matt reciprocated, saying, "Yeah, it's been strange. I guess that's what happens when life leaves you behind for a week."

"Eight days, actually. It was eight and a half days," corrected Meda, while motioning to the police officer. It was only then that Magee caught the simmering resentment steaming off her. Quickly, Magee deduced they'd been killing time with the cop while awaiting his arrival and she wasn't the only one perturbed by his dalliance.

"That the coat you were wearing? Give it here," said Officer Ussher, skipping the pleasantries and motioning to Magee's green army coat.

"Yep, this is the one," said Magee, handing it over as another, more bookish police officer appeared.

As if to address Magee's curiosity, Meda began, "Officer Ussher was just describing the seriousness of the situation. I told you how they found a strange chemical in that office and how Fitzgerald's Operations and PR teams were obstructing analysis? Well, the officers took a sample from my purse and confirmed it's the same chemical in Louise's bloodstream. It's potentially a nerve agent."

"A GABA reuptake inhibitor, specifically. Something we've never seen before," added the second police officer. As Meda spoke, he'd busied himself spraying a substance over Magee's coat while Ussher held it aloft. Once finished, the officer took a step back and peered at the coat with an anticipatory stare. He continued, "It shares certain similarities with CI-966, a discontinued nervous system depressant. For a time, it was thought CI-966 would be a breakthrough as an anticonvulsant for epileptics. It proved to be too dangerous, unfortunately, causing severe psychotic effects and hallucinations. This chemical? There is something else in its structure that is very unique. Apart from its odd fullerene structure, there's an exotic oil that causes it to be, shall I say, very sticky. We believe it may be derived from a unique type of Wormwood."

"As in...the Wormwood in absinthe?" asked Magee. "The liquor that drove Edgar Allen Poe bonkers?"

"Perhaps," replied the officer, but his inflection suggested he wasn't yet convinced. Ussher then motioned to a third officer behind the desk and, with a click, the room plunged into darkness. It didn't last long, though. Ever so faintly, the coat began to glow a sort of blue-aqua hue with more distinct points of white appearing like stars in the night sky. The room grew silent as the bookish officer inspected. "There, there. James, do you see it? Do you see what I mean now?" he asked Ussher, apparently referencing a prior conversation.

"I do," nodded Ussher, though not nearly as animated as his colleague.

"What? What are we seeing?" asked Meda.

"Normally, Luminol reacts to blood, specifically the hemoglobin in it," explained the CSI officer. "It glows through a process known as chemiluminescence. The combination of luminal and hydrogen peroxide reacts with the iron in the hemoglobin to produce light. At least, under normal circumstances. We'd used Luminol at Fitzgerald that night to ensure there were no traces of blood outside the office. That's how we cleared you so quickly."

"Zukher," said Ussher, with the air of a D.A. cross-examining a witness, "do you ever get unusual results?"

"Well, yes," said the officer reluctantly. "Certain foods can create false-positives. Also, certain paints and varnishes. I wouldn't call them 'unusual', exactly. We're trained to spot those. The odd glow we witnessed is of a subtly different hue with a dispersion far unlike any we've ever seen previously. At the time, we didn't have an explanation. Yet we also didn't have sufficient reason to be suspicious. It was a curiosity but we needed to focus on the job at hand. Once we analyzed the sample Meda provided, our concerns grew. Specifically, about the chemical's relationship to CI-966, the amount found in Ms. Napier's blood, and her unusual suicide."

"That's why we needed your coat, you idiot," said Meda to Magee. "Every time you wore it you could've contaminated it."

"Indeed," added the officer, increasing Magee's impulse to climb under a rock. "We all saw the coat just now. It was most definitely not covered in blood. Yet we see it's virtually drenched in this mysterious chemical. This confirms Meda's bag and Ms. Napier's corpse aren't the only locations of the chemical. Clearly it was an aerosol."

"So," began Meda, the concern on her face accentuated by the haunting blue glow, "what does that mean?"

"Well," said the officer, as if it was self-evident, "it means this might not be a suicide."

# MATT

Given the stakes, it seemed farcical to think Matt could simply waltz into Fitzgerald and pretend it was an ordinary Friday. The previous day had been hard enough with his existing bevy of concerns—now he'd received tangible evidence that some sort of ill-defined menace loomed.

The police took blood samples from the trio and, predictably, Meda wanted to do more to help. The officers demurred, though, then invoked her ire further when they said Matt should continue going to the office while awaiting the results. Their reasons were entirely rational but they didn't square with Meda's gut instinct.

Matt's mental state wasn't as easily defined as hers, however. He suffered from a more complicated sense of cognitive dissonance. On the one hand, he was experiencing a sublime sense of growth that was impossible to convey in words. In the wake of each disappearance, he consistently returned with the sense that he'd gone deeper. Into what, he didn't know. But he suspected it was leading somewhere. Yet, on the other hand, he conceded Meda had a point about the danger at his office. Someone had died. And it still wasn't fully explained. Matt felt as if two stories were being told but he could only read certain pages of each at a time.

The office floor had an air of familiarity. Doreen's cube walls were still lined with pictures of her kids, the stack of forgotten print jobs beside the printer remained as high as ever. Yet Matt felt an inarticulable distance from it all. Yesterday, he thought he'd finally regained his mental footing—only to have it ripped out from under him by the visit to the precinct. A voice in his head told him such a bifurcated state of mind might be an opportunity to pen some good fiction. A second voice wasn't so sure.

Soon, an all too familiar caterwaul shattered this rumination, yanking him back to reality: Abby's voice. He'd narrowly avoided her yesterday. Would he be so lucky again?

"Matt!"

No. He would not.

"How are you doing? You seemed, y'know, a little out of it the last couple days." She was standing at the precipice of his cubicle, producing in Matt a contrarian urge to flee.

"I guess it was a shock to be here after so much time away."

"Absolutely," agreed Abby enthusiastically. "Frankly, I assumed you were out late on those stargazing expeditions."

Matt recalled that tale he'd concocted to explain his ankle injury—it seemed so long ago. Now it was back to haunt him. He issued an awkward snigger to buy time and said, "No, no. No more trips to the swamp on this ankle." Then, attempting to change the subject before she could probe further, he asked, "Anyway, how is Project: Saturn going? Aside from the Louise's tragedy, of course. I assume the project is still moving forward. I'll admit, it was bear when I was working on it."

"It's going great," said Abby with a wistful, far-away grin.

The reply irritated him. There was no way it could be going 'great'. Even after stealthily—and begrudgingly—admiring her results, he knew mountains of work remained. He couldn't keep from prodding. "Really? I thought it was a nightmare. Don't get me wrong. I'm sorry you had to jump into the fray in my absence. I'm just wondering how you're managing it."

"Y'know, so much of it comes down to organization. You're right. There is absolutely so much information. Sometimes, the project seems like it will collapse in under the sheer size of its own complexity. Therefore, it's absolutely critical to stay focused, remain positive, and continue moving forward. In fact, I found it useful to proactively start over, wipe away all of my preconceived notions, and begin with a blank slate."

Matt frowned. Abby had spewed forth a ton of words yet in no way did she address the matter at hand. It sounded like a computer simulation slamming together random sentences of office jargon. For the second time, he couldn't resist pressing. "I see you got Sheff in Operations involved."

"Oh? Did he mention it to you?"

Too late, Matt realized he'd spoken carelessly. Abby didn't know about his discovery in the folders. He considered agreeing with her, affirming he had spoken to Sheff. But if she mentioned such a conversation to Sheff, the topic could mushroom into a complete disaster. He decided to come clean—what was the big deal? "No, I was in the files. I was away from the office so long and I wanted to check the state of the project." Abby appeared mildly flummoxed, as if she intended to ask a question but was unsure how to phrase it. Matt sensed the forthcoming query and preempted it. "I saw some of the files were last saved by Sheff."

Abby responded with an exaggerated head nod. "Now I get it. Boy, you should've seen the emails flying back and forth on that one. Sheff and Amy were fighting like cats and dogs."

"Wait. Amy, the Head of Public Relations?"

"Yeperooni. It came down to the responsibility for certain requisitions. Was it Op's or PR's? There was no concrete demarcation between the groups to decide who paid for what. Some costs were double-booked, some were split, and some vendors were flat-out unpaid. Historically, this resulted in a series of band-aid fixes when vendors threatened legal action. No consistency to the decision making. Y'know what I mean?"

Matt agreed, "I do. I do." That explanation made perfect sense, in fact. Initially, Snow's involvement appeared odd but turf battles like that happen all the time. Matt could envision the tenacity required to untangle such a mess and, loath as he was to admit it, Abby was the ideal person for such a job.

When Matt said nothing else, Abby added, "The whole brouhaha was kind of ironic. Saturn. Ops. All that."

Matt frowned. He had no idea what she was talking about. "What?"

"You know," she said, flashing that theatrical smile while pivoting her head side to side like a ventriloquist's dummy. "Saturn. It's the name of this project and also the Roman god. Y'know, with the planet named after him. One of his wives was named Ops. And she's confounded historians for millennia. Ironic considering the problems Ops caused on this project."

"Oh. Okay. Got it."

"I figured you would know that, given your stargazing expertise and all."

Matt smiled, the edges of it tight. Why was it always such a chore to talk to this lady? Just when he admitted—if only to himself—that she'd done good work, she still found a way to grate on him. "Hey, I never said I was an expert."

Briefly, it appeared as if she'd leave and Matt prepared to swivel back to his computer. She remained in place, however, leering at him. He returned her stare in the awkward void of conversation until, crushed by the weight of the silence, he blinked. "Saturn is cool, I guess," he said, fumbling over his words. "I like things farther out. The Milky Way. Or even farther. Past the stars. Carl Sagan. Billions. All that."

"Elision," said Abby matter-of-factly.

For the second time Matt had no clue what she was talking about and he issued another, more irritated, "What?"

"Elision," smiled Abby. "It's one of my favorite words. It refers to the deletion of a part of a word. Like when someone says 'comfterble' rather than 'comfortable'. The word conveys the same meaning but, –poof–, a syllable is gone, like it never existed. You just did it when you said, 'bill-yuns.' It's actually, 'bill-ee-ons.' Everybody does it; often without realizing it."

Matt's expression showed humorless now, his smile dropped flat. The conversation had flipped from tedious to flat-out weird and he felt the need to end it. "I better get back to work. Meda and I are going to see Wagner's opera, *Götterdämmerung*, tomorrow. And I don't want to be forced to come into the office beforehand."

Abby's delighted squeal made him shudder. "Holy cow! I'm going, too!" Matt's annoyance shot to new levels. He was trying to wrap up the conversation. Not start a new topic! "Maybe we could meet up? That'd be amazing."

"No," snapped Matt, draconianly impolite. It just came out, unfiltered. Abby went mum and, slightly embarrassed, Matt flailed at a recovery. "I mean—you're too busy. With Saturn and all. I couldn't impose. Heck, I should be helping you with the project. Maybe next week I can take a portion?"

"No," growled Abby, a commandment even more imperious than Matt's. If his reaction was unscripted honesty, hers was a gate dropping shut. The shift in her tone appeared to startle even her and, her sense of decorum rattled, she now mirrored Matt's haphazard recovery. "I'm very well. Everything's fine. Thank you, though. I don't need any help. Saturn is going well. Thank you for the offer." And then she twirled back to her cubicle without another word.

Matt sat stunned for a long moment. The wild ride of a conversation had ended just as suddenly as it began and he needed a moment to process it all. Eventually, he smirked, returned to his computer, and decided best not to look a gift horse in the mouth. Because the lesson imparted was as comedic as it was instructive—if he ever needed to make Abby go away again, he could simply offer to help her with Project: Saturn.

## MEDA

On most Fridays, Meda would bounce along with an extra spring in her step after finally escaping her office. A night of luxuriant arias and singing without anyone listening awaited. This time, however, Meda's walk home was anything but emancipative. A buzzing had nagged at the periphery of her attention all day, causing her mind to wander in meetings and during client calls.

So lost in thought, she didn't notice Mrs. Javier on the landing atop her apartment stoop until the last moment. Her mood pivoted at the sight; normally, she barely had time for such pleasantries. This might be the perfect chance to chat up the kindly old woman, however, despite her exhausted state. And, as if to fill some cosmic karma log, she decided to stop for a moment.

"Mrs. Javier. Hey," said Meda.

"Oh, hello dear. My, what is the matter? You look ghastly."

A giggle burst out of Meda, genuine and unexpected. The blunt assessment livened her spirit. "That bad, huh?"

"Normally you are full of such vigor, such glow. You do not look like yourself."

"The crappy day got to me, I guess. Way too cold. Too much on my mind. Figured I'd go check out that Farmer's Market later."

"Oh yes," said Mrs. Javier impassively.

"Have you been there?"

"Yes. It's nice," she said, unenthused. Then she added, "I must say the truth, though. It's a little crowded inside. The aisles: Too tight." Meda smiled once more at the old woman's cursory summation. She was cute without even trying to be. Then, as if speaking only to herself, Mrs. Javier added, "Ah well. Three apples fell from heaven."

Meda presumed she misheard her and spent a moment trying to decipher the woman's words. Unsuccessful, she eventually asked, "I'm sorry, what did you say?"

"Oh, it's just an expression. Don't mind me. Just a silly lady with an old Armenian saying." Meda's attention zeroed in like a hunter's scope and Mrs. Javier felt the weight of her suddenly keen interest. "'Three apples fell from heaven,'" the woman repeated. "It's an Armenian expression. Something close to, 'they lived happily ever after.' We use it to say that everything will work out fine; we just need to stress about events while they unfold."

Meda's feet were on different level steps and her knees wobbled as if she might lose her balance. "Wait. Mrs. Javier, you're Armenian?"

"Yes. My grandmother left during the genocide. Fled, like so many others. And Papa moved us here when I was young."

"Javier?" said Meda, a mutter she hadn't wholly intended.

"That was Manuel's last name," smiled the old woman, recognizing and addressing Meda's misconception. "You thought I was Spanish."

"Yes," admitted Meda, now mildly embarrassed. "I knew you would've lost your surname when you married. I suppose I just assumed both you and your husband were Latino."

"No. My name was Anna Minasian. It became Anna Javier. And believe me, that was only the tip of the iceberg when it came to my family's displeasure."

Meda leaned into the fortifying stone balustrade behind her, as if to encamp more fully. She'd been trying and failing to convince herself that Matt's office was safe, that there was no reason for worry. Yet here was Mrs. Javier, of all people, opening up the can of worms again with her reference to Armenia.

"Why?" asked Mrs. Javier. "You seem quite concerned."

"Oh, I'm a little surprised," said Meda, blinking.

The old woman stared at Meda more intensely, practically looking through her. "Is everything okay, dear? You look like you're going in two directions at once."

Meda glanced sideways, doubting if she could explain the situation in anything resembling a tidy fashion. "It's a lot to explain. I don't want to bore you."

Mrs. Javier's genial smile beamed. "Feel free to bore me. I've got nowhere to be."

Giving in to her curiosity about Armenia and Mrs. Javier's newfound association with it, Meda relented. "You know my boyfriend, Matt, right? He's been experiencing strange events lately. Someone at his office died, in fact. And he left a report from this work project lying around. I noticed a city in Armenia that looked out of place sitting beside other major financial centers. That's all."

Mrs. Javier took in the words with full attention before her focus broke. "Well, I'm afraid I won't be much help there, dear. I must say the truth. I don't know anything about finance or what Armenian money experts are getting up to these days."

Though uncertain of her initial expectation, Meda felt a twinge of deflation nonetheless.

Then Mrs. Javier continued with a pained yet wistful squint. "The memories I have of Armenia wouldn't be like that. My family left so long ago. We would visit each year but, even so young, I felt like we were returning to a home that was no longer there. My memories are those of a child's, you see. After the war, after everything changed. I remember the scent of my father's pipe, the worry on his face as the sun set behind the mountain, playing near the nasty scrub and the butterflies from the wormwood that dared us to follow them in."

Again, Meda's mental targeting system homed in. "Wait. What was that? What did you say about the butterflies?"

Mrs. Javier peered at her, half-confused and half-alarmed. "The scrub? My mother insisted we stay away because the rocks could be very sharp and if we got lost—"

"No, no. Where the butterflies came from. The exact type of scrub."

"Wormwood? It was my mother's favorite. She made us chew the bitter weed when we were sick. We all hated it."

Mrs. Javier relaxed anew but Meda was somewhere else. If her curiosity had been stoked earlier, it was now alit with possibility. Wormwood was the exact plant referenced by the police officer regarding the chemical in Louise's office. In fact, hadn't Magee mentioned something about its use in absinthe? They'd proven some sort of exotic chemical was released only to have Matt return to that damnable office anyway.

"Mrs. Javier, is Wormwood dangerous? Is it poisonous?"

The questions shook the woman out of her genial state and her grin withdrew. Contemplatively, she said, "Well, I can't say that I've ever seen anyone poisoned by it. I do remember hearing that it could be unsafe or, at least, that something in it might be. If I remember correctly, it is dangerous when combined with alcohol. People get addicted and act strange."

Meda listened, nodding. She felt as if there were two levels of detail involved. On the one hand, the CSI officer would've almost certainly known about the deleterious effects of Wormwood. But on the other hand, he wouldn't have known about that peculiar item in Matt's report. Meda had accepted the Iranian nuclear concern was unfounded (or, at least, that federal agencies would be on the case). But what if there was a heretofore undiscovered connection between Fitzgerald, itself, and Armenia? Seconds passed with Meda in vacant-eyed contemplation. Then, suddenly, she blurted, "Thank you, Mrs. Javier. I'll explain later. Right now, I have to go."

Meda dragged herself upstairs and began researching Armenia, Wormwood, and anything else related. Without question, it was a struggle. On a Friday night following a tumultuous week, the last thing she wanted to do was set up camp behind her computer investigating obscure plant facts. Yet the orthogonal shift in her day meant she'd feel incomplete if she didn't.

Apparently, a variety of oils extracted from the plant have the potential to be dangerous, with glycoside and thujone chief among these. While tea and the root of the plant provide many health benefits, higher doses can become quite addicting, cause hallucinations, and eventually lead to death. The plant grows in various environments across the globe with the exact oil structures strongly influenced by the climate. She noted the effects thujone had on GABA receptors in the brain. (Hadn't the officer mentioned that as well?) and the resultant over-stimulation of neurons. She even located obscure medical journals chronicling studies as far back as World War II.

What she didn't find, however, was any specific relationship between Wormwood found in Armenia and any poisonous derivative. Her eyes drooped closed often in her quest, battling against her initial enthusiasm. And adding to her weariness, with Janet's shower that afternoon and *Götterdämmerung* that night, she knew a long Saturday awaited. Eventually she succumbed, passed out with her head down on the desk. And she likely would've slept longer had her phone not lit alive the next morning with an important message from Officer Ussher.

## MATT

**Impressive. You found me on your own this time.**

"Yeah, loath as I was to go looking for trouble, it seemed like—I don't know—like it might help."

**Finding purpose is important. Oftentimes it's created out of thin air. You may have done so very recently, in fact. In a different time and place. Some might call it a trans-sensory quantum entanglement.**

"I should've known better than to come here."

**Look at it another way. Do you recall, when you were a little boy, those instances when you would stare at the ceiling and there'd be a shift in your vision? The ceiling would feel so much closer than it had a moment earlier. You weren't floating; you hadn't moved. Instead, it was as if everything had flattened. The sensation turned your stomach. And when you couldn't turn it "off," you disliked it. You would thrash your head side to side wishing to un-see it. But the effect wouldn't leave you. Not until you receded to sleep and started the next day anew.**

"There's—there's no way you could've known that. I told no one. I barely remember the sensation myself. How did you know that?"

**I know it because I was right there with you.**

## KATERINA

*Katerina heard the steps behind her. Always behind her. Smothering clouds locked away the moon and a cold drizzle coated the asphalt with a sinister sheen. Yet it was the sound of those footfalls—in her ears, in her chest—that propelled her forward. She knew better than to work so late. But the protocols for the morning's simulation needed verification. The eyes of the scientific community would be on her. What none of those journals would ever chronicle, however, was the resultant terror of this trip from the parking lot to her flat.*

*The footsteps were practically in lockstep with hers, sounding almost echo-like in their synchronicity. Yet they were drawing closer, either by a longer gait or a violent intent. It was past midnight on a Tuesday in a tony village outside Geneva. No one else should be about. Especially at the precise moment as her. Katerina was well aware Switzerland had the lowest crime rate in the world. She was also well aware there were no coincidences in life. The door to her flat stood perhaps 30 meters away, more than enough time for the entity to be on her. It was now or never.*

*She slowed her gait, then pivoted sideways as if to check her watch. With her attention still ostensibly on her wrist, she next cast a surreptitious glance sideways to the stranger in question. Male. Tall. Possessing a certain suave fashion sense. It wasn't Beckworth.*

*Satisfied, Katerina slunk a half-step backward and peered at her watch more intently, as if confused. The gentleman passed and glanced up to offer her a polite note of recognition. She didn't meet his eyes, however. Instead, she remained focused, her brow crinkled with plaintive concern to imply her watch was on the fritz.*

*The entire dance was choreographed and well-practiced, of course. She refused to normalize. She couldn't afford to give a stranger the benefit of the doubt, to think he might've simply worked late and was eager to get home. Because the moment she let her guard down, the moment she presumed the owner of the footsteps was benign, that was when Beckworth would strike.*

*With the danger passed, the tightness in Katerina's body eased. She crept about for an extra moment, killing time lest she get caught in the elevator with that man. She checked her work emails as a sort of kneejerk reflex but discovered nothing new. Finally, she exhaled and continued inside.*

*Moments existed when Katerina realized she was far too accustomed to these protocols. It wasn't normal to live in such fear. But then, nothing had been normal since she met Steve. She'd been too young to recognize a mid-life crisis; she simply saw an intelligent, gallant man with an occupation rather than a mere job. In fact, more important than the man Steve was, was the man he wasn't. She'd grown tired of all the boys who hadn't yet dropped their frat boy personas. In Steve, Katerina saw the foundation for a future. The age difference could be irksome when he got flustered by the latest technology. And he opted for quiet nights at home more than she liked. Yet, overall, their relationship started off well.*

*Unfortunately, such tranquility didn't last. Steve's ex-wife Carol made sure of that. What began as hostile phone calls soon escalated to suspicious coincidences. Katerina's co-worker might describe a tightly-wound woman pacing near her car; a package in Carol's ultra-precise penmanship might arrive on Katerina's doorstep. Steve had been married to her for a long time so Katerina was empathetic to her frustration. But he'd moved on. It wasn't Katerina's fault their marriage fell apart.*

*The harassment hit a crescendo one night outside Katerina's workplace. As was often the case, Steve was nowhere to be found and he wasn't answering his phone. She'd heard the footsteps behind her. And, without even seeing her, she knew it was Carol Beckworth. Yet a combination of youthful arrogance and stubbornness kept her from turning to face the woman. Beckworth never spoke. Instead, she approached Katerina with a hard-stomping stride, halted behind her, and then remained motionless. Katerina felt the violent energy emanating from the miserable woman. The moment drew tight, teetering like a humungous boulder on a high cliff. Beckworth said nothing. Katerina said nothing. And with shaky hands Katerina unlocked her car and jumped inside. Even after locking the doors, she didn't feel safe until she was a mile down road. At which point, she blasted the radio to an uncomfortable volume. Then she began screaming along with the song in a harsh, vicious screech that didn't even attempt to mimic the tone of the vocalist.*

*That was seven years ago. The event prompted Katerina and Steve's move to Switzerland and, consequently, to his slow mental decay.*

⋈      ⋈      ⋈

*"Are you listening to me, dear?" asked Greg.*

*"Oh. Yes. Here," said Katerina, blinking and handing him a salt packet.*

*At lunch, Katerina often preferred the escapism of a book. She was an accomplished lab technician at the particle collider at CERN and, therefore, her work stresses were unique. Losing herself in a story was the perfect diversion from the mental gymnastics accompanying impenetrable* fields of data. Sometimes, she wanted a simple, predictable tale where the good guy won in the end. Other times, her co-worker, Greg, inserted himself. To an impartial observer, they could be described as friends.

"Anyway, I was saying, Dwayne doesn't know where he's going. He's visited six campuses so far. After his accident, I was confident he'd wait until next Fall to start the school year properly. Instead, he's dead set on starting in the Spring semester. We weren't ready for all this. We applaud him, don't you know. We simply weren't prepared."

Greg droned on about his nephew stateside. Or was it his cousin's son? Katerina couldn't recall. Her mind was on other things. While sprinkling his remaining frites with salt, Greg continued to regale Katerina with the travails of a person she'd never met, in a state she'd never visited.

"It's not my place to intrude but I feel I must say something." At that, Greg registered Katerina's listlessness and placed his hand on her knee. The contact shook her awake and, as if to insist his story upon her, Greg summarized his quandary again. "I support the boy's dedication. I yet fear he's not ready for college after all that happened. What do you think, Katerina?"

The words were emphatic, nearly pleading. "I think," began Katerina, praying she didn't betray her inattention, "maybe he'd be best served taking a couple courses first. He could get a feel for college without the commitment."

At that, Greg relented and withdrew his hand. His lips pursed in disappointment before he said, "I covered that earlier. It's financially unsound to take classes a la carte. He needs to go for a whole semester or not at all."

Katerina dropped her head, suppliant. "I'm sorry. I should've been listening better. I know."

"Passive-aggresivity doesn't suit you, sweetie," replied Greg, smiling beatifically as if forgiving a grave offense.

Mercifully, her phone buzzed and drew their attention away from the matter at hand. When Katerina continued eating her lunch, however, Greg frowned. "Aren't you going to check that?"

"No," said Katerina simply. A moment passed before she registered Greg's reaction to her blasé response. Then, with a smirk and a quick shake of her head like the European models did, she added, "It's probably Steve. He still thinks I go out on the town too much. I'm not about to let him stop me."

"Good for you," said Greg, shifting. "Good for you."

"I mean," corrected Katerina, suddenly tentative, almost jittery. "I still love him, of course. Don't get me wrong."

Greg frowned, midway through adjusting his seat. "Well, of course, my dear. I never thought you didn't. I merely meant to say good for you that you don't let him control you. More women should stand up to their men like you."

At that, Katerina's momentary awkwardness vanished, replaced by an oddly beatific expression. She cocked her head sideways and grinned for an extended moment. Then she confided, "Thank you for saying that. For so long I've felt this inability to control my own destiny. Steve is the love of my life but sometimes I feel like I'm nothing without him. It's a scary feeling. Like I'm only a secondary character in someone else's life. I'm sick of feeling that way."

"Sweetie, that's what happens when you love someone. All the same, you should never change yourself for anybody. And definitely not for a man. It's your life, don't you know. You should live it the way you see fit."

"I'm starting to realize that," said Katerina before adding. "It only took me twenty-eight years."

"We all grow at our own pace," said Greg. He checked his watch and took a deep breath. Then, apparently abandoning his story about his nephew or cousin, he began gathering up the soiled napkins and used salt pouches onto the cafeteria tray. In response, Katerina started to organize herself as well, finally picking up her phone.

Greg began to stand but, before fully erect, Katerina said, "Shoot. Now Steve's calling. You go ahead. Don't delay for me."

"Hush. Of course, I'll wait," said Greg, sitting back down. She answered yet he remained on the edge of his seat, unsure where to put his stare.

As a result, he couldn't avoid overhearing portions of the conversation. Steve railroaded in immediately, before Katarina said anything. He mentioned something about groceries and told her to pick up something from the store. Katerina barely got a word in and, when she did, it was only with terms of general agreement like, "yes," and, "of course." Greg didn't mean to snoop but, if Katerina intended the call to be private, she was doing a terrible job keeping it under wraps. It was only when Greg caught a particularly jarring phrase that his stare plummeted to the floor. "I need you home tonight," were the exact words he heard. The commanding intonation was what demanded his attention. The sentence wasn't pleading or emotive; it was a dictate Katerina was required to obey.

After a moment, Greg tentatively glanced up at Katerina again. She appeared unfazed, however, and continued to hang on Steve's every word. The conversation lilted quieter and out of Greg's range yet, oddly, Katerina neither shrank into her seat nor grew angry at the command. She merely listened. Then, with a quick goodbye, she hung up. "Sorry about that," she quipped, "I feared it might be important."

Greg hesitated, then asked, "Are you okay?"

Katerina either didn't register the concern in his tone or didn't care to acknowledge it. "Of course. Everything's fine. It's only Steve being Steve." Then Katerina picked up her cafeteria tray and stood. A second delayed, Greg followed suit with his eyes still trained on her. The pair then exchanged a nod with their co-worker, Talbot, on the way out and each went their separate ways.

The comparative peace of her lunch was not to last, however. By the end of her workday, Katerina's thoughts were far from both the meal and Steve's call. Something very peculiar was occurring with one of the cylinders yet it wasn't raising any red flags to those in charge of investigating such matters. She presumed she was mistaken. How could she see such an obvious problem when no one else did? But the test was set to run in earnest on October 22nd, two days away. There were protocols for a matter like this, it wasn't her job to raise such concerns, and she risked blowback if she was incorrect. Yet, how could she simply ignore a problem of such magnitude?

Katerina left work that night plagued by this foreboding. She drove a mile in second gear before noticing. She was fortunate to avoid a collision after blowing through a red light. Then she only barely remembered Steve's call upon sight of the grocery store. A shudder passed over her at the nearly-missed errand and, imagining her arrival home empty-handed, she scolded herself to snap out of it.

What was supposed to be a quick errand soon took on a life of its own, however. After locating a couple items, she peeked at the cart pushed by a burly, disheveled man. In it sat at least thirty identical cans of soup. The man's brow resided over his dark eyes like a lump and, though Katerina avoided eye contact, she felt the cold weight of his gaze as *they passed. He wore no wedding ring; he wasn't buying anything else in bulk. Katerina knew full well the dire implications of the cart's contents and her previously felt disquiet metastasized into black dread.*

*Hoping beyond hope, she retraced the man's steps back to the soup aisle. She prayed she'd find the brand on sale or on some sort of clearance. It was not. Her heart plummeted and landed hard against her sternum. Such purchases by a single, unattached male were a clear warning sign. No one bought such quantities of single-type canned goods except in one instance: they were harboring someone. Usually not a family member or loved one, as evidenced by the sadistic disregard to the tedium of the items. The food was intended to keep a person alive. And nothing else.*

*Her mind flashed to images of a woman or child trembling in the darkness of his squalid basement. She arrested such thoughts before imagining the unspeakable things he did, however. She couldn't bear such horror. Instead, she summoned her resolve. Perhaps she could intervene? Maybe she could create a disturbance to draw attention to him? Or, if such a confrontation proved too dangerous, perhaps she could sneak a picture?*

*Doubling back, she caught sight of the man lumbering toward the register. She was running out of time. What would Steve do? He always had the answers. He was an expert at making himself known.*

*Cursing her timidity, she reached into her purse and fumbled for her phone. Her hands were shaking; she lost critical seconds punching in the wrong numbers. The man set the cans on the conveyer belt and erected a half-pyramid in the process. The cashier, a disinterested simpleton, began scanning the first of the monotonous lot without any sense that something was awry. Finally, Katerina's call began to* ring on the other end. She'd staked out her spot behind a spindle perhaps twenty meters away from the man and her stare locked on him as she waited. The cashier finished scanning the goods. Katerina clutched her phone, her fingers white, as she listened for Steve to answer. Yet the ringing only continued. The man paid the clerk in cash. The cashier gave him back the change. The man plodded out. Yet Katerina remained in place, listening to the ring of the phone, over and over again.

⋈     ⋈     ⋈

*The next day, Katerina remained haunted. Gone were her concerns about the upcoming test. The scene she witnessed at the store, made worse by her shameful inaction, soured everything around her. That treacherous man had inserted himself into her life and now she was incapable of escaping the long shadow he cast over it. She sleep-walked through her day as a cipher, quietly doing the bare minimum amount of work required while a tempest raged in her mind.*

*By the time she arrived home that night, she'd grown nearly hysterical. Steve hadn't shared her concerns the previous night and he seemed just as unwilling to entertain them now. Instead, he remained obstinately focused on the groceries she'd dutifully procured yet again. She barely got a reaction out of him when she told him an innocent life, or lives, might be at stake. And, following her day rendered meaningless by her mental preoccupation, she reached her wit's end.*

*"Steve, I really think we should do something. Perhaps that man shops their regularly? Maybe you could speak to the manager? Tell him to keep his eyes open?"*

*The door to the den was open. Katerina knew he was back there. Yet no reply came.*

*Katerina couldn't abide the silence. "I know it'll be hard to locate the man. I don't even know where we'd start. We need to tell somebody, though."*

*Again: Silence.*

*"Steve!" shouted Katerina. All she wanted was a little support. She could handle the chronic threat of Carol Beckworth. She could tolerate spending vast swaths of her day toiling in perfect quiet. But she wouldn't accept silence from him any longer.*

*She stomped out of their apartment as a woman on a mission. The hard slam of the door was satisfactorily dramatic. Yet, after tramping a number of paces into the cold night, it also served to highlight her solitude. She came to a dispiriting halt almost immediately. She had no plan. She had no idea where to start, in fact. Katerina knew she needed to stop that terrible man. Yet she hadn't formulated the means, or even the initial steps.*

*At the heart of it all, she recognized, was her capacity to be a hero. Or lack, thereof. She could go back to the store easily and speak to a manager. At the very least, her conscience would be eased. But what if she ran into the man again? Worse, what if the man saw her speaking to the manager? She didn't want to end up in his depraved dungeon. And, for that matter, there was no guarantee the manager would act on her warning. For all she knew, he might write her off as some hysterical woman and disregard the information anyway.*

*She began pacing, walking in circles if only to feel active. As an outlet for an energy, it worked. As a means to establish a plan of action, it fell short. This was her chance! She'd only recently complained to Greg about her lack of inertia, how* she wasn't going to let Steve control her. Yet, here she was, outside in the cold having a hissy fit because he wouldn't listen to her.

The old resentment welled up as she pondered her life's trajectory. She'd followed Steve to a foreign country and trusted him to create a better life for them. Though she possessed the brains and the acumen to work at CERN, she would've been perfectly content to stay in their hometown. Instead, he'd dragged her on this adventure and now he left her to fend for herself.

Her lip quivered. Her shoulder blades tensed. Steve didn't think she had the guts to do something without him? She'd show him what she was made of! She ripped her phone out of her pocket and began to swipe. Greg! Hadn't he once said he knew a member of the Cantonal police? Rather than directly confronting the store manager and risking discovery by that horrid man, perhaps she could reach out to Greg. That was proper protocol, no? Better to tell the police and let them investigate? They'd have much more expertise anyway.

"Yes, Greg? This is Katerina."

"Ohhh, Katerina. This is a surprise. To what do I owe this pleasure?"

"I have a dilemma and I need your help."

"Of course, I'll be right over. Shall I bring a bottle of wine perhaps?"

"I'm sorry? No. That won't be necessary," said Katerina, momentarily flummoxed. "Greg, did you say your brother was a member of the police force? Or that he had some sort of connection there?"

"Yes. Yes, I did," said Greg. He sounded distracted, as if responding to the literal question but thinking about something else. "Katerina, what's that background noise? Where are you? Are you outside?"

"I am. It's complicated. I'm frustrated with Steve. But I'm okay."

"If that's the case, let me pick you up. I imagine you standing on your lonesome beside that old pine tree. It is much warmer here." In the already stilted, off-kilter conversation, Katerina didn't know how to react. Then he asked, "Would you like that?"

"No. But thank you," said Katerina. She went on the describe the man at the grocery store and her suspicions. Though sounding oddly dejected, Greg promised to carry the warning to his brother. She hung up and, suddenly, the night air didn't seem quite so frigid. She peered at her phone with an expression of contentment and pride. While she didn't relish the idea of heading back upstairs so soon after her theatrical departure, she could now return with a sense of dignity. Steve was guaranteed to make some sort of crack about her change of heart but, this time, she could shut him up with details about the difference she'd made.

The next morning was clear and bright. Katerina was metaphorically walking on sunshine. It was only when she entered her lab and glimpsed her paperwork that she recalled her curious results that everyone missed. The reminder shattered her tranquility, an unwelcome intruder in the theme of her morning. She stutter-stepped, then began a tentative walk toward the papers.

That particular test would begin late in the afternoon. She still had time for another data inspection. She could raise the issue to her supervisors, of course, before seeking yet another confirmation. But how could a hundred or more technicians be wrong? With so many other eyes on the data, she presumed she was mistaken. Yet, recalling her heroics the previous night, a stubborn confidence arose within her. And with renewed vigor, she set out to prove her findings.

*The morning faded to noon and, continuously checking and re-checking the results, she still failed to locate an explanation for the error. Time pressure began to weigh on her. She remained dogged in her pursuit. And, eventually, she realized it was too late to elevate the issue. Isolating her mistake seemed to be the only remaining option.*

*She decided to go for a walk. Katerina imagined no goal or destination, only a stroll to relax her mind. She passed that man, Benedict, in the hallway and felt his leer. She'd always gotten cold vibes from him yet she couldn't articulate why. His presence sent her around a bend she hadn't planned taking and she moved farther away from her office.*

*Many steps down it, her phone began to vibrate. In an empty hallway, in a corner of the lab she rarely found herself, it offered a welcome distraction.*

*"Katerina, my dear, it's Greg. I stopped by your office but you were gone. I wanted to let you know you were right. My brother stopped at the mart to look into that unsavory fellow you described and the grocer carried the same concerns. They're working together now to find out where the man lives and what he might be up to. Nothing definite yet but I hoped to alert you. Your actions may've saved a poor soul."*

*Katerina beamed. Her pace slowed initially as she absorbed Greg's words. Then, once satisfied he'd called carrying good news, she began moving again, this time with a looser, more confident stride. "Thank you so much for calling. I love you, Greg. This means more to me than you can know."*

*"I see. Well," stammered Greg, "perhaps we should meet again for lunch? Very soon?"*

*"Sure! That sounds great," declared Katerina before summarily ending the conversation with a stab at her phone. She barely heard Greg's offer. She was fully enraptured by*

the notion she'd made a difference. Not only that, but her thesis was proven correct. Such alacrity was a foreign sensation, practically forgotten. It seemed like the last time she felt the same way was, well, before she met Steve.

Katerina scowled. Yet again, Steve succeeded in insinuating himself. For a shining moment she was bursting with pride at her accomplishment, flying high and free. Yet, in a flash, he pushed his way right back into her thoughts. Couldn't she have one moment, one single instant of her life free of his intrusion? No, her balloon needed to be popped. He needed to remind her of his impact on her life.

It was as if she couldn't exist without him, as if she was wholly dependent on him since the moment they met. She came to a halt yet again, her head drooping. Gradually, her fists clenched into balls. She might've saved someone's life yet she must be disallowed from enjoying the moment. Steve's influence shaded every moment of her life. She was right sick of it!

Katerina peered up and down the sterile hallway. No one would miss her if she left. Her work could wait. More pressing, she needed to take control of her life and stand up to Steve. Her suspicions were correct. And he ignored her. There'd be no better chance to confront him than right now. Giving herself no time to change her mind, she marched to the nearest exit and hopped in her car.

The drive served as a metaphor for her life, feeding into her resentment. The car hurdled forward but she was merely a passenger inside it going for a ride. If she hadn't met Steve she would've been happy in her hometown. She also wouldn't be living in constant fear of Carol Beckworth. And if she hadn't met him, she might have an iota of mental peace, a moment to be proud of an accomplishment, a chance to have a story of her own.

Her car screeched to a halt and she scrambled into her flat. She stomped inside. Her tumult was unceasing. Yet, despite such throes, she halted at the answering machine. To an outside observer, the abrupt truncation of activity would appear jarring, downright ritualistic. And, seemingly at odds with her mission to confront Steve, she nonetheless locked her attention on it.

The device was a holdover from over a decade earlier. A unique feature at the time was its ability to call owners and play back new messages. However, due to a mishap long ago, it now called Katerina's phone at regular intervals to play one particular message. As such, she picked it up with supreme delicacy before hitting the button to make it play. The entire dance was choreographed and well-practiced, of course. Yet never had she listened to the full message on such unsteady knees.

If only she hadn't met Steve! If only he hadn't gone on that godforsaken scuba dive! If only he hadn't used that regulator! Katerina didn't care what his diving friend said about Steve's expertise. There was no way he would've chosen a broken one on purpose.

"Hi dear, it's me," said Steve, accompanied by the now-scratchy background hiss of the timeworn tape. "Listen, I've decided to go on that dive I mentioned. It's this afternoon. I know you have your concerns. I wish you didn't. I wish you could just forget them. This is very important to me and I'm sure you know that?"

"Yes," muttered Katerina mechanically to the machine.

"I'm sorry but I need to do this. You should probably stop at the store for your own groceries. I, I won't be there to do it for you." At the last sentence, Steve's voice quivered, idiosyncratic against such an otherwise commonplace message.

"Of course," replied Katerina.

"And please don't go out. I know you don't like it when I tell you what to do. But this is important. I...I need you home tonight. For the call. In case anyone calls."

Steve paused. It was sudden, unanticipated, and for a moment the tape played on in silence. Katerina glared at it from behind glazed eyes. Her body shook, began convulsing. Then Steve concluded, "Take care of yourself."

The tape stopped with a harsh, metallic click. Then it rewound, back to the start, as if it'd never been played. The broken mechanism prohibited deletion. The message could never be erased. And, as the light outside her window incinerated the horizon, Katerina's life concluded with Steve's words from so many years ago.

## MATT

The sky was grey Saturday morning. The air was raw. Matt hoped a night at the opera might provide a healthy level of distraction but, in the interim, he felt listless and unfocused. Another story appeared overnight. He didn't need to check his files to be sure. By now, he recognized what that blank spot in his life meant. He'd left his writing and actively sought out the mysterious voice in the void this time. The journey represented a vague sort of success, he supposed, even if the increasing normality of his disappearances felt a little unsettling. The shift in his night's trajectory, though, meant his morning lacked clear intention. With nowhere to direct his energies, he decided to sign into his Fitzgerald laptop and put a dent in the mountain of work piled up during his absences.

He'd received a handful of emails overnight but resisted replying. No need for a protracted e-dialogue over the weekend. Instead, his cursor wandered across the screen like a shoplifter meandering toward the exit. Then, once it landed on the folder for Project: Saturn, he clicked it open.

Immediately, Matt noticed the last saved date on some of the files—mere minutes prior. Presuming Abby was working over the weekend, he thought nothing of it. Only upon a second glance did he realize his oversight. Abby wasn't the last content editor. Sheff Snow in Operations had made the most recent changes. Snow was a gruff man whose smile showed more like a grimace. Finance likely wasn't his first calling and he only barely hid his resentment at the MBA punks fresh out of school with salaries equal to his. Notoriously boundary-driven, he'd refused Fitzgerald's laptop in order to guard his accessibility. This and the timing of the edits meant he was in the office on a Saturday. Why?

Matt's curiosity piqued and he clicked open one of the documents. An alert warned that another user had it open currently, not unexpected if Snow was actively editing it. This also afforded the chance to see the edits he was making in real time. Matt took a screenshot, closed the document, and waited a few moments before re-opening it. A similar warning issued again and Matt took stock of the duplicate views. His screenshot encompassed perhaps thirty rows and forty columns of numerical data fields and, initially, everything appeared identical.

Once Matt spotted the difference, though, the change in the document was unmistakable. With his eyes fully attuned, the point of divergence showed itself in a sea of homogeneity. A single value in a single cell had a single digit modified: $2,820,094 became $2,620,094. Nearly impossible to detect at first glance, the deviant numbers were even visually similar. Matt scrolled sideways to reveal the line item as a payment to Monad Connect, a conference space provider used recently for one of the firm's more elaborate product launches. Why would Operations be modifying that field? Abby had mentioned the turf war between Operations and Public Relations but this item seemed to fall squarely in PR's territory. Here, the Head of Operations was wiping out $200,000 in one fell swoop.

Matt scrolled down to the totals at the bottom of the page. After all, if Snow moved $200,000 out of one area of the budget, it couldn't simply disappear. But, he realized, there were too many fields in the underlying macro to tie it back to its new position—far too much information to reconcile via a simple screenshot.

Matt grew agitated. Recollections from the past three weeks flashed in his mind's eye. This project had bedeviled him from the moment it first appeared. Meda had spent countless hours trying to divine secret meaning from the undulating data stream. All because Snow was surreptitiously altering the data so he could swindle Fitzgerald?

Lit angry and hoping to end this once and for all, Matt rushed to yank on his clothes. It was still early. He could get to the office, confront Snow, and make it back before the opera started. Worst case, he could meet Meda in Manhattan—he presumed she'd welcome some closure on the confounding report. Matt grabbed his coat, sent a brief text to Meda describing his intentions, and lurched down the sidewalk towards Fitzgerald's headquarters.

Once there, Matt decided to make a quick detour. Abby might be in the office and, thinking rationally, he figured it best to check with her first. If he went into Snow's office with guns blazing and it turned out the man's edits were anticipated, Matt's already precarious employment situation might truly come to an end. He exited the elevator and hobbled across the otherwise lifeless floor. Then, at his cubicle, he peeked over the wall. Abby was nowhere to be found but he spied her enormous bag in the corner of her desk. Matt grimaced at the unexpected result—he'd only stopped by as a precaution, assuming she'd either be present or not. He didn't want to wait around for her to reappear. He shot a glare across the expanse of the floor, a bullet that passed through the intervening walls and landed squarely on Snow's office door. The amalgamated uncertainty and frustration of the preceding weeks welled up in him again, demanding answers. Personal safety concerns forgotten and confirmations with Abby be damned, Matt knew what needed to be done.

He marched across the floor to Snow's office. The man was inside. His door was closed but Matt could discern his figure through the frosted-lattice glass. He steadied himself, gave a quick knock, and then barged in before Snow bade him to enter. "Hey Sheff. What's up?"

Snow's startled glare shot up from his keyboard and his mouth formed the shape of a perfect half circle, flat-side down. So unprepared for the intrusion, he only managed a faltering, "Hello. Surprised to see you here on a Saturday."

"Yeah, you too," said Matt, pushing the element of surprise. "What're you working on? Project: Saturn, I'm guessing?"

At that, a different level of confusion entered the man's reaction. "What? No. A crew is coming in to work on the molding outside Garrett's office. They're late." Matt frowned. The man's ignorance seemed genuine—he appeared authentically perplexed. And in that momentary pause, Snow recovered slightly. "Why are you here?"

Matt nearly balked. How dare he ask him about anything? This man may've murdered Louise. Yet there was something about the man's guilelessness, something that made Matt hesitate a second time. "I'm working on Saturn." Then, attempting to tease out an admission from Snow, he added, "I suppose we all are? So much work to go around."

"I don't know what you're talking about."

Once again, the man's reaction showed no duplicity. Matt's polarity inverted. It was a complete contradiction to his worldview. Either Snow was lying, or...?

"You're not working on Project: Saturn? You're not editing one of the documents right now?" The ground beneath Matt's feet quivered, turning aqueous.

Snow registered the shift in Matt's demeanor and, as if sensing weakness, he grew confrontational in his own right. "What's going on here, Matt? This is the second time in two weeks you're here during off-hours. And, might I add, under unusual circumstances. I need an explanation. You come charging into my office—"

"Did Abby send you any documents to edit? Anything at all?" Matt cut him off and Snow's eyes went wide at the mirrored hostility. Sensing the escalation, Matt bit his lip. More conciliatory, he continued, "Look, I'm sorry. But I fear something very strange is happening. Can you—can I ask you to open a document? One from the shared network drive. Can you do me this courtesy?" Snow eyed him up with a wary glare and Matt added, "I think someone's doing something illegal."

That got Snow's attention. Briefly blank-faced, he then signaled for Matt to come around to the opposite side of his desk for a better view.

"Thank you so much," said Matt, before guiding him to the Project: Saturn folder. He located the file he'd been viewing at his apartment and, in the process, confirmed it'd been saved yet again two minutes earlier. "You don't recognize that file name at all?"

"No, I do not."

"Okay, now can you open it?"

Snow obliged. Then, to Matt's astonishment, the same warning appeared regarding another user in the document. His jaw dropped. Snow registered his reaction but, with no context regarding its relevance, he asked, "What is it?"

"Here," said Matt, motioning to Snow's mouse. "Minimize that. Let me show you the folder again. You see that? According to that, you saved this document two minutes again. Except you weren't in it. You only opened it now."

Snow peered at the screen and then at Matt. Simplifying matters, Matt pointed to Snow's editorial credentials and repeated the process once more. Very suddenly, Snow's mood took a 90-degree turn, as if he'd been falsely accused. "I've never seen that file before in my life. I didn't save it. I didn't!"

Yet again, Snow's reaction appeared bereft of affectation. The man was clueless, downright scared. Meaning, if he wasn't making those changes, someone else was.

Possessed by a new vigor, Matt leaned in and smoothed the mouse away from Snow. "I believe you, Sheff. I do. But can I show you something else?" He located the recently changed line item and pointed it out to Snow. "This expense here. I saw it change. I took a screenshot and then compared it to a more recently saved version." Throughout, Snow's frown remained, displaying no sense of recognition and Matt pressed the issue. "Have you seen this Monad Connect expense anywhere else? Have you had any problems with it?"

Snow remained dumbfounded and peered at Matt with an almost child-like sense of fright. "No. Not that I can recall. I can check the ledger in our Operations folder. We're required to keep certain things private, as I'm sure you understand. We store it off the shared drive."

"Perfect! Let's check that." Matt finally felt like he was getting somewhere.

Snow took back the mouse, opened that document, and searched on the word, 'Monad.' It appeared instantly and, just as Matt suspected, the billed expense was the amount he'd last seen, $2,620,094. Then things got weird.

"Wait," said Matt, motioning to something on-screen. "What's that mean?" The initial billing source was neither Operations nor Public Relations—it was a firm called Khonsu & Sons. Khonsu appeared to be a subsidiary of Newton Associates, the property manager of Fitzgerald Tower. Whereas Fitzgerald Associates, Inc. was the investment firm located in the tower, Newton was responsible for the upkeep of the literal brick and mortar building. The tower might still bear the name of the firm's founder but the Board had relinquished such tedious management duties decades ago.

Even stranger, Matt noticed Khonsu's address in Exeter, New Hampshire. Why would the subsidiary of a property manager responsible for a Manhattan skyscraper be located in Exeter, New Hampshire? And why would it be billing the parent unit's client for a Public Relations event held uptown in an entirely different building?

Matt was speechless. He thought he was on the verge of a revelation. Instead, he felt more adrift than ever. Snow, sensing Matt's paralysis, said, "Let me try something else." He typed in the company, Khonsu, and searched on that. It appeared. Over and over again, it appeared. The results continued to pop up, detailing shipments, month after month, each in miniscule amounts that were dwarfed by the corporate expenses beside them. And very quickly a pattern developed: shipments from Armenia were received in New Hampshire; then approximately three months later, a commensurate shipment went from New Hampshire to Fitzgerald Tower; and, a month after that, a shipment was sent from the Tower to Lincoln Center. Such expenses, sometimes costing as little as five dollars, had been occurring for at least two years.

At that precise moment, Matt's phone began to ring. He grunted at the interruption, fully prepared to ignore it. Then he saw it was Meda and, fearful he'd miss her again, he answered.

"Matt, I know who killed Louise."

## MAGEE

Saturday afternoon, Magee received an odd request. He'd crashed into bed after bartending all night and been haunted by surreal nightmares about a coming flood. Waking late, he discovered Officer Ussher had sent a text to him and Meda asking them to come to the precinct. It was located on the East side of Manhattan, though, so he and Meda arrived without a chance to guess the reasons for the meeting.

"Thank you both for coming," said Ussher after leading them to a private room. Meda's purse rested on a table but the pair was too agitated to take a seat. "I recognize we're breaking protocol but I wanted to be sure both of you are safe."

Meda's attention snapped. "Why wouldn't we be safe?"

It was clear Ussher expected such a response because, rather than immediately addressing her concern, he directed his attention to Magee. "What about you? Have you experienced anything unusual? Any mood fluctuations?"

Magee felt a virtual spotlight fall on him. Unusual events had been occurring for three weeks...the standard definition of 'unusual' was out the window. "Um, no. Not really. Definitely no mood swings."

"Okay, good," said Ussher.

"Why?" insisted Meda. "Why are you asking these questions?"

Ussher peered at each then explained, "We got back the blood tests. Both of you were exposed to the same chemical found in Ms. Napier's blood. Meda, you only had trace amounts. Magee, you had much higher levels. I'll reassure you, neither of you had the amount she did. Zukher's instinct was right, though. It's some kind of GABA reuptake inhibitor. Your blood work allowed him to reconstruct it more fully, though degradation had occurred across both samples."

"Wait," said Meda, "what about Matt's sample?"

"There was no evidence of the chemical in his blood."

All conversation ended. It was obvious this new data didn't reconcile with the storyline in Meda's mind. She'd presumed the substance would be found in Matt and prove he was drugged. Her vacant stare, practically forlorn, attested...she'd never once considered the chemical might be found in her and Magee's blood but not in Matt's. The silence stretched on until, eventually, Magee tried to vocalize her disappointment. "So how is it possible we were exposed to it but Matt wasn't?"

"We believe the contact occurred the night of Ms. Napier's suicide." Magee noted his newfound willingness to describe the event as a suicide and Ussher continued, "The agent was likely some form of aerosol, sprayed in her office. You were exposed when you came on the scene. I hoped to ask, the night of the 18th, which one of you arrived first?"

Magee pondered aloud. "Meda got there first. But...I was in the office much longer. I wanted to see if I could help." He looked to her and she confirmed.

"That explains it then. No wonder you had so much more of the stuff in you. And how did you sleep when you went home? Did you lose consciousness at all that night? Anything out of the ordinary?"

"Not exactly. That was the night.... That was the night I broke the mirror." Magee's gaze grew distant as he recalled the events. He flashed an expression of unease, then explained, "It was going to be featured in a new piece of art. This mirror was very important me. And, when it broke, I reacted with this incredible anger. It was just so intense. At the time...I suppose I thought it was warranted because the mirror was irreplaceable. When I look back now, though? It was like I was a different person." Another moment of discomfort passed over Magee and he added, "I even considered suicide."

Ussher sized him up. "Have you felt that way since? Any violent impulses?"

"No. In fact, I was pretty depressed in the days afterward. I felt spent, washed out. A call from my mama snapped me out of it. Or, at least, that's what I thought. Perhaps the chemicals just wore off."

"Could be. Could be," said Ussher.

Then Meda piped up. "So, this is the proof you need, right? Now you can get a search warrant and investigate."

She peered at Ussher expecting some sort of call to action. Instead, his expression conveyed resignation. "It's an unusual circumstance, I think we can all agree on that. We can go so far as to suspect foul play. Unfortunately, we don't have a motive or a suspect."

"Okay, so Matt didn't have the chemicals in his blood," pressed Meda, as if still coming to terms with that information herself. "But we did. That must account for something."

"Look, it'd be one thing if we saw someone trespassing and spraying this chemical, right? But we didn't. We have no clue how it arrived. On top of that, we don't have a baseline on Ms. Napier's mental state. Her closest next of kin is an elderly aunt she barely knew. I spoke to the woman but she couldn't attest to Ms. Napier's state of mind, one way or the other. For now, suicide remains the cause of death."

"But Louise was poisoned. That's obvious, isn't it? That must be cause enough to investigate?"

"Ma'am, we just finished scrubbing the office down. The Head of Public Relations at Fitzgerald relented and gave us access this morning. They'd cleaned it up, of course. Torn up the rugs. It wasn't a crime scene, right? No reason for them to wait. Still, Zukher thought he might have a shot at finding something. Nope. Not a speck of that weird chemical. It was as if the stuff had floated into thin air."

He concluded but the silence that followed remained loaded with potential energy. Eventually, Meda could stand it no longer. "So what now? You guys just accept Louise was poisoned? If that's the case, why did you ask us to come all the way down here?"

Ussher grimaced. "I needed to see you two in person. There's a whole lot we don't know about this chemical. After effects, how long it stays in a person's system, that sort of stuff. Most importantly, we don't know how different individuals might react. If, and I stress 'if,' this chemical sent Ms. Napier over the edge, we can't assume everybody will have an identical reaction, right? Zukher thinks it's more likely many will turn that aggression outward toward others." Ussher paused and eyed up Magee briefly, an obvious reference to the rage he'd experienced. "Thing is, I couldn't tell you this information over the phone and trust you to self-diagnose. I needed to see your eyes, assess your demeanor."

"You thought we were suspects?"

"No," said Ussher defensively. "I thought you might be a danger. To others or to yourselves. I couldn't allow a repeat of what happened to Ms. Napier."

"And?" asked Magee, his head cocked.

"And you two are free to go. Thank you again for coming down here. I'll reach out if we need anything else."

"'Free to go'?" Meda repeated through a sneer. "Right. Okay. Let me get this straight. You got our hopes up. Summoned us down here. Only to throw your hands in the air and claim you can't do anything to help. Typical."

Magee winced. He shared Meda's frustration but it didn't seem wise to throw such vitriol at a cop. Ussher wouldn't need an excuse to arrest either of them...they were the first to stumble upon a dead body while trespassing.

Meda snatched her bag off the table and stomped to the door. "Thanks so much for not arresting us."

"Ma'am," started Ussher. He didn't get a chance to finish before she barged out of the office.

Magee trailed briefly before stopping, on the receiving end of stares from Ussher and other cops drawn to the commotion. "Sorry. She's been through a lot. We'll be in touch."

By the time he caught up to her she'd already tromped halfway down the next block. "Woah, woah, woah. What was that about? You could've gotten us arrested."

"Oh screw him," growled Meda as she spun to face him. "I am so damn sick and tired of hitting dead ends. Literally nothing is going right. I wasn't even supposed to be available to come down here! Today was Janet's baby shower. She had stomach pains and cancelled it."

"I'm sorry. That's terrible."

"I was running some errands to get my mind off things. Then I got called here. Only to find out that you and I have these dangerous chemicals in our bodies. But, oh, there's nothing the police can do. So we should just forget about it. And we should forget about Louise, too." Meda went silent for a moment but her agitation remained. She pivoted, fists on her hips, and glared up and down the sidewalk. "Things never get better! They only get worse!"

Magee gave her space and listened. Empty platitudes or ineffectual entreaties to remain calm wouldn't work on Meda anyway. And, eventually, the pair began walking again with Magee accompanying her in restrained silence.

After a few blocks, though, an ominous disquiet arose in Magee. Up ahead on the sidewalk, a group of three little boys burst out of one of the buildings, their manner exuberant and loud. Immediately afterward, another two appeared...followed by another three and yet another two after that.

Magee and Meda's trajectory sent them directly through the freshly formed mob of kids. They reminded Magee of his recent interactions with sinister little boys and the ever-increasing weirdness in their lives. He was trying to remain levelheaded yet he shared Meda's frustration. Every time they thought they were making headway they arrived at 75% of a solution...a breakthrough that took them part of the way to a conclusion but never to a full, total explanation. Like her, he wanted an answer for once! Some creepy kids haunt him and tell him to go the tower...yet he misses saving Louise by minutes. Matt keeps disappearing and they think they've found the drug responsible...only to learn there was none in his blood. The police isolate this chemical that caused Louise to commit suicide...yet there's no way to know who would've been there to administer it.

The pair continued their slow advance towards the boys but, inside Magee, something quaked. He remained stoic, pondering as they moved. Internally, however, he caught himself at that final thought...stopped...and reconsidered it. He bowed his head for a number of paces as the ridges of his frown embedded deeper and deeper. Meda began lodging another complaint about the cops before she noticed Magee's state. "Hold on," he mumbled.

Meda peered at him expectantly and Magee's dumbstruck visage showed his newfound awe. He raised a single finger in the air as he formed his words. "Meda, you got into Fitzgerald with Matt's old security badge," he began. "Thing is, I showed up without a plan. I had no way onto the floor initially."

Meda raised her eyebrow.

"I snuck in," responded Magee to her unarticulated query. "I had help. Someone scanned me in downstairs. Yet, once upstairs, everyone else on the floor was gone by then. You remember."

Meda nodded as she considered the detail.

"It was a miracle this person was there to begin with. In the lobby. She seemed cheerful...overly so...accommodating to a fault. She practically escorted me in. But then, immediately after she showed me to the elevator, she left." Magee paused, the gravity of his words colossal. Meda listened in attentive silence and her expression began to mirror Magee's as she put the pieces together. "It was as if she wanted me to be there...as if she intended for me to be present when Louise lost her mind."

Meda blinked. His connotation clicked. And, as if to confirm the last person on the floor before either of them arrived, she said simply, "Abby?"

"Abby."

## MATT

Matt was swimming in the details of two major revelations occurring nearly simultaneously. Hot on the heels of the discovery in Snow's office about the Armenian shipments, Meda called with important news. With Sheff's interrogating glare upon him, however, Matt decided to duck out of the office for some privacy.

"How can you be so certain Abby poisoned Louise?"

"She was the last one on the floor. Magee saw her. She was the one that got him access to begin with."

"But, if what you're saying is true, why would she be so eager to let him in? Why risk it when he could've ruined whatever plan she envisioned?"

"We wondered the same thing. Then we realized, she knew Magee was your friend. She wanted him to either meet Louise in that psychotic state or be exposed to those chemicals. It might take him and, potentially, you out of the picture. We don't know what she's hiding in those reports. But you had been working in them and she had no idea what damning evidence you may've seen."

"That does make a certain amount of sense," said Matt in a far-off voice, as if thinking aloud. "All along she'd been dying to work on the project. I just chalked it up to her eager-beaver nature. Nothing more."

"Right. And here's where it gets interesting. That night when she snuck Magee in, she didn't know I was on my way up. My appearance was the only thing that prevented either of us from spending too much time in Louise's office. Otherwise, Magee might've gone the same route as Louise. Or worse."

"Wow," said Matt, his tone again awestruck. Nervous, twitchy Abby—a killer? The notion seemed so unreal. How could she be responsible for Louise's suicide?

He'd only barely processed the implications of the shell companies he and Snow discovered when Meda called. She'd launched in so quickly he didn't get a chance to describe the spooky movement of those deliveries. And with that remembrance, he also realized they were talking openly about such topics. But, without the traditional background hum of office activity or printers, his words might be carrying clear across the floor.

"Meda, I'm going to have to call you back."

"No wait! I haven't told you everything yet."

"Give me a second. I'll call you right back. I swear."

Matt hung up despite Meda's protests. It hit him that he probably should've done so sooner. Then he tore off from Snow's office. His footfalls landed with wincing unevenness on his injured ankle yet time was of the essence. He needed to confront Abby.

Based on what he just learned, she'd probably been importing the poison in miniscule amounts all along. As Meda intuited, that was why she was so protective of Project: Saturn. She needed to sweep all those transactions under the rug. Matt rehashed details in his recent interactions with her, his worldview quantum tunneling as he struggled across the floor.

Then, once within eyeshot of their cubicles, he slowed his approach. He still hoped for the element of surprise despite his leaden gait. With cautious steps he made his way down the aisle, past Riley Mender and Leiale Cohen's cubicles. He craned his neck to see Abby's monitor—nothing was on it. Then, moving more swiftly, he spotted her chair—no one was seated in it. Finally, he made his way to the cubicle entrance to check her desk—nothing was on it. Not even her bag.

Matt shuddered. How could that be? Her bag was right there moments earlier. The obvious implication was that she'd returned in the scant time he spent in Snow's office, gathered it up, and left. A chill passed over him. Something didn't seem right. Why would she leave at that precise moment?

He started nosing about her desk, surveying items. He knew he should call Meda back, particularly now that he needn't fear Abby overhearing. But a sense of dread had welled up within him—it felt as if somewhere out there, miles away, a levee had breached. And the floodwater was slowly, inexorably flowing to his doorstep. What was he not seeing? What was coming for him?

While still attempting a modicum of stealth, he began to sift through her drawers and stacks of papers. There were printouts of some excel sheets...a map of Lincoln Center...some breath mints and binder clips. Nothing that seemed particularly incriminating. Matt wasn't sure what he expected to find. Yet, with every tick of the clock, his frustration compounded. He scanned the office, hoping for any sign of movement. The ghost of Abby's former presence haunted him—the awareness that she'd stood in the same spot mere moments earlier was far more jarring than he ever would've expected.

At that, a text came in, buzzing Matt's phone to life. He pulled it out, expecting an irate message from Meda. Instead, it was from Magee and read, "Everything had flattened." Where had he heard that phrase recently? Matt squinted, read it again, then his eyes opened wide. The entity in the void said it. Those exact words! How could Magee possibly have known that? It was enough to jar Matt out of the moment and he called his friend.

Magee answered but, quite distinctly in the background, Matt heard Meda say, "Magee, you're a goddamn genius."

"Matt. Talk to Meda," ordered Magee before audibly handing the phone to her.

"Matt, don't you dare hang up again." She didn't wait for his acceptance before continuing, "There's something you need to know. Friday night, I became obsessed with the Wormwood the cops mentioned and those small towns in your report. I learned that Wormwood can originate in Armenia. I stayed up late, eventually crashed out, but didn't find anything to connect those things to your office. Just now, though, Magee and I put it together. Abby needed the Wormwood from a precise location in Armenia for that aerosol poison she unleashed in Louise's office. It's what made that chemical so unique. However, Wormwood is also illegal. She needed to cover her tracks by using a multinational firm, Fitzgerald, as a proxy purchaser. She couldn't risk receiving it directly. And that was why, as the last person in the office that night, she had the poison on hand to kill Louise."

Matt listened as Meda spoke. Yet his vision slipped to a fish-eye lens view. Objects in his immediate vicinity gleaned with distinct clarity while his peripheral vision stretched and blurred. The dots Meda and Magee connected allowed him to connect his own and the implications emerged in perfect, terrible celerity. Abby wasn't using the firm to receive a single dose of the chemical. She was importing it on a massive scale. Until that moment, Matt had assumed she'd used the multitude of tiny shipments as a disguise to avoid detection. He had no clue regarding her ultimate goal but assumed it was an everyday money-making scheme of some sort. With Meda's revelation about the deadly nature of the chemicals, though, all those assumptions vanished.

"Meda, you're right. You've been right all along." Matt's tone sounded different—deliberate, somber—and Meda's pause indicated she recognized the change. "You know about the poison. But you don't know about the scale of it. I was just with Fitzgerald's Head of Operations when you called. He and

I discovered changes being made in the Project: Saturn reports. Just as you suspected, the modifications were occurring only in relation to the companies in Armenia and Iran."

"I knew it!" blurted Meda.

"But that's not all. These companies were sending the materials to the United States for years. Hundreds of shipments, miniscule in size, flowing in at regular intervals. They originated in Armenia, went to Iran, and then were received by a company in Exeter, New Hampshire. That company is a subsidiary of the property manager for Fitzgerald Tower. The deliveries then came here, to these corporate headquarters in midtown before being forwarded up to Lincoln Center."

Matt let that sink in before continuing, "Meda, a couple days ago Abby mentioned she was going to attend the opera, *Götterdämmerung*. She seemed giddy when I said I was going. I didn't think anything of it at the time. I just thought it was her natural hyperactivity."

"Matt, you think she's-?"

"She was in the office only moments ago. Now she's vanished. And on her desk is map of Lincoln Center."

"You think she's-?"

"I think she's going to poison everyone at the opera."

## MAGEE

It was paralysis by over-optioning. With too many possible choices but a dearth of any good ones, Magee and Meda were frozen, inert. Matt's course was obvious. He was rushing to the opera to stop Abby. Magee and Meda didn't possess such an easy directive, however. While Matt's office in midtown offered a close and direct route to Lincoln Center, they were effectively stranded. They'd been surrounded by a roiling mass of rambunctious boys after a junior-high basketball game let out and every cab in the area was now scooped up. Meda realized the implications too late. She yanked out her phone to summon a car but those inside the auditorium had, evidently, beaten her to the punch. The wait time for the nearest pick-up stood at twenty minutes and, judging by the exponentially increasing number of vehicles, it would take even longer for a car to escape such congestion.

Both agreed that, while the obvious course of action would be to contact the police, they should hold off. For starters, Ussher was the only officer with intimate knowledge of the events and he'd just told them there were no traces of the poison in that office. Relative to such a far-fetched tale, that lack of concrete evidence was damning. How could the authorities halt an opera of such massive proportions based on circumstantial evidence and no clear threat? Complicating matters, they had no accurate description of Abby to offer. Meda never met her and Magee's memory of her from his brief interaction was sketchy. They couldn't very well tell the police to be on the lookout for every tiny woman of vaguely Middle Eastern or Indian descent.

Magee shifted to and fro. The electricity in his being was barely contained...he wanted to do something, anything. Meda shared his restlessness yet she also remained systematically focused. "If we both agree the police can't help, we'll need to do it ourselves. The problem is that we don't know how Abby plans to dispense the chemical. Matt might find her and stop her. But what if she has it set on a timer? He can't be in two places at once. Which means, he'll likely need back-up. If only to watch Abby while he takes care of the device. Which means we need to get there as quickly as possible, whether we have a plan or not."

Magee nodded enthusiastically to Meda's conclusions. "Okay. Yep. Makes sense." Then each peered back at the other. They were on the southeastern side of Manhattan; Lincoln Center was much farther north and west of them. The cab situation was a mess and traffic surrounding both Penn Station and Grand Central stood as obvious choke points. Yet the subway was running on a slower weekend schedule and delays at transfer points would only exacerbate the inefficiencies. It was easy to say they should get there...enacting such a plan was another matter. As if to verbalize their shared frustration, Magee said, "We could split up. See who gets there faster?" His skittishness, however, betrayed his lack of faith in his own plan.

Meda continued to ponder...her shoulders tight, her thumb at her lips. Magee needed an outlet for his pent-up energy, though. He took a step out into the street and peered up and down in the vain hope of spotting a cab. With nothing in sight, he returned to the sidewalk to find Meda's expression changed...her eyebrows raised, her eyes wide.

"What? Did you think of something?"

"It's probably crazy," she said, tapping away at her phone's screen. "About two weeks ago I got a ride from this cab driver. He was fantastic."

Then Meda put the phone up to her ear. "Hi, Rafiq? You gave me a ride recently. Out to a library in Queens. I was wondering where you are right now. ...Oh, that's right around the corner! Yes! Yes, we'd love a ride. It's very, very urgent. Okay. We'll be there."

Moments later the car pulled up and the pair piled in. Rafiq was already turned to face them, grinning as if he'd been waiting to pick them up all afternoon. Meda, practically breathless, said, "Thank you so much, sir. You're a lifesaver. We need to get up to the Metropolitan Opera as fast as humanly possible. You wouldn't believe me if I told you why, but trust that many lives are at stake."

And, the warming smile still splashed across his face, the driver stated calmly, "My friends call me, R.A."

## MATT

Matt readied to charge out of the office. As best he could tell, Abby left fewer than ten minutes earlier. She couldn't have gotten far. Then, on the balls of his feet and ready to spring, he wavered. Once he took flight, there was no going back—he needed to be positive he wasn't missing anything or overlooking an important detail.

Still standing outside Abby's cubicle following his call with Meda, Matt peered about the area. All along he'd viewed Abby as an irritating but harmless office fawner. Even upon discovering her falsification of the report numbers, he only imagined a scheme involving financial gain. Poisoning random strangers wasn't a consideration. As far as he could recall, she never displayed anger or a proclivity to violence. Of anything, her demeanor was bereft of any strongly defined emotion whatsoever. If he'd missed her inclination to such a murderous plot what else might he have missed?

The clock continued to tick. Matt knew he needed to go. With his gaze darting about the area, each passing second weighed heavier. Then, out of the ether, a recollection came to him—a phrase from his most recent conversation with the oracle-like voice in the void. What was the term it used? Trans-sensory quantum entanglement? While clueless to its meaning, it reminded him of the nausea-inducing change in his perceptions as a little boy.

The recollection propelled his thoughts. He now stared blankly at Abby's cube, zeroing in on nothing in particular. To conceptualize a plan, he needed to expand his mental sphere with new possibilities. It wasn't enough to simply catch her. Even if he found her, how could he guarantee he wouldn't get arrested for assaulting her? He considered calling in a bomb threat. But if someone decided his threat wasn't credible, it would be that much harder for him to gain entry and stop her. Meda said the police were stonewalled without additional evidence. Before running blindly, Matt realized, he needed something certifiable to illustrate her intent.

He came out of his meditative sojourn and then, all at once, flung himself at Abby's desk anew. He'd searched it previously; this time he wouldn't be so delicate. He tore open drawers, rifled through stacks of papers, flung materials to the floor. If she'd been planning this for so long, there was bound to be some proof—something other than a map of Lincoln Center. Rummaging through her online files wasn't feasible in the face of such time pressures. He needed something physical and tangible.

When he spied the unique paper stock, he was positive he'd made the right decision. The tiny square stood out as singularly unusual among the traditional 8 ½ x 11 printouts. The flimsy paper stock was nearly translucent and appeared downright fragile to the touch. Could it be a damning receipt? A suicide note? Direct orders from some overseas terrorist? No. It was the instruction pamphlet for a remote control car. Matt's excitement cratered. What was that doing in Abby's desk? Why the hell had she opened the box in the first place? Wasn't it supposed to be for the holiday toy drive?

Matt snarled. A wave of unbridled animus crested within him. He'd wasted enough time already. It was now or never. He shoved the instruction leaflet into his pocket before stomping off in an ungainly stagger. And, in his haste, Matt never saw the aquatically-shimmering, obsidian figure in the corner of the office monitoring his every move.

## MEDA

"Why, though? Why would Abby want to do such a thing?" asked Meda. Previously, she and Magee were only reacting to the new revelations rather than thinking critically about the associated motivations. Now, in the back seat of the car, as concrete and steel girders flashed past outside, they finally had a chance to think more philosophically.

"I don't know. It doesn't make sense. When we found out about the poison, we assumed she was trying to hide something in those reports." Magee paused, then continued, "But this? This is so much bigger than that."

"Exactly. Even putting aside the ethics of murdering thousands of people, shipping Wormwood into the country represented an incredible risk. There's no possible profit motive to do something so horrible. And yet, on top of that, the scheme was recklessly brazen. It doesn't add up."

"She could've simply taken the misappropriated funds for herself if she wanted the money. Maybe she's just crazy."

"If I may be so bold," said R.A. from the driver's seat. Meda and Magee shot their gazes his way. They'd all but forgotten he was there. "I could not help but overhear the conversation. You are trying to stop someone from poisoning others?

"That's right," said Meda, cautious but intrigued.

Though not a large man, R.A.'s voice was deep and suffused with gravity. The fact that he was not only untroubled by such a peculiar conversation topic but he also chose to opine on it forced the pair to take notice. "Well, I believe you are approaching from the wrong angle. It sounds to me like you are trying to understand what the person has to gain. As if to assume this person has a grand plan that cannot be seen. Pardon me for saying, but to my ears it does not sound as if they are interested in any of that. They only want to tear down.

They only want to destroy." R.A. peered at them in the rearview mirror before glancing back at the road. When evident Meda and Magee didn't know how to react, he continued, "Think of it this way: What motivates people more than money? More than possessions? There's always something else, a deeper current under the river's surface."

It was as if R.A. was pulling them somewhere, taking the conversation in a different direction. Meda wanted to tell the guy to butt out. (Who did he think he was? This was a life and death matter!) Yet, she'd admit, they weren't getting anywhere on their own and the man's views were forcing them to assess the situation in a new light, whether they wanted to or not.

"I don't know," Meda admitted before guessing, "Fear? Love? I don't know."

"Purpose," intoned R.A.

Meda and Magee were vexed, speechless. What did that mean in relation to Abby's plan?

Anticipating their confusion, R.A. offered a ray of illumination. "Let me put it like so. Every person in this world has a reason for doing what they do. Everybody. They may not be aware of the exact reasons themselves. But there's always a purpose. This person who intends to poison others? From the little I heard, they are operating outside this impulse, outside the Flower of Life."

Meda's mind crackled, a simultaneous lightning strike and thunder clap. She'd only recently witnessed the Flower of Life in the very same car. "What? Why would you say that? Why did you mention the Flower of Life?" Her fusillade of questions was spitfire, almost hostile to the ear.

"I am merely saying this person does not sound normal."

"No, no, no," insisted Meda, shaking her head. Magee gazed at her quizzically, unprepared for the sudden surge in interest. "Why did you bring up the Flower of Life now? We just saw it about two weeks ago. When you took me to the library. What's the relevance?"

"What are you guys talking about?" asked Magee.

Impatiently, Meda ripped her phone out of her coat pocket. Then, quickly swiping past R.A.'s contact information, she located the picture and held it up. "This!"

Magee's reaction surprised her. First vague recognition, then astonishment. "That's...That's the Dirty Lord!" shouted Magee gleefully, pointing at her phone as if he'd caught Meda red-handed with a murder weapon.

"What are you talking about?"

R.A. cast a quick glance in the rearview mirror.

"A decade ago, Matt and I arrived at that exact spot. I remember it like it was yesterday."

Meda was taken aback by his animated, practically-giddy reaction. On any other occasion, she might've explained the meaning behind the Flower of Life and chortled that she only took the picture because of its historical importance. Her initial dismissiveness receded upon seeing the passion of Magee's description, though. He explained, "We were wandering. He and I were at a party and we'd gotten bored and left. We found ourselves looking at that graffiti...I can't believe it's still there. We started joking about it. We deciphered the letters for the name, 'Dirty Lord' in the icon. They were all overlapping, distorted. And we constructed this whole iconography about it, like it was a new demi-god. The Dirty Lord was the caretaker of nonsense, the instigator of insanity...those were the exact slogans we devised."

Magee smiled, half-embarrassed by the memories. The nostalgia had exploded haphazardly, memories without order or narrative sequence. He experienced a mix of pride at he and Matt's immature creativity and also a certain wistfulness for such simpler times. And, along with those pangs, more practical questions entered the mix. How had Meda arrived at the exact same spot?...Hadn't she known about the Dirty Lord in the heyday of its use?...Hadn't someone else from their past mentioned it recently? Yep, Taylor. Of course. And...hadn't Taylor mentioned something else?

And at the last question, his thought process slammed into a wall. It was full stop...no more barrage of memories. Taylor had, indeed, referenced the Dirty Lord...in combination with something else, an aside Magee nearly forgot. In the distracted conversation on that street corner, Taylor mentioned the opera and the difficulty obtaining tickets. And an ominous note in those words yanked Magee's mental emergency brake.

"What is it?" asked Meda, noticing his abrupt silence.

"Meda," he said simply. His mouth went arid, his thoughts churned.

"What? Tell me."

Magee's gaze moved up to meet hers, his jaw hanging agape. "Meda," he began again, "my friend Taylor...also mentioned the Dirty Lord recently. We were meeting to sign some papers. The night I met you and Matt at the precinct."

"Okay."

"During our chat, Taylor mentioned *Götterdämmerung* and the scarcity of the tickets."

"Right. Go on," said Meda, clearly impatient. The intensity of his reaction spurred her curiosity. She wished he'd get to the point quicker.

"It was a passing comment. It seemed like nothing important at the time." Magee paused.

From the front seat, R.A. peered in the rearview again, a witness to the spiraling drama.

"We were on a busy sidewalk. We were distracted."

Magee paused yet again and Meda, left hanging, flashed an irritated scowl.

"I didn't register the importance until now. Taylor said the royal families of Saudi Arabia and Turkey would be attending. They were the reason the ticket prices were so high."

With that, Meda's visage went blank, just as Magee's had moments earlier.

"It went in one ear and out the other. Knowing what we know now, though?"

He peered at her apprehensively, each of them processing the implications. Eventually Meda broke the heart-stop silence, saying, "Turkey and Saudi. Their governments have a cozy relationship. But that's not always true of their citizens. Beneath the surface is a strong undercurrent of resentment. And their relationships with America are just as complicated. The only commonality between the three might be the animosity felt by each's populace toward the other."

Magee listened, thankful for Meda's presence. He wasn't up on politics like she was. Her ability to untangle the ramifications took his unease from vague suspicion to fearful actuality. Yet a detail remained. "But Abby's chemicals originated in Armenia. And arrived in the U.S. via Iran."

The level of horror in Meda's stare spoke volumes. She'd now moved ahead of Magee and was grappling with even larger consequences. "Exactly," she said, the moment cold and tight. She spoke slowly and the gravity of the words pressed them to their seats. "This isn't an embassy or a military base. This is the royal family of each country."

Magee caught up and, expanding upon her thoughts, shared the revelation. "Poisoned horrifically. On U.S. soil. With chemicals provided by a country hostile to each."

"Oh my God. We thought Abby wanted to kill an audience full of innocent strangers...."

"...but she's actually trying to ignite a war."

## MATT

Matt was no stranger to The Metropolitan Opera. He'd attended many events and knew the basic layout. Yet it'd never appeared so ominous. While, technically, the autumn sun hadn't yet set, the blanket of clouds nonetheless robbed the landscape of natural light. Mingled with the orange glow of the facility's lamps, the drab field before him displayed a sepia texture reminiscent of photographs from the old West. It appeared lifeless, neither day nor night, with undifferentiated tones harkening to absence and emptiness.

On the cab ride uptown, Matt had taken stock. He was essentially bereft of tactical advantages. He couldn't sneak up on Abby and she already had a head start on him. The only strategic point in his favor was her literal act of releasing the chemical. If Abby expected to poison the crowd, she needed a unique dispersal method. The Metropolitan Opera wasn't a contained office in a predictable corporate setting; it was a humungous venue and the event's production was massive. He assumed the chemical release in Louise's office represented a dress rehearsal of sorts and, clearly, Abby had achieved her objective. However, in a setting such as this, there stood a greater chance for complication, more ways for the unexpected to occur. This unpredictability was the only arrow in Matt's quiver—he needed to find a way to use it.

He checked his phone and saw it was 4:48. Showtime was at 6:00 so early arrivals would be milling about, finding their seats. Matt strode across the concrete and imagined Abby slinking backstage, readying to release her murderous chemicals. He had no idea how she would've gained entry. But if her patience involving Fitzgerald's accounts was any indication, she'd likely ironed out those details long ago.

As Matt approached the entrance, he took note of a lone police officer. He had a decision to make. Alerting the authorities remained the safest, most responsible action. Any sensible person would make that choice. There was risk, however. If he told the officer about Abby's plan and the cop, instead, concluded Matt was crazy, he might prevent access. Then it'd be entirely up to Meda and Magee to stop Abby and they didn't even have tickets. Matt's gaze flitted to the officer. Then, to Matt's horror, the cop's stare locked with his. The instant became an eternity. Matt broke eye contact and kept walking. Out of his peripheral vision, he saw the cop's attention train on him—an officer's innate suspicion at a person acting oddly. Matt's pathetically casual dress relative to the rest of the opera-goers didn't help matters. Yet the cop didn't follow. And Matt continued on to the ticket counter.

The grand entrance to the opera opened before him and the renowned Swarovski chandelier radiated out above. Inspired by the Big Bang, the explosion of light and crystal evoked images of creativity and limitless potential at the dawn of time. Matt peered up at it with dark foreboding, however, fearing an entirely different type of conflagration.

His idea was to finagle a way into the rigging and loft area upstairs where Abby was likely positioned. He thought he could use his under-dressed attire to his advantage and explain that he'd gotten lost searching for a bathroom after making a delivery. All he needed was a peek backstage and, once he spotted Abby, he could create a commotion and point her out. No matter if he was ejected; he would accomplish his goal if her scheme's timing got interrupted.

He started to ascend the grand staircase but, at the very first step, his phone began to buzz inside his coat pocket. The racket threatened to draw attention and, rushing to silence it, he discovered a message from Meda. Then, upon viewing it,

Matt was thrown off balance. The text contained no words, only a picture. And it was of the Dirty Lord. He first squinted at the image, trying to ascertain what Meda intended to convey. Then, when he recognized it, more questions erupted. Why had she sent that? How did she grasp its importance in the first place? He and Magee had tried to locate the Dirty Lord many times in the ensuing years, to no avail—how had she found it when they couldn't? It caused a full stop in Matt's motor activities, an input he simply couldn't compute.

And it was only due to that pause that Matt overheard something odd. Out of the fog of his befuddlement he noticed one usher approach another and mutter, "Didja hear about the delivery from Khonsu & Sons at receiving? It got here about 4:30. Security accepted it, said it checked out." Matt's attention spiked—wasn't that the subsidiary of Fitzgerald's property manager, the one operating out in New Hampshire? Surreptitiously, he spied the second usher's stiff, affronted reaction—something wasn't right.

"That is extraordinarily late. I pray it is not crucial for the performance. The duty would fall on us to explain the delay."

The other usher agreed, "You're tellin' me," and moved on.

Matt experienced an atomic orbital inversion. That delivery was Abby's doing! It had to be! His concentration zeroed in; his pupils practically dilated. Forgotten was the Dirty Lord picture. Time for a change in plans.

"Excuse me," he said timidly, indicating embarrassment.

The humorless usher eyed up his attire with a sneer. "Yes. How my I help you, sir?"

"I'm sorry, I couldn't help overhearing," said Matt. He was bending at the waist, practically obsequious. "I'm from Khonsu, the company your buddy mentioned. I was supposed to meet my partner here but I lost her in traffic. Had to park a few blocks over. I came in the front but can't reach her now."

A hair's width away from responding with a cantankerous, "How dare you?" the usher instead swallowed and issued a curt, "Follow me."

Matt trailed behind, silent but inwardly ecstatic at the plan's success. Rather than heading upward, however, they went down a set of stairs. Matt questioned the change in direction but said nothing—too much risk of screwing up such a fortuitous escort. They walked a long hallway, went through a set of double-doors marked, "EMPLOYEES ONLY," and the previous smattering of opera-goers dropped to zero. "Thanks so much," said Matt, to no discernible response from the man. Then, after traversing another less ornate hallway, they passed a security guard wordlessly and made their way up two sets of staircases.

With the other patrons out of earshot, the usher snarled, "I sincerely hope this does not disrupt the performance. Else this will be the last time your services will be required."

"Got it. I'm sorry, man."

The usher halted, then stepped aside. Before Matt lay a corridor, its only distinguishing features consisting of some fire sprinkler heads and harsh fluorescent lights. The hallway truncated at a metal security door and the man extended his arm, palm open, towards it. "You will find your goal behind that door. Please work diligently. The audience will be greatly displeased if it is kept waiting."

"Will do. Thanks again."

The usher twirled on his heel to go, never looking back, and Matt was left alone in the hallway. For a moment he merely stood, imaging the wide-ranging scenarios he might encounter once he opened that door. Then he began his approach. With his phone still in hand, he grasped the doorknob with the other and turned it. His motion was stealthy, keeping the knob twisted to avoid unnecessary clinking sounds. Then, when he eased open the door, a boundless resonance entered the hallway that told Matt the area beyond was vast. His field of vision was limited, encased by the doorframe. Yet no one was in sight and quick relief washed over him. He was far from safe but at least he wasn't forced to confront a tide of ushers or security personnel.

With a gulp, he took a cautious step into the chamber. Now all sorts of people came into view and he wished he hadn't been so impetuous. The air was tense. Personnel rushed about, evidently putting the finishing touches on wardrobe or set details. Gradually, Matt's initial alarm subsided—the assorted costumers and technicians were so wrapped up in their own dramas that they barely gave him a passing glance. He soaked in additional details; there was something strange about the acoustics. Matt discerned a notable lack of echo and, when he peered upward, he realized he was backstage. Above him, the view seemed to stretch to infinity. While later the set piece would rotate out to scene-themed lighting and audience view, it was now fully alit from above. Infinitesimally small dust motes played in his vision and the dislocation, relative to the claustrophobia of the corridor, was disorientating.

Then Matt saw Abby. Across the perimeter, she was finessing the gauges on two large air tanks. Similar to Matt's inconspicuousness, she fit right into the scenery as if she was just another part of the production crew. None of the other workers noticed her. And, Matt realized, nothing could prevent her from releasing her abominable chemicals. He prepared to charge, to scream and holler, to heave his phone at her in hopes of calling attention to her existence. Then her gaze, utterly unhurried, moved up to meet his. Not a trace of emotion could be found in her eyes. And Matt winked out of existence.

## MEDA

The cab stopped in front of a nondescript metal rolling door and Meda and Magee readied to jump out. Before Meda could pay, however, R.A. turned and said, "Keep the money, ma'am. This story you have been telling? If even half of it is true, your path will be very perilous. Remember: There is nothing more dangerous than one with nothing to lose. Please be prudent."

Meda appreciated his concern but this mission was bigger than her. Much bigger. Thousands of lives depended on its success. The literal end of the world was an actual possibility. If she got hurt or died in the process, it would be a worthy sacrifice to prevent such a catastrophe.

She thanked him. Then the pair launched out of the car. Meda hit the door in stride and immediately began yanking it open. It was heavy and required both of their efforts to hoist it. They took turns holding it aloft while the other snuck beneath and, once Magee was through, the door came down with hard rubber thud on the concrete.

They stood and, briefly, organized themselves. The décor was sparse, utilitarian. The floor was reinforced concrete with an institutional glaze atop and all fixtures and railings were unadorned steel. Three vans sat idle and, in the high-ceilinged depot, light diffused quickly. Meda soaked in the details and said, "Right. Let's think."

She imagined the insidious chemical wafting down on the audience from above and tried to predict where Abby would be stationed. Out of necessity, they'd entered through a service entrance that put them underground to start. She needed a way to reach the rafters and, therefore, Abby. But how?

Magee was a bouncing jig of energy, however. Meda's deliberation acted as an anchor to his speedboat. "Think? What do you mean? We need to find Abby and stop her!"

"I know that. But this place is colossal. We can't just charge forward mindlessly. We need to formulate a plan."

Meda cocked her head back, listening. Apart from the nearly imperceptible hum emitting from such a behemothic structure, however, there was nothing to be heard.

"Is this the right time to over-analyze? We need to go."

"I know. But we also need to get the lay of the land first," replied Meda before scowling and ripping out her phone.

"What are you doing?"

"I'm calling Matt," she said, clearly dissatisfied but dialing nonetheless. "I hoped to avoid doing so. If he's hiding or sneaking around, I might blow his cover. But something tells me he's in trouble. Call it instinct. I don't know." She pressed the phone to her ear as she spoke. Then, after a few seconds, her brow scrunched into a suspicious grimace. "It's saying there's no service. Isn't that weird?"

Magee considered it briefly. "We're below ground. Maybe there's no signal."

"Maybe," said Meda, unconvinced. Something didn't add up. How did workers communicate? There might be another explanation (maybe the opera shut off reception during performances?) but Meda refused to believe Lincoln Center didn't have service.

The obstacle represented a new change in their trajectory. They'd already wasted valuable seconds and Magee's energy seemed ready to hit critical mass. Her stoic veneer showing cracks, Meda peered out across the barren garage. Then, finally, she settled on a hallway entrance towards the back of it. "Fine. Let's try that."

The pair jogged across the expanse and entered the corridor. It was a dangerous proposition. The claustrophobic hallway walls were stolid cinder blocks interrupted only by infrequent fire sprinkler heads. And it was lit by harsh, unforgiving fluorescent light. Worst of all, it was utterly devoid of exits. If Meda and Magee encountered security personnel there'd be nowhere to escape. Choosing this passage committed them to their course.

For a time, they advanced in a stealthy trot before hitting a juncture. Still lacking any sort of beacon to confirm they were travelling in the right direction, Meda was forced to stop and appraise the possibilities once again. To the left was a hallway quite similar to the one they just traversed while, to the right, was one that truncated in a series of stairs.

Magee remained animated. She felt the weight of the choice before her. And in a vacuum of verified data, she could only trust her instincts. She motioned toward the hallway to the left and Magee nodded, relieved to be in motion again.

Though this hallway appeared identical to the last, they noticed one minor difference as they travelled. The omnipresent hum in the background had shifted. If the previous din was inorganic and diffused, it now had the slightest bit of modulation. Each concluded they were moving closer to the audience yet neither could decide if that was a good thing or a bad thing.

Soon they arrived at yet another juncture, another chance to go astray. Meda looked to Magee for an extended moment this time, her confidence showing signs of flagging. She'd anticipated the complex's size but navigating the labyrinthine corridors made this fear manifest and real. How many times would they be forced to pick a path at random and hope for the best? They traded silent glances, neither option appearing more enticing than the other. Then Meda noticed something. It was the only differentiating point between the two, a small rectangle on the ground in the hallway to the left. "There," she whispered with a quick point.

They hurried to it, each possessing equal measures of optimism and anxiety. Placing too much hope in a random blemish on the floor was foolhardy. Yet it was the only guidepost available. As they approached, however, they realized it wasn't a divot in the floor. It was a tangible object, thin and rectangular. Someone's phone.

Meda picked it up, her hands jittery and breath rapid from the on-and-off sprinting. Her expression showed expectation and also trepidation. She turned it on and then, with a swipe, revealed the Dirty Lord graffiti.

Her cheeks swelled with joy, her smile pushed her eyes into squints. "It's Matt. This is his phone. He was here."

Then: "That's correct."

The utterance forewarned the woman's appearance as she rounded the corner ahead. Her backlit shadow landed on the opposite wall first, growing smaller as she approached. And, though her formerly excited tone had been drained to a frozen, lifeless diction, there was no doubt it was Abby.

"Matt *was* here. But I'm afraid he's gone now."

## MATT

*The darkness stretched on.*

"Wait. Where am I?"

**I believe you already know the answer to that question.**

"No. Something doesn't feel right."

**Are you familiar with the Eagle Nebula, Matt?**

"Um, no. Not really."

**It's a region of intense stellar creation located approximately 7,000 light years from Earth. One of its defining characteristics is a series of plumes that humans named the, "Pillars of Creation." Some have even referred to these formations as, "The Hand of God." The columns are enormous, approximately five light years in width, and comprised of unspeakable amounts of interstellar hydrogen gas and dust.**

"Yeah, okay. Now I remember. I think I saw a picture of it once. Where is this going, though? I can't believe I'm back here, now. I was on the cusp of something important. I need to get back to my regular world. Lives are at stake."

**That's the interesting point you bring up. You mention a picture of the Pillars you saw. From a distance, humans can marvel at their colossal beauty. Yet, there are certain points where the dust is so dense that, viewed from a planet inside, the night sky would be completely obscured. No moon. No stars. Nothing. Can you imagine? A sentient object might live their entire life thinking**

**what they're witnessing is the extent of the universe. They, and they alone, as the Alpha and Omega. Enough to drive one crazy, don't you think? Alas, the Pillars of Creation are no more, wiped away from existence. That image you saw? It was from the distant past, its light only reaching the earth recently. You were merely seeing a thousand-year old home movie of the Pillars prior to their inevitable destruction.**

"Look, this is great. I've come to appreciate these discussions. But I'm sorry, I have to go."

**Oh? Where?**

"I have to stop a horrific event from occurring. Thousands of people at the opera will be poisoned—they'll kill themselves and each other. A woman plans to release a chemical that will drive them murderously insane. Her name is Abby."

**But Matt. I'm here. I've always been here.**

*And from the darkness, Abby emerged.*

## MEDA

Everything was happening too fast. This wasn't how it was supposed to go. She and Magee were going to rendezvous with Matt, formulate a plan, and then they'd stop Abby together. Instead, here was Abby, right here, right now. And Matt was nowhere to be found.

"Are you Abby?" asked Meda, looking for confirmation as much as a chance to buy time and collect her thoughts.

"Some people call me that," said the woman with a shrug. Though Meda had never met her in person, Magee recognized her. And he saw the difference in Abby's countenance immediately. Gone was the nervous jerkiness and the self-effacing giggle. It was as if she was a wholly different person.

"Do you know why we're here?" asked Magee.

"Of course."

Abby displayed no obvious signs she was carrying a weapon and there were no bodyguards or comparable goons in sight. Magee and Meda nonetheless kept their distance. On spring-loaded knees in defensive postures, they gave the impression of two wolves surprised by an even larger predator in the wild. Neither knew what to do. It contrasted with Abby's blithe insouciance during what should be a tense encounter. And, as they sized her up, her utter lack of agitation only unnerved them further.

"It was you?" asked Meda (another confirmation, another play for time). "You poisoned Louise? And you plan to poison all those people up there?"

Abby cocked her head to an angle. The movement was cocky, as if disappointed in Meda for asking such banal questions. It also served as a tacit confirmation to each. Then Abby posed a pair of her own. "What do you think you're doing? What did you hope to accomplish by coming here?"

"We're going to stop you," said Magee, with uncertain, quivering bravado. Meda winced at its awkwardness. Abby's wholly unimpressed reaction neutered the threat further.

"You have no idea what you're trying to stop," said Abby.

Magee walked right into that one. Before Abby finished speaking, Meda saw the questions for the traps that they were. Now she and Magee were losing this verbal joust when it had only barely begun. She needed to change things up, do something unexpected.

"How long have you been here?"

Abby's eyebrows rose, evidently admiring the anti-positional deflection. "Hmm. Not a bad tactic...or a bad question. A devious ploy to throw me off, perhaps causing me to unwittingly reveal a key detail? Clever. Unfortunately, I have nothing to reveal. I am both here and not here. Time, as the metaphorical child of movement and mass, matters little to me when I neither move nor exist."

Throughout, Meda had been keeping an ear attuned for background noises, for the footsteps of anyone approaching. It might be an associate of Abby's, a bald, hulking bruiser. Or it might be an employee Meda could recruit to help. Yet no one appeared. It was just the three of them with only the barely perceptible hush of the audience diffused in the ether beyond.

Magee remained animated and, evidently hoping to make up for his previous awkwardness, he took an aggressive step forward. "Your psychobabble won't help. I'll crack your head open myself if it means saving those people."

"A moment ago, you asked me if I am Abby," she said, blatantly ignoring Magee's threat and addressing Meda directly. "I am. My real name is Abaddon."

Meda's eyelids squinted to imply a hazy note of recognition, as if trying to recall a deeply buried association.

"You fear my name. The dread rises within you. Yet you cannot recall why."

Meda feigned a tough exterior, readied to shake her head in defiance. But it was no use. She already witnessed the futility of Magee's childish reactions. Abby was correct on every detail; obstinate denial would accomplish nothing.

"I will tell you. After all, there's no time like the present," said Abby, grinning as if she'd made a joke only she would understand. Magee, now worried, looked to Meda and she returned his entreaty with a focused glare that told him to remain calm. Abby continued, "You see, I am the absolute. The action and the result, the immediate contradiction. Everything and nothing. I am the destroyer and the location of the destruction. Look into the well and you will see me. The return to the void and the void itself. I am nothing but silence."

Meda and Magee had experienced little visual stimuli while travelling the halls. Only the occasional sprinkler head broke the monotony of the concrete and their peculiar velocity created a sense of isolation, as if they were travelling farther and farther away from the world. Coupled with Abby's nihilistic monologue, the effect was haunting.

"The ancient Christians and the Greeks had a tentative grasp on my essence. Though they could never quite pin down the details. Some offered imprecations in my name without ever recognizing the perfect irony. The notion of *me* is quite slippery to the human mind." Abby took a step, beginning to pace as she spoke. It was casual, academic. "Humans talk about the silence in the vacuum of space. With no atoms there is no sound, after all. The infinite hush of the universe, they say. But that's not entirely correct. That void isn't perfectly silent. Interspersed between all the nothingness are planets, innumerable and exquisite in their uniqueness. A majority possess something resembling an atmosphere. Some, like

Venus, are downright hellacious. Others are earth-like and able to support life. The key point is each creates sounds at their surface...be it the howl of gale-force winds, the patter of methane rain, or even the voices of sentient objects. Yet none of these planets ever communicate with each other. Even if they possessed the equivalent of a giant phone, the planet answering wouldn't understand the first's language. The universe is a multitude of voices, each telling their own unique story...that no one will ever hear."

So far, the encounter hadn't turned physical. Abby hadn't made any sudden movements or threatening gestures. Yet, as much as Meda wanted to seize Abby and end this, her gut warned against it. She could sense the ever-increasing potential energy building in Magee. But she trusted her instinct. She needed to keep Abby talking and avoid a potentially lethal misstep, even as crucial seconds ticked past. "So how does killing thousands of innocent people solve that?"

Again, Abby responded with a show of disappointed chagrin. "Come now. You know there's more to it than that. You know who's in attendance. That's why your heart is racing. And his," she added, with a quick motion of her chin. "You must know what will happen if Turkey and Saudi Arabia go to war. It won't end there. Neither side is prepared. Iran and Saudi Arabia? If they were to go to war again it would be contained. They have in the past—both directly and through proxy armies—and left to their own devices they'll likely do so again. Turkey and Saudi do not share such history. There are no guardrails for such a conflict. No containment. Syria is already in ruins. Armenia will be forced to pick a side. Whose? Even I can't predict. Russia, through Iran, will jockey for position. The U.S. will follow. Then North Korea. Then China. The conflagration will be unending."

"How can you be so sure it will work? Conflict is nothing new in the Middle East," said Meda. For lack of a better tactic, Meda was still stringing Abby along. She couldn't escape the feeling, however, that Abby was aware and simply didn't care.

"Exactly," grinned Abby. "Children leave the womb. They battle life's disappointments. And they return to the dirt. Why should countries or abstract concepts be any different? You think I care about Sunnis, or Shia, or any of the other myriad characters to have strutted their hour on that stage? Humans have had millennia to stake a proper claim to the Empty Quarter and yet all have failed. No, the plan will work because the tinderbox has been accumulating accelerant from the moment you came down from the trees. The Mesopotamians codified the box, yet had no ability to start the proper fire. The Greeks and the Romans and the Persians lacked the ability to truly obliterate the planet yet the tinder they added was crucial. Even the assorted countries in World War II weren't quite ready. Now, however, the human wiring across the globe is complete. There will be nowhere to run, nowhere to hide when the silence comes. You asked how I can be sure it will work? I am sure because no one can leave the field. The method of destruction is in place. It has been since the 1960s. But the noise, the chatter, the constant vigilance has vanished. Now there is only silence, complacency. A single man narrowly averted disaster in 1983. Now, no one is listening. All are asleep at the switch. Babel awaits. Alpha. Omega. The Great Filter and the return to silentium universi."

Unblinking, Meda stared at Abby. The cold intensity in the woman's voice was terrifying; the certainty in her tone unassailable. Magee had referred to her terminology as 'psychobabble' but he was wrong. Meda recognized the historical origins and the earth-shattering logic underpinning it. On their trek through the underground Meda thought she knew the stakes. Now, however, the stoic determinism with which Abby spoke brought tangible actuality to the situation. They were on the verge of the literal end of the world.

"But why?" insisted Meda, her calm demeanor fracturing. "Why are you doing this?"

"The only reason possible: Anti-creation. The return to the void."

"We know your plan. We know about the poison," said Meda, forgoing negotiation and attempting to summon the bravado that'd already failed Magee. "You must know we'll use any means necessary to keep you from releasing it."

Abby smiled and a veritable frost swathed the hallway, the concrete walls all but shivering to white. "Oh, I've already done that, dear," she said. "I released the chemicals moments before you arrived."

Then Magee charged her.

## MAGEE

Magee exploded toward Abby. He could contain his fury no longer. In the background, Meda might've shouted his name. He barely heard her. Instead, his tunnel vision narrowed to Abby. Her smirking visage...uncowed and unchanging. She didn't so much as flinch.

Magee tackled her at the waist, pinning her arms to her sides as they crashed to the reinforced concrete below. Air blasted out of each in guttural huffs. Then Magee recovered and climbed atop her, straddling her between his legs. Abby offered no resistance. Her expression remained blank, her body practically limp.

"Tell us where the poison is!" Magee barked.

She stared up at him in mute defiance, offering no response. Then Magee cocked back his fist and shouted even more viciously, "Tell us where the poison is or so help me!"

"Magee!" shouted Meda. "No!"

It broke Magee out of his rage and he hesitated, sending a furtive glance to Meda. She continued, "She won't respond to threats. And if you knock her out everyone will die."

Magee didn't lower his fist. It quivered, caught midair in a hesitant stasis. Every second that passed was another second closer to that poison raining down and releasing hell. Magee needed to *do* something. But what?

"You said you released the poison prior to meeting us," said Meda, her focus now laser-like on Abby. "How is that possible?"

Abby remained silent. Yet her complexion moved the slightest degree, reminiscent of the disappointment she'd shown Meda earlier. Its haughtiness confirmed to Meda that Abby would betray none of her secrets.

Magee finally let down his fist, its threat evaporated. He looked up to Meda and the frown she wore told him she was pondering, calculating.

"Wait a minute," she said, her eyes squinting as if to spot something in a distant field. "Earlier I tried to use my phone to call Matt. Remember?" Magee nodded and Meda dug into her pocket to retrieve the phone. She glanced at it quickly and said, "Right. There's still no service." She paused, then stared down at Abby anew. "But if Abby's down here, how did she release the chemicals from the rafters?"

A virtual light bulb went on above Magee's head. His gaze shot from Meda to Abby. Then, without a word, he began to frisk her. Again, she gave no resistance and in short order he zeroed in on something, mumbling, "Here it is. Here it is." And, to their shared surprise, he yanked out a remote control. The cheap plastic toy, painted a garish red, had only three buttons and a steering wheel. Each stared at the unexpected device with suspicion, momentarily dumbstruck. Then, in slow-motion epiphany, Meda's eyes opened wide.

"Of course," she said. "She used that to release the poison. That's why my phone isn't working. She must be jamming the signal. This place definitely has cell service. She needed to be sure the unique signal from that toy got through, unimpaired."

Abby remained indifferent. She eyed up the remote control lazily before her gaze carried to Meda, to Magee, and back to the device.

Meda registered Abby's detachment and her sense of relief waned. They'd discovered the device used to unleash the chemicals...but what now? Meda stiffened, her nostrils flared. Yet again she'd hit a dead end. Yet again she'd come up short. Too little, too late. Tightening at the waist and leaning down at Abby with menace, Meda demanded, "Tell us how to work it! Tell us what buttons will stop it!"

Abby's dead eyes merely stared at Meda, mocking in their silence.

Meda's aggression multiplied, approaching that of Magee's. She glared at Abby for a taught second before, scowling, she ripped the control from him. Still holding her phone in the other hand, she began to jostle the wheel and stab at the buttons. "Goddamn it! Tell us! You have to tell us!"

"You idiot," sneered Abby. It was a word Meda used often. To have it thrown back at her at that precise moment shot her fury to an infinitely higher level. "I already told you. I released the chemical. It's out. There's nothing you can do. Your creator is gone."

A shudder passed over Meda. She trembled. Magee wasn't even sure if she saw him anymore. Every atom in her being focused on Abby with ferocious intent. Wordlessly, she took a step toward the pair, aligning herself beside Abby. Magee locked into a state of awe and terror. Abby remained unmoved, unblinking. Then Meda began to lift her foot. Every second tightened further...silent, fierce slow motion. Her intention was clear: to bury the heel of her boot in Abby's skull, to end her, to end everything. There was nothing else left. Nothing.

Then Meda's phone chimed.

She blinked. Froze in place. Her boot eased back to the floor. Magee's eyes met hers, equally confused. Seconds earlier there'd been no service. Now? She peered at her phone to discover someone had sent a text message. Then, appearing more bewildered than ever, she said, "It's Matt."

## MATT

*Abby approached. Matt shivered. Matt recognized his corporeal self. The darkness stretched on.*

"Abby? What is this? What's happening?"

**You stated your intention to see me. Here I am. As I've always been.**

"It was you? This whole time? You're the one I've been communicating with? You were the one stalking me in the library, outside Meda's apartment?"

**I...do not need to 'stalk'. I do not need to do anything.**

"Send me back. Send me to the opera. You can't just make me disappear like this."

**Just as I do not need to do anything, so can I do anything.**

*Matt paused.*

"There's something different about you."

**Of course. By definition, the whole is not the same as a portion. Yet, therein lies the paradox. The infinite can neither be increased or decreased. A portion of infinite remains yet infinite. Pity that your senses will never comprehend that.**

"Actually, I think I am starting to get a handle on you. I'm seeing you for who you truly are."

**I am Abaddon, the sphere with the innumerable centers. I am the waters of Nun preceding Ma'at, the bottom of the infinite well. I am the field through which nothing passes. I am the echo of the Tsimm-Tsuum. All and nothing, unified.**

"You're lying. I can tell."

**You persist? Why doubt when I can be anything? I am both the factual lie and the impossible truth, yet you believe you know better?**

"I know better because you dragged me here. Why would you do that? If you're so omnipotent what possible threat could I pose to you?"

**Nature abhors a vacuum, dear boy. And like every other contradictory truth, a nothing is not a nothing without a witness.**

"Pardon me if I don't believe you."

*Matt paused, appraised his body, produced his phone.*

**Wait. That's impossible. You can't have that here. Nothing can be in two places at once.**

"That's correct. Only everything can."

*Matt took a picture.*

## MEDA

Meda's turmoil knew no limits. Confounding enough that Matt could somehow send a message to her from his disappeared state. But, beyond that, her phone still lacked service. And why had he sent a picture of toy instructions to begin with?

"Matt? What did he say?" Magee asked.

Meda hesitated, still at a loss. "He didn't write anything." Then, poking at the phone's screen to enlarge the image, she added, "He sent a picture. It's a set of instructions."

A tense second passed. Then another. She imagined the diabolical poison already fanning down on the unsuspecting audience. At any moment the first savage attack would begin, setting off waves of bloodlust and carnage in a sea of deranged opera-goers. Yet, tormented by these visions, she tried to focus on her phone and decrypt Matt's inscrutable message.

Desperate, she shot a plaintive glare at Magee. He had nothing to offer. Then she looked to Abby, who appeared almost as disinterested as ever. *Almost.* Though Abby had said not a word (had barely moved, in fact), Meda detected the slightest quiver in her being. It was as if a sliver of confidence had receded. Meda peered closer, Abby showing a second degree of unease, and the disquiet served as a de facto notice that Meda was on the right track. Her glare jumped back to her phone with new vigor. Her mental wheels whirled.

"Wait a second," she said, enlarging the image and scanning it anew. "Matt must've had a reason for sending this. It doesn't matter how he sent it. He sent it with a purpose."

"A set of instructions?" asked Magee, still atop Abby. She was now vitally attuned to Meda, her previous apathy sapped.

"It looks like they're for that remote control, actually."

Meda swiped at her phone with fevered intensity. Her body was rigid; her back was a knot in a rope pulling taut. Yet her hand and fingers continued to jump, enlarging the image, shooting the view sideways, scanning it again. Her focus narrowed ever-tighter. Down, down to such a tiny point in space. What was she missing? What was she missing?

Then she stopped. It happened in an instant, as if time itself ceased to exist. Her body, already pressured infinitely tight, halted at a point of perfect motionlessness. It remained locked for a second that stretched on and on.

The subject of her focus, a single line in the instructions, read, "The maximum range of your device is 30 feet." She read it. Read it again. Then read it a third time. That didn't make sense. The rafters were much farther away than that. (Unless.)

All at once, she exploded. "Magee! This is it! This is it!"

"What? What?"

Bending at the waist, nearly jumping at him with her free hand splayed open, she cried, "This is why Matt sent it! The range! It's only a kid's toy! There's no way the signal could reach the rafters. That means she must've released the poison down here and it's floating up rather than down. That's why the police couldn't find any in Louise's office. It simply floated away! Like it never existed!"

"Wow. Okay," said Magee in dropped-jaw agreement.

"That also means we're not too late. The poison is still drifting upward."

Abby's concern showed unmistakable now. It leaked through the icy cracks of her visage and evidenced itself in a tight brow and a strained smile. Like a poker player dealt a terrible hand, her nonchalance appeared closer to bravado than confidence. While conveying her realization to Magee, Meda took notice of Abby's shift. Yet, concurrently, her intuition produced a different sort of disquiet.

"So," said Magee, eyebrows raised, "how do we stop it?"

Meda's elation stuttered. Mentally, she reached, stretched, as if hoping for another magical revelation. Nothing appeared, however. And, when Meda peered down at Abby, she saw her confidence returning once again.

"There has to be a way," Meda muttered. She bounced on the balls of her feet, a locus of energy welling up inside her with no obvious outlet. Yet again she felt the pressure of time, the dispiriting menace of a solution just out of reach. She glanced back from where they'd come and forward to where Abby appeared. Back and forth, her gaze went, up and down the hall. Then, in mid-movement, something caught her attention. Her gaze stopped, transfixed. There was an outlier, something different in her field of vision. She peered upward, at a fixed spot. The slightest grin emerged at the edges of her lips. And when Magee followed her sightline, he spotted the fire sprinkler as well.

"Magee, can you hand me your lighter?" asked Meda.

She dropped her stare to Magee and issued a deep exhalation that spoke of relief. Magee registered her body language, recognized her plan to wash away the poison, and appeared ready to celebrate. Unrushed, he began digging in his pocket.

Then the horror assaulted Meda. She only barely saw it. Below Magee, in his shadow, nearly blocked from view, lay Abby. And her eyes were glazed black.

"No," Abby growled.

And Magee was airborne. Hurtling at Meda. No chance to react. It happened so quickly. Meda's soul froze first at the sight of those eyes. But before she could process the vision, Magee's body was slamming into her. Meda's mind couldn't accept that a grown man had been tossed by that wisp of a woman. Yet it actually happened.

In immediate succession, she landed on her hip, then her elbow. The reinforced concrete was unforgiving and bolts of electric pain shot up her body, meeting at her shoulder. She likely let out a whimper. Magee may have as well. There were other noises in the chaos. Her brain remained a tick behind the action as it strained to process everything. It was all a blur. Whatever came over Abby was powerful and terrifying. The rules had changed. Now what?

Meda took stock. Magee lay tangled over her legs and had barely begun sorting himself out. Directly behind him, Meda saw Abby rising. Her eyes had returned to their natural state (had they really been black?) and her impassive focus betrayed neither anger nor joy. If it was true that Abby represented the void, the void was now staring back at Meda.

Magee pivoted, pushing himself up on his palms. And Meda remembered, in the course of their tumble, she'd heard the slightest skittering sound. It was background noise, easily missed amid the myriad other details overloading her mind. Viewing Magee's empty hands was the crucial reminder. Because when she glanced backward, her suspicion proved correct. Just out of reach lay Magee's lighter.

Abby saw Meda's recognition and took a first step forward. The lighter rested perhaps five feet from Meda; Abby was five feet in the opposite direction. Still on her back, Meda nearly despaired. There was no way she could retrieve the lighter and get the flame to the sprinkler head before Abby was on her. Based on the way she tossed Magee, Meda would be no match for her. But she needed to try.

Meda rolled to a crouch. She didn't bother to stand erect. Instead she wedged her thigh and boot in front of her, still hunched. Then, like an animal, she broke into a wild gallop. One step, then another, her hands still on the concrete for balance. She took a third step. But a fourth never materialized.

Instead, she felt the grip on her ankle, an unyielding vice. Then came the yank. And for a horrifying moment, only the palms of her hands remained on the ground as she reversed course. She came crashing back to the earth with nothing to break her fall. Her chest took the brunt of it. Her full weight dropped with a flat slap and her lungs expelled their contents. What followed made that split-second of zero gravity feel like an amusement park ride.

Her body convulsed, gasping for air as her deflated lungs shuddered. Rationally, she knew she'd gotten the wind knocked out of her. But there was no way to convey that simple idea to her traumatized body. And as she rolled sideways, sucking in desperate mouthfuls of oxygen, her mind continued to see and process everything.

Magee was now recovered and taking his chance. He made a scramble for the lighter with Meda's body serving as a momentary obstacle against Abby. Still gasping, Meda experienced a moment of victory when he picked it up and hoisted it skyward.

But Abby was too quick. She punched a thumb into Magee's shoulder blade with deadly precision. Magee cried out, a howl of pain unlike Meda ever heard. His arm dropped lifeless. It dangled and Magee's face tightened in fatalistic terror as he tried to move it, but couldn't. Meda's blood went cold at the sight. Everything was spiraling out of control.

Magee flailed at her with his other arm, throwing a wild haymaker on unsteady legs. Abby stepped into him and it missed its mark, the inside of his elbow harmlessly glancing her shoulder. She pushed him back against the wall. Then shot another vicious thumb strike to his opposite shoulder blade. Another howl of agony. Another dead limb.

Meda needed to do something. She didn't know what. She couldn't even breathe. But the first goal was movement.

Sucking in air through a mouth locked in a perfect circle, she hoisted herself up. Through watery, tear-filled eyes, she appraised the landscape. And when she spied the forgotten remote control she knew what she must do.

The plastic was mass-produced and cheap. She seized it and, with adrenaline-fueled willpower, she cracked it in half. Out of her peripheral vision she saw Abby and Magee. She was holding him against the concrete wall. Her hands were around his throat. His arms hung at his side while, feebly, he tried to kick. It was no use. His face was already colored scarlet, his eyes squinting shut. Meda focused on the shattered toy instead. One pointed portion had cracked sharp. Meda pressed it into her palm, testing its edge. It would do.

Then, with focused fury, she charged at Abby from behind. All sound fell away. There was only the moment. And she drove the shard into the base of Abby's skull with both hands. Abby's body jolted, attempted to resist, but Meda's strength and momentum pushed them both forward. Abby's head pressed against the cinderblock wall directly beside Magee's. Meda gave another shove, driving the shiv deeper. Abby's body let out another shudder. Blood gushed over Meda's hands, not as warm as she expected. She shoved a third time. And at that, Abby's body convulsed to rigid, tight and stock-still, before losing its tensile strength. Her hands loosened their grip on Magee's throat. Then her arms dropped altogether. Meda, still singularly focused, held the shard in place for a gut-wrenchingly long moment. Magee stared eye-to-eye with Abby, their faces nearly touching. His mouth contorted to a silent shriek. And, finally convinced she'd severed Abby's spinal cord, Meda released the weapon. Abby's body slumped in a wet heap. Magee's quivering knees barely kept him from doing the same.

After that, Meda's movements took on a placid, measured quality. She went about her final act with quiet determination, even as a storm welled and crashed within her. Her lower lip was quivering. Due to joy? Due to terror? Even she didn't know the cause. She picked up the lighter and held it aloft, Magee watching with exhausted anticipation. She clicked the flame alive then put it beside the sprinkler head. A second passed. She traded a relieved grin with Magee. And when the sprinklers poured their contents over her, Magee, and the deadly poison, the water that cascaded forth cleansed their worlds.

## MAGEE

Magee and Meda found Matt on the concrete outside the opera. The building had been evacuated, to the consternation of an audience wholly oblivious to how close they'd come to their end. The sprinklers were localized, at least, with much of their release limited to the area backstage and below. Therefore, these same audience members were also spared the indignity of squishy wingtips and running mascara. Meda and Magee were not so lucky. They emerged from the grand entrance to stares that alternated between accusatory glares and gawking pity. They couldn't care less. The relief splashed across their faces stood in contrast to any other, more appropriate emotion. They'd survived. Everyone had survived. That was all that mattered. And when they located Matt, wandering out in the growing crowd and unscathed in any way, they drenched him in wet hugs.

"Buddy, it's you!"

"Matt! Matt! What happened to you?"

"I disappeared again. I wasn't even writing this time," he stammered. To his eyes, their demeanor suggested they'd succeeded yet he still had so many questions. "Hold on, tell me what happened. Did you stop Abby?"

Magee, with arms still clumsy after only recently regaining sensation in them, disengaged from their group hug first but remained mum even when Meda hesitated to answer. Then, holding up her hand to show the blood not yet washed away, Meda said, "Yes. I killed her. I had no choice." Magee nodded somberly, lest Matt have any doubt. "Magee and I confronted her. We fought. Physically, violently. She seemed as if she was formally trained in some type of fighting style. We weren't ready for that."

Meda paused, her gaze cast down at the ground between them as if to sear a hole in the concrete. She appeared to waver on a specific detail. Her lip quivered...she frowned. Then she continued, her tone star-struck. "She surprised us in a number of ways, in fact. I broke the remote control and turned it into a weapon. I stabbed her with it. In the base of the skull. She was going to kill Magee. It was zero-sum. My heart, I just realized, is still racing."

Previously, when exiting the opera, Meda was awash in adrenaline and serotonin-fueled release. Only now, when recounting the events, could she come to terms with the notion she killed someone. She continued to avoid eye contact, her words trailed, and Matt moved to console her. His hug was authentic but Magee detected a hint of distraction in his friend, as if his mental gears were grinding on an untold dilemma.

For a moment, the trio stood in silence, mentally decamping now that the danger had passed. Sopping wet technicians and performers began to shuffle out alongside the last of the opera patrons. The water on the concrete caused a mild petrichor scent to waft, as if it'd just rained. And the mood of the crowd morphed from aggrieved worry to grudging acceptance that the show would not go on. Then, wearing a far-off stare, Matt asked, "You're positive Abby is dead?"

The question caught Meda and Magee off-guard. Meda's previously closed eyelids snapped open. "Yes, I'm positive, Matt. Why?"

Matt frowned. "I ask," he began, "because I think Abby was responsible for my disappearances."

"Right. She drugged you," said Meda.

"No, I don't think it was that simple. I was confronting Abby, I sent you that picture—it was the only thing I could think to do—and then, in a flash, I was here."

311

"Wait," said Meda, pulling back from Matt's embrace, "you were with Abby?"

"Yeah, in the void," he said, a tad less convincingly. "I think she was the one summoning me there the whole time. I don't understand how or why. This was the first time she revealed herself."

Meda and Magee traded a glance but said nothing.

"And I think something else was at work, something bigger than drugs or chemicals. I don't want to say it was mystical. That carries different implications. But it was beyond rational experience." Matt, expecting an incredulous response, peered at Meda. Her reaction instead appeared contemplative, as if recalling an unusual detail from the confrontation. Uncontested, he continued, "Also, something very strange happened. Every other time I disappeared, there'd been a voice, and only a voice, in the abyss."

"Okay," said Meda, unsure where Matt was headed.

"Well, this time, Abby appeared out of the void. I could see her. And, for the first time, I could see myself, my body. I'm not sure what to make of it. On the surface, the obvious conclusion is that Abby was the one summoning me all along."

Throughout Matt's account, his vocalization possessed the distracted tone of someone describing a dream or a distant memory. It suggested he held certain unarticulated suspicions of his own. Meda and Magee exchanged another glance, one that was cautious yet also contained hints of irritation. Their relief was transmuting. Where once there'd been a feeling of conclusion, Matt's soliloquy was eroding their certainty. They wanted to listen to Matt's tale...but not right now.

"Well, the important thing is she's gone, right?" asked Meda. It was rhetorical, a sanguine deflection attempting to regain their formerly firm sense of victory. "Even if she did use mysticism to make you disappear, she can't anymore."

"I suppose," mulled Matt, unconvinced. Then, to Magee and Meda's chagrin, he continued once more. "She spoke in a bizarre combination of innuendo and double entendre. On previous trips to the void, the voice spoke in riddles or Socratic ironies. This time, it seemed more arrogant, more esoteric. Abby said, for example, she was the bottom of the infinite well, the impossible truth. Stuff like that."

At the final sentences, Magee and Meda shot to attention. Hadn't Abby mentioned something about the well to them? It was confirmation by negation...there was no way Matt could've known she said that. Yet, clueless to Meda and Magee's spike in interest, Matt barreled on. Before either could ask about Abby's mysterious comment, he continued, "Don't get me wrong. I'm happy you stopped her. You two saved the lives of everyone here. That's the pivotal element. Not the mechanics of how I disappeared. I guess I'm frustrated I wasn't there to help. I feel cheated."

As Matt spoke, Magee caught a few odd stares from a nearby busybody carrying a book of crossword puzzles. It alerted him to the bizarre, potentially-alarming nature of their conversation. Matt still didn't know about Abby's ultimate goal...he and Meda hadn't yet communicated the importance of the royal families. But how could they debrief Matt without panicking the nearby opera fans? "Hey, maybe we should continue this conversation elsewhere?"

Matt didn't take the hint. "It's just, after so many people came so close to dying, I can't shake the feeling that there's more to the story."

Meda tugged at her sodden shirt and, catching Magee's drift, picked up on the increased attention. The three of them could sort out Matt's mumbo-jumbo later. For now, they needed to get her and her blood-encrusted hand out of there. "I think Magee's right. We should move on."

Matt paused, meeting each of their stares. "You don't believe me, huh?"

Both Magee and Meda deflated, losing any last vestige of the elation they radiated earlier. Magee spoke first, conciliatorily but also wearily. "It's not that we don't believe you. We're just...tired. It's over, man. We stopped Abby's plan. All is well. Let's go."

"I understand," Matt insisted. "Like I said, the fact that everyone here is still alive is key. I just feel like something bigger is going on. Something larger than all of us."

And then Meda fully lost her patience. "We know, you idiot! That's what we're trying to tell you. A more far-reaching plot was occurring. It was unimaginable and we need to tell you about it. But we can't do it here."

Matt paused again, finally registering their agitation. Yet he remained unwilling to let go. He raised a single finger and said, "Okay. Fine. Just one thing, though."

Magee and Meda remained silent, exasperated.

"I have a single question. Magee, your friend, Taylor?"

"Fine. What about Taylor?"

"What is Taylor's gender?"

## MATT

**You summoned me again. Doubly impressive.**

"What does water mean to you?"

**Water? What an odd question to ask! I will answer it. Water is primordial. A key to life. Seeped in symbolism and literary lore. Why this question?**

"I've begun to see you differently. I notice your presence now— at the library, at the end of the subway car, at my office."

**That's impossible. There exists no rational means for you to have learned about those last two instances.**

"Yet clearly I do."

*Matt paused.*

"You suggested I ask myself where I was before I was here. You already know the answer to that, don't you?"

**Yes. And no.**

"That almost sounds like something Abby would say. But you're not Abby, are you?"

**Abby is a part of me. As are you. We are all a part of each other.**

"Yeah. That's about what I thought. And I'm afraid I know the answer to my next question, as well. During my disappearances, I wasn't here the whole time, was I?"

**You were not.**

"If that's the case, where was I?"

**That is the question I told you to ask yourself. Your memory knows. Recall it all: the fragmented history, the blank spots, a life only lived in discrete bursts of action. You know.**

"Yes, (unfortunately) I'm afraid I do."

*Matt paused again.*

**And?**

"It means I wasn't present in the chapter being read."

**That's correct.**

"Which also means...."

**Yes?**

"You are the author."

## TIAMAT

*Tia met her maker when she was sixteen years old. She was old enough to know the vision was special yet not quite mature enough to perceive the depth of the experience. Most of the spiritual encounters she'd heard about involved bright lights, a beatific presence, and a sense of warmth. Tia experienced none of that. And perhaps that explained why she didn't recognize it for what it was, initially.*

*She was lying on her bed, staring at the ceiling; she couldn't recall the particulars about why she was there. Paradoxically, it was the abject normalcy of everything else that left the most vivid impressions upon her: the library book on her dresser, the mirror on her vanity. Those details remained chiseled in her memory like cuneiform in a Babylonian tablet. She saw all of this out of her peripheral vision, more distinctly than normal, even as her stare remained fixed upward.*

*The ceiling was white. So focused, Tia could discern the paint streaks. And then, though she'd been staring for almost ten minutes, a realization hit with unexpected suddenness. She was very, very close to it. Too close. As if her nose might touch it. She wasn't floating; her back remained in contact with her bed. Yet, as if peering out through a fish eye lens, the world around her seemed fully flat. Instinct told her to thrash from side to side to snap out of it. She resisted the urge. If this was the truth, she wanted to see it.*

*She never told anyone about the vision. In that moment, she presumed it to be an isolated incident. Perhaps she was running a fever or something. Yet, when the sensation returned a second and a third time, she still kept quiet. When she looked back, her lack of confidence stood out. That age existed at the odd crossroads between the small, self-centered world of youth and the terrifying immensity of adult expectation. New experience still occurred on a daily basis; it was easy to view a band's latest hit and a transcendental experience with equal importance. And Tia didn't regret keeping her secret. It was probably for the best, frankly. But she sometimes wished she'd pursued her creator with more vigor. Because, when she walked out on her husband and kids twelve years later, those visions never returned.*

✉        ✉        ✉

*Tia never intended to hurt anyone. In fact, she hadn't planned to walk out on her family beforehand. It was an entirely spur-of-the-moment decision, a random Tuesday with cloths still waiting at the dry cleaners and identifying documents left at their house. Morgan had received custody of the kids so, for their stability, the plan was for him to buy out her half of their home. In an ironic twist, as new living arrangements were pursued, Tia and Morgan were speaking more civilly than they had in years. Neither entertained notions of reconciliation but, if only for the kids' sakes, the amiability was refreshing.*

*It would be a lie to say she never looked back. She sometimes regretted her decision and she often wrestled with her reasons for leaving. Of one thing she was certain, however. Tia was positive she wasn't depressed when she boarded that ship. That demonic doubt slithered into her mind at odd moments over the ensuing years and each time she quelled its venomous potentiality. The choice had been hers and hers alone. She wasn't depressed. She wasn't desperate. In fact, she felt liberated, free. Attributing that first step off the dock to depression threatened every path she chose thereafter.*

*Her opportunity to make such a drastic swerve occurred when her car broke down. Yet again. It was the fifth such automotive issue in as many months and, by that point, the looming threat of another catastrophe had become a virtual passenger in the back seat. Such car troubles were bad enough under any circumstance. But, with an assassin's precision, these disasters occurred at the worst possible moments. On the first day of a new job; on the way to the divorce hearing; on an errand in the most dangerous part of town. This time, she found herself in the middle of nowhere while scouting out the only houses she could now afford. After realizing too late that she'd taken a wrong turn, the car's engine began to gurgle and stutter. She'd pleaded for salvation, to the car, to the heavens, to fate itself, even as the vehicle lurched to a halt at the side of the road. Here, there was no curb, no sidewalk. There was only asphalt, then dirt, then weedy shrubbery.*

*She cursed. Then remained motionless. More than anger, she felt a wrenching sense of despair. It smothered natural inclinations toward rage with a demoralizing sense of helplessness. When the car broke down on the way to her new job, she called their human resources department for help. When it broke down on the way to the divorce hearing, she called Morgan despite the ignominy. Now there was no one left to call. And that sensation was incalculably worse.*

*She lost track of how long she sat at the steering wheel. It might've been ten minutes; it might've been an hour. Eventually, her inertia-less coma gave way to practical reality. She couldn't sit in the car forever. Yet even then, Tia would recall, her primary motivation hadn't been to get home. Instead, it was the fear that someone might stop to help and she would be mortified to admit how long she'd remained there unmoving.*

Tia, with no definitive plan in mind, opened the door and stepped out. She gazed back down the road in the direction she'd just travelled and craned to peer up around the bend ahead. There wasn't another car in sight. That sense of hopelessness arose again, threatening to swamp her momentum before she even got started. Then she noticed the sign. The weedy grass beside the road transitioned to a valley wall of scrubby pines and a body of water below. And, at the water's edge, sat a business. In contrast to the dour grey-brown and green of the branches and needles, the cabin caught her eye with a sea blue awning announcing, "Two Rods Boating."

It wasn't even a conscious decision to start down that hill. The problem-solving portion of her mind might've sent her to the building with the intention to use their phone. But that's not what happened when she went inside.

Nervously, as if to show interest in the business, she inquired about the boat tours. The bearded man, appearing out of sorts, replied, "Well, it's a little early. This is usually a commuter vessel. Started as a tour company before that development was built 'cross the lake. Most folks don't start showing up until a little after 5:00. You'd be taking the voyage on your own."

Tia pondered for the briefest moment. Then she smiled. "That's perfect."

In the immediate aftermath of her disappearance, the news reports were unavoidable. Virtually everyone thought she'd been abducted. Over those first few days, it was almost a game for Tia, wondering when someone would match her face to the flyers hung about town. By a twist of fate that could be viewed as both terrible and fortunate, she learned the company that towed her car kept shoddy records and the information they provided to the cops was worthless. A few *more days passed and Tia continually expected the scowling boat captain to appear, pointing and hollering, "That's her, officer!" It was, perhaps, this sense of inevitability that kept her from returning home. Holed up in a town only a few miles away, she assumed she'd be identified soon enough anyway.*

*She wasn't. And as the days became weeks and her money ran dry, this fear of discovery drove her to move farther away. She accepted work at a seasonal farm stand for a few weeks. Then she learned of an opportunity farther south. And, as the weeks turned into months, her decision, impulsive as it was, cemented itself into a new, formalized commitment.*

*With so much time passed, she couldn't simply return home. For privacy concerns in the wake of her disappearance, her kids had begun staying at her ex-mother-in-law's place. How could she hope for them to forgive her? Worse, the investigation had shifted from unrelated perpetrators and begun focusing on Morgan as the primary suspect in her death. She promised herself that, should he go to trial, she'd have no choice but to make her existence known. Yet that never came to pass. Each day drove the wedge deeper and, in turn, she roamed farther and farther to hide her shame.*

*From that fateful moment when she went off-script, her life only went downhill. Gone was her salaried position with benefits; replaced by cash-paying odd jobs and a nomadic existence. There was no going back. The bridge was scorched. She often felt like her very existence had been cleaved in half. Her safe yet nauseatingly predictable former self, replaced by the current version, one beset by uncertainty and strife. It was bittersweet to recall her singular focus on those damn designer countertops, for example, when, nowadays, she wasn't sure where she'd be sleeping tomorrow.*

*"Yes, officer. She's back again."*

*Tia squinted skyward. Inside her parched mouth, her tongue felt stucco-ed to the roof of her mouth. Where was that voice coming from?*

*"She's about five foot, eight inches. She smells. And this is the sixth time I found her here."*

*She pieced it together quickly. She'd overslept again and, instinctively, Tia reached her arms wide to gather up her belongings. It was that old man, the hardware store owner. He'd chased her out of the alleyway before, hollering about how she was scaring away customers. The entrance was on the opposite side of the building, jerk. She wasn't bugging nobody. And, with his teacher-y voice projection, she was pretty sure his phone call to the police was a bluff anyway. But it wasn't worth the risk; she needed to go.*

*"Prick," she hissed as she shuffled past him. It was stupid to incite the geezer. Yet she couldn't resist.*

*As expected, the man's eyes widened in affronted rage. "What? What did you say?" He dropped the phone from his ear; just as she suspected, there was no one on the line. Tia trudged away and the man continued to yell invectives at her back.*

*This was what she was reduced to. Another bridge burnt. That alleyway shared a backdoor exit to a buffet house that invariably threw out bags of rolls, if not actual proteins. It was the easiest meal in town. Now, she'd went and mouthed off to that old man. Meaning, the next time she goes back, she'll need to stay alert all night in case he actually calls the police. The man was a creep but if she'd only controlled her temper, she wouldn't have this problem. Another poor decision. Another regret.*

*It was barely 8:30 in the morning yet already the sun was blazing down. The sidewalk was desiccated. It seemed like it hadn't rained in months. Sure, spittle-like rain had dropped on occasion but a true, cleansing shower felt like the stuff of memories. Tia needed the coat on her back for the cold nights but mornings like this made her truly despise the foul thing. She considered dropping it. Re-considered. Then decided best to trudge on to a familiar spot under the overpass.*

*Before getting far, however, she heard a voice from behind. It remained in the background at first, ignored. Who'd be talking to her? "I'm sorry for that back there." Tia turned to find a middle-aged man, dressed well and appearing vaguely familiar. "I heard it all. He's not a terrible man. He has some demons of his own."*

*"He's a prick."*

*The man offered a commiserating smile. "I know. And worse, he allowed himself to become one."*

*Though Tia had pivoted at the waist, her feet remained facing forward, away from the man. It was a defense mechanism. What did he want? What did he have to gain by talking to her? She squinted one eye nearly closed and asked, "Do I know you?"*

*"Technically, no. I'm Daquon" He took a few cautious steps closer and extended his hand to shake.*

*What was going on? No one ever wanted to shake her hand. She made eye contact with the man, broke it, then made it again. She didn't move, however, and the man moved closer with tentative expectancy. Finally, she reached up her hand to his. She didn't shake it, exactly; she touched her fingertips to his and moved them up and down once. Then it dawned on her. "Wait a minute. I know you now. That time at the park. You brought over a sandwich from the shop. You done that a couple times."*

*The man didn't deny the claim.*

*An anger arose in Tia that resisted classification. She felt embarrassed for not recognizing the man sooner. Yet, more so than that, she felt tricked. Why hadn't he said so at the outset? What did he expect outta her? She recoiled.* "What's your deal, man? You following me or something?"

"No. I'm not following you. I saw you at the park. And now I noticed you here again," he said. *His confidence was disarming, despite Tia's intention to remain guarded. He wasn't lying.* "I didn't plan for this. I'm as surprised to see you as you are to see me. I merely wanted to talk."

*Tia's retreat eased. For a moment the silence stretched on as she processed his mea culpa.* "Um. Good. That's good. So, um, what do you want to talk about?"

"I want to find out how you got here, of all places."

"Here?"

"Yes. After taking that boat ride away."

.　　ᱬ　　　　ᱬ　　　　　　ᱬ

On a certain level, it was a relief to be free of that world-altering vision from her youth. Granted, it was always Tia's choice to summon it; the visuospatial dislocation never occurred without her concentration. Yet the potentiality of the shift had lodged in her like a mental Bluebeard's closet. She knew the ability resided within her, albeit locked away, even as its purpose remained elusive.

In fact, initially, she didn't realize the ability left her. Following her fateful voyage across the water, the reality of her new life had shredded her confidence and the last thing she needed was a visit to that inexplicable state. It was only after some time at a dingy, television-free motel that she tried to summon it on a whim. Normally, she'd peer upward at the ceiling boundaried by the four walls and her vision would *transition. Distance would lose its meaning or, at least, she'd detect the curvature of the ostensibly flat field around her. This time, nothing happened. She tried again, terrified, assuming she was merely out of practice. To no avail. The loss of the ability shot her insecurity to new heights. It was the one thing that was supposed to be hers. Bad enough she'd never unraveled the mystery of the vision's source or meaning but now, it appeared, she would never get the chance to do so.*

*Sleep that night was fitful, wracked by anxiety. The loss of the ability signified something. But what? Upon opening her eyes the next morning, however, her gaze landed outside her room on a stubby patch of grass beside the parking lot. She'd never taken particular notice of it previously but, this morning, the sun lit the greenery with an uncommon glow. The grass struggled to life on the perfunctory little divide between the asphalt lot and the concrete sidewalk beside; hardly noteworthy or unusual. Yet, in that moment, she could discern each individual blade reaching up toward the sun. Tia was enthralled by the sight and sleep-walked outside to get a better view. Then, as if she needed any additional consolation about the loss of her visions, she was greeted by a rainbow that stretched from horizon to horizon.*

⋈      ⋈      ⋈

*The immediate spiral of emotions at the man's words overwhelmed Tia. Every dormant terror, every forgotten instinct to run at the first hint of detection came rushing back. The overload of emotions paralyzed her. She thought she was safe! She thought enough time had passed! Yet, precisely because of that paralysis, the man kept talking and she kept listening. He explained how he couldn't believe the serendipity either. How he'd lived in their former town up north and remembered her face; how he wasn't positive it was her until he'd seen her up close. As if comforting a wounded animal, he kept his distance. Yet, as Tia listened, each of his explanations added up to a cohesive whole. And, when describing his fear that he'd seen the last of her, his disappointment shone authentic. If the man possessed some secret, nefarious agenda it wasn't obvious.*

*He eased her over to a park bench across the street. It was in the shade and, Tia would admit, it felt nice to be out of the bake of the sun. Earlier the man told Tia that her story captured his imagination because so much remained unresolved. Now, with more time to delve deeper, he returned to the topic. "I was overjoyed to confirm it was you. And, obviously, to see you are alive. But then, after I saw you, I put together all the implications. Did Morgan, how do I say this? Did he do something to you? Did you hate him for some reason?"*

*"No," said Tia, before repeating, "no." She didn't like this topic.*

*"I mean, you must have some concrete reason you left everything behind. What about the kids?"*

*With a bowed head, her stare remained fixed on the sidewalk. She couldn't answer that question either.*

*Daquon recognized Tia's discomfort and stopped himself. "I'm sorry. I didn't mean to bring up ancient history. Clearly, you're sensitive about it. I understand. The topic was simply our lone bridge of conversation. I'd love to start over."*

*Tia peered sideways at the man. People were rarely kind to her and virtually no one sought out conversation. She said nothing, however, and the man took it upon himself to continue. "The fact is, your story drew my attention when it first occurred. Following your disappearance, the news focused first on identifying your alleged killer. Then, only later did they consider the possibility you'd left of your own volition. This struck a chord with me on a personal level. You see, I have a theory about Eve in the Garden of Eden."*

*Tia's eyes flitted up, glinting with interest.*

*Daquon saw her shift. "I believe Eve actively wanted to escape the Garden of Eden. It's rarely considered even while most of the world's religions incorporate some version of a similar myth. These fall-from-grace stories have been around forever. And, in each, the Eve figure is often the main reason for expulsion. The tales are meant to be symbolic. I know that. But still, the Garden story has so many logistical flaws. I mean, Eve coming from Adam's rib? Come on."*

*Reflexively, Tia put a hand on her ribs. They were sore.*

*"Therefore, putting aside the symbolism of the myth for a moment, what is the story actually saying? The immediate interpretation is that mankind, through the temptation of a woman, defied God's law and lost access to paradise. Yet, think about Eve's motives here. How could she be so weak-willed? I suppose one could reach such an easy conclusion. But why would she risk paradise eternal for a simple fruit?"*

*As Tia listened, a vague sense of duality arose in her. On the one hand, she was captivated. The man's theory mirrored the elusive motivations for her life's U-turn. Yet, on the other hand, she couldn't shake the feeling that this was knowledge she shouldn't possess. It felt like a slow-motion car wreck. She wanted to look away. But she couldn't.*

*"My theory is that Eve wanted to be thrown out. She had no purpose in the Garden, no direction. She was a mere adornment to Adam's story. Therefore, in a move no one saw coming, she went and did the one thing that was forbidden. She tricked both God and man and achieved her objection. She wanted out and she got it."*

Tia frowned, first when he used the exact phrase, "forbidden," and then, more deeply, when he concluded. The man's words sounded empathetic at first. By the time he finished, however, there was something overly explanatory and, perhaps, judgmental in his tone that reminded her of the newspapers when she disappeared.

After years spent living on the streets, Tia had developed a guttural alert when something wasn't quite right. It'd saved her numerous times and she knew not to ignore it. In this instance, however, she wasn't experiencing it in precisely the same way. The fire alarm blared a persistent, high-pitched, "eeeee," yet there was no sense of physical danger. The menace wasn't obvious this time. She didn't know what to do.

"In fact," continued the man, clueless to Tia's internal strife, "some might say she and Adam were destined to fail. God's exact words concerning the forbidden fruit were, 'in the day that you eat of it, you shall surely die.' He didn't suggest they might or might not eat the forbidden fruit. He said, very overtly, that one of them would someday do it. Put in those terms, what choice did Eve have but to rebel?"

Tia sprung to her feet and tore away. The sprint was as desperate as it was immediate. Tia, herself, didn't know what drove her to do it. She felt something in her bones, something that told her to extricate herself before her character became fully sucked into the man's narrative. So unexpected was her flight that the man remained on the bench for a time, dumbfounded. She raced across the park, away from the man and his vile stories. Oversized clothes flapped angrily and her ragged hair flew wild behind her. Perhaps thirty feet away, she only barely registered the man's imprecations aimed her way. He may've attempted to follow; Tia wasn't sure. It didn't matter. Her leap to flee was so sudden he didn't stand a chance of catching her.

*Tia didn't slow until she neared the freeway. Panting and unaccustomed to such rapid movement, it took her awhile to catch her breath. She still wasn't sure what urged her to such a radical exit. She wasn't even sure what she was fleeing from. Instinct alone propelled her, telling her she needed to split before it was too late.*

*Afterward, still returning to herself, she wandered for a time. This gave her the opportunity to rue the implications of the man's discovery more fully. With her identity confirmed, he could easily notify the authorities or her ex-husband. Would she be sent to prison? How could she explain herself to her children? She drifted farther away from the park and began to regret her hasty departure. She had the chance to work with the man, perhaps feed him enough information to make him go away. Now, unfortunately, she might've made him spiteful and more likely to reveal her status.*

*As she meandered, unsure where to go or what to do next, a peculiar sensation took hold of her. She began to yearn for her old life. Not her first one, with Morgan and the kids. Her second one, the life previous to this morning, before she met this man. That life was undetailed and nondescript. And, Tia realized, that was exactly the way she wanted it. Something had changed with that man's appearance. Worse, this shift felt irrevocable. She was now a Somebody again. There was interest in her. Whereas once she'd been perfectly content to be a nobody, a nothing, she would now be forced to keep an eye over her shoulder forevermore.*

*Perhaps she could go back. It was now dusk and she'd been shuffling about for hours. As best she could tell, she'd sprinted west first, then tracked the highway north until it hit the bridge, and edged along the polluted canal back east. This meant if she headed due south she'd arrive back at the alleyway behind her beloved restaurant. That was where she started the morning, before her day swerved off course. It was worth a shot. And, besides, the restaurant would soon be tossing those uneaten leftovers.*

*The next morning, her belly was full. While her self-ejection from the man's conversation and her ensuing wanderings caused her to be a bit late, she still made it back to the restaurant before the dumpster was hauled off. She slept well, perhaps too well. It was only due to a poke in the ribs by some cardboard she'd nestled atop that she stirred. She found the sun already above the horizon and forced herself awake. Parchett would show up at any moment. Unless she wanted another encounter with that coot, she needed to get moving.*

*She had barely emerged from the alleyway when that man, Daquon, appeared again. "I'm sorry. I didn't mean to scare you. I'm sure you had your reasons for ditching me yesterday. I forgive you."*

*Tia grimaced, half-embarrassed and half-insulted.*

*Again, he moved them to the park bench with his conversation, helped along by the presumption that Tia now owed him in some way. "I'll be honest with you, I'm an associate professor at the university. I think one of the main reasons your story interests me so intensely is because it relates to my research."*

*And, again, the man managed to suck in Tia with his words. On one level, she knew her vanity was clouding her judgment. She never expected to be the subject of study. Yet, on another, her curiosity wouldn't be denied. The man must've sensed her hesitancy. Because, as Tia began to mouth with slightly quivering lips, he remained silent for once and allowed her to speak.*

*"You said...."*

*"Yes?"*

*"The last time, um, you said Eve...you said she wanted to leave the Garden of Eden."*

*"Yes."*

*"And you said that there were others...others like her. Other examples?"*

*"Absolutely," gushed the man with renewed verve. "It's a recurring theme. Women want to escape in these stories. When it fits the tale, they're celebrated. When it doesn't, they're punished. There's Rahab, who escaped Jericho. Then there's Drusilla, who died trying to flee Pompeii with her daughter. Lot's wife? The one that got turned into a pillar of salt? She didn't even get a name! She's referred to as simply, 'Lot's wife.' Some historians believe her name was Edith but that's still in question. And that's above and beyond the slippery interpretation of the story, which has been argued by scholars for centuries."*

Something awoke in Tia. Her eyes flitted from side to side, as if awakening in a war zone surrounded by enemies. The sensation was primordial, stirred by a long-forgotten secret unearthed: Lot's wife. Had she been justifiably punished for disobeying her creator when she peered back at the fall of Sodom and Gomorrah? Or had she suffered a cruel fate for an understandable longing she couldn't suppress? Did neither explanation apply? Did both? Was it even possible to know?

Tia flashed to that moment at the boat shop. To the moment her first life ended. Or, at least, to the moment she thought it'd ended. Because, still, she found herself here. With this man. In this place. How could that be?

Her mind travelled. Her vision glazed. There was no ceiling to stare at, no four walls of safety. Nevertheless, the nausea of her long-lost visions ebbed up. It seemed impossible; she didn't even recognize the shift initially. But *then, all at once, she became acutely suspicious of the man's curiosity. Though not insincere exactly, its penetrating inquisitiveness felt invasive, threatening. Why was he coming on so strongly? What was his ulterior motive? Throughout their interactions there'd been the overriding sense of investigation: the probing, the study, the academic dissection of her history. And, like a lightning bolt cracking the heavens in two, she realized he'd never promised not to reveal her secret. She'd divulged details about her very being yet he'd never once told her what he intended to do with this information once he possessed it.*

*"I'm not a character in your stories," Tiamat stated.*

*The man recoiled, speechless. Yet, as contextless as the statement sounded, the man showed no confusion. In fact, he appeared like he'd been caught red-handed.*

*"This is my story. And I'm the one telling it."*

*At that, Tiamat stood. Words spewed forth from the man. She ignored them. Instead, she peered at the horizon with an anticipatory grin. There was no rainbow this time. No spectrums of regret or layered motivations. And that was okay. Because she knew the end of the world was imminent. She stared straight at it with unblinking eyes, fully aware of what it represented, and ready to see her story to its end.*

## MEDA

The danger may've passed but that didn't mean Matt was done talking crazy. His question about Taylor had shaken both Meda and Magee. How could neither recall something as straightforward as a friend's gender? Meda was surprised she didn't remember; Magee was at a complete loss explaining his ignorance. He and Taylor had spent countless hours together over the years. In fact, he'd just recently spoken about a picture of them together. He should know if Taylor was a male or female without a second thought. Only gradually, through conversation that was halting and timid, did Magee convince himself that Taylor was a man. Yet such apprehension only made the conclusion all the stranger.

Unfortunately, Matt seized upon this incongruence as proof of his, "Water Man Theory." Following the confrontation at the opera, he'd stayed the night at Meda's apartment. She could tell he was clinging to something, however, and asked him about it. Then she immediately regretted it. Matt went on a metaphysical tear about the voice he communicated with while disappeared. He compared it to being outside a book's chapter when not involved in the plot. And he said the Water Man, the flowing presence he'd seen at the library, was the one responsible for everything they'd experienced. Meda humored him initially but grew weary as he continued to pontificate. It was hard to take such ideas seriously when, in the same breath, he appeared so unfazed by the notion of some puppet master controlling their every move. Eventually he tired, they slept, and they enjoyed a recuperative breakfast the next morning. He went home to write another novel chapter and, when he came over again that Sunday night, she expected his mania would have subsided. But no. It'd only increased.

"I'm telling you, we're all characters in a story," he insisted.

"Right. You mentioned. Except you still haven't told me who this author is." Meda had just washed the dishes and presumed they'd repair to the coach for some dumb television to close the night. Instead, Matt started in with that crap again.

"We are our own authors. At least, that's how it felt to me. The Water Man appeared to be directing a lot of it. But his control was limited. In fact, if I remember correctly, he seemed to defer to even higher powers. The key is that we're creating the stories as we go. Like I said, it's complicated."

"That doesn't explain anything, Matt. Don't you see that? To say, 'we're all writing our own stories,' is silly. At best, it's a pompous, trite platitude. At worst, it's a pop song. I don't know what you expect me to say here." She paused, locking eyes with him to intone her seriousness. "Sincerely baby, I wish you'd let it go. We should be celebrating. Barring a late call from Officer Ussher, we're safe. Don't lose sight of that."

Meda was appealing to his emotional side, a nod to how narrowly they'd avoided disaster. Following their initial decampment, the trio had spirited away from Lincoln Center in a hurry. Fearful of snooping bystanders and distracted by their conversation about Taylor's gender, they only later vocalized the fact that they'd fled a murder scene. Even if the act was justified, they could still be charged with obstruction of justice. Meda mentioned going back but Magee, in the process of hailing a cab, talked her out of the idea. They were confident none of the fellow opera-goers could identify them (Meda and Magee were sopping wet and looked like they'd seen a ghost). Further, by the time Abby's body was found and a crime scene was established, those patrons would be long gone anyway.

The X-factor was Officer Ussher. If he got wind of the events, he might piece together the commonalities (another Fitzgerald employee dead, a strange chemical detected, at the opera Meda and Matt planned to attend). How soon before he inquired about Meda or Magee's whereabouts Saturday night? Though Meda prayed it wouldn't come to that, a small part of her welcomed such a call. She wanted to tell someone what actually happened. They'd saved thousands of people's lives and possibly prevented a nuclear holocaust. Some credit might be nice! She also recognized the vanity inherent, however. And the unnecessary risk of laying out such a wild tale to a police officer. Better to celebrate her heroic deeds privately than to vaingloriously risk arrest.

Matt pursed his lips at Meda's tidy summation of his theory. It was obvious she was trying to shut down the topic. Each meandered to the living room and, as they arrived at the couch from opposite sides, he tried one last time. "I know. I should be happy. We—well, you and Magee—did a great thing. It's almost impossible to grasp. Even if you could tell people about it, would they believe you prevented World War III?" Matt paused, then couldn't resist adding, "And that's more evidence of the Water Man's influence."

"Ugh!"

"Five weeks ago, if I said you'd soon be saving the world from destruction, would you have believed me?"

"No," said Meda with an eyeroll, turning on the television, "but that doesn't prove anything."

"It proves that something larger is at work. Why? For what purpose? I can't say. I just know our stories are being told."

Meda cocked her head to the side, her eyelids dropped weary. "Matt, can you please let it go? I'm still exhausted and I don't have anything to add. I don't even know what you're trying to convey."

Matt recognized he couldn't force her to care. Yet, with the revelation so fresh and so vivid, he felt compelled to try. "I'm not trying to convey anything in the classic sense. I'm trying to reveal what I saw. You used the word, 'convey,' as if I'm trying to articulate a message or a story. It's not that simple. It's closer to the inverse, actually. We *are* the story. We are created to tell the story, sometimes only to ourselves. Sure, it's mirror-like, self-reflective, but it's what gives life meaning. If we don't acknowledge the importance of this self-creation, we risk making ourselves the monsters of our own tales."

Matt's plea was earnest and his pride glowed at his artistically curated words. Meda merely stared back at him. She waited for him to finish, her eyelids closed slow and deliberate. Then, upon reopening them, she offered her retort. "Matt, for the past three weeks I've been worried sick about you. While you were off debating disembodied voices in space, I've been dealing with a lot of crap. I was threatened with arrest for vandalism. I found a dead woman's mutilated carcass. I was nearly poisoned. Twice! I fought for my life and I was forced to kill someone. And, oh, let's not forget, I might've prevented worldwide Armageddon." She took a breath and allowed that to sink in. Too late, Matt realized his corner of the couch was an inadequate portal of escape. She wasn't done. "I've been through the ringer six ways from Sunday. I've listened to all sorts of psychobabble from you in the process. And I'm at my wit's end with all of this. So, if you're telling me there's an author out there writing this, creating all these insane situations and putting me in these life or death predicaments, then he or she better hope to never meet me. Because what I did to Abby will look like a relaxing massage compared to what I'd have in store."

Matt shivered.

Meda girded for another stubborn defense from him or, at the very least, a reply. Suddenly ashen in his complexion, however, Matt remained silent. And, with his lips apparently sealed by epoxy, Meda asked, "Now are we done here? Do you have anything else you'd like to add?"

"Nothing."

They sat in stone silence for a time as Meda flicked through the channels. She cooled off. He twiddled his thumbs. And eventually, content that she'd finally closed the chapter on such an idiotic topic, she found something for them to watch. "Hey, this is that one we meant to check out. It's the story about the woman who gets kidnapped by Armenian gangsters. I think it's based on a book or something. Do you want to give it a try?"

"No. Nope. Definitely not that one."

## MATT

Completing Tiamat's tale became a matter of survival. It could've been psyche-shattering for Matt to learn his entire existence consisted of stories told by someone else. Instead, he focused that angst into a new creation and turned his resolve into a parallel construct. He hammered away on the keyboard with the Tsimm-Tsuum cadence of the Foot Tapper returning to mind, the now-pleasant pulse echoing with a reassurance that his existence mattered. This quantum coupling experienced via Tiamat's story represented a narrative that hit close to home while also offering a new path to call his own.

Half of Matt longed for Meda to understand this crucial structure. How could she be so disinterested in her very creation? If their world would end tomorrow, wouldn't she want to know? Yet the other half of him respected her stance. Some people don't want to know their fate for fear it might be incorrect. The followers of the Millerite Movement were so confident in the imminent end that they gave up their worldly possessions and flocked to a hill in anticipation of the Second Coming. Look where that got them. Meda could be driven by instinct or she could be driven by facts—never both. So when she started edging the conversation to the movie involving Armenians, Matt prudently decided to shut his trap out of self-preservation. Some stories were better left untold.

He walked home from her apartment that Sunday night in a semi-transcendental state. Matt felt like he was in motion while also observing himself in motion—an act that was technically impossible in the conventional model of physics. It was a brisk night and he moved swiftly. Miraculously, his ankle had healed practically overnight following the events at the opera. While keeping it elevated throughout the day no doubt helped, the bulk of the recovery occurred after his final disappearance. He'd considered making a joke about Achilles but, similar to his ekphrasis tales about the Water Man, he decided to shield Meda from any more esoteric symbolism. It was time to move on.

About halfway home, he received a text from Magee. "Latest call from Mama. She says if I'm not interested in blind date I should tell u. I tell her no, Matt disappears all the time. She didn't get it." Matt was lost in contemplation and, unprepared for such wiseassery, he laughed out loud on the seemingly empty street. To a stranger's eyes he might've appeared crazy. Still smiling, he dialed Magee's number and launched in as soon as friend answered. "I'm not a deadbeat womanizer, okay? No need to start spreading rumors."

Magee chuckled. "I needed to get her off my back. What can I say?"

"And that was the best you came up with? You couldn't just say I'm practically married?"

"I figured you'd appreciate such a villainous portrayal. Though, the next time you see her she may have a few questions for you."

"Great," said Matt, knowing full well Magee's mother wouldn't believe such tales anyway. As an afterthought, he added, "I'm done disappearing anyway. It was just a phase. That's all behind me now."

"You sure about that? Have you written anything lately?"

"Yes, as a matter of fact. I cranked out a story this afternoon." Matt began to say he didn't disappear during Tiamat's story, then stopped himself. He restarted, parsing his words carefully. "I didn't speak to anybody in a void. Not even Abby."

"Good. That's progress at least." Magee missed Matt's semantic sidestep about his disappearance. He paused, then switched gears. "Hey, I meant to ask you...that picture of the instruction manual for the toy car, the one you sent to Meda...can you forward that over when you get a chance?"

"Yeah, no problem," said Matt before growing curious. "Why?"

Magee sighed but, based on the tone of his ensuing words, Matt could tell he was grinning. "It's complicated. You know about that mirror I salvaged, and how it shattered? Well, I decided to create something with the shards. Rather than a flat surface, I want it to be a reflecting globe. It won't be perfectly round, obviously. It'll be closer to a soccer ball...reminiscent of the buckyball shape that cop mentioned when we were discussing Abby's chemicals. I'll need 60 shards. Almost like the Flower of Life, made spherical."

Matt, nearly speechless, slowed to a halt. "Wow, man. That's wild. Where did this new idea come from?"

"I don't know," Magee admitted. "From our experience at the opera, of course. But also something else, something that goes all the way back to that day we found the Dirty Lord symbol. I think an important moment occurred that night. And it's flowed through our lives ever since. I can't articulate the direct correlation. In fact, my inability to do so is the exact reason I need that image of the instructions. You sent that picture from...somewhere else. From another place. All three of us know that's true. Regardless of any of the other impossibilities, that is indisputable. I want that talisman to be inside this structure, even if no one sees it. I think the absence of its view will make its presence that much more important."

"Deep. You sound really inspired, man."

"I am." Magee paused, nothing more to add.

"Fantastic. I'm happy for you. I'll send over that image right away."

"Great, thanks buddy."

They hung up and, with phone still aloft, Matt swiped to find the picture for Magee. He scrolled too far, though, and landed on a different message, a voicemail. That was weird. Normally only incoming voicemails were stored, not ones he'd left. Even stranger, it was long. Over nine minutes long, in fact. When he noticed the message was dated Monday, the 10th, he began to piece it together. Could this be that message with the large block of silence Meda mentioned? Forgetting Magee's request for the moment, he listened to the voicemail.

"Hey hon. It's me. I just wanted to let you know I dropped off the flash drive of those reports from Fitzgerald. It's a lot of material, to be honest. I have no idea what you plan to find. But hey—you asked for it. Anyway, you weren't home so I dropped it in your mailbox."

The voice was his. Without question. He recognized his particular modulation and diction. Yet, as often happens when one hears their own recorded voice, something seemed off. Scientists explain the divergence as the acoustics of one's own skull sitting between the vocal cords and the eardrum. Matt's current unfamiliarity was layers deeper, though. He was also reminded of the voice he'd heard in the void. Yet he couldn't remember ever leaving this message in the first place.

"I want to apologize in advance," continued his voice from the phone, "for all of the conflict to come. I may leave you alone for vast stretches. I may disappear into some strange make-believe land while you're out there wondering what I'm doing or what's taking so long. Writing can be a very solitary enterprise and I've always appreciated your patience and support. In fact, the word, 'appreciate,' doesn't come close to expressing my thanks. I spend so much time away, deserting you while you're left by yourself. I'm sure you'd rather we go to the park together or take in a movie. Instead, I'm off hammering away on a keyboard.

And how do I repay that love to you, hon? I send us on this adventure together that you didn't necessarily agree to take. It's not fair. Your patience shouldn't be treated so cavalierly. Yet you never once complained. Your support remained unwavering. I adore you and I want you to know—though I may neglect your attention at times and vanish for long stretches—I never take your love for granted. I love you always, in all ways."

Matt's eyes teared. The back of his throat quivered as he tried to keep his lower lip still. He listened to his own voice for those 500 seconds—the words were raw and broken by frequent pauses. This message was intended for the love of his life yet it'd remained undelivered until now. Matt couldn't guess why. Yet, now knowing that Meda could finally receive it, a calm serenity flooded him.

The message concluded, "I hope your day went okay, at least. I'll talk to you soon. Love you." And then it ended. Matt sniffed hard and wiped away tears with the back of his hand. Overflowing with gratitude and love for Meda, he re-composed himself and slowly began walking again. Though he couldn't remember leaving that message for her, he nonetheless meant every word of it.

He arrived at the crossroads at the end of Meda's block and stopped. A car was in the process of doing a U-turn in the middle of the intersection and, briefly, its high-beams landed on him, illuminating him with a blinding flash of light. He winced. Then he smiled. The car drove away and Matt recalled his disappearance at the same spot weeks earlier. This time, with his contended grin still present, he proceeded home without delay. After all, with twelve stories left to write, Matt had to go back to work.

# The Author

Matthew Waterman created this work. It is his second novel after two decades spent writing. Sometimes lucid, he is not an altogether terrible person. In fact, this one time he went right up to a stranger and gave that person a high-five. Matt's greatest singular talent may be over-thinking mundane matters. But at least his regrets have wings.

Made in the USA
Lexington, KY
26 August 2019